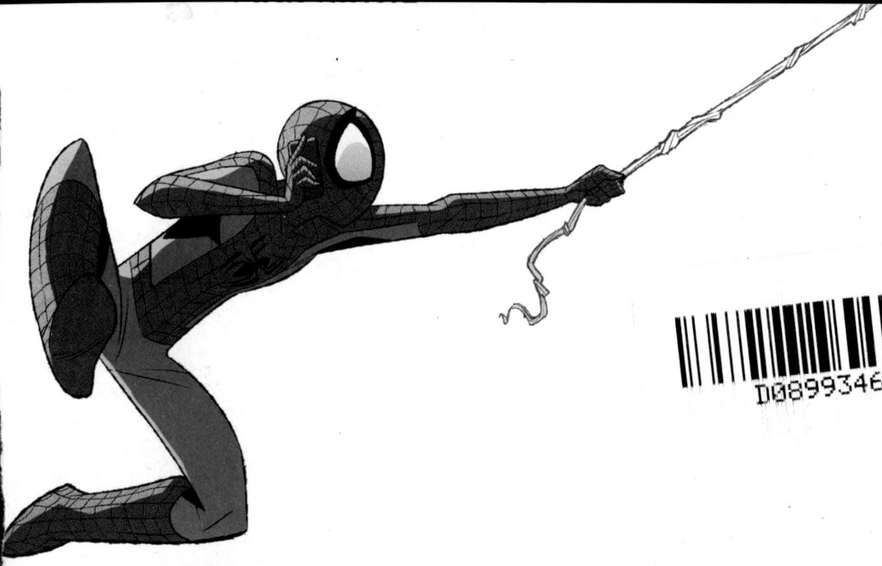

PETER PARKER & MILES MORALES

SPIDER-MEN: DOUBLE TROUBLE

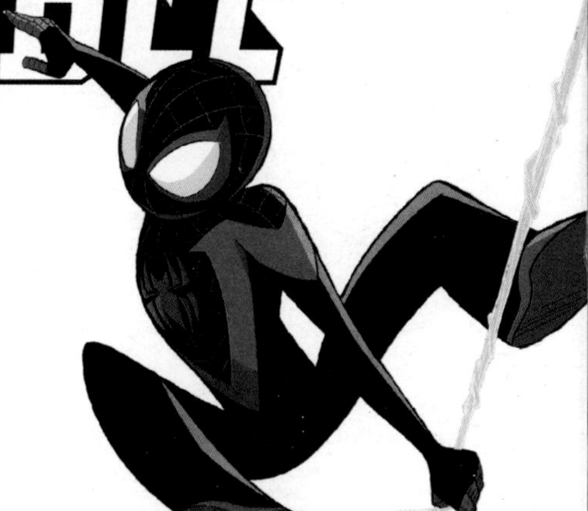

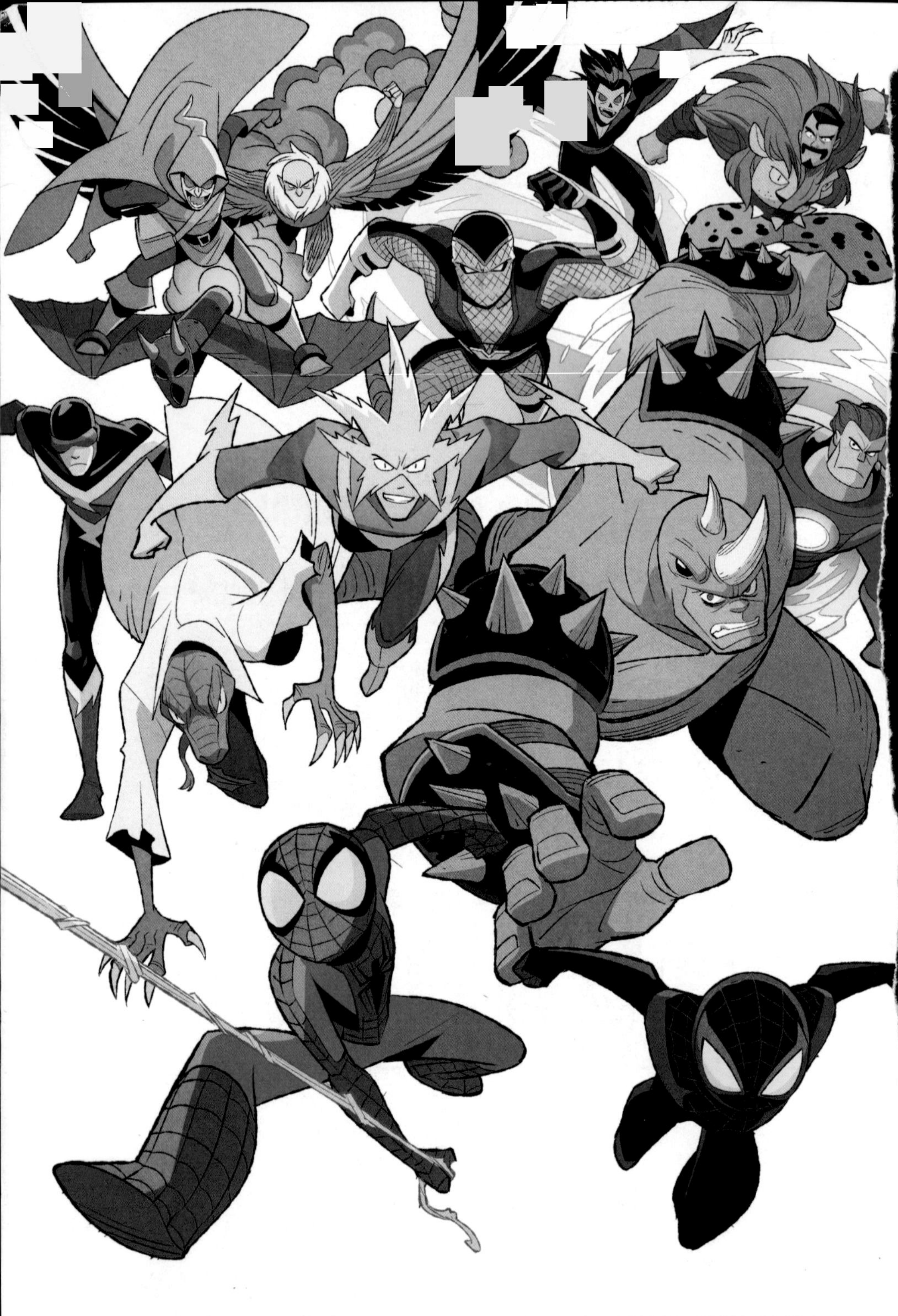

PETER PARKER & MILES MORALES: SPIDER-MEN DOUBLE TROUBLE. Contains material originally published in magazine form as PETER PARKER & MILES MORALES: SPIDER-MEN DOUBLE TROUBLE (2022) #1-4 and SPIDER-MAN & VENOM: DOUBLE TROUBLE (2019) #1. First printing 2023. ISBN 978-1-302-93147-6. Published by MARVEL WORLDWIDE, INC., a subsidiary of MARVEL ENTERTAINMENT, LLC. OFFICE OF PUBLICATION: 1290 Avenue of the Americas, New York, NY 10104. **Printed in Canada.** KEVIN FEIGE, Chief Creative Officer; DAN BUCKLEY, President, Marvel Entertainment; DAVID BOGART, Associate Publisher & SVP of Talent Affairs; TOM BREVOORT, VP, Executive Editor; NICK LOWE, Executive Editor, VP of Content, Digital Publishing; DAVID GABRIEL, VP of Print & Digital Publishing; SVEN LARSEN, VP of Licensed Publishing; MARK ANNUNZIATO, VP of Planning & Forecasting; JEFF YOUNGQUIST, VP of Production & Special Projects; ALEX MORALES, Director of Publishing Operations; DAN EDINGTON, Director of Editorial Operations; RICKEY PURDIN, Director of Talent Relations; JENNIFER GRÜNWALD, Director of Production & Special Projects; SUSAN CRESPI, Production Manager; STAN LEE, Chairman Emeritus. For information regarding advertising in Marvel Comics or on Marvel.com, please contact Vit DeBellis, Custom Solutions & Integrated Advertising Manager, at vdebellis@marvel.com. For Marvel subscription inquiries, please call 888-511-5480. **Manufactured between 3/10/2023 and 4/11/2023 by SOLISCO PRINTERS, SCOTT, QC, CANADA.**

10 9 8 7 6 5 4 3 2 1

PETER PARKER & MILES MORALES

SPIDER-MEN:
DOUBLE TROUBLE

MARIKO TAMAKI & VITA AYALA
WRITERS

GURIHIRU
ARTIST

VC's CORY PETIT
LETTERER

GURIHIRU
COVER ART

KAITLYN LINDTVEDT
ASSISTANT EDITOR

ALANNA SMITH
EDITOR

SPIDER-MAN & VENOM: DOUBLE TROUBLE

MARIKO TAMAKI
WRITER

GURIHIRU
ARTIST

VC's TRAVIS LANHAM
LETTERER

GURIHIRU
COVER ART

DANNY KHAZEM
ASSISTANT EDITOR

DEVIN LEWIS
EDITOR

NICK LOWE
EXECUTIVE EDITOR

SPIDER-MAN CREATED BY **STAN LEE** & **STEVE DITKO**

COLLECTION EDITOR: **DANIEL KIRCHHOFFER** ASSISTANT MANAGING EDITOR: **MAIA LOY**
ASSOCIATE MANAGER, TALENT RELATIONS: **LISA MONTALBANO** DIRECTOR, PRODUCTION & SPECIAL PROJECTS: **JENNIFER GRÜNWALD**
VP PRODUCTION & SPECIAL PROJECTS: **JEFF YOUNGQUIST** BOOK DESIGNER: **STACIE ZUCKER**
MANAGER & SENIOR DESIGNER: **ADAM DEL RE** LEAD DESIGNER: **JAY BOWEN**
SVP PRINT, SALES & MARKETING: **DAVID GABRIEL** EDITOR IN CHIEF: **C.B. CEBULSKI**

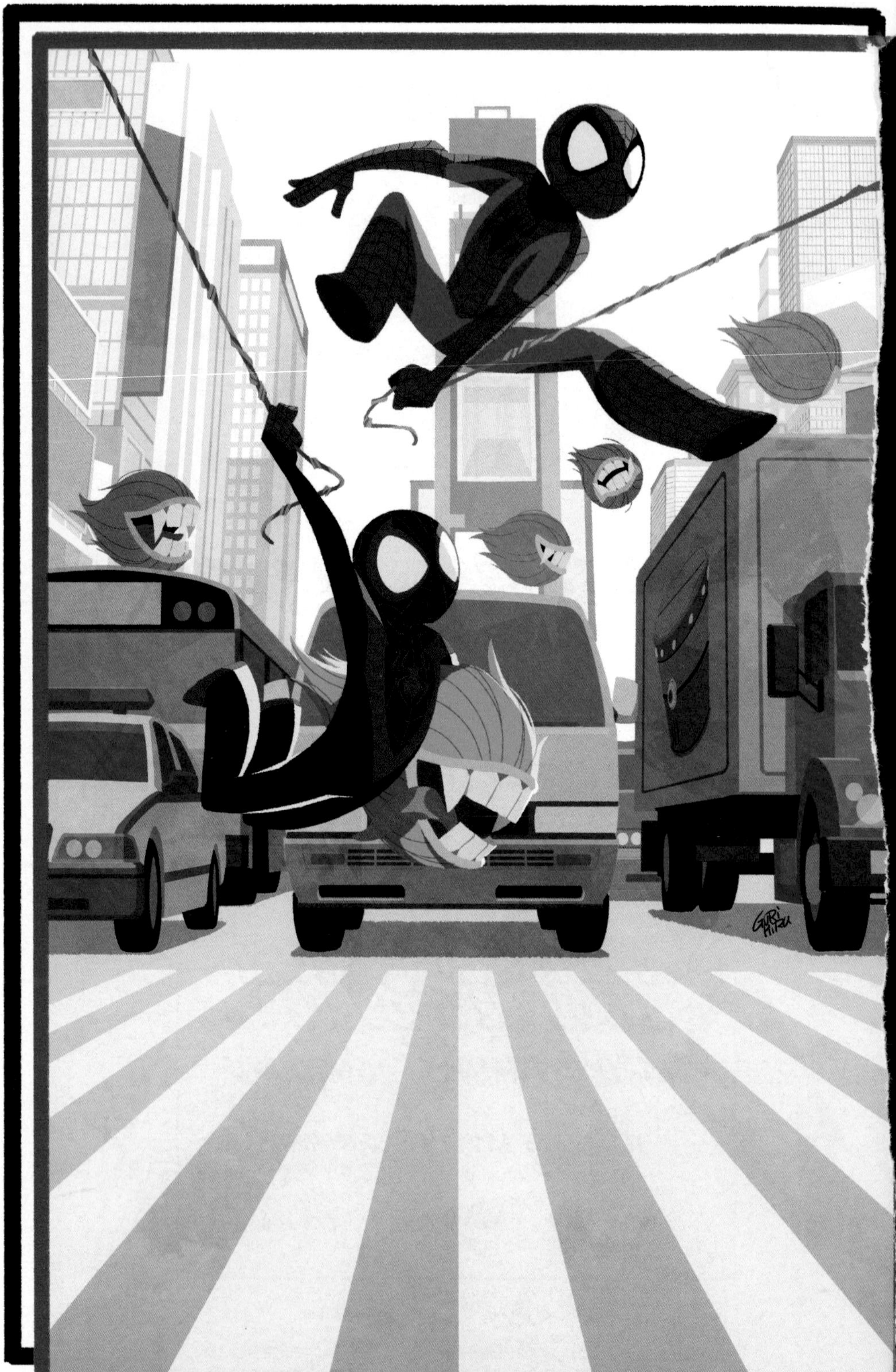

1

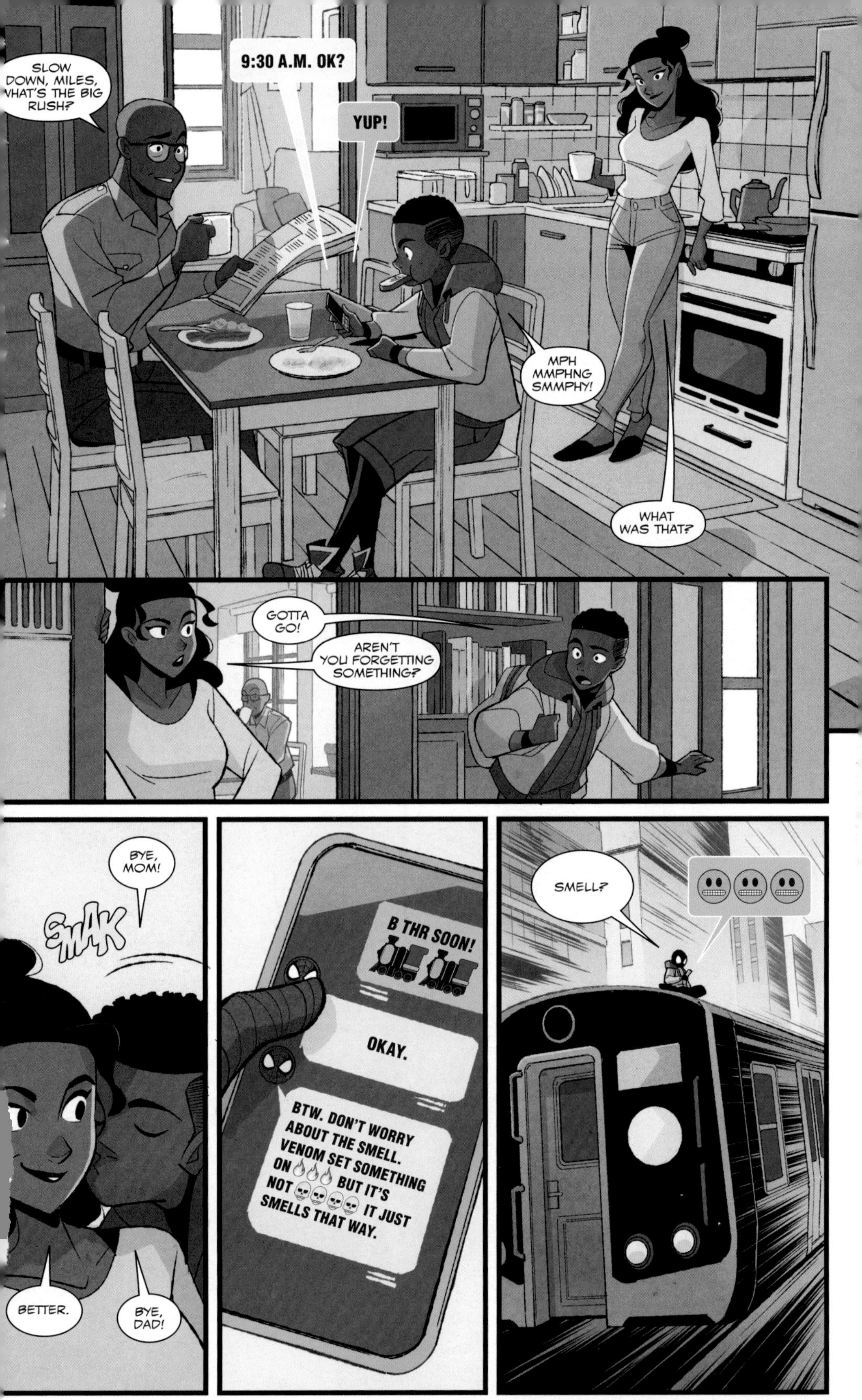
SLOW DOWN, MILES, WHAT'S THE BIG RUSH?
9:30 A.M. OK?
YUP!
MPH MMPHNG SMMPHY!
WHAT WAS THAT?
GOTTA GO!
AREN'T YOU FORGETTING SOMETHING?
BYE, MOM!
SMAK
BETTER.
BYE, DAD!
B THR SOON!
OKAY.
BTW. DON'T WORRY ABOUT THE SMELL. VENOM SET SOMETHING ON BUT IT'S NOT IT JUST SMELLS THAT WAY.
SMELL?

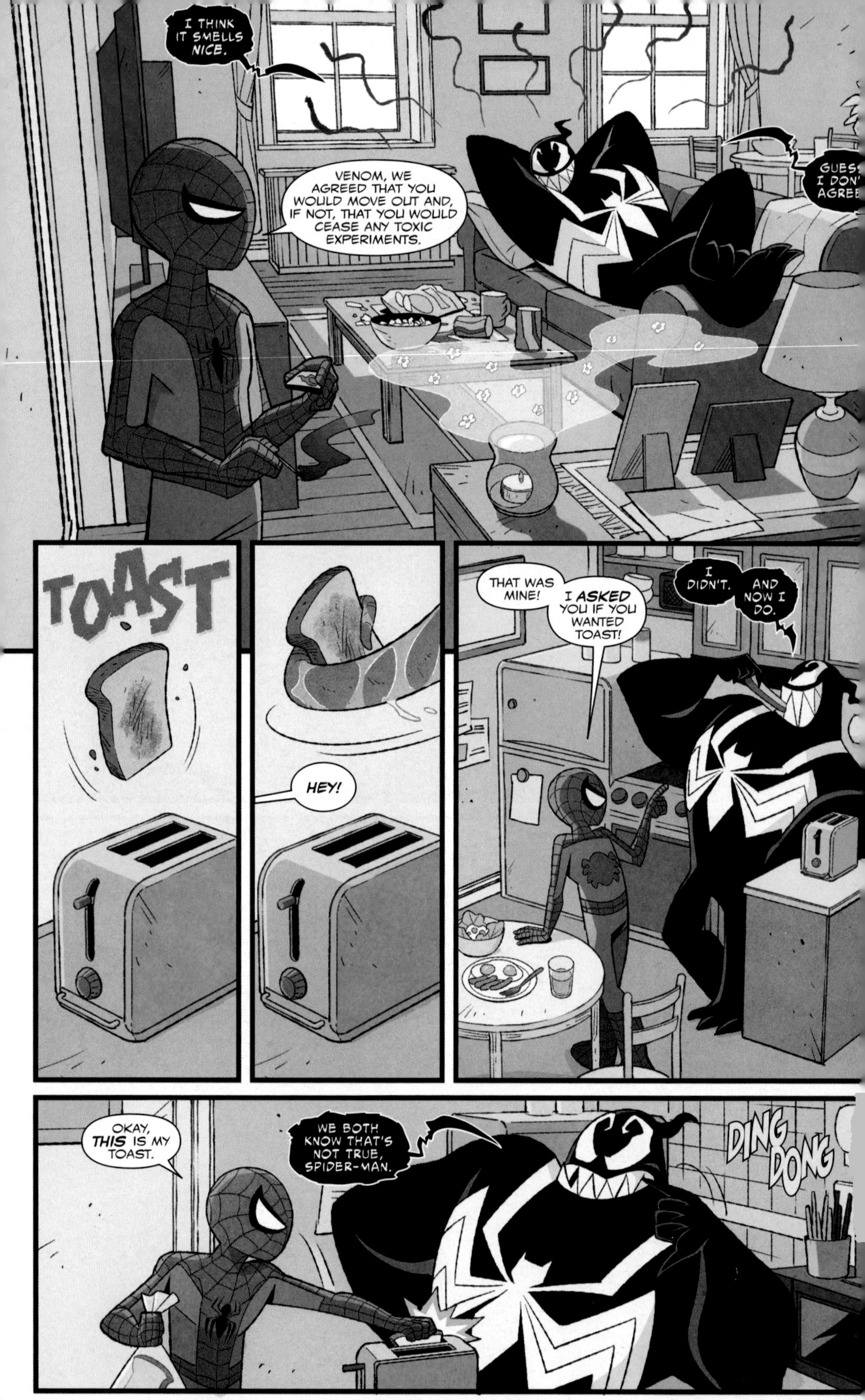
I THINK IT SMELLS NICE.
VENOM, WE AGREED THAT YOU WOULD MOVE OUT AND, IF NOT, THAT YOU WOULD CEASE ANY TOXIC EXPERIMENTS.
TOAST
HEY!
THAT WAS MINE!
I ASKED YOU IF YOU WANTED TOAST!
I DIDN'T.
AND NOW I DO.
OKAY, THIS IS MY TOAST.
WE BOTH KNOW THAT'S NOT TRUE, SPIDER-MAN.
DING DONG

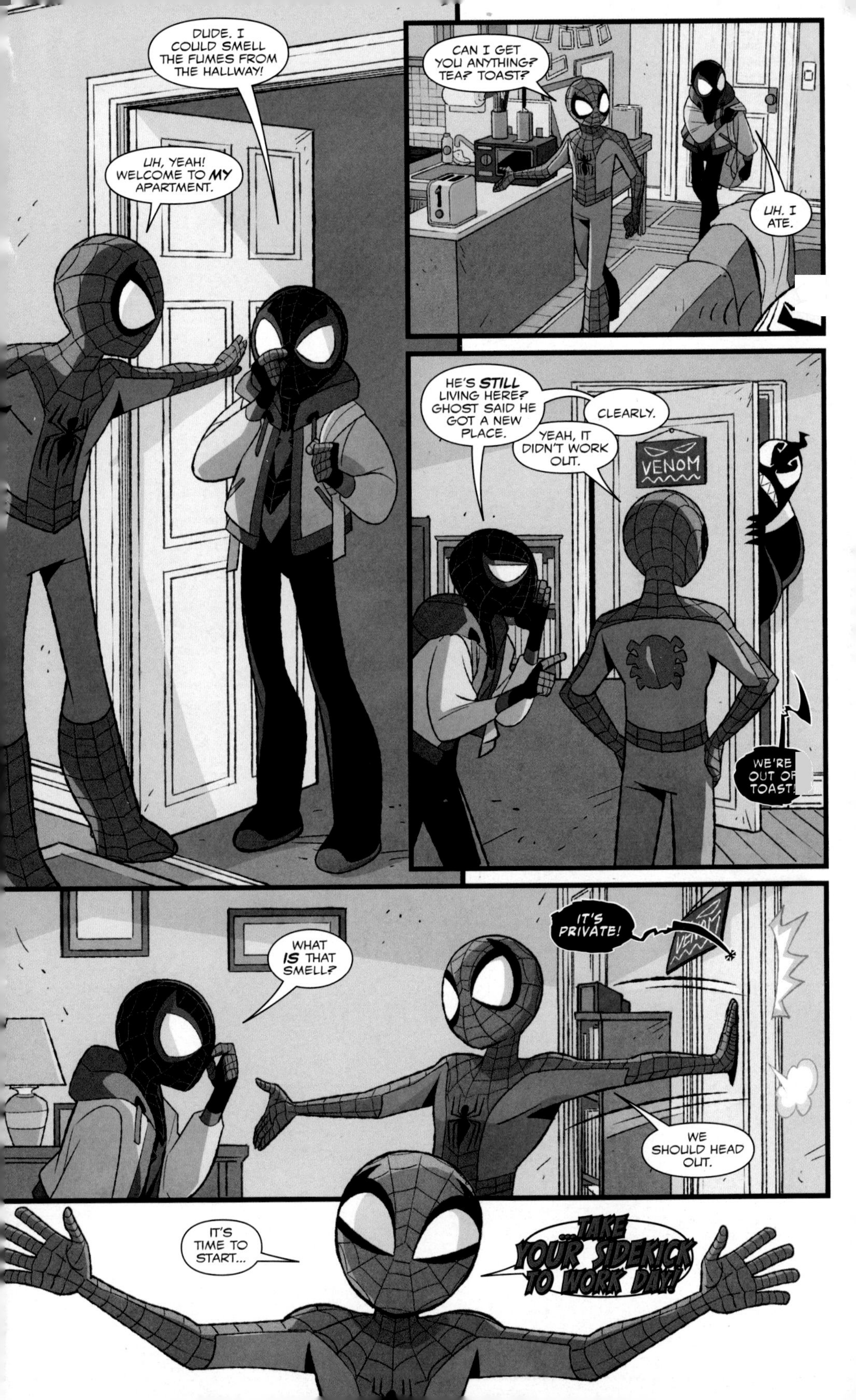
DUDE. I COULD SMELL THE FUMES FROM THE HALLWAY!
UH, YEAH! WELCOME TO MY APARTMENT.
CAN I GET YOU ANYTHING? TEA? TOAST?
UH. I ATE.
HE'S STILL LIVING HERE? GHOST SAID HE GOT A NEW PLACE.
CLEARLY.
YEAH, IT DIDN'T WORK OUT.
VENOM
WE'RE OUT OF TOAST!
WHAT IS THAT SMELL?
IT'S PRIVATE!
WE SHOULD HEAD OUT.
IT'S TIME TO START...
...TAKE YOUR SIDEKICK TO WORK DAY!

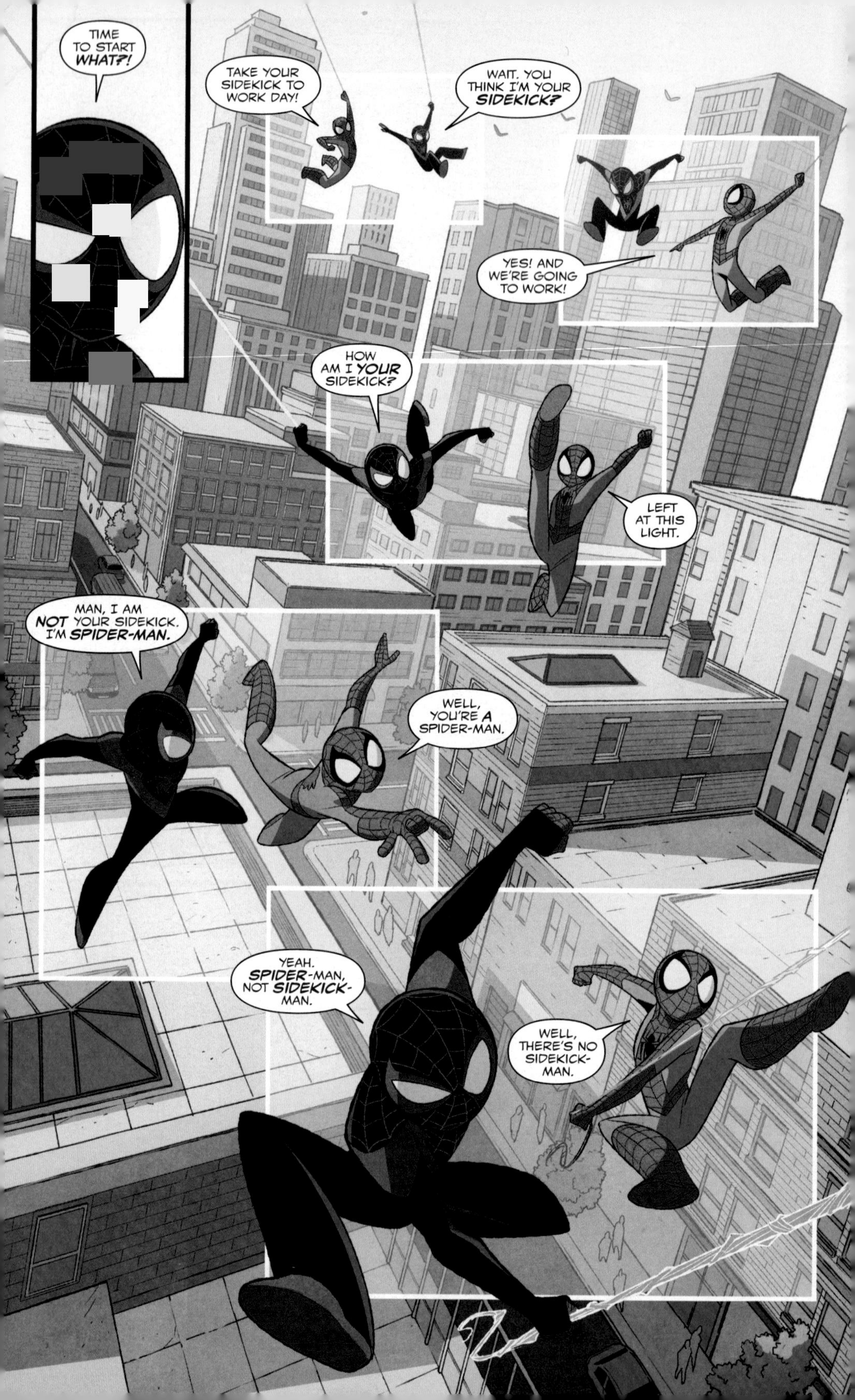
TIME TO START WHAT?!
TAKE YOUR SIDEKICK TO WORK DAY!
WAIT. YOU THINK I'M YOUR SIDEKICK?
YES! AND WE'RE GOING TO WORK!
HOW AM I YOUR SIDEKICK?
LEFT AT THIS LIGHT.
MAN, I AM NOT YOUR SIDEKICK. I'M SPIDER-MAN.
WELL, YOU'RE A SPIDER-MAN.
YEAH. SPIDER-MAN, NOT SIDEKICK-MAN.
WELL, THERE'S NO SIDEKICK-MAN.

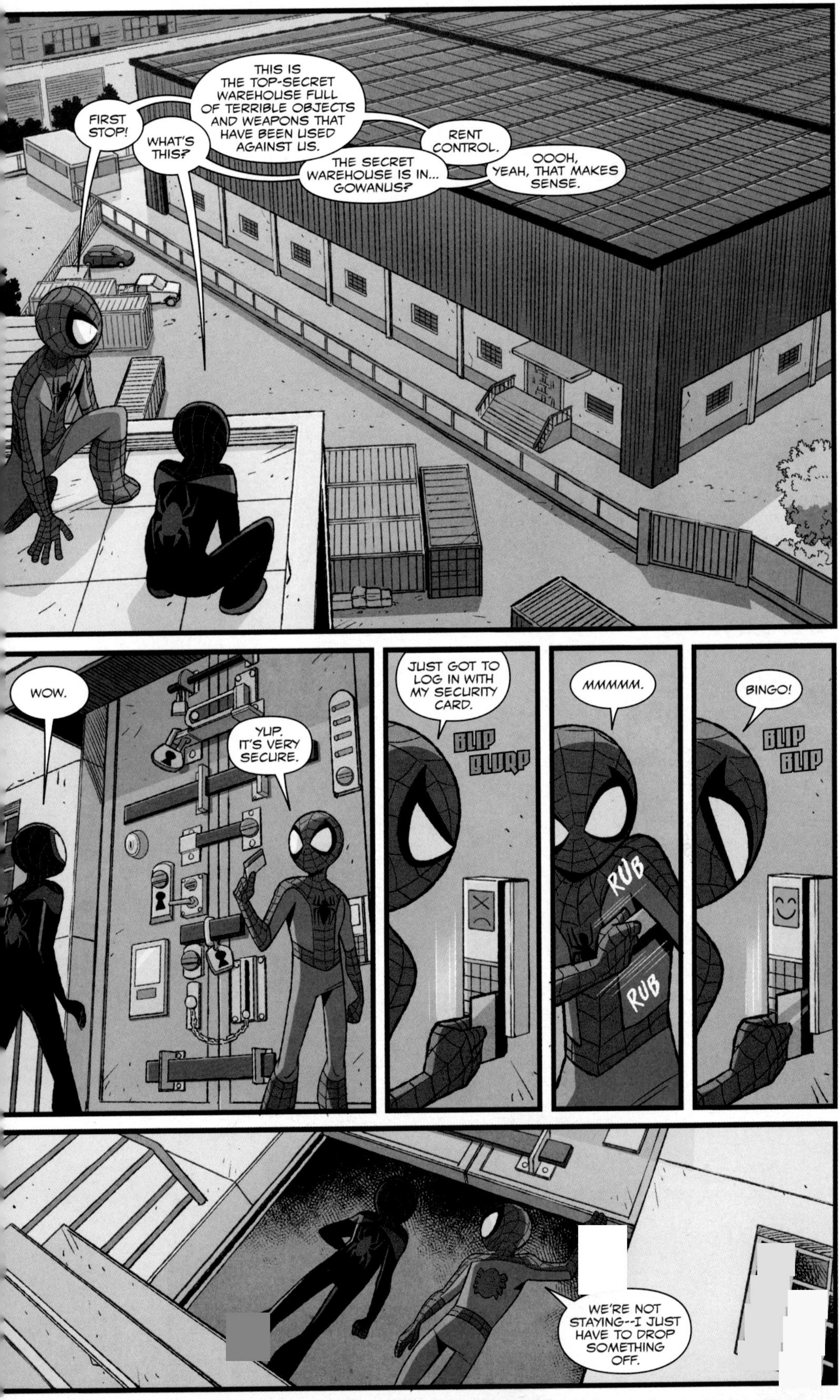

FIRST STOP!
WHAT'S THIS?
THIS IS THE TOP-SECRET WAREHOUSE FULL OF TERRIBLE OBJECTS AND WEAPONS THAT HAVE BEEN USED AGAINST US.
THE SECRET WAREHOUSE IS IN... GOWANUS?
RENT CONTROL.
OOOH, YEAH, THAT MAKES SENSE.
WOW.
YUP. IT'S VERY SECURE.
JUST GOT TO LOG IN WITH MY SECURITY CARD.
BLIP BLURP
MMMMM.
RUB
RUB
BINGO!
BLIP BLIP
WE'RE NOT STAYING--I JUST HAVE TO DROP SOMETHING OFF.

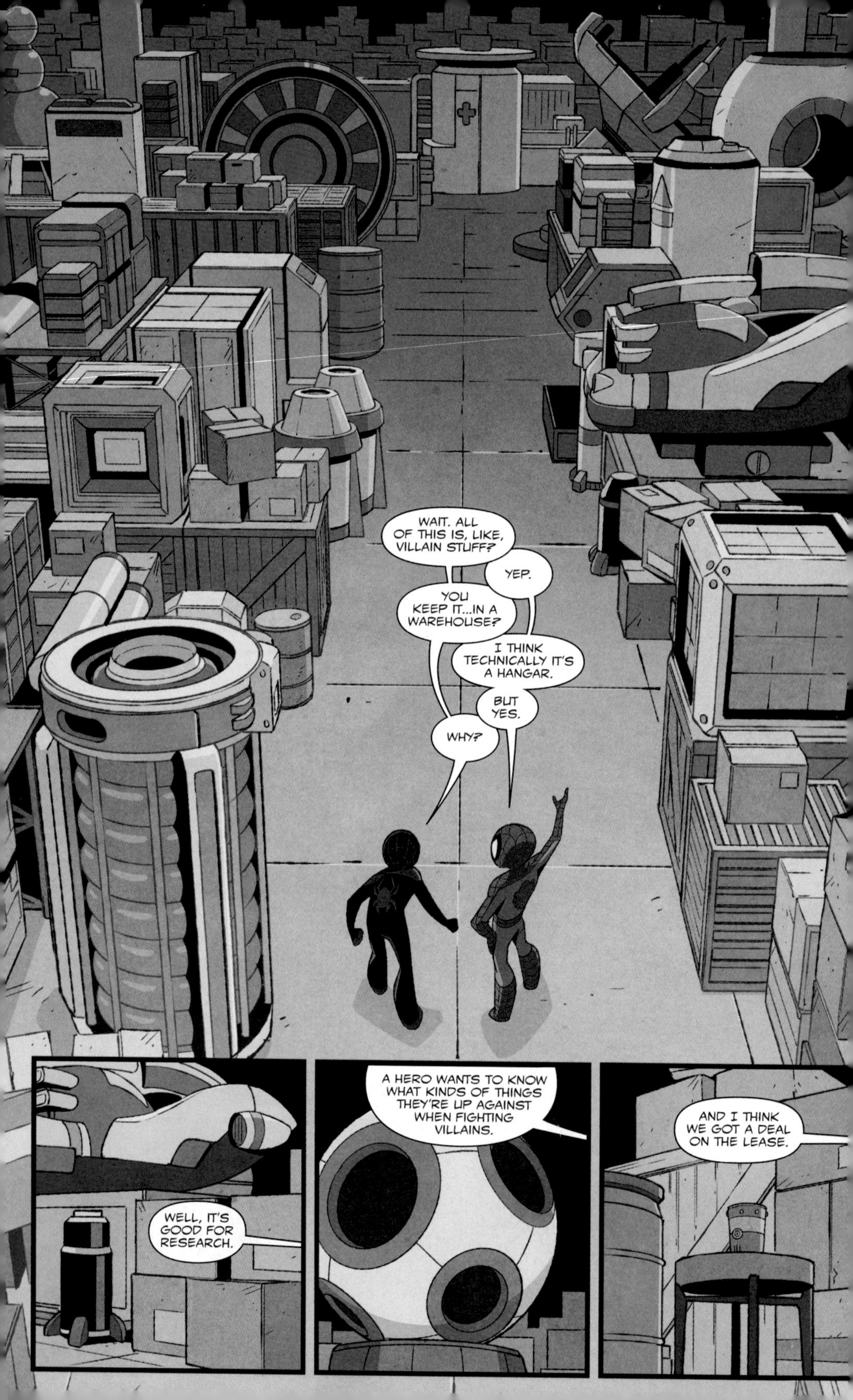
WAIT. ALL OF THIS IS, LIKE, VILLAIN STUFF?
YEP.
YOU KEEP IT...IN A WAREHOUSE?
I THINK TECHNICALLY IT'S A HANGAR.
BUT YES.
WHY?
WELL, IT'S GOOD FOR RESEARCH.
A HERO WANTS TO KNOW WHAT KINDS OF THINGS THEY'RE UP AGAINST WHEN FIGHTING VILLAINS.
AND I THINK WE GOT A DEAL ON THE LEASE.

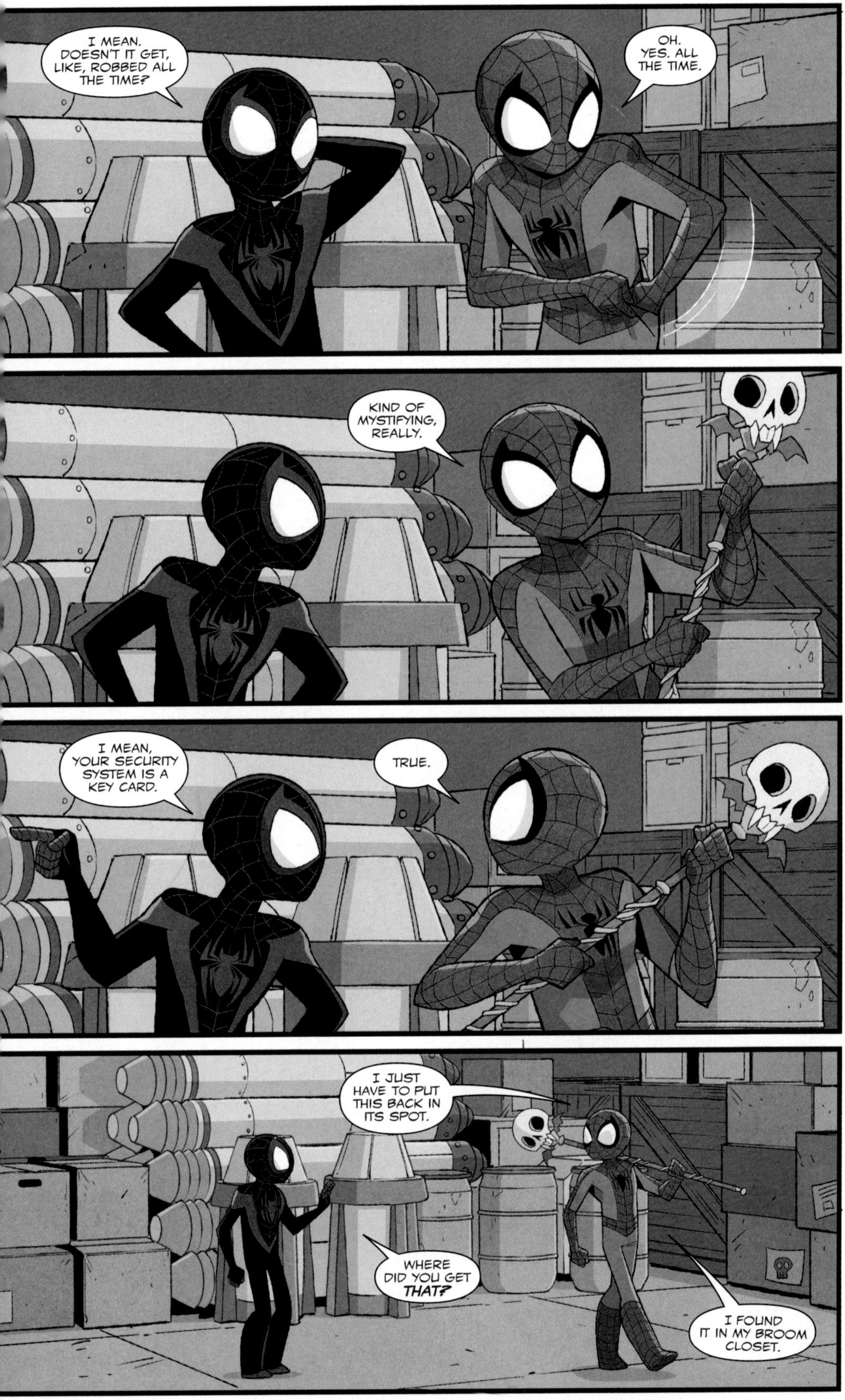
I MEAN. DOESN'T IT GET, LIKE, ROBBED ALL THE TIME?
OH. YES. ALL THE TIME.
KIND OF MYSTIFYING, REALLY.
I MEAN, YOUR SECURITY SYSTEM IS A KEY CARD.
TRUE.
I JUST HAVE TO PUT THIS BACK IN ITS SPOT.
WHERE DID YOU GET ***THAT?***
I FOUND IT IN MY BROOM CLOSET.

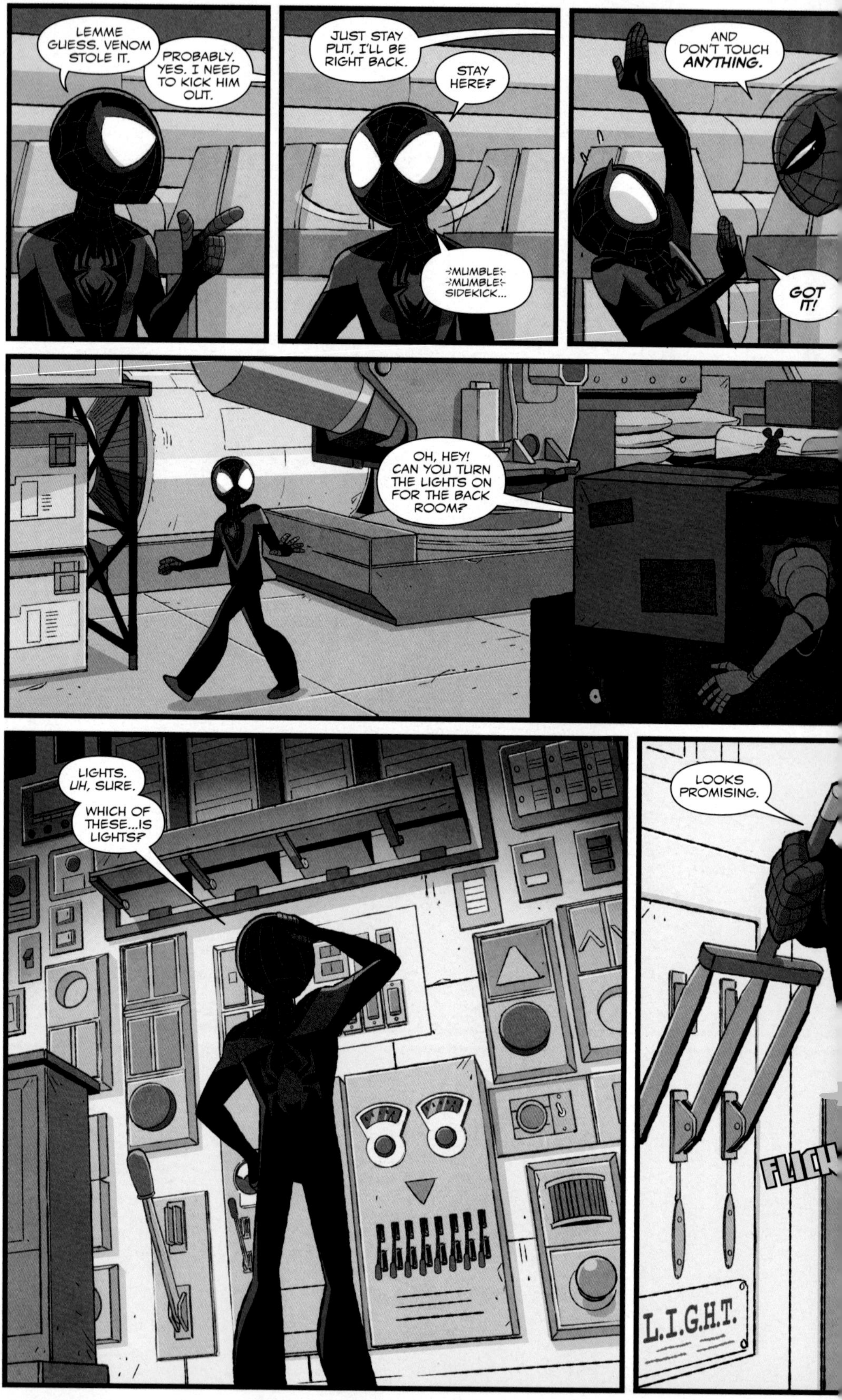
LEMME GUESS. VENOM STOLE IT.
PROBABLY. YES. I NEED TO KICK HIM OUT.
JUST STAY PUT, I'LL BE RIGHT BACK.
STAY HERE?
-MUMBLE- -MUMBLE- SIDEKICK...
AND DON'T TOUCH ANYTHING.
GOT IT!
OH, HEY! CAN YOU TURN THE LIGHTS ON FOR THE BACK ROOM?
LIGHTS. UH, SURE.
WHICH OF THESE...IS LIGHTS?
LOOKS PROMISING.
FLICK
L.I.G.H.T.

WHRRRRRRRRRRRR

WHAT?!

WHHHHRRRRRRRRRRRRRRRRRRRRRRRR

MILES?!

HORRIBLY DANGEROUS THING

MILES?

WHAT DID YOU DO???

UM.

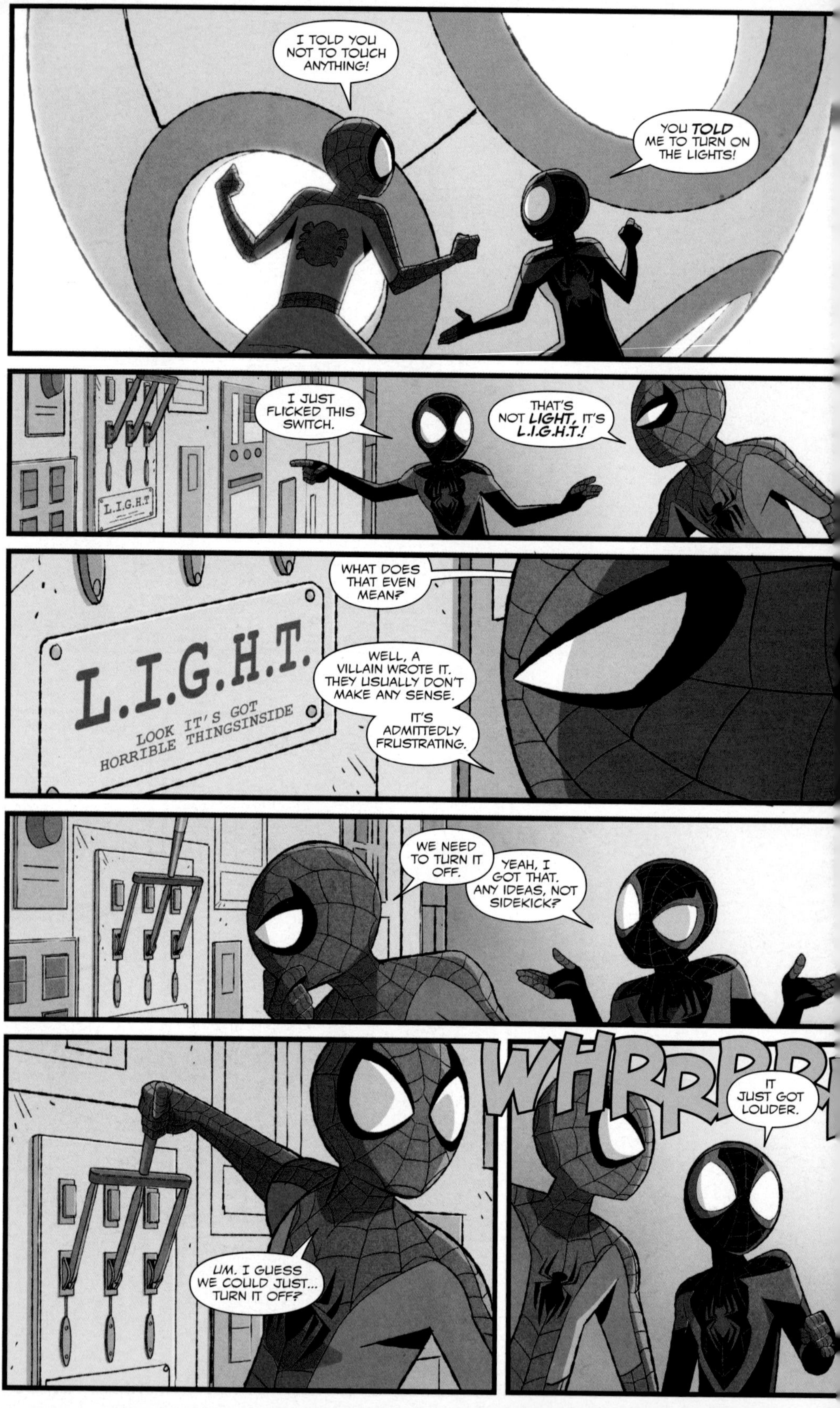

I TOLD YOU NOT TO TOUCH ANYTHING!
YOU TOLD ME TO TURN ON THE LIGHTS!
I JUST FLICKED THIS SWITCH.
THAT'S NOT LIGHT, IT'S L.I.G.H.T.!
L.I.G.H.T.
WHAT DOES THAT EVEN MEAN?
L.I.G.H.T.
LOOK IT'S GOT HORRIBLE THINGSINSIDE
WELL, A VILLAIN WROTE IT. THEY USUALLY DON'T MAKE ANY SENSE.
IT'S ADMITTEDLY FRUSTRATING.
WE NEED TO TURN IT OFF.
YEAH, I GOT THAT. ANY IDEAS, NOT SIDEKICK?
UM. I GUESS WE COULD JUST... TURN IT OFF?
WHRRR
IT JUST GOT LOUDER.

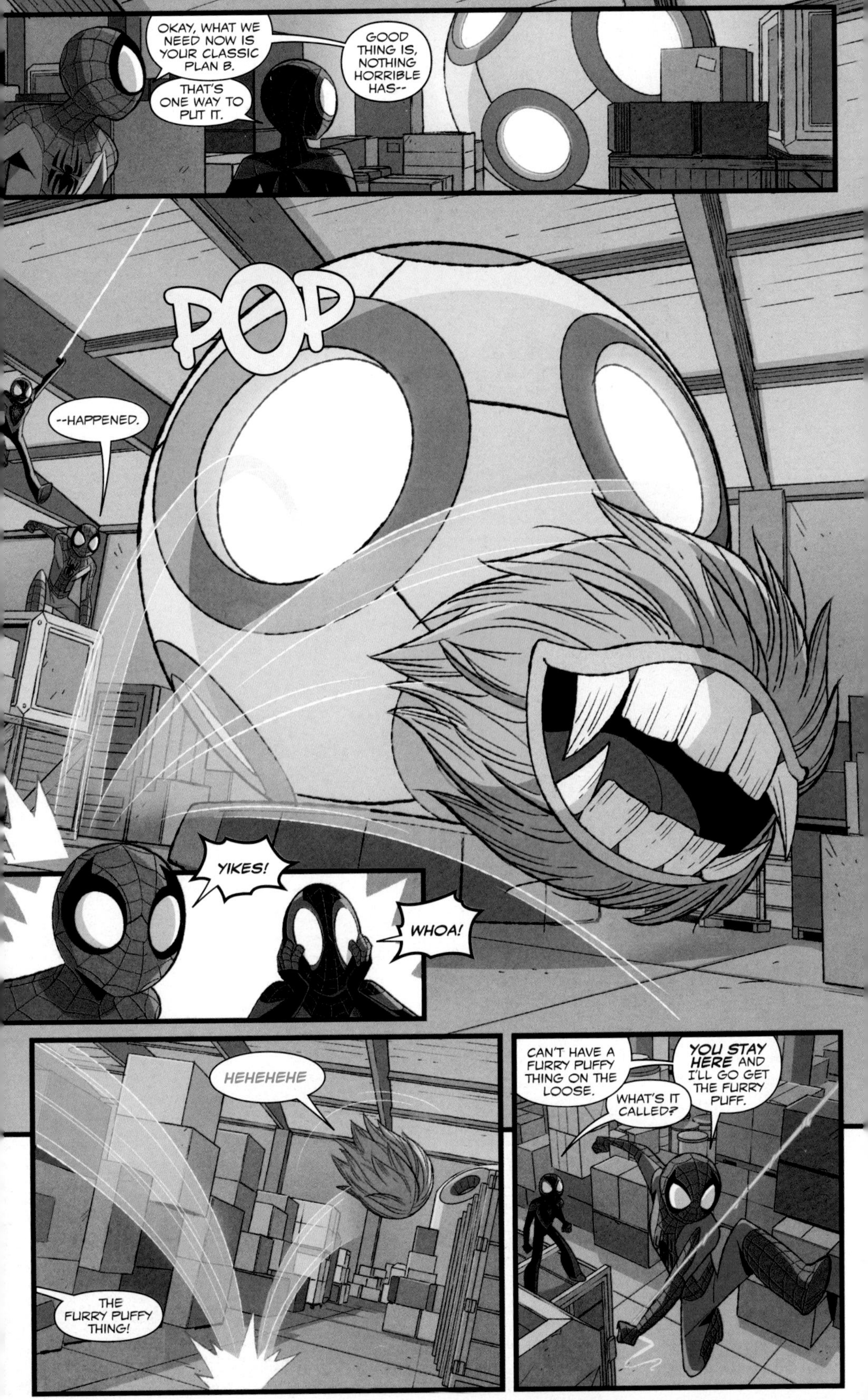
OKAY, WHAT WE NEED NOW IS YOUR CLASSIC PLAN B.
THAT'S ONE WAY TO PUT IT.
GOOD THING IS, NOTHING HORRIBLE HAS--
POP
--HAPPENED.
YIKES!
WHOA!
HEHEHEHE
THE FURRY PUFFY THING!
CAN'T HAVE A FURRY PUFFY THING ON THE LOOSE.
WHAT'S IT CALLED?
YOU STAY HERE AND I'LL GO GET THE FURRY PUFF.

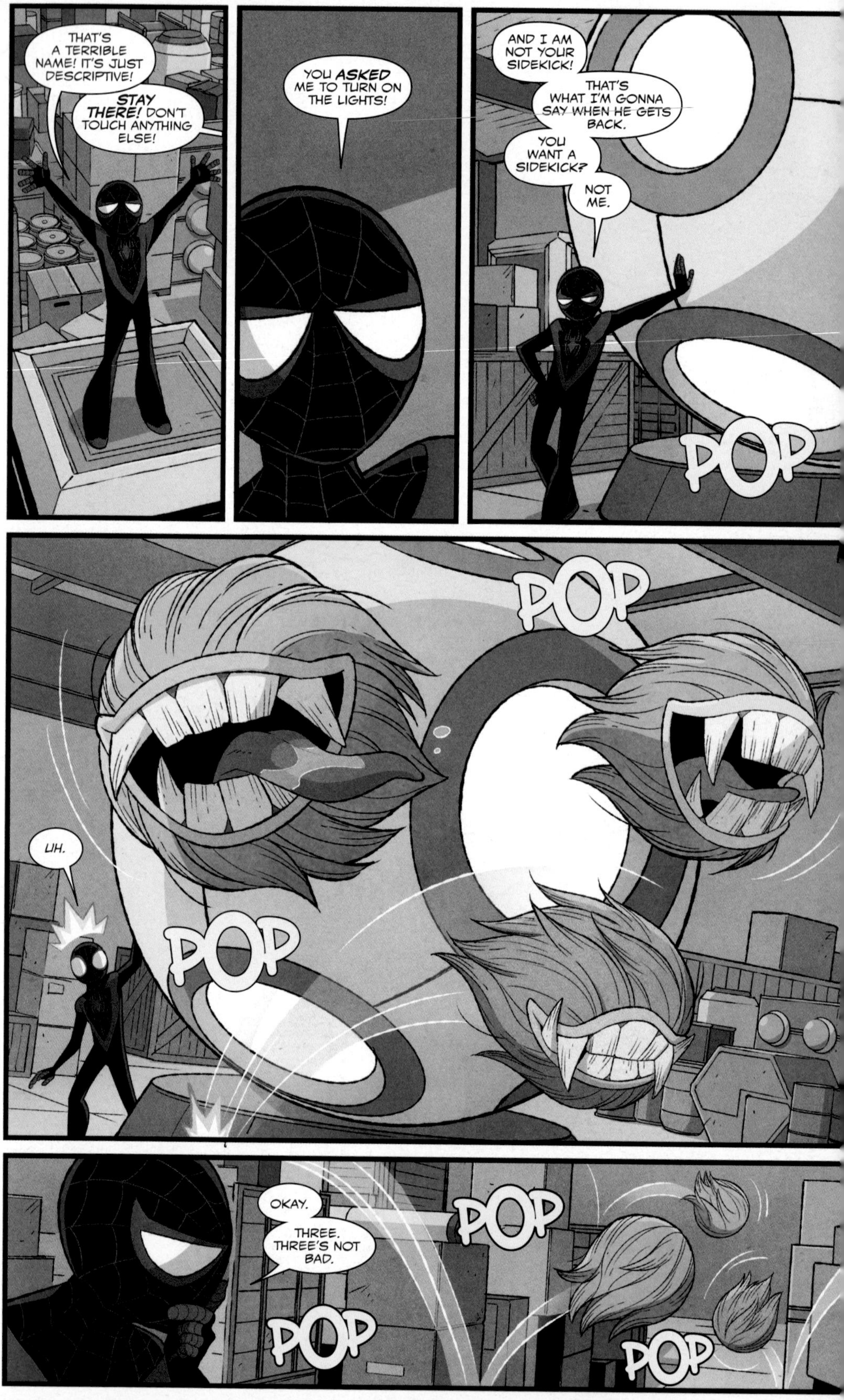

THAT'S A TERRIBLE NAME! IT'S JUST DESCRIPTIVE!
STAY THERE! DON'T TOUCH ANYTHING ELSE!
YOU ASKED ME TO TURN ON THE LIGHTS!
AND I AM NOT YOUR SIDEKICK!
THAT'S WHAT I'M GONNA SAY WHEN HE GETS BACK.
YOU WANT A SIDEKICK?
NOT ME.
POP
POP
UH.
POP
OKAY.
THREE. THREE'S NOT BAD.
POP
POP
POP

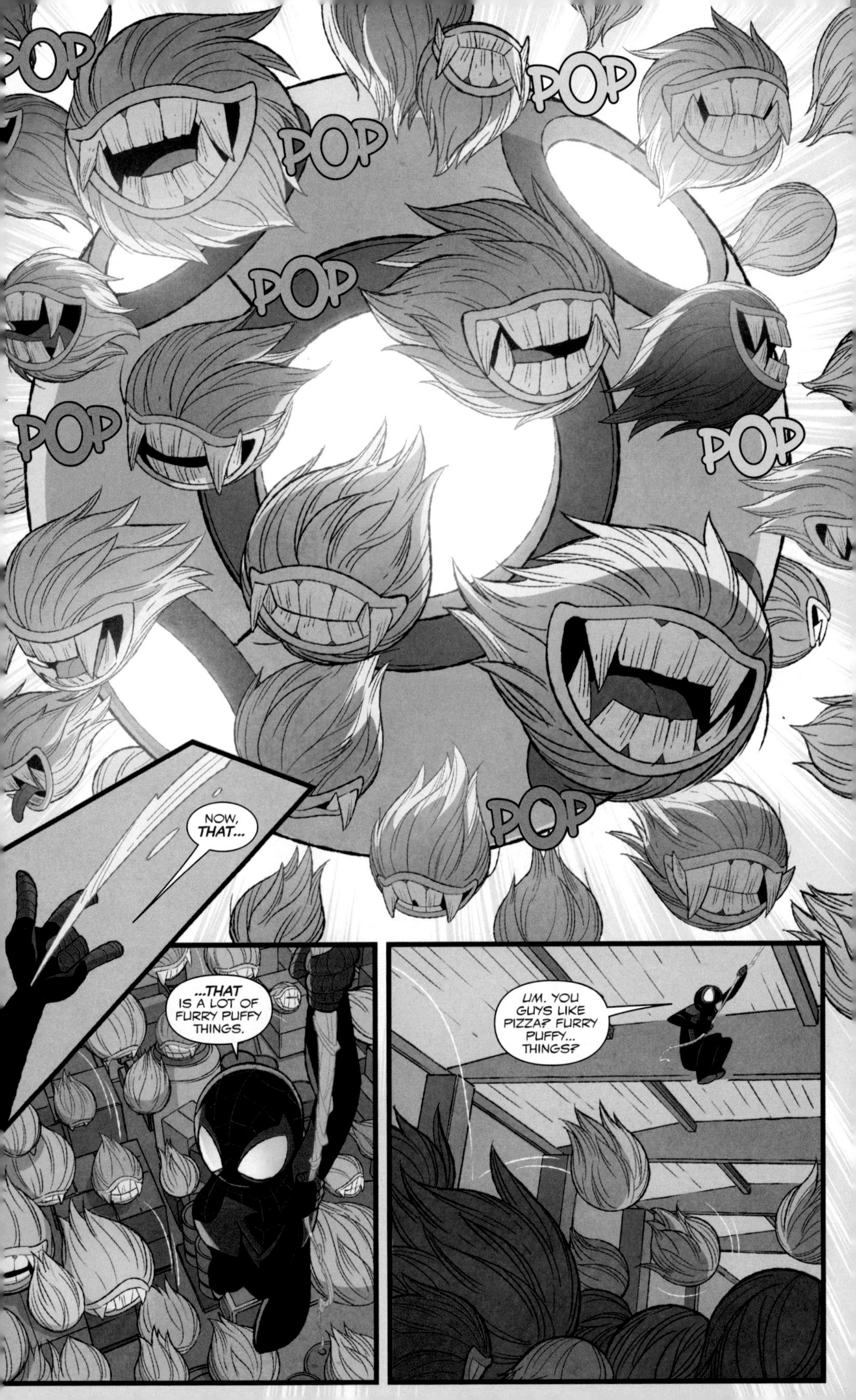
POP
POP
POP
POP
POP
POP
POP
POP
NOW, THAT...
...THAT IS A LOT OF FURRY PUFFY THINGS.
UM. YOU GUYS LIKE PIZZA? FURRY PUFFY... THINGS?

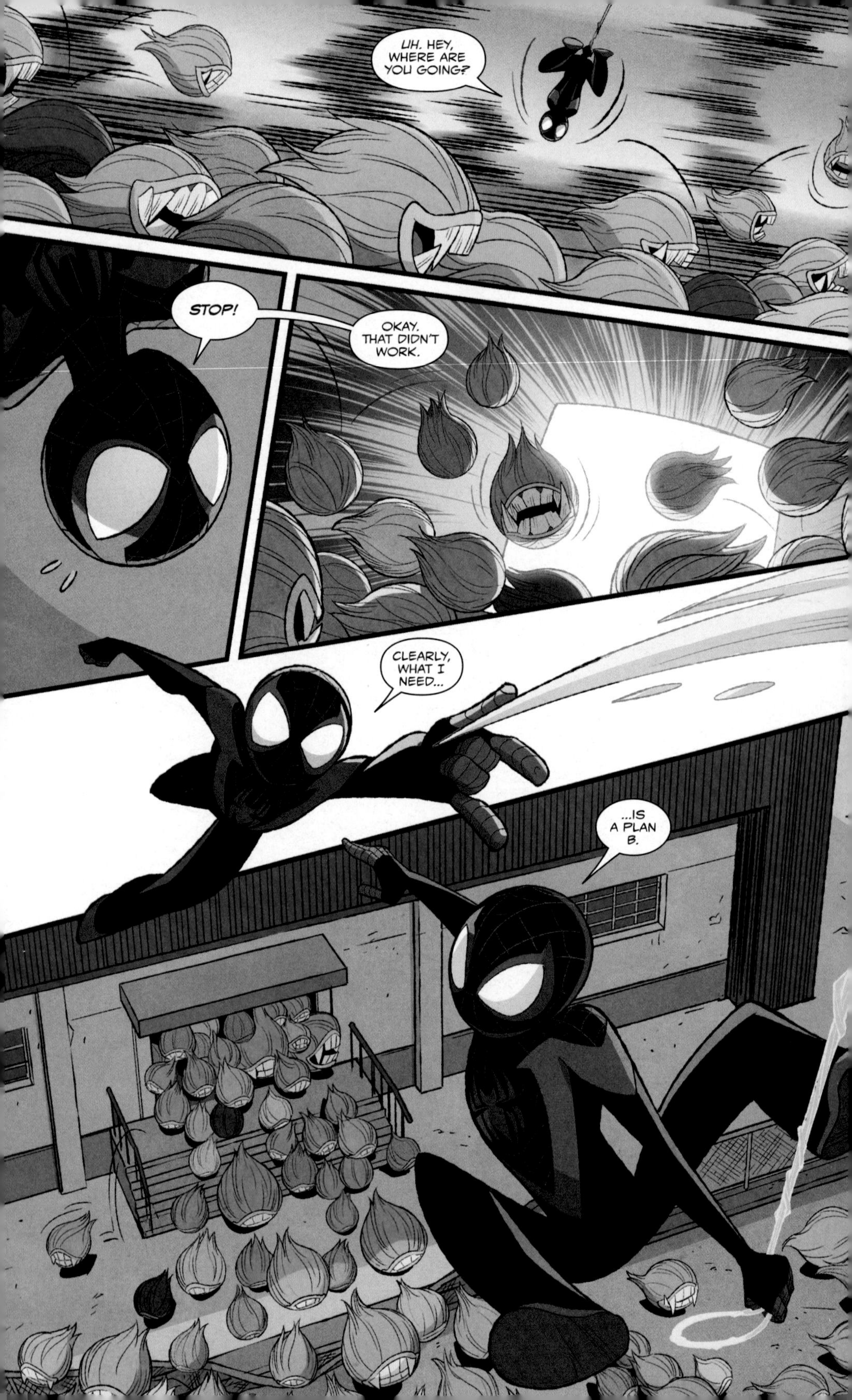
UH. HEY, WHERE ARE YOU GOING?
STOP!
OKAY. THAT DIDN'T WORK.
CLEARLY, WHAT I NEED...
...IS A PLAN B.

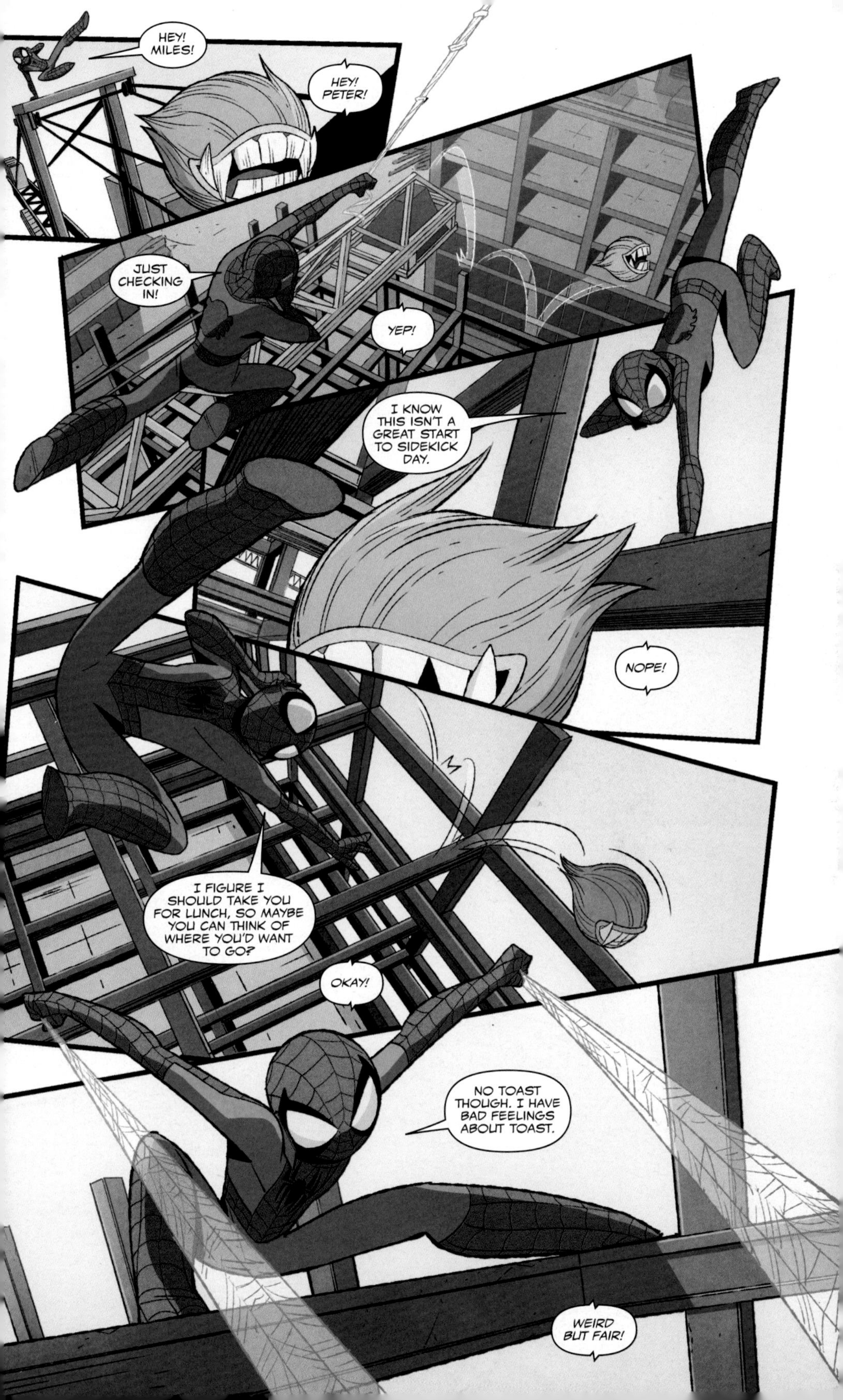

HEY! MILES!
HEY! PETER!
JUST CHECKING IN!
YEP!
I KNOW THIS ISN'T A GREAT START TO SIDEKICK DAY.
NOPE!
I FIGURE I SHOULD TAKE YOU FOR LUNCH, SO MAYBE YOU CAN THINK OF WHERE YOU'D WANT TO GO?
OKAY!
NO TOAST THOUGH. I HAVE BAD FEELINGS ABOUT TOAST.
WEIRD BUT FAIR!

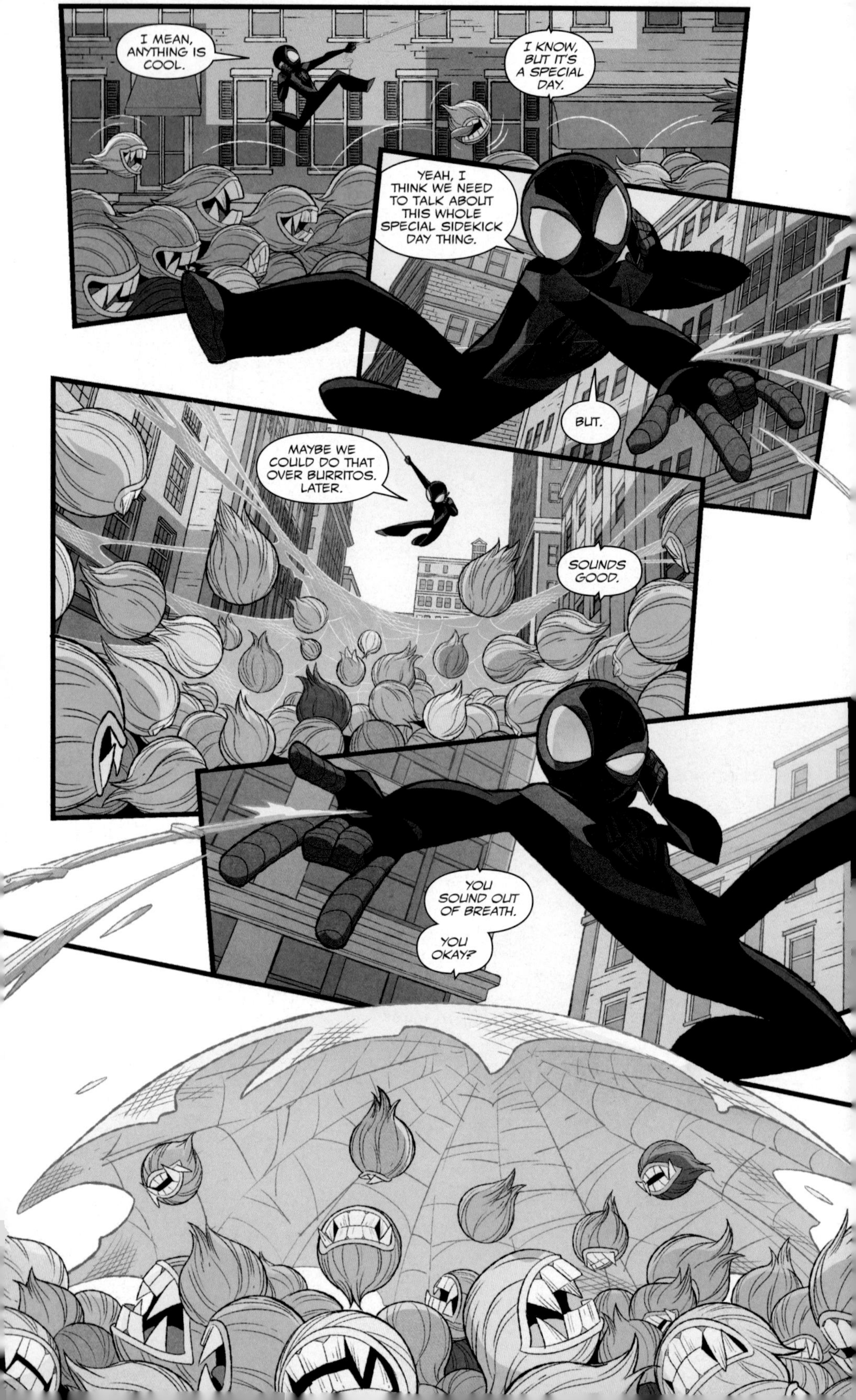
I MEAN, ANYTHING IS COOL.
I KNOW, BUT IT'S A SPECIAL DAY.
YEAH, I THINK WE NEED TO TALK ABOUT THIS WHOLE SPECIAL SIDEKICK DAY THING.
BUT.
MAYBE WE COULD DO THAT OVER BURRITOS. LATER.
SOUNDS GOOD.
YOU SOUND OUT OF BREATH.
YOU OKAY?

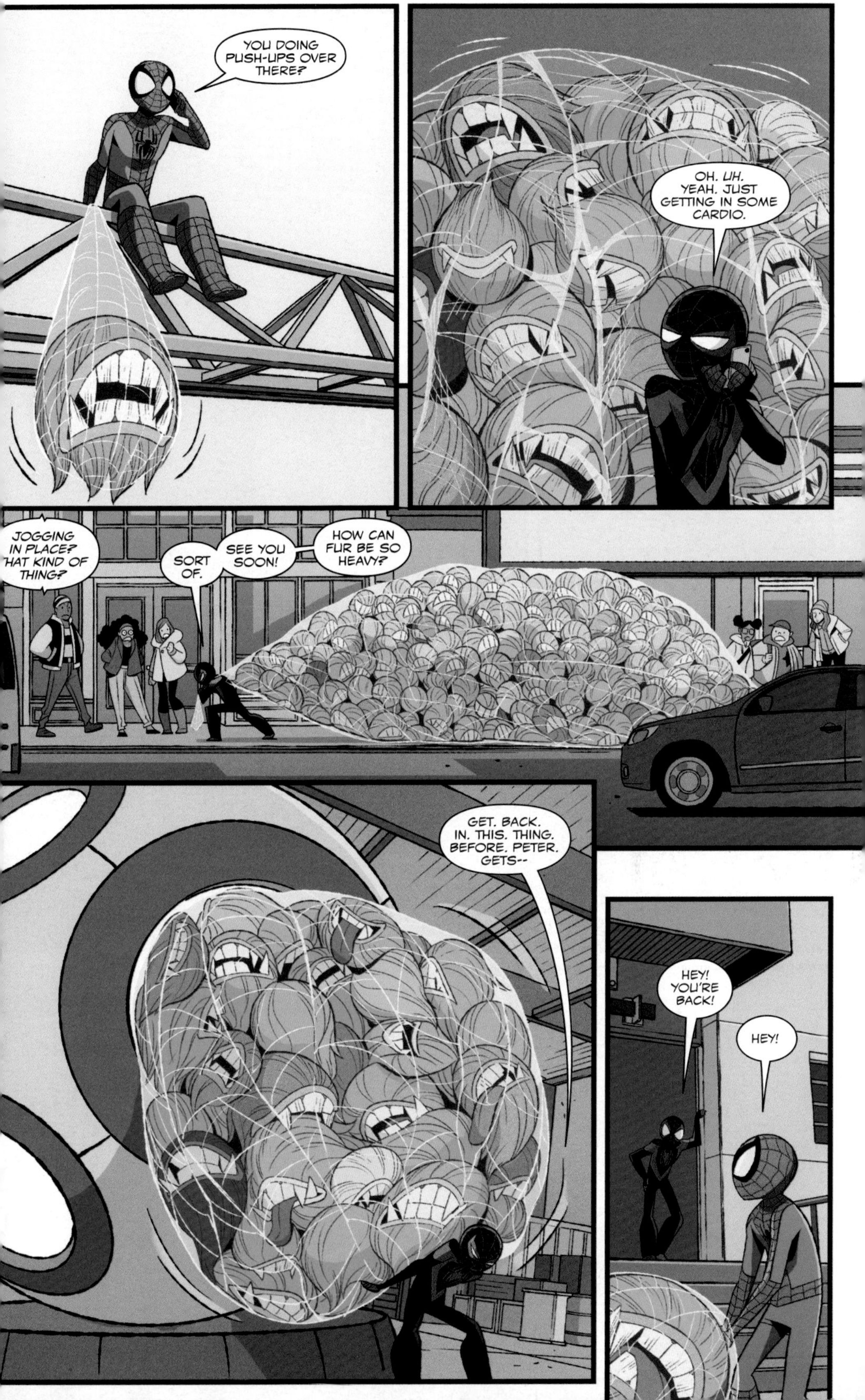
YOU DOING PUSH-UPS OVER THERE?
OH. UH. YEAH. JUST GETTING IN SOME CARDIO.
JOGGING IN PLACE? THAT KIND OF THING?
SORT OF.
SEE YOU SOON!
HOW CAN FUR BE SO HEAVY?
GET. BACK. IN. THIS. THING. BEFORE. PETER. GETS--
HEY! YOU'RE BACK!
HEY!

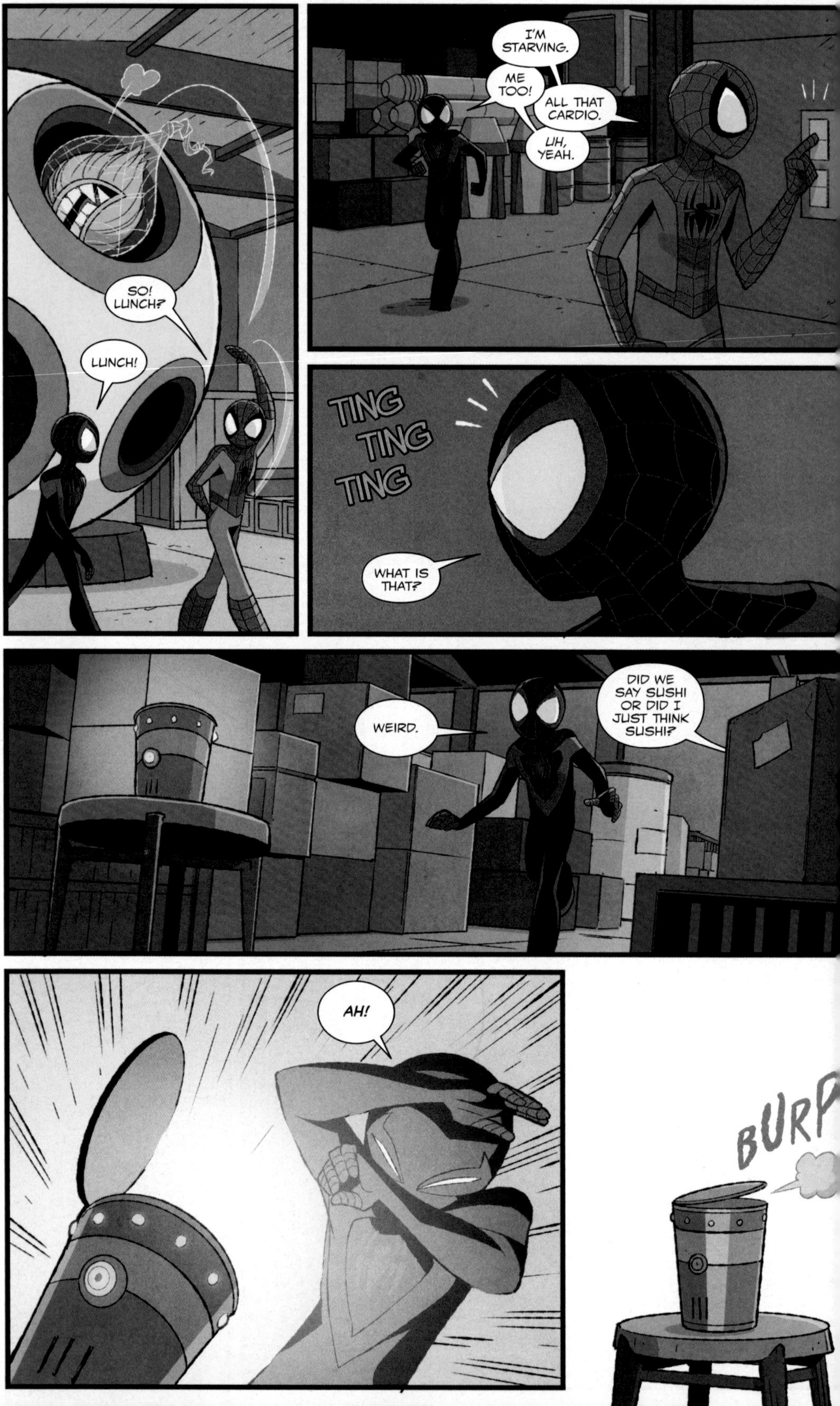
SO! LUNCH?
LUNCH!
I'M STARVING.
ME TOO!
ALL THAT CARDIO.
UH, YEAH.
TING TING TING
WHAT IS THAT?
WEIRD.
DID WE SAY SUSHI OR DID I JUST THINK SUSHI?
AH!
BURP

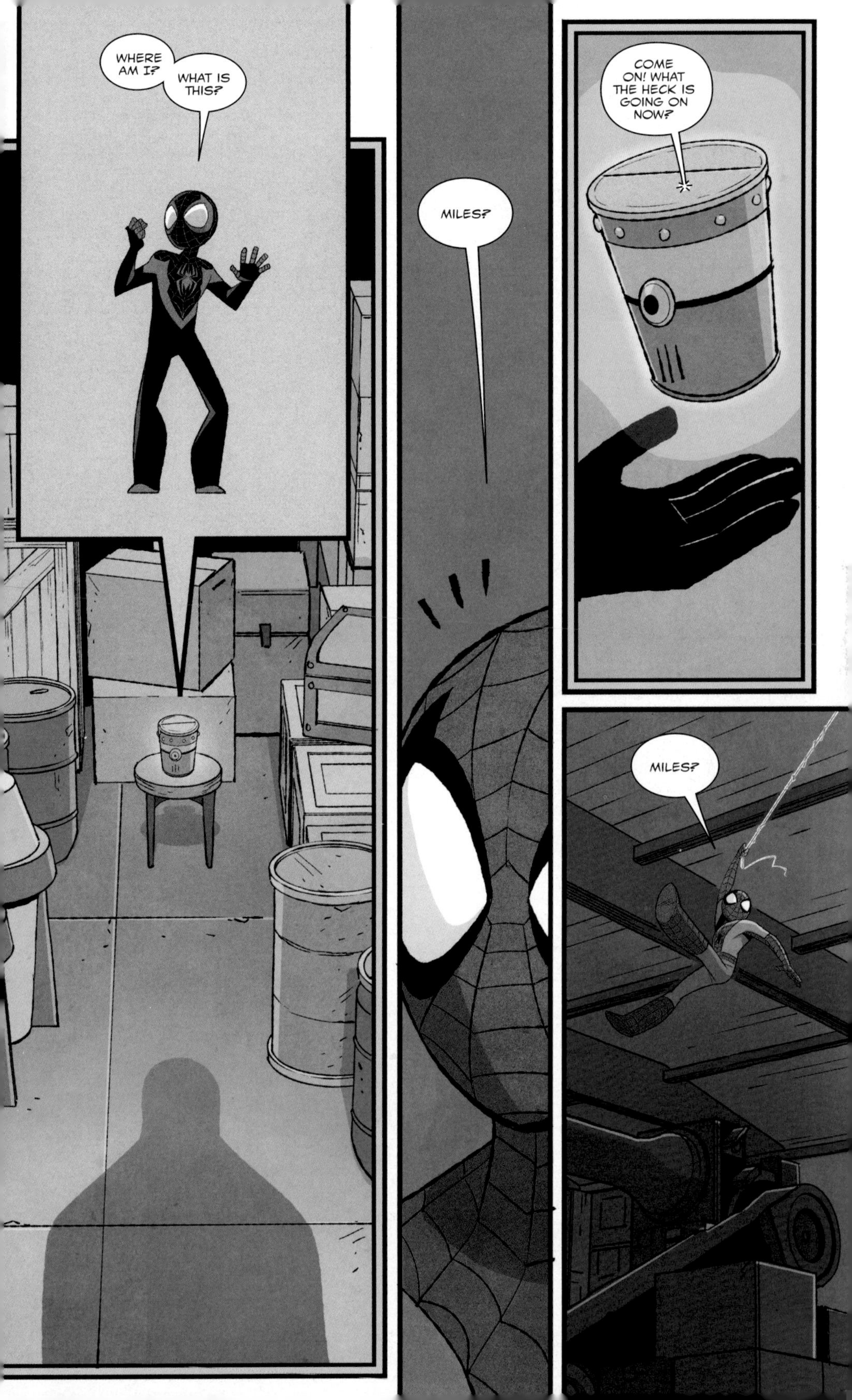
WHERE AM I?
WHAT IS THIS?
MILES?
COME ON! WHAT THE HECK IS GOING ON NOW?
MILES?

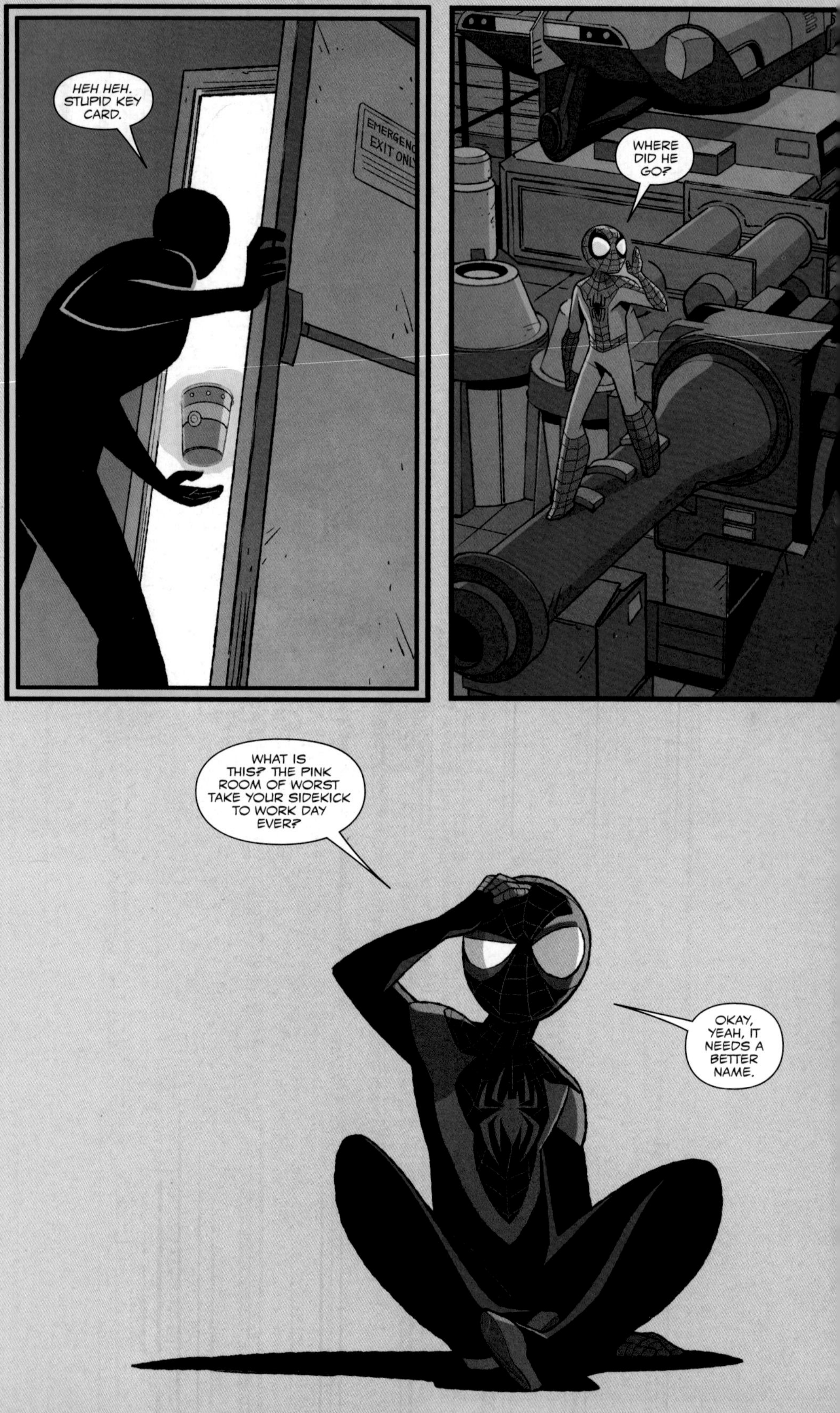
HEH HEH. STUPID KEY CARD.
EMERGENC EXIT ONLY
WHERE DID HE GO?
WHAT IS THIS? THE PINK ROOM OF WORST TAKE YOUR SIDEKICK TO WORK DAY EVER?
OKAY, YEAH, IT NEEDS A BETTER NAME.

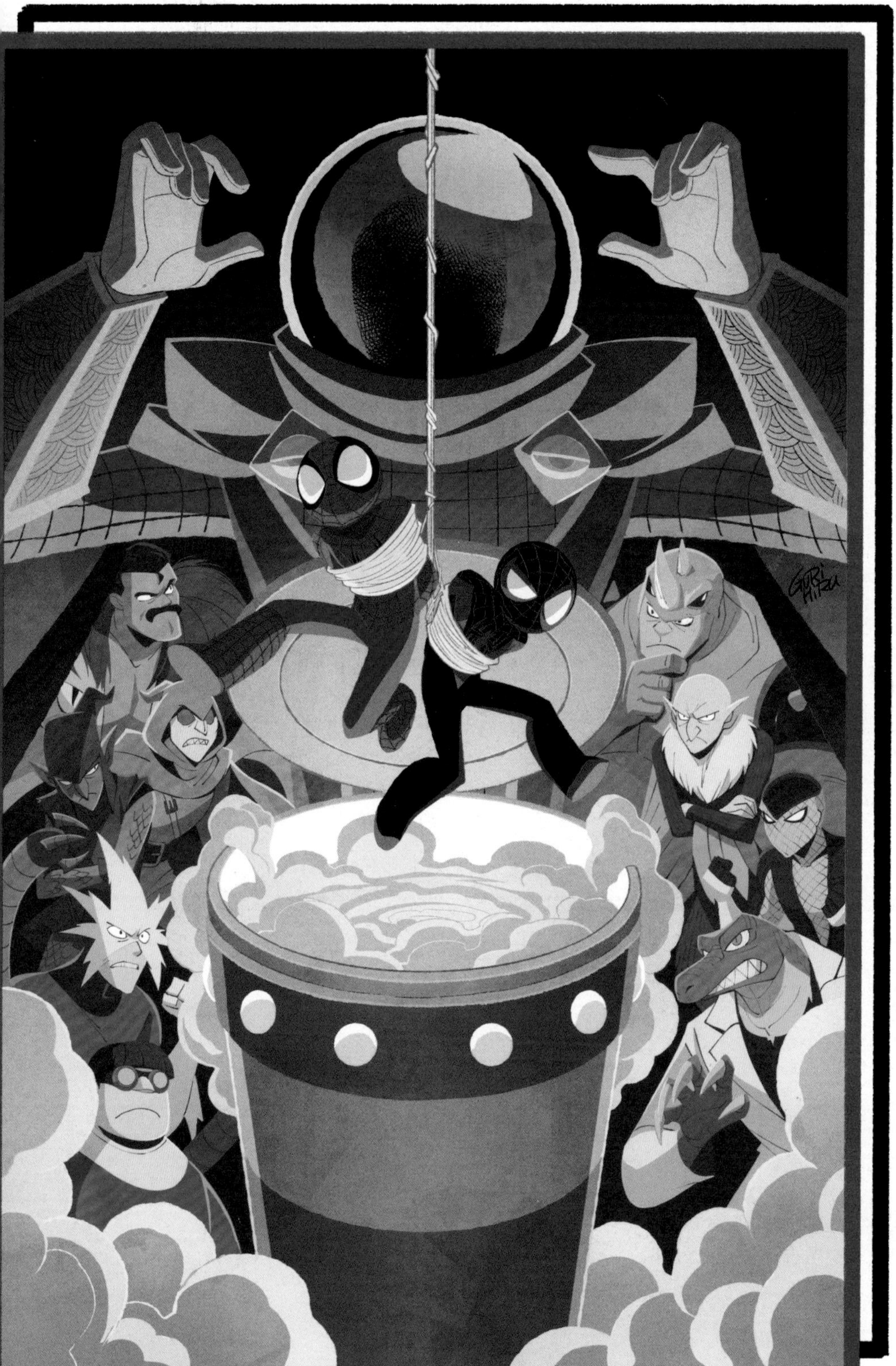

2

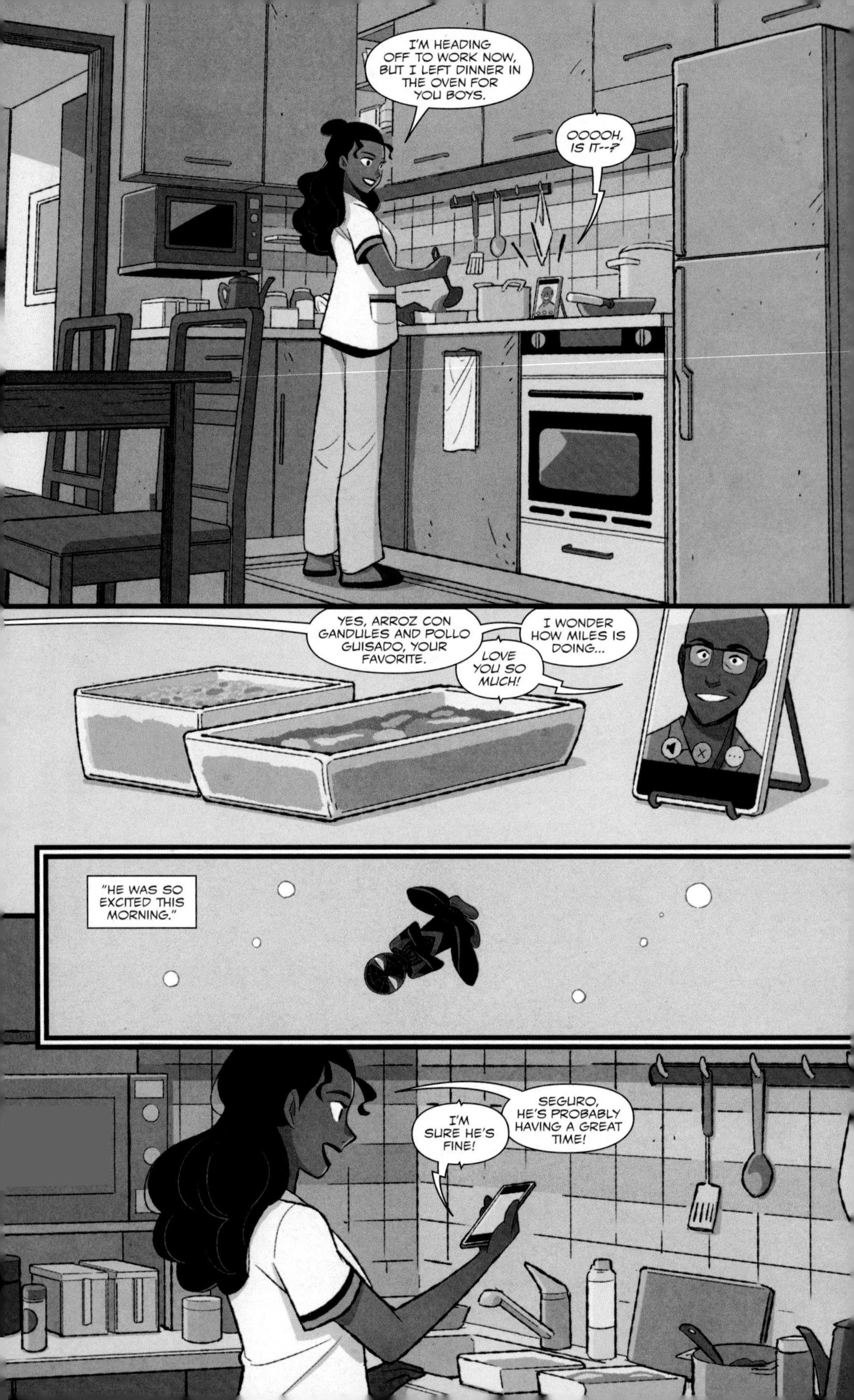
I'M HEADING OFF TO WORK NOW, BUT I LEFT DINNER IN THE OVEN FOR YOU BOYS.
OOOOH, IS IT--?
YES, ARROZ CON GANDULES AND POLLO GUISADO, YOUR FAVORITE.
LOVE YOU SO MUCH!
I WONDER HOW MILES IS DOING...
"HE WAS SO EXCITED THIS MORNING."
SEGURO, HE'S PROBABLY HAVING A GREAT TIME!
I'M SURE HE'S FINE!

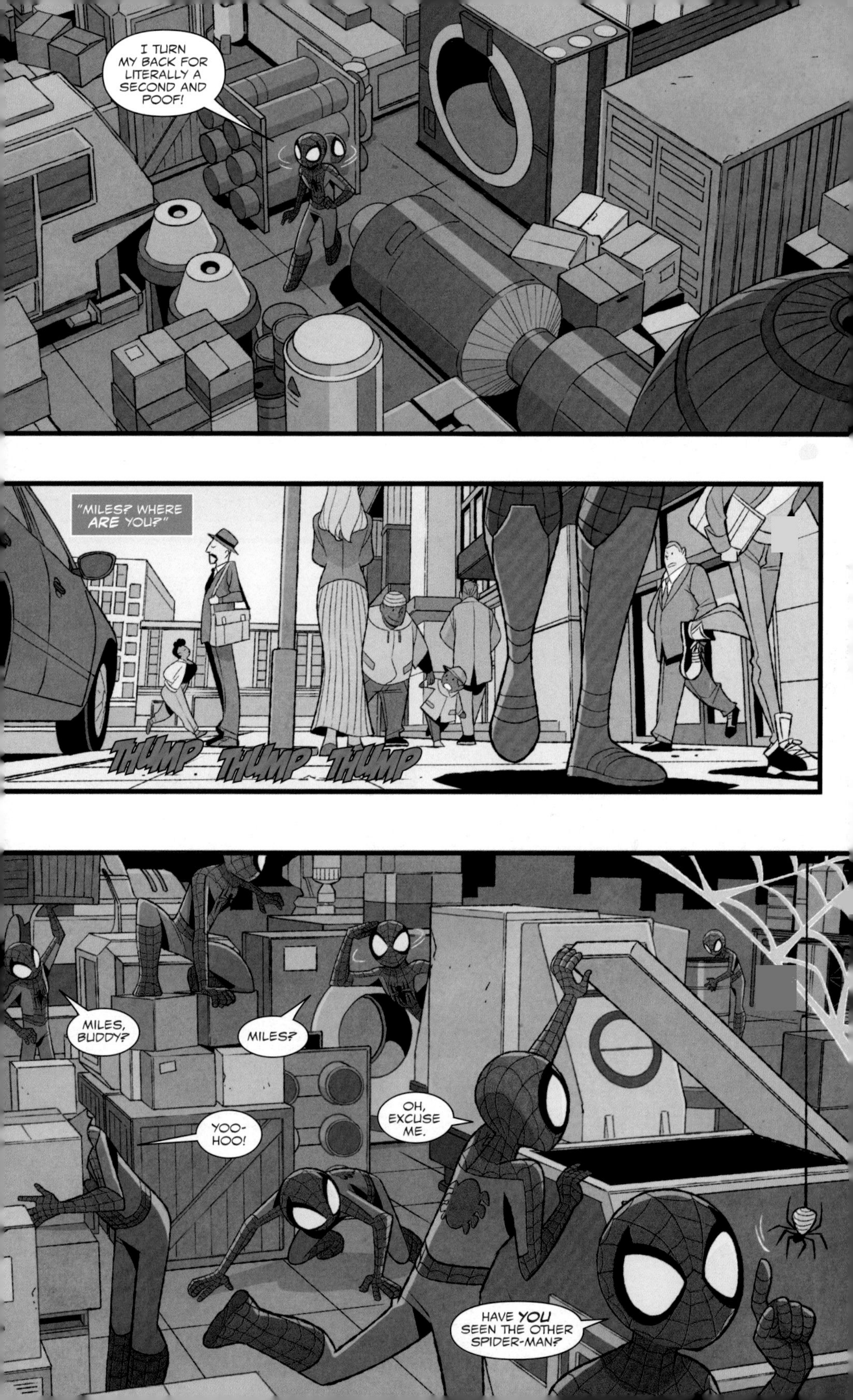
I TURN MY BACK FOR LITERALLY A SECOND AND POOF!
"MILES? WHERE ARE YOU?"
THUMP THUMP THUMP
MILES, BUDDY?
MILES?
YOO-HOO!
OH, EXCUSE ME.
HAVE YOU SEEN THE OTHER SPIDER-MAN?

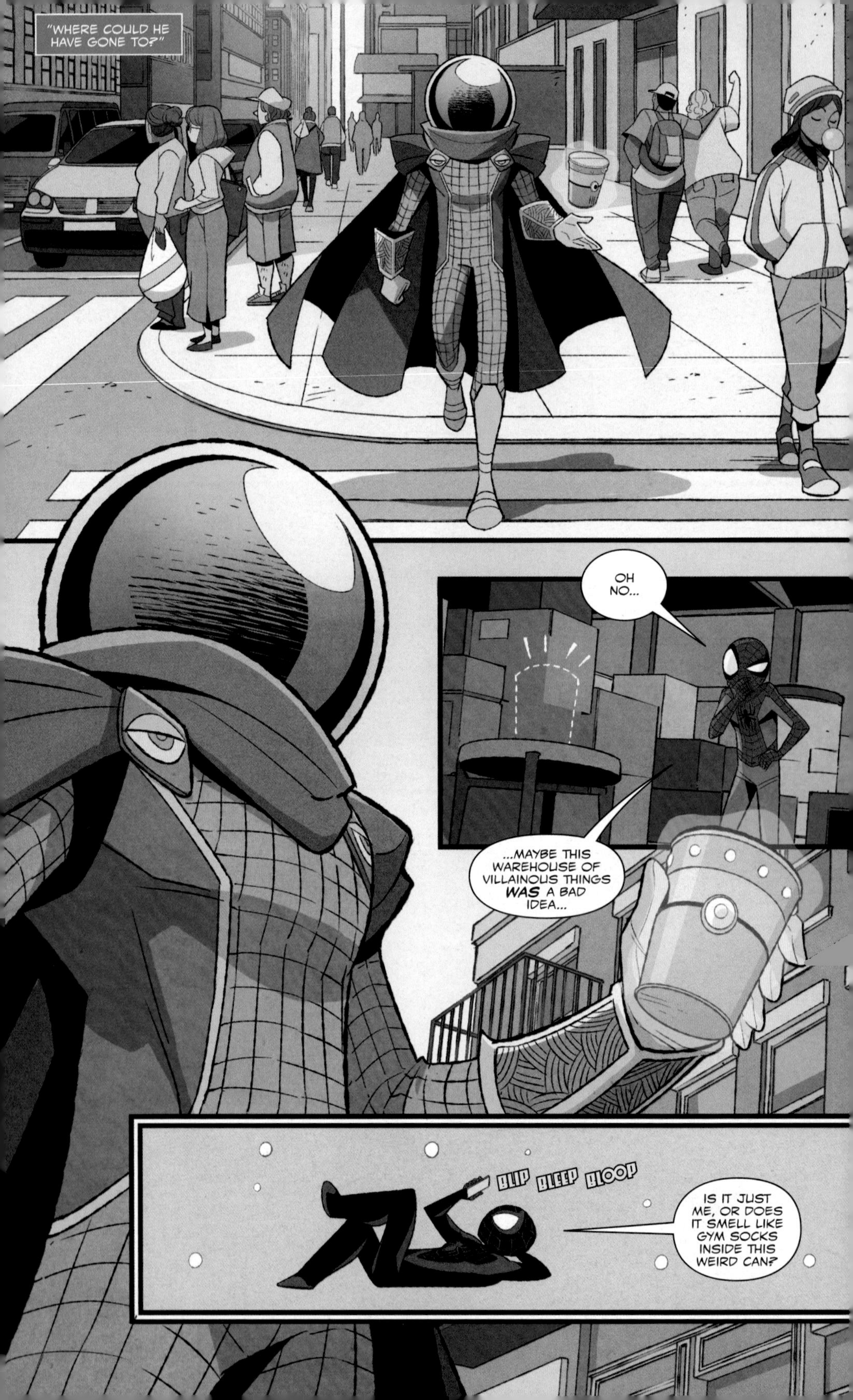
"WHERE COULD HE HAVE GONE TO?"
OH NO...
...MAYBE THIS WAREHOUSE OF VILLAINOUS THINGS WAS A BAD IDEA...
BLIP BLEEP BLOOP
IS IT JUST ME, OR DOES IT SMELL LIKE GYM SOCKS INSIDE THIS WEIRD CAN?

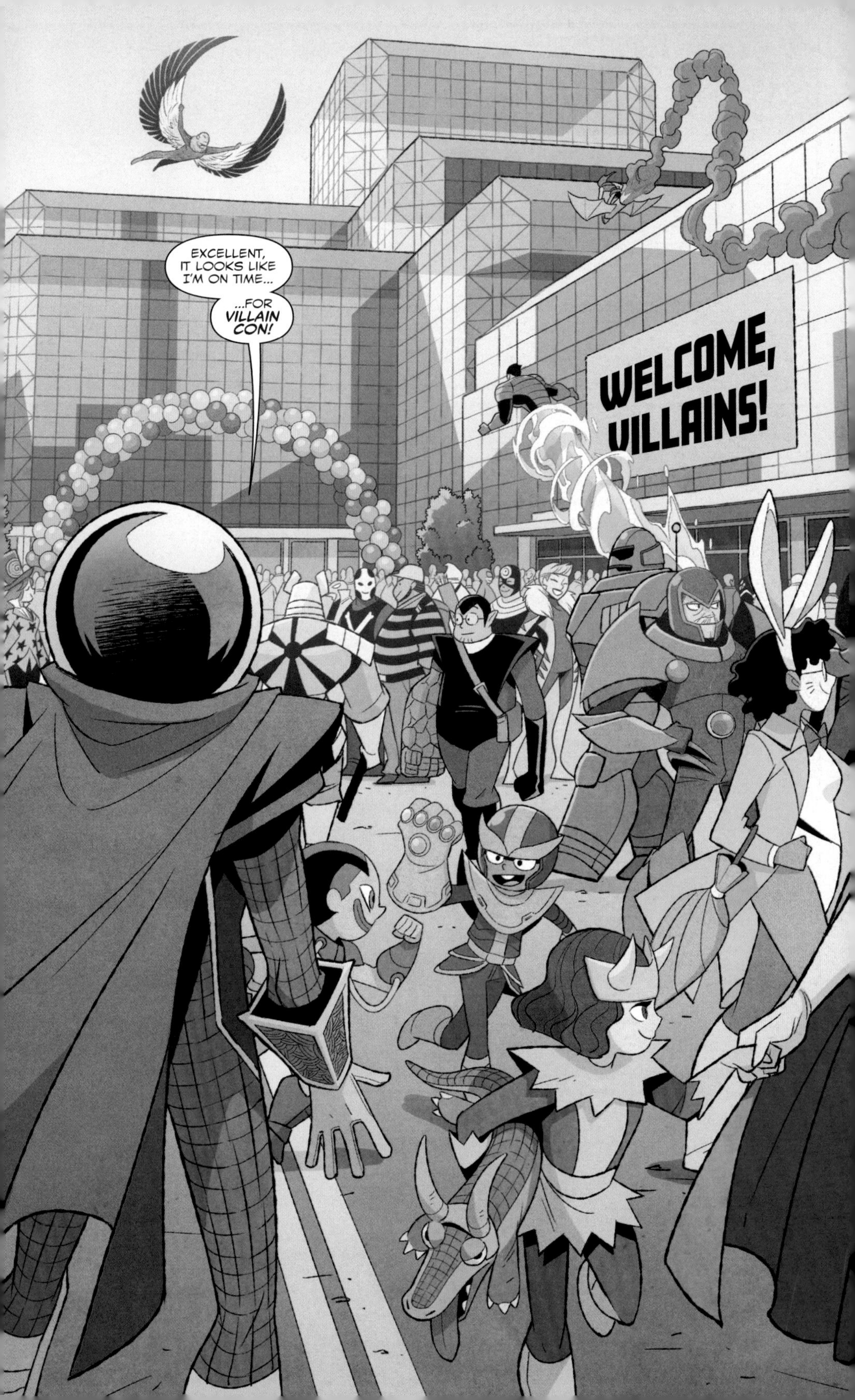
EXCELLENT, IT LOOKS LIKE I'M ON TIME...
...FOR VILLAIN CON!
WELCOME, VILLAINS!

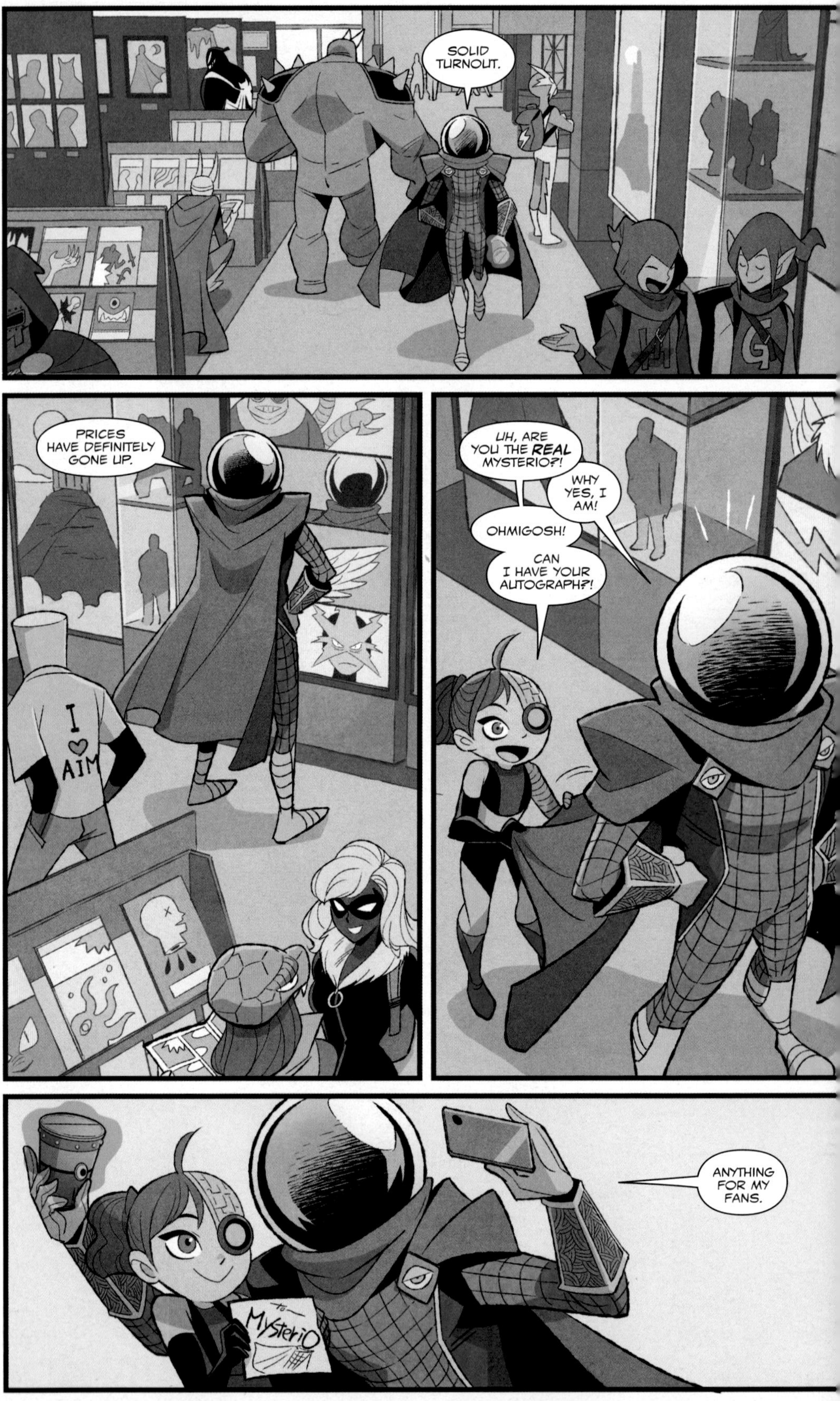
SOLID TURNOUT.
PRICES HAVE DEFINITELY GONE UP.
I ♥ AIM
UH, ARE YOU THE **REAL** MYSTERIO?!
WHY YES, I AM!
OHMIGOSH!
CAN I HAVE YOUR AUTOGRAPH?!
ANYTHING FOR MY FANS.
To MysteriO

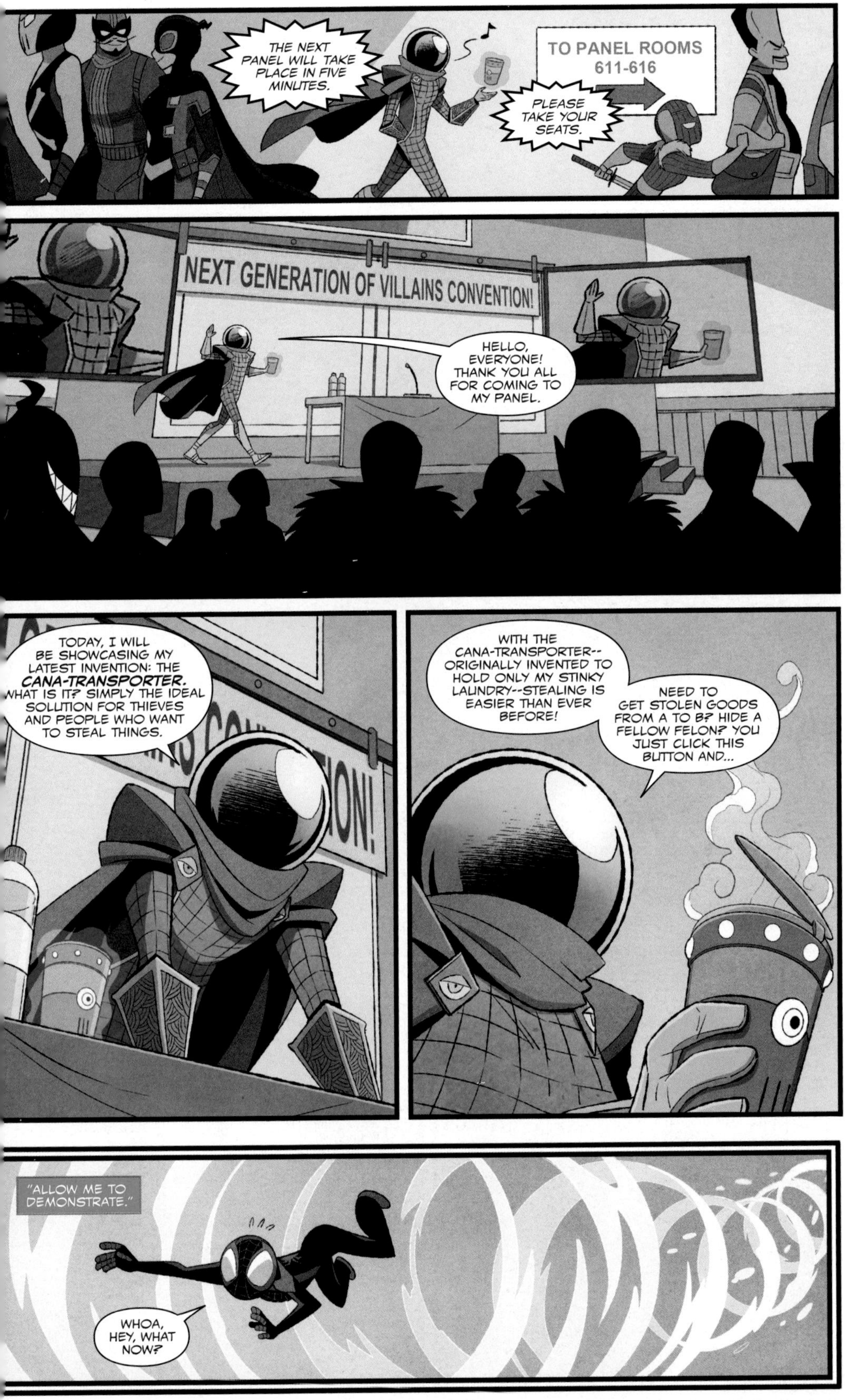

THE NEXT PANEL WILL TAKE PLACE IN FIVE MINUTES.
TO PANEL ROOMS 611-616
PLEASE TAKE YOUR SEATS.
NEXT GENERATION OF VILLAINS CONVENTION!
HELLO, EVERYONE! THANK YOU ALL FOR COMING TO MY PANEL.
TODAY, I WILL BE SHOWCASING MY LATEST INVENTION: THE ***CANA-TRANSPORTER.*** WHAT IS IT? SIMPLY THE IDEAL SOLUTION FOR THIEVES AND PEOPLE WHO WANT TO STEAL THINGS.
WITH THE CANA-TRANSPORTER--ORIGINALLY INVENTED TO HOLD ONLY MY STINKY LAUNDRY--STEALING IS EASIER THAN EVER BEFORE!
NEED TO GET STOLEN GOODS FROM A TO B? HIDE A FELLOW FELON? YOU JUST CLICK THIS BUTTON AND...
"ALLOW ME TO DEMONSTRATE."
WHOA, HEY, WHAT NOW?

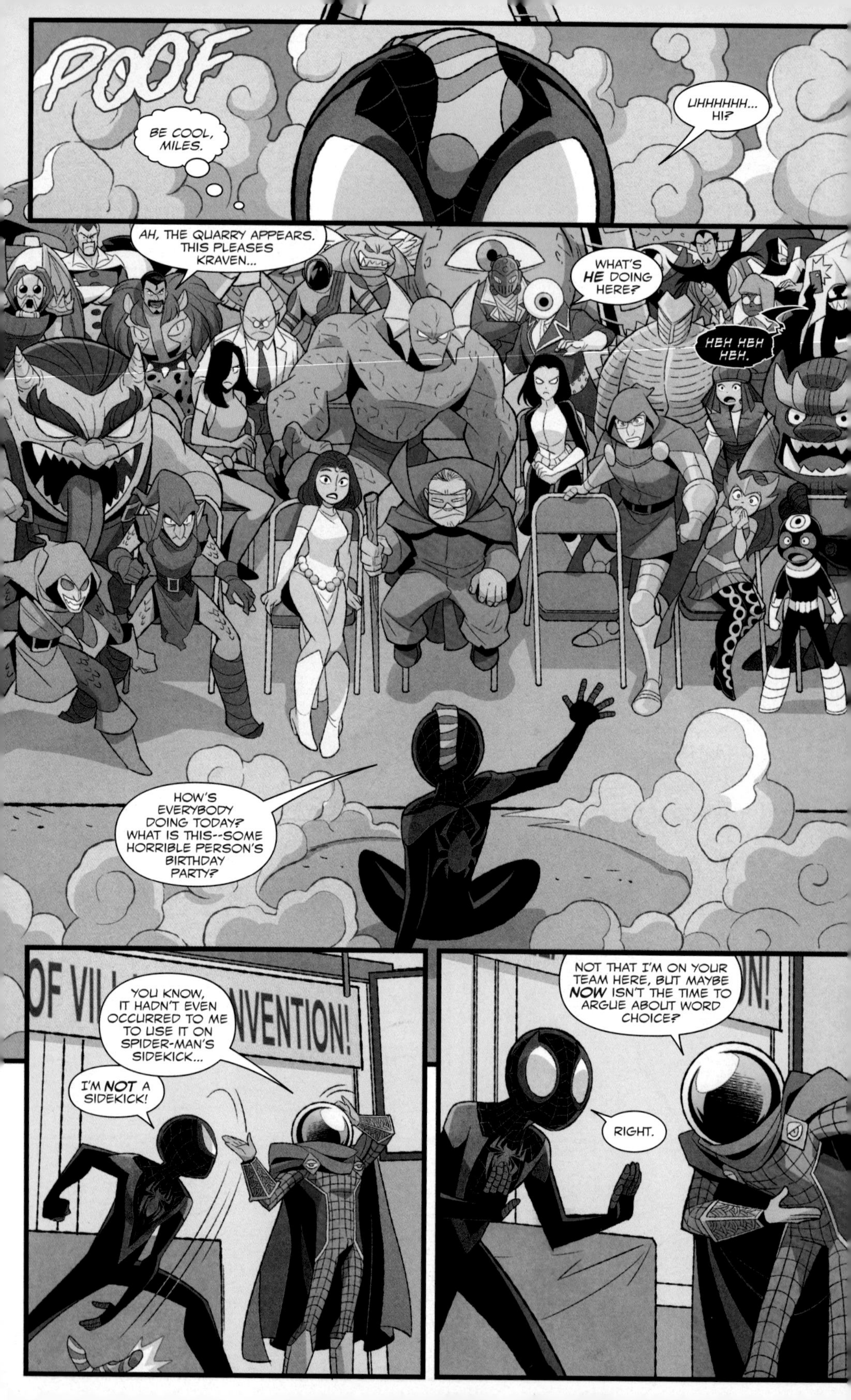
POOF
BE COOL, MILES.
UHHHHHH... HI?
AH, THE QUARRY APPEARS. THIS PLEASES KRAVEN...
WHAT'S HE DOING HERE?
HEH HEH HEH.
HOW'S EVERYBODY DOING TODAY? WHAT IS THIS--SOME HORRIBLE PERSON'S BIRTHDAY PARTY?
OF VIL... ...NVENTION!
YOU KNOW, IT HADN'T EVEN OCCURRED TO ME TO USE IT ON SPIDER-MAN'S SIDEKICK...
I'M NOT A SIDEKICK!
NOT THAT I'M ON YOUR TEAM HERE, BUT MAYBE NOW ISN'T THE TIME TO ARGUE ABOUT WORD CHOICE?
RIGHT.

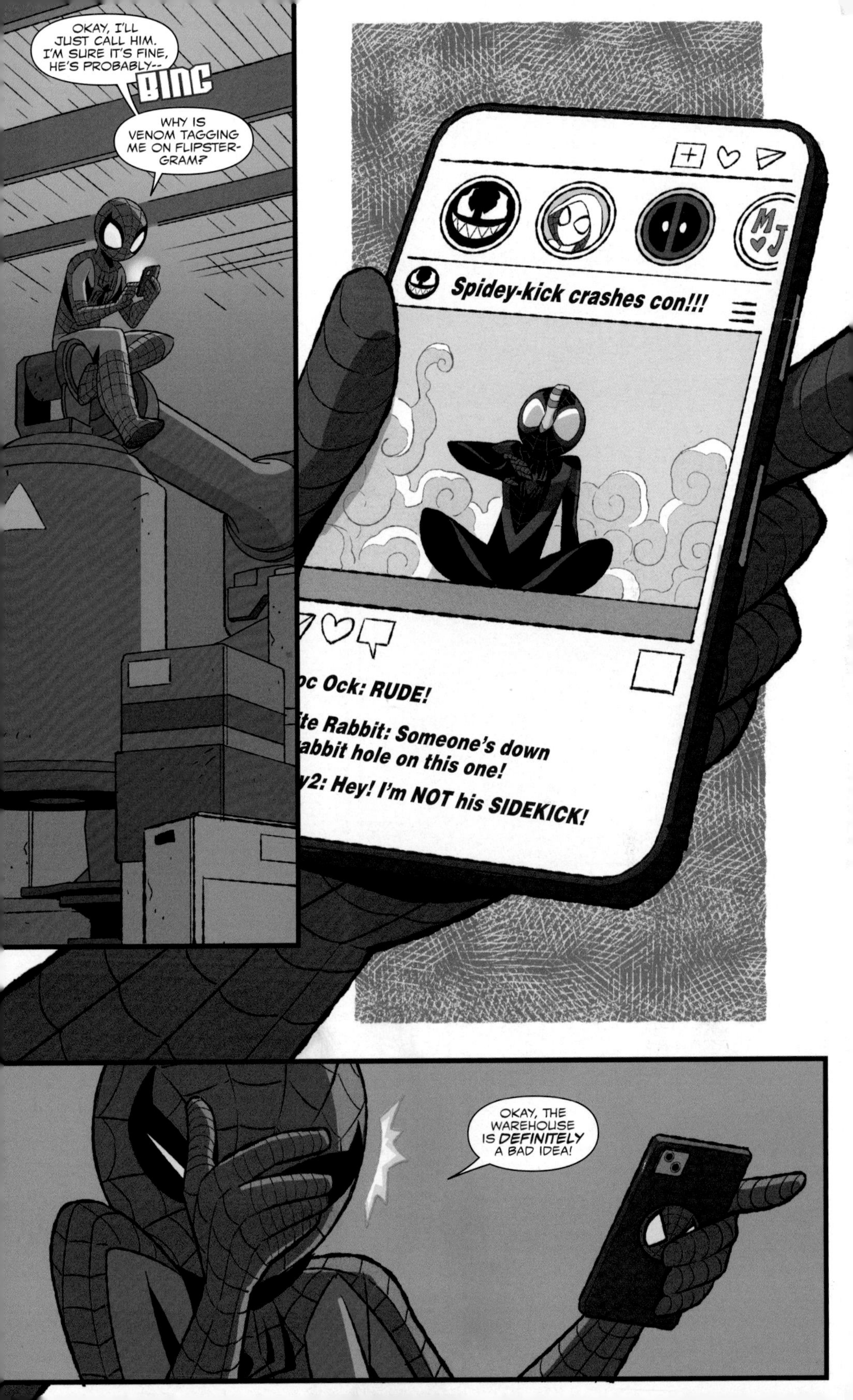

OKAY, I'LL JUST CALL HIM. I'M SURE IT'S FINE, HE'S PROBABLY--
BINC
WHY IS VENOM TAGGING ME ON FLIPSTER-GRAM?
Spidey-kick crashes con!!!
MJ
oc Ock: RUDE!
ite Rabbit: Someone's down abbit hole on this one!
y2: Hey! I'm NOT his SIDEKICK!
OKAY, THE WAREHOUSE IS DEFINITELY A BAD IDEA!

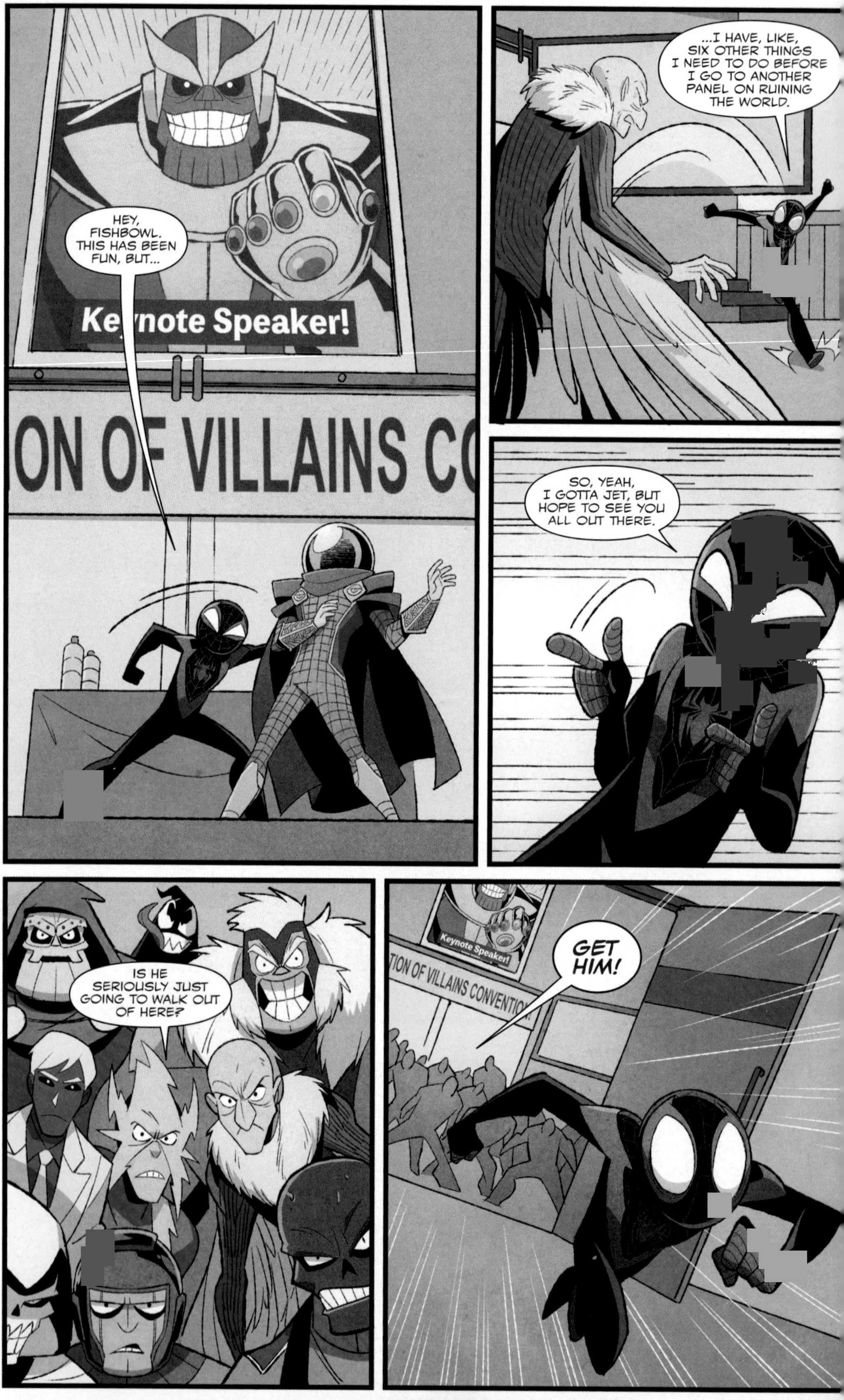
Keynote Speaker!
HEY, FISHBOWL. THIS HAS BEEN FUN, BUT...
ON OF VILLAINS CO
...I HAVE, LIKE, SIX OTHER THINGS I NEED TO DO BEFORE I GO TO ANOTHER PANEL ON RUINING THE WORLD.
SO, YEAH, I GOTTA JET, BUT HOPE TO SEE YOU ALL OUT THERE.
IS HE SERIOUSLY JUST GOING TO WALK OUT OF HERE?
Keynote Speaker!
TION OF VILLAINS CONVENTIO
GET HIM!

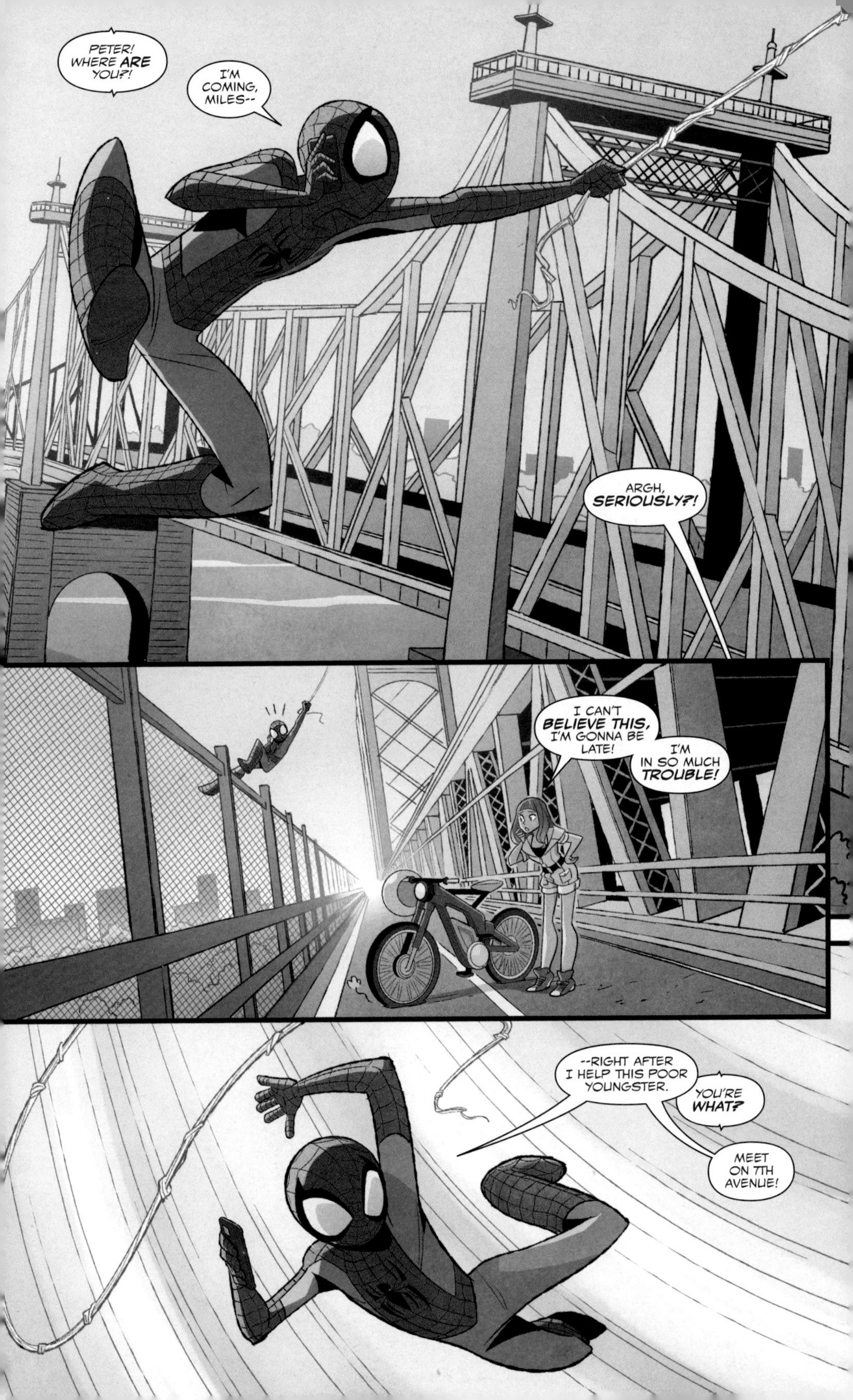
PETER! WHERE ARE YOU?!
I'M COMING, MILES--
ARGH, SERIOUSLY?!
I CAN'T BELIEVE THIS, I'M GONNA BE LATE!
I'M IN SO MUCH TROUBLE!
--RIGHT AFTER I HELP THIS POOR YOUNGSTER.
YOU'RE WHAT?
MEET ON 7TH AVENUE!

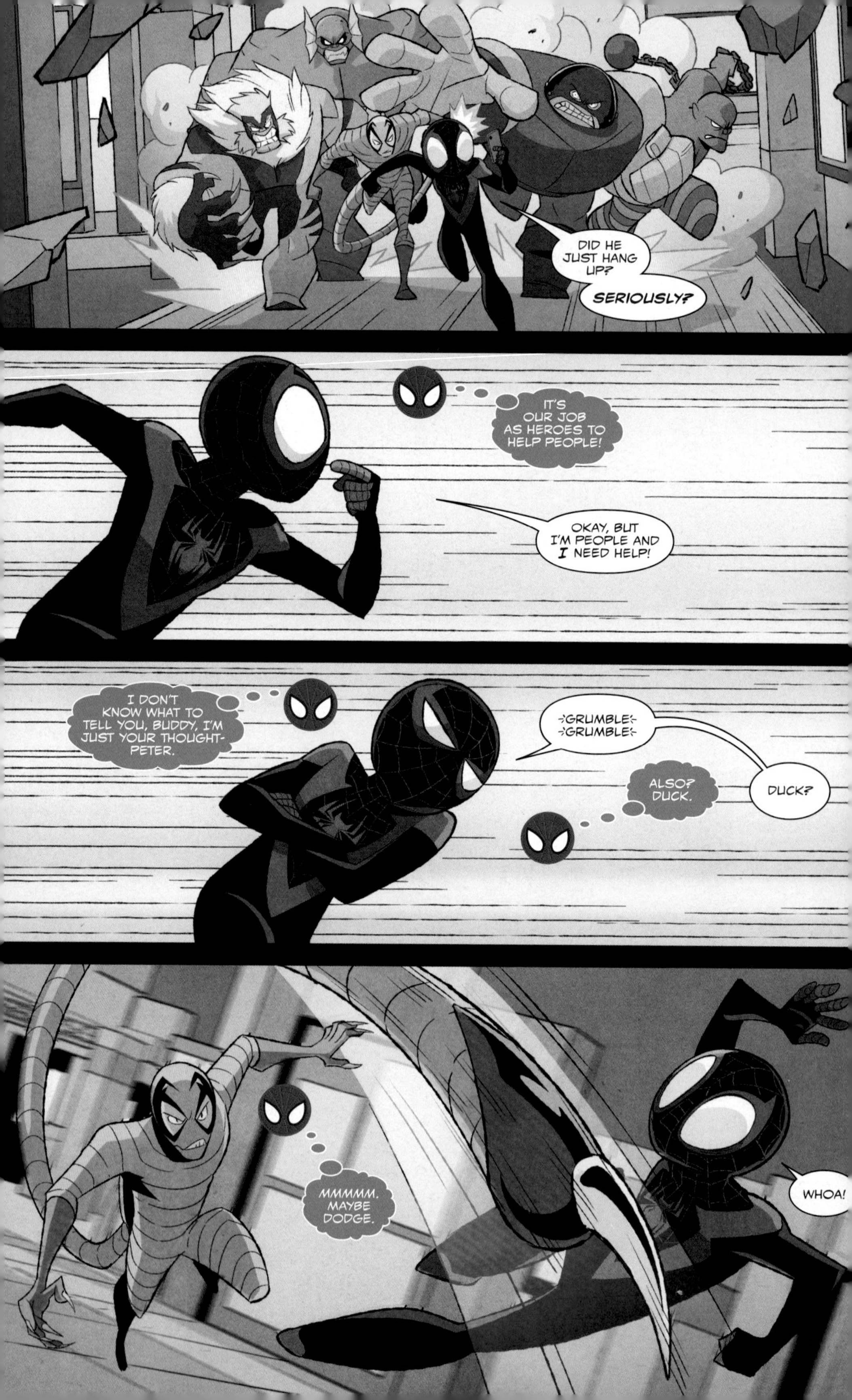
DID HE JUST HANG UP?
SERIOUSLY?
IT'S OUR JOB AS HEROES TO HELP PEOPLE!
OKAY, BUT I'M PEOPLE AND I NEED HELP!
I DON'T KNOW WHAT TO TELL YOU, BUDDY, I'M JUST YOUR THOUGHT-PETER.
GRUMBLE GRUMBLE
ALSO? DUCK.
DUCK?
MMMMM. MAYBE DODGE.
WHOA!

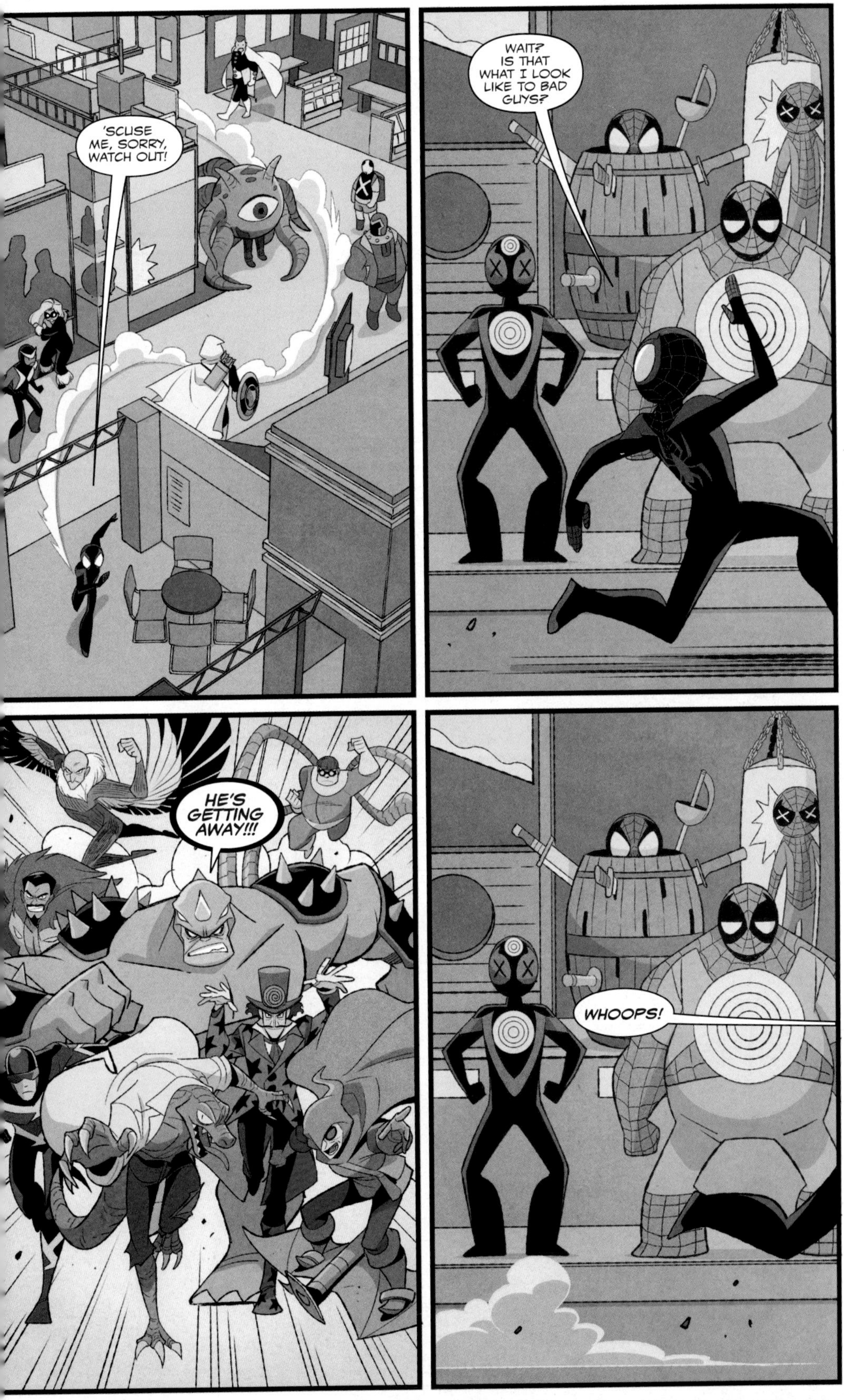
'SCUSE ME, SORRY, WATCH OUT!
WAIT? IS THAT WHAT I LOOK LIKE TO BAD GUYS?
HE'S GETTING AWAY!!!
WHOOPS!

GREAT CON!

HEY THERE, INNOCENT CITIZENS I NEED TO PROTECT.

YOU HAVE TO GET SOME DISTANCE, OR ELSE PEOPLE COULD GET HURT.

OKAY, ONE, I ALREADY THOUGHT OF THAT. TWO, IF I GET THEM TO FOLLOW ME TO 7TH, THEN REAL YOU CAN BACK ME UP. RIGHT?

THAT'S THE SPIRIT!

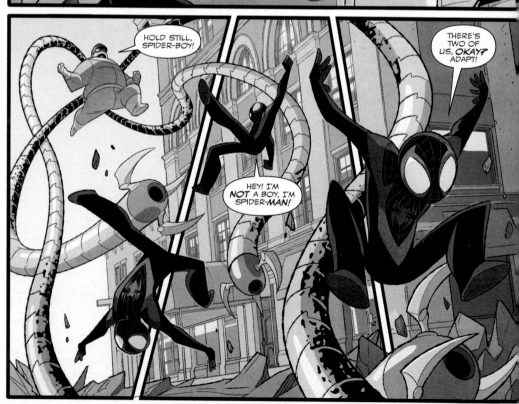

HOLD STILL, SPIDER-BOY!

HEY! I'M NOT A BOY, I'M SPIDER-MAN!

THERE'S TWO OF US, OKAY? ADAPT!

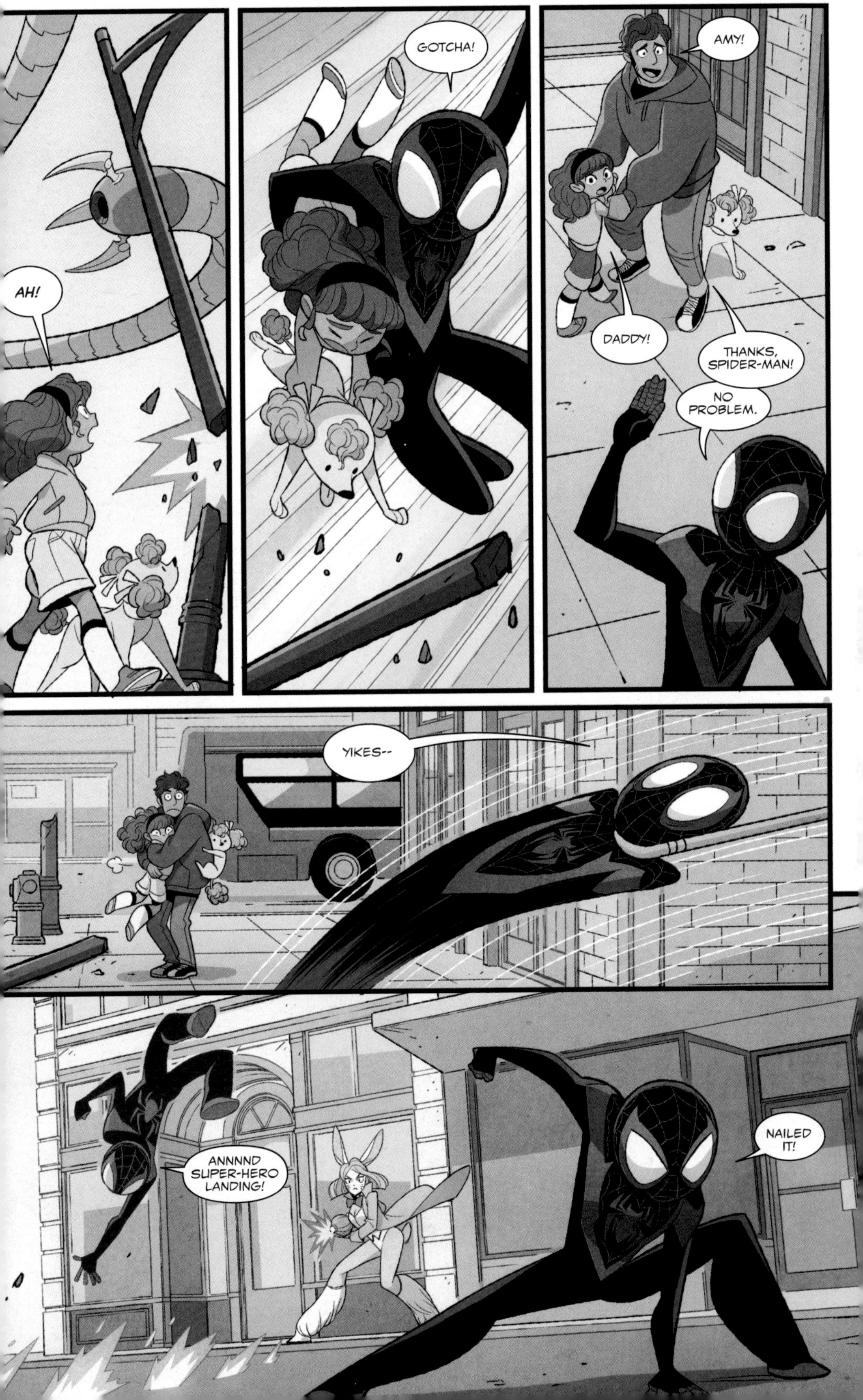
AH!
GOTCHA!
AMY!
DADDY!
THANKS, SPIDER-MAN!
NO PROBLEM.
YIKES--
ANNNND SUPER-HERO LANDING!
NAILED IT!

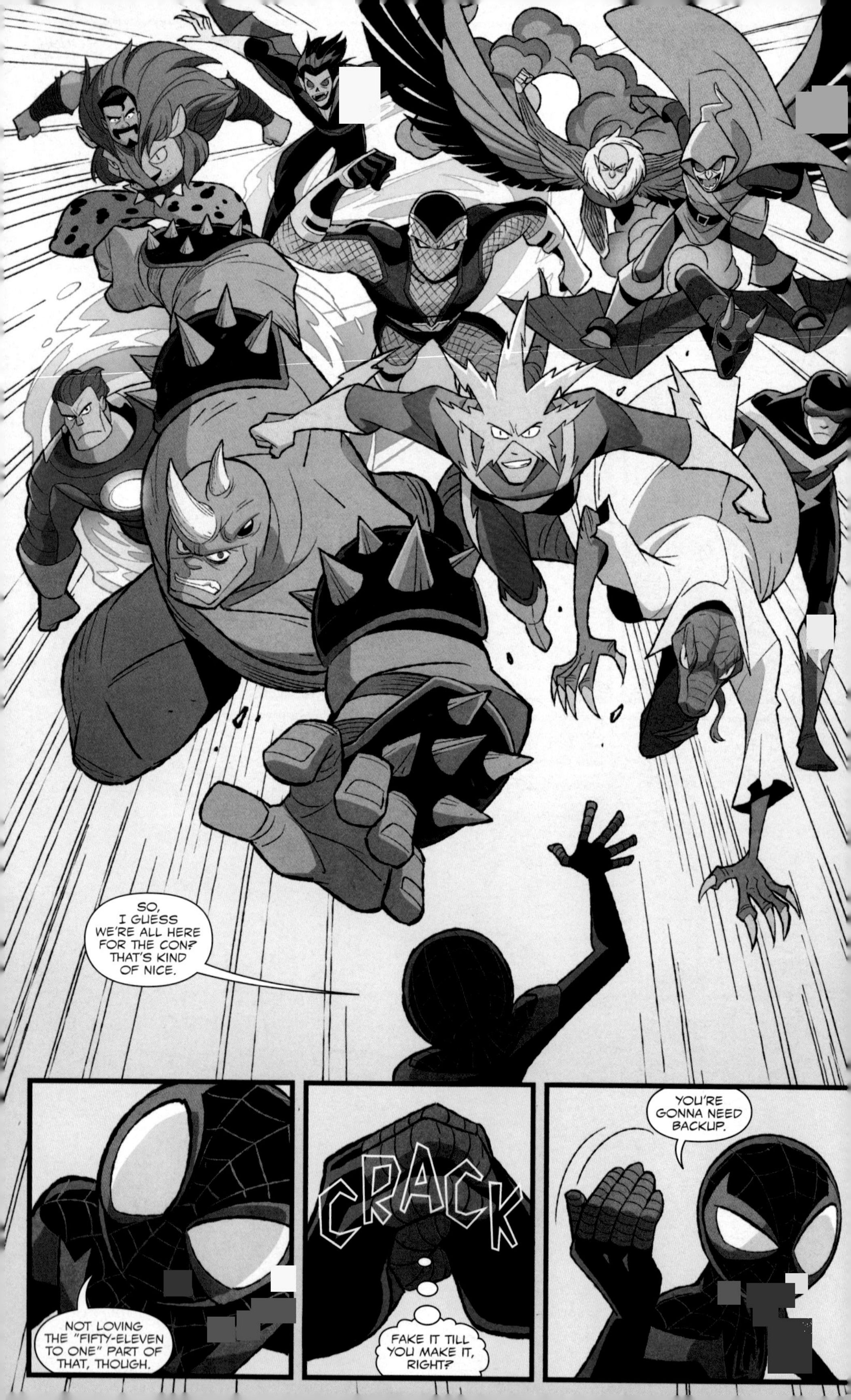
SO, I GUESS WE'RE ALL HERE FOR THE CON? THAT'S KIND OF NICE.
NOT LOVING THE "FIFTY-ELEVEN TO ONE" PART OF THAT, THOUGH.
CRACK
FAKE IT TILL YOU MAKE IT, RIGHT?
YOU'RE GONNA NEED BACKUP.

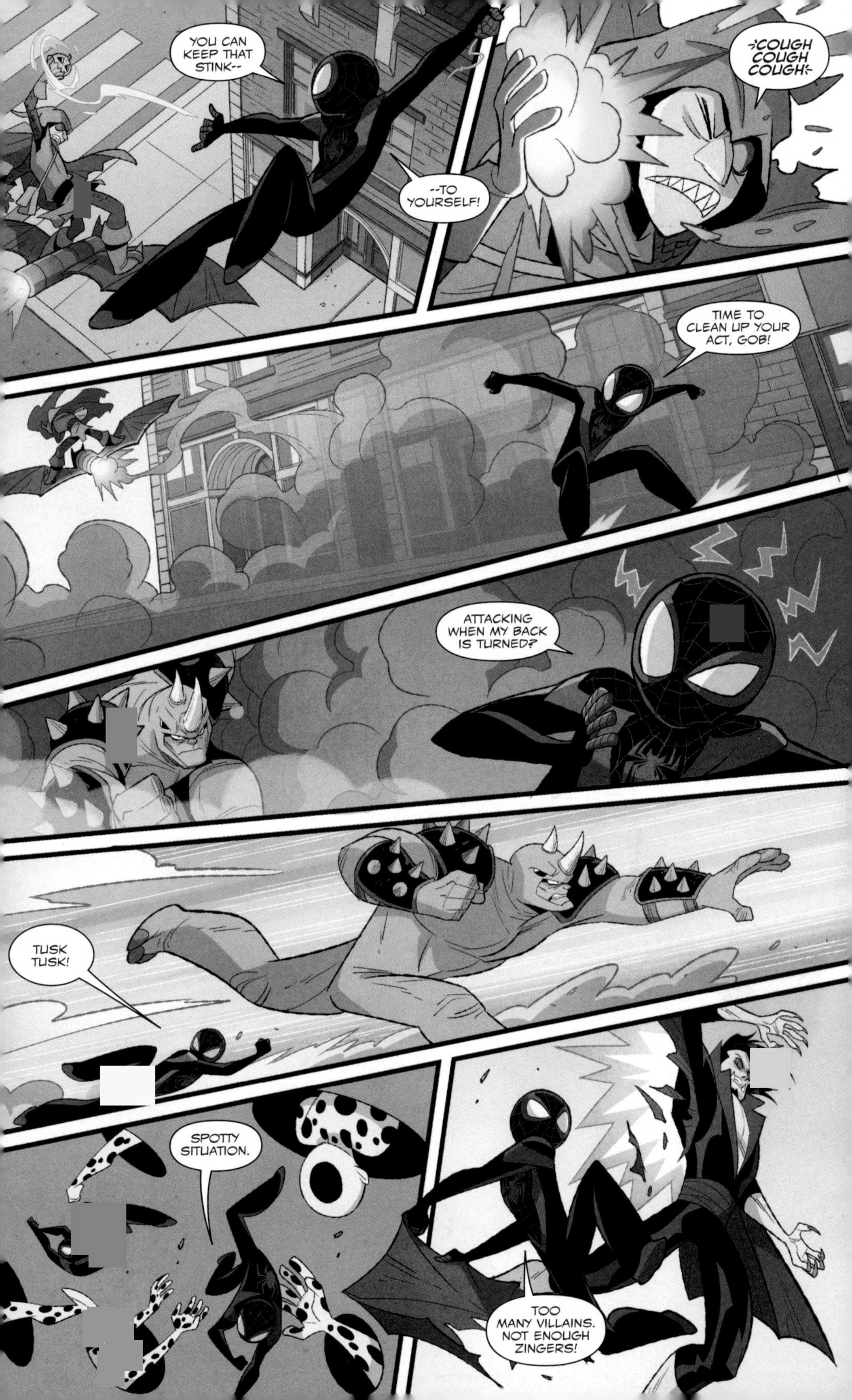
YOU CAN KEEP THAT STINK--
--TO YOURSELF!
COUGH COUGH COUGH
TIME TO CLEAN UP YOUR ACT, GOB!
ATTACKING WHEN MY BACK IS TURNED?
TUSK TUSK!
SPOTTY SITUATION.
TOO MANY VILLAINS. NOT ENOUGH ZINGERS!

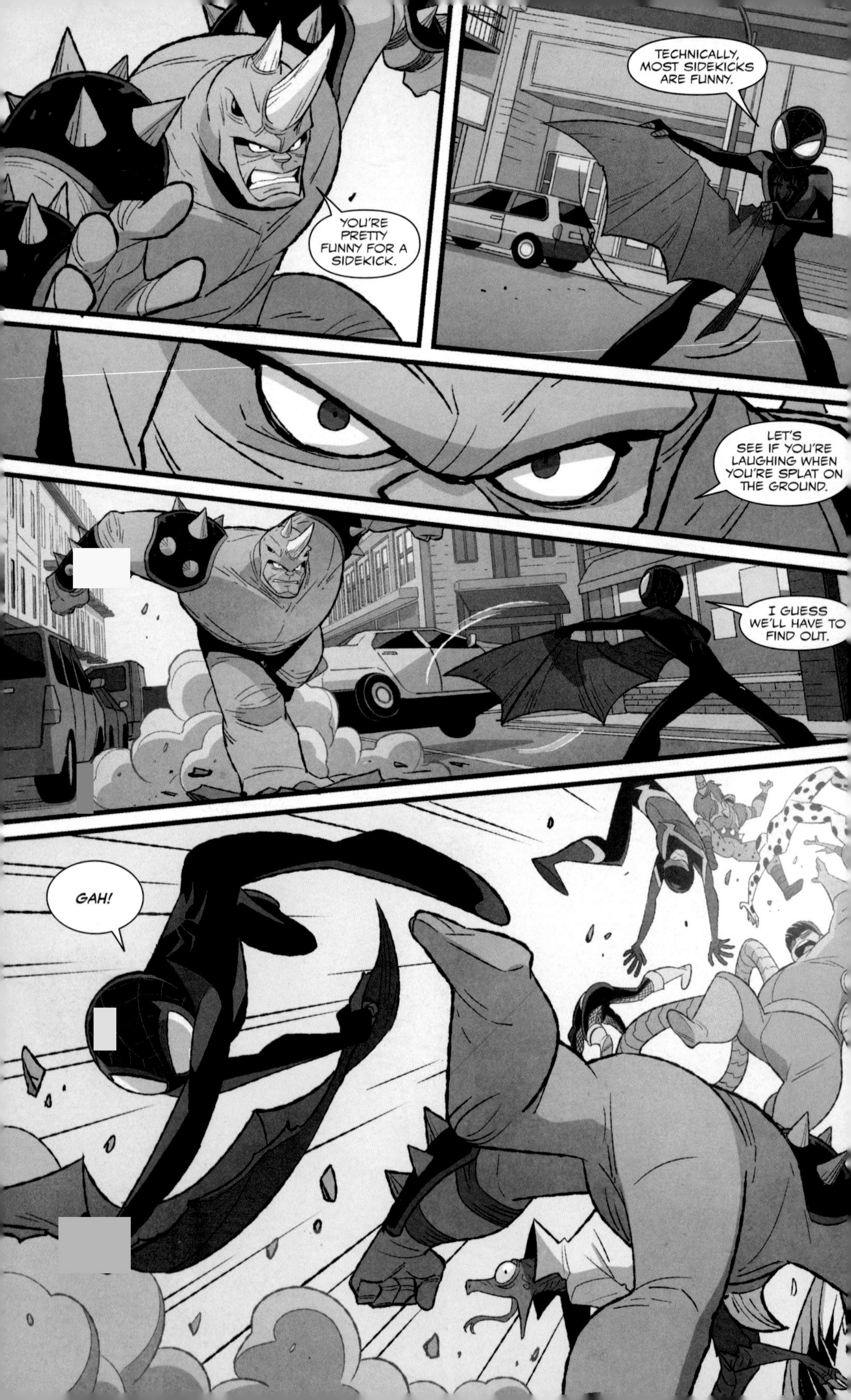
YOU'RE PRETTY FUNNY FOR A SIDEKICK.
TECHNICALLY, MOST SIDEKICKS ARE FUNNY.
LET'S SEE IF YOU'RE LAUGHING WHEN YOU'RE SPLAT ON THE GROUND.
I GUESS WE'LL HAVE TO FIND OUT.
GAH!

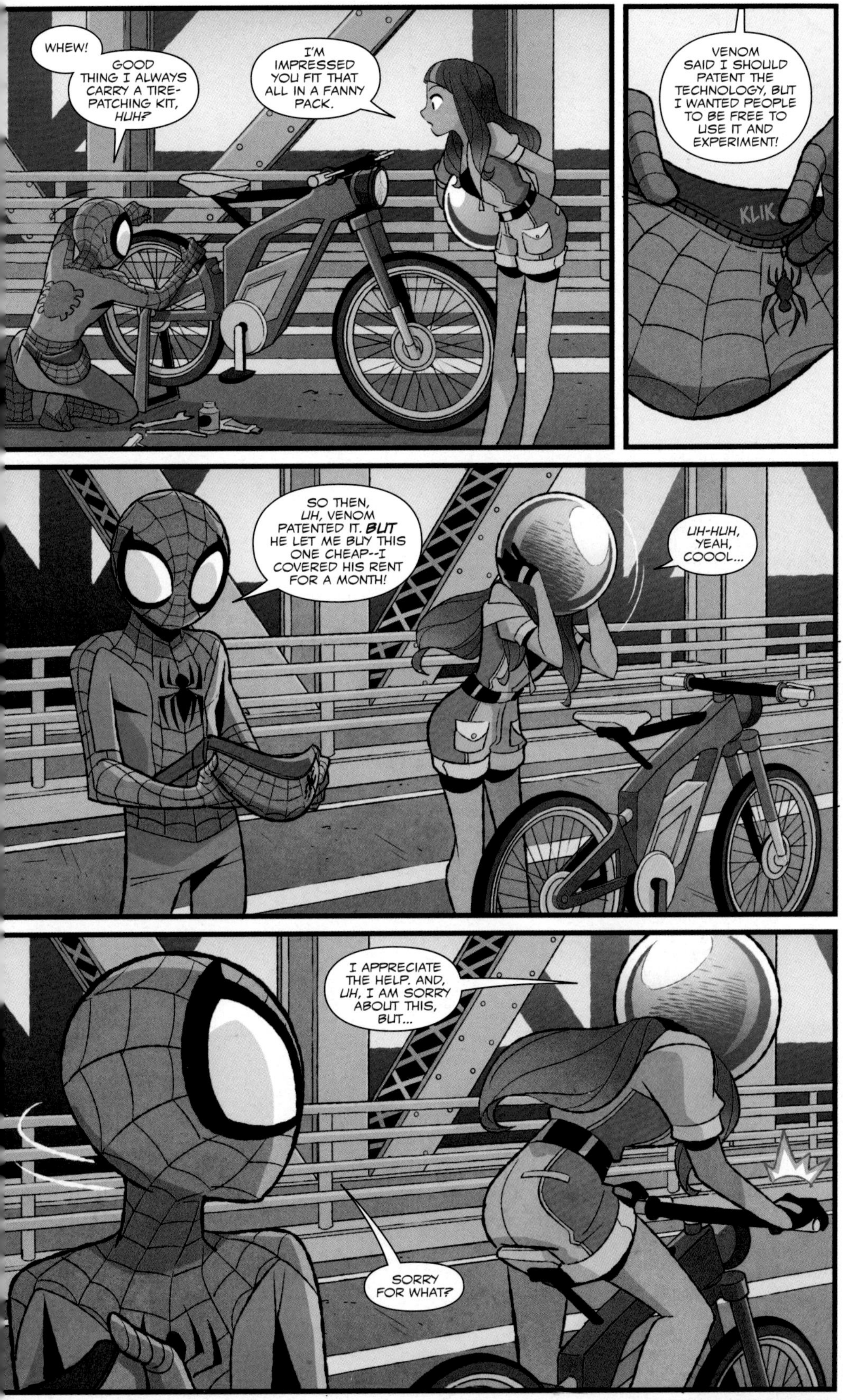
WHEW!
GOOD THING I ALWAYS CARRY A TIRE-PATCHING KIT, HUH?
I'M IMPRESSED YOU FIT THAT ALL IN A FANNY PACK.
VENOM SAID I SHOULD PATENT THE TECHNOLOGY, BUT I WANTED PEOPLE TO BE FREE TO USE IT AND EXPERIMENT!
KLIK
SO THEN, UH, VENOM PATENTED IT. BUT HE LET ME BUY THIS ONE CHEAP--I COVERED HIS RENT FOR A MONTH!
UH-HUH, YEAH, COOOL...
I APPRECIATE THE HELP. AND, UH, I AM SORRY ABOUT THIS, BUT...
SORRY FOR WHAT?

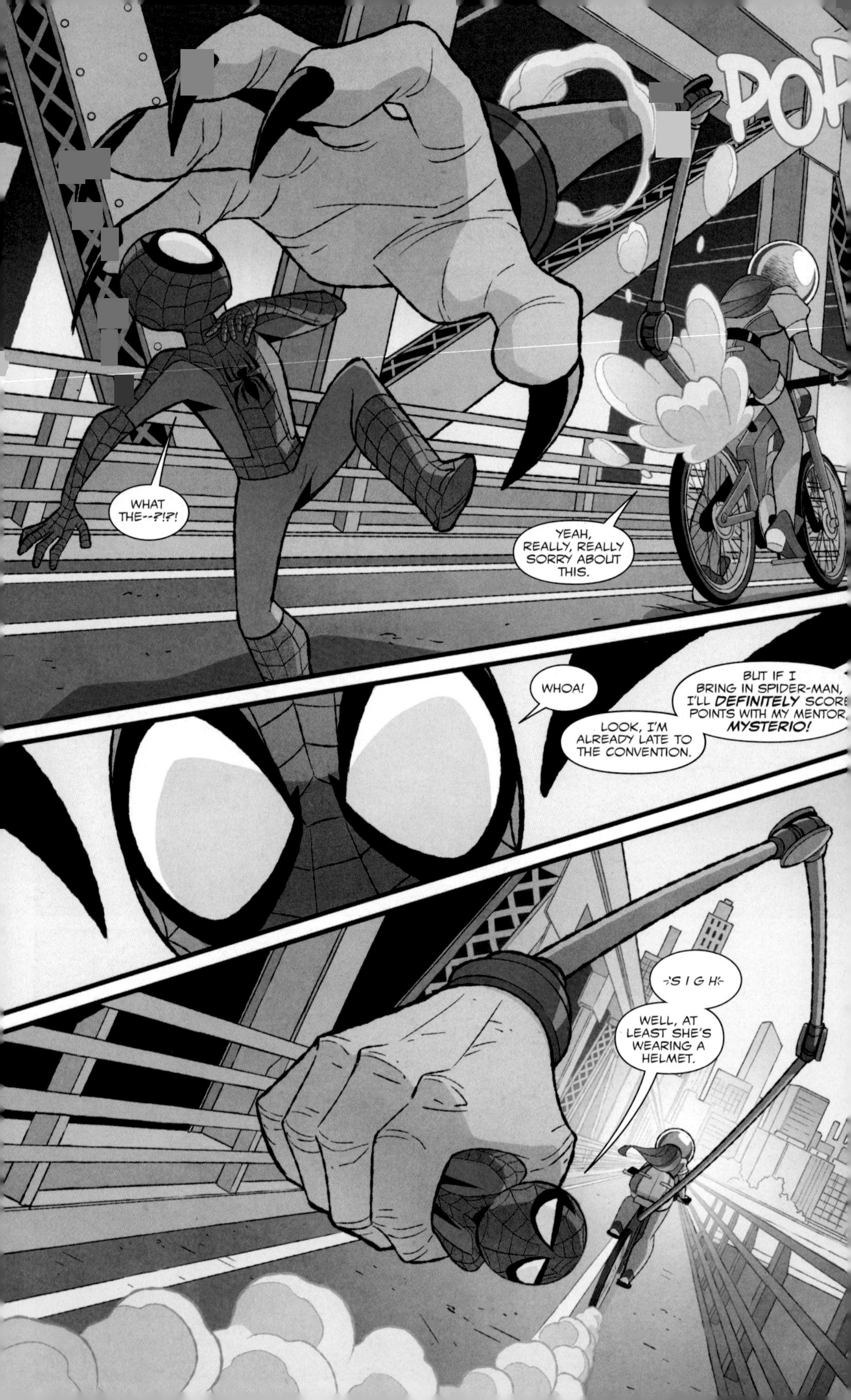
POP
WHAT THE--?!?!
YEAH, REALLY, REALLY SORRY ABOUT THIS.
WHOA!
LOOK, I'M ALREADY LATE TO THE CONVENTION.
BUT IF I BRING IN SPIDER-MAN, I'LL *DEFINITELY* SCORE POINTS WITH MY MENTOR, ***MYSTERIO!***
-SIGH-
WELL, AT LEAST SHE'S WEARING A HELMET.

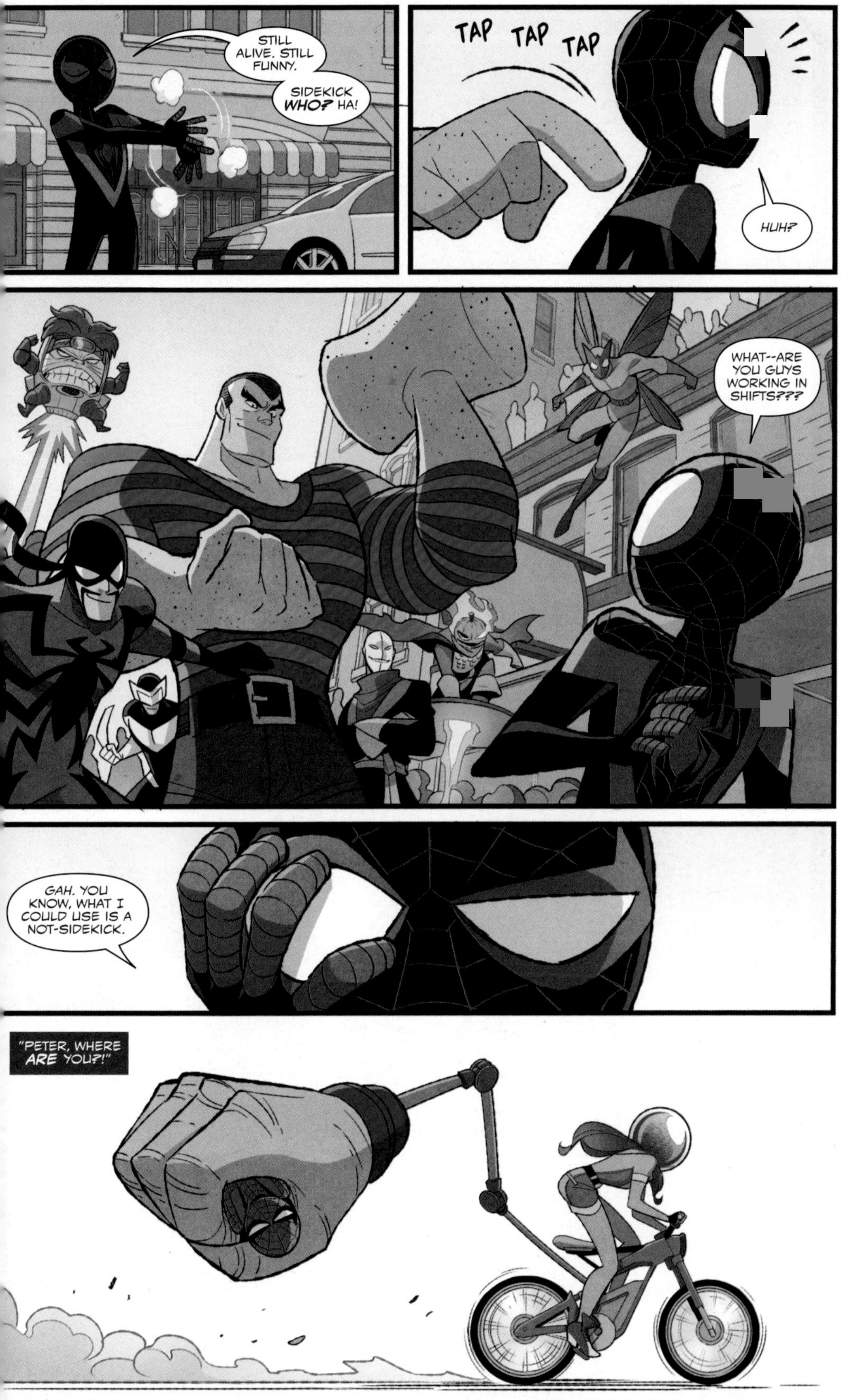
STILL ALIVE. STILL FUNNY.
SIDEKICK **WHO?** HA!
TAP TAP TAP
HUH?
WHAT--ARE YOU GUYS WORKING IN SHIFTS???
GAH. YOU KNOW, WHAT I COULD USE IS A NOT-SIDEKICK.
"PETER, WHERE **ARE** YOU?!"

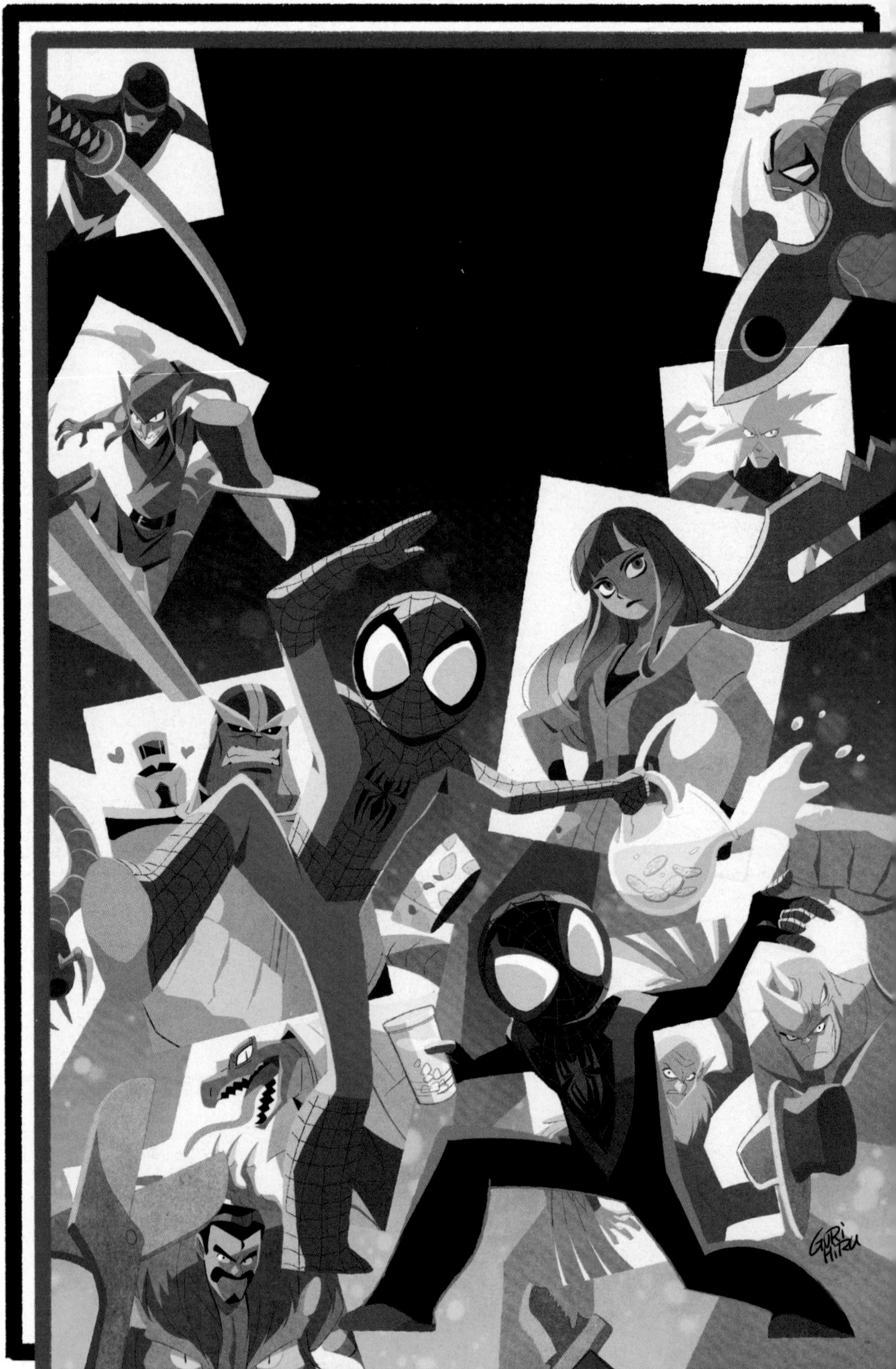
GURI HIRU

3

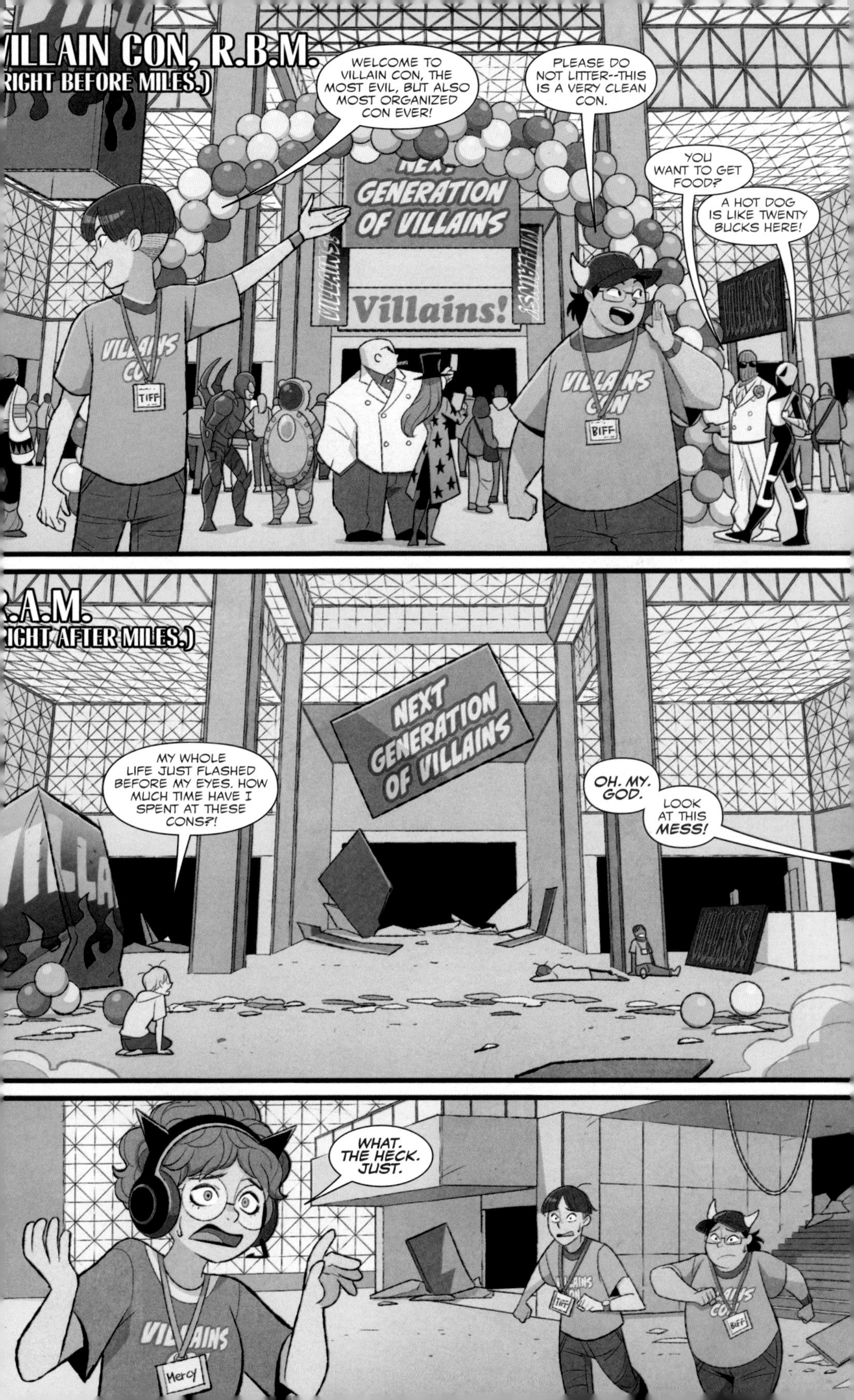
VILLAIN CON, R.B.M. (RIGHT BEFORE MILES.)
WELCOME TO VILLAIN CON, THE MOST EVIL, BUT ALSO MOST ORGANIZED CON EVER!
PLEASE DO NOT LITTER--THIS IS A VERY CLEAN CON.
YOU WANT TO GET FOOD?
A HOT DOG IS LIKE TWENTY BUCKS HERE!
NEXT GENERATION OF VILLAINS
Villains!
VILLAINS CON
TIFF
BIFF
.A.M. IGHT AFTER MILES.)
NEXT GENERATION OF VILLAINS
MY WHOLE LIFE JUST FLASHED BEFORE MY EYES. HOW MUCH TIME HAVE I SPENT AT THESE CONS?!
OH. MY. GOD.
LOOK AT THIS MESS!
WHAT. THE HECK. JUST.
VILLAINS
Mercy

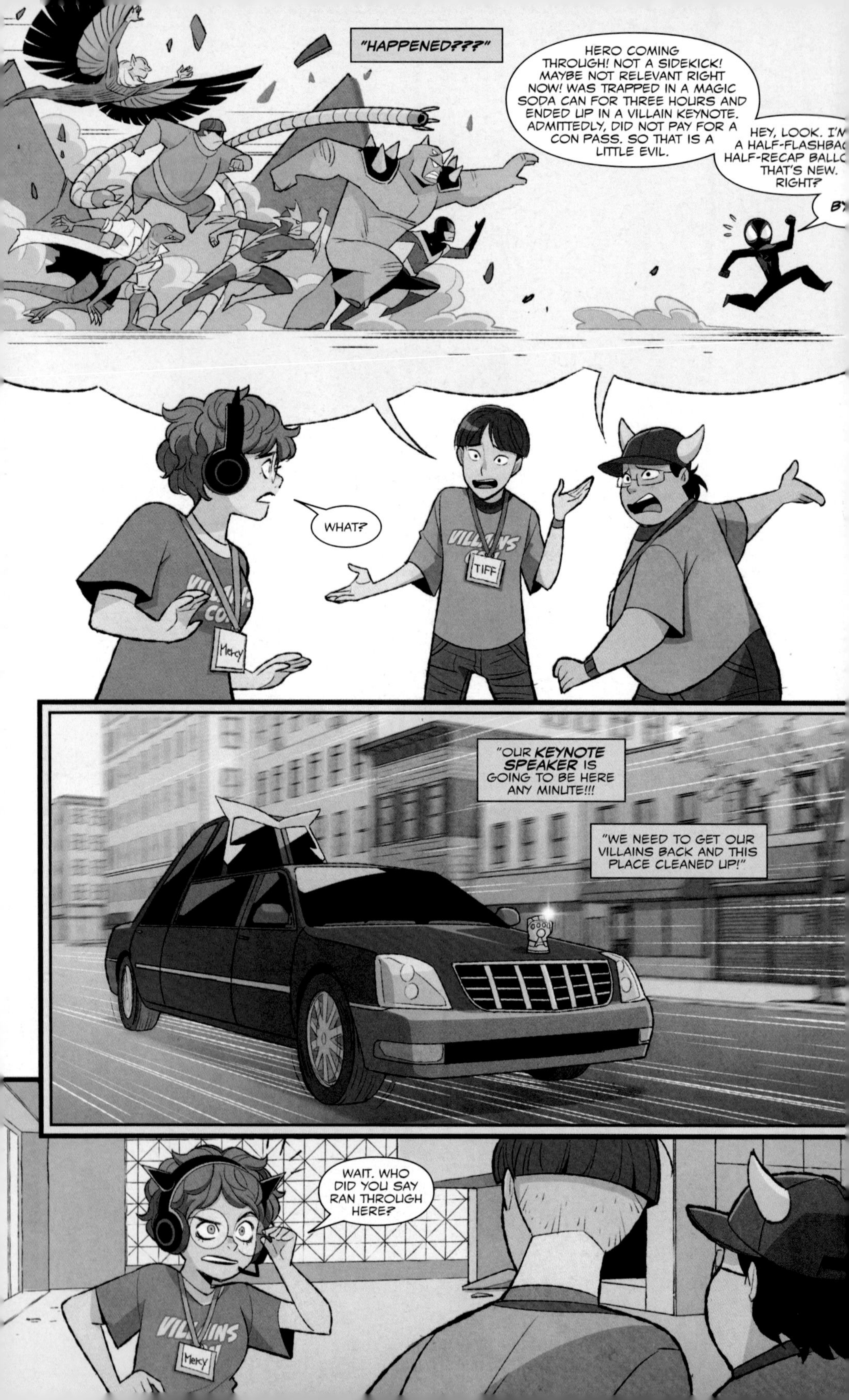
"HAPPENED???"
HERO COMING THROUGH! NOT A SIDEKICK! MAYBE NOT RELEVANT RIGHT NOW! WAS TRAPPED IN A MAGIC SODA CAN FOR THREE HOURS AND ENDED UP IN A VILLAIN KEYNOTE. ADMITTEDLY, DID NOT PAY FOR A CON PASS. SO THAT IS A LITTLE EVIL.
HEY, LOOK. I'M A HALF-FLASHBAC HALF-RECAP BALLO THAT'S NEW. RIGHT?
WHAT?
TIFF
Mercy
"OUR KEYNOTE SPEAKER IS GOING TO BE HERE ANY MINUTE!!!
"WE NEED TO GET OUR VILLAINS BACK AND THIS PLACE CLEANED UP!"
WAIT. WHO DID YOU SAY RAN THROUGH HERE?
Mercy

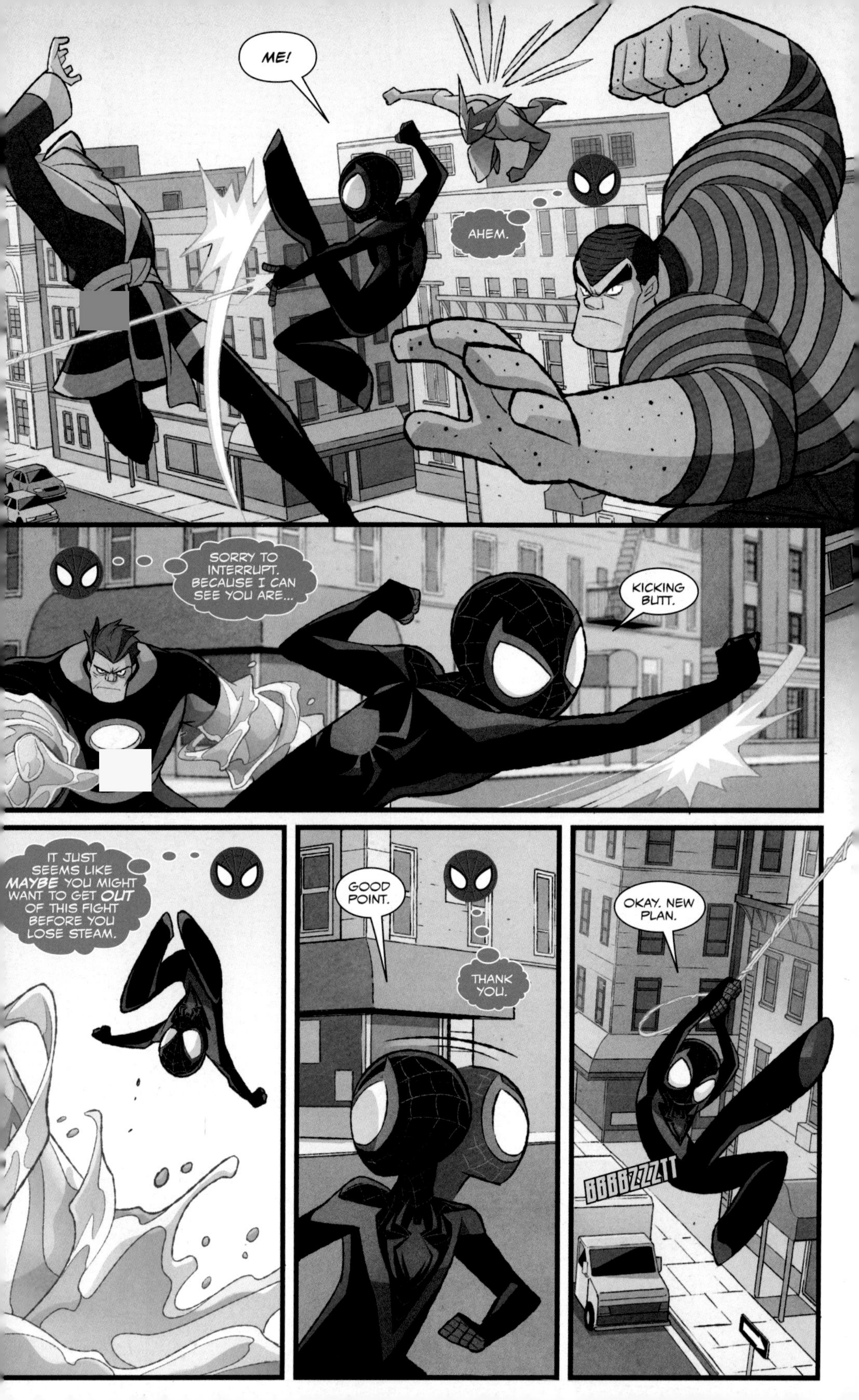
ME!
AHEM.
SORRY TO INTERRUPT. BECAUSE I CAN SEE YOU ARE...
KICKING BUTT.
IT JUST SEEMS LIKE **MAYBE** YOU MIGHT WANT TO GET **OUT** OF THIS FIGHT BEFORE YOU LOSE STEAM.
GOOD POINT.
THANK YOU.
OKAY. NEW PLAN.
BBBBZZZZTT

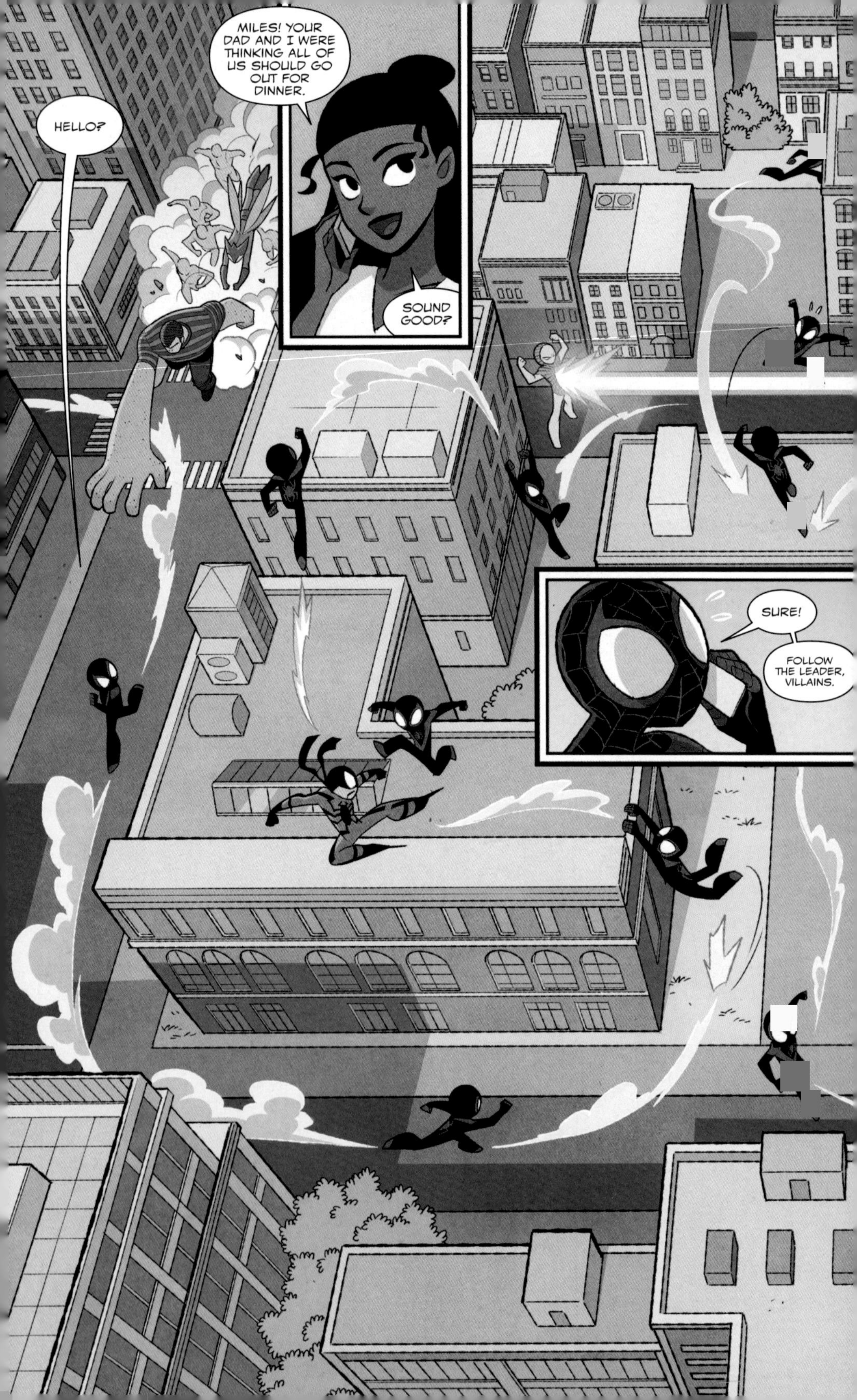
HELLO?
MILES! YOUR DAD AND I WERE THINKING ALL OF US SHOULD GO OUT FOR DINNER.
SOUND GOOD?
SURE!
FOLLOW THE LEADER, VILLAINS.

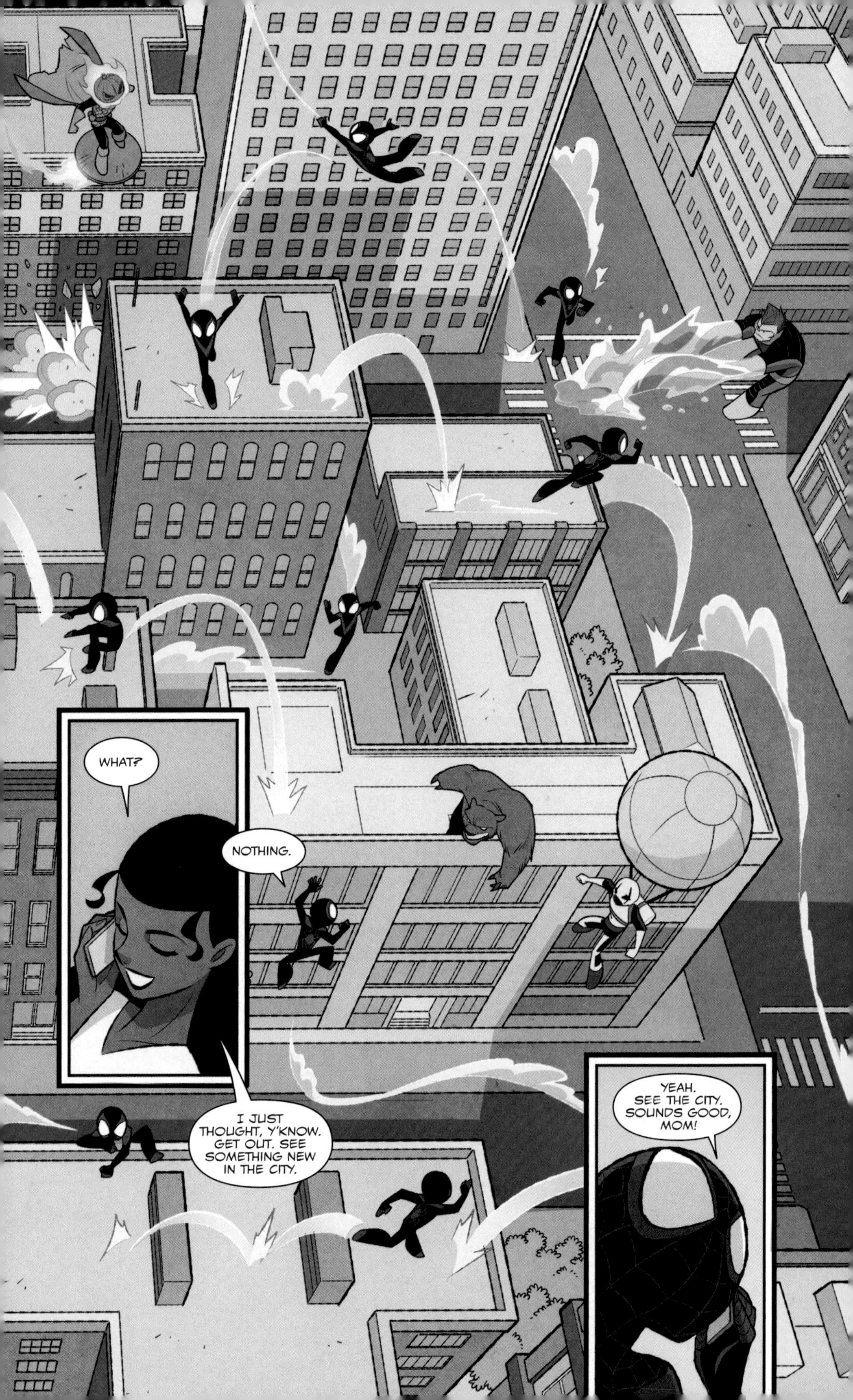
WHAT?
NOTHING.
I JUST THOUGHT, Y'KNOW. GET OUT. SEE SOMETHING NEW IN THE CITY.
YEAH. SEE THE CITY. SOUNDS GOOD, MOM!

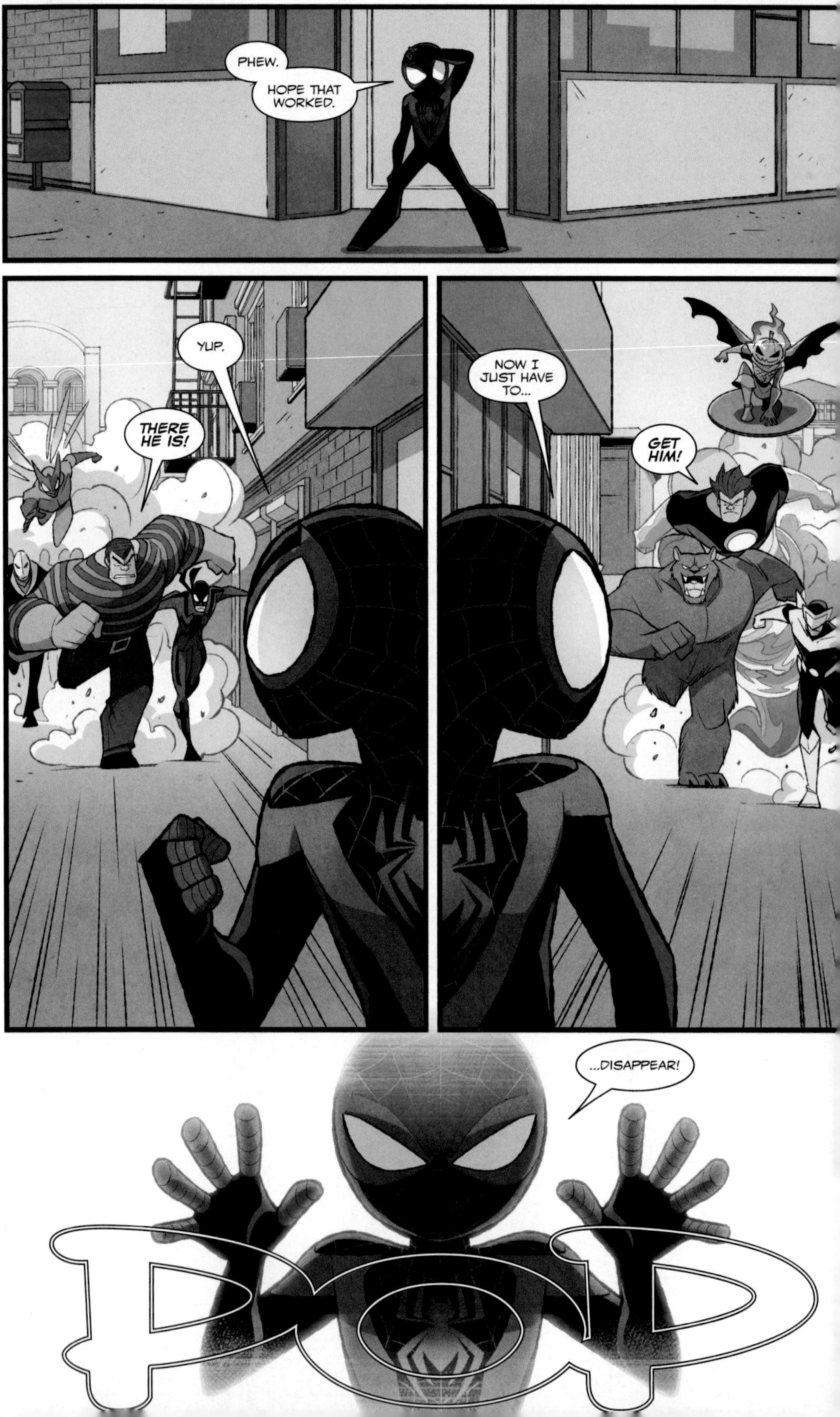
PHEW.
HOPE THAT WORKED.
THERE HE IS!
YUP.
NOW I JUST HAVE TO...
GET HIM!
...DISAPPEAR!
POP

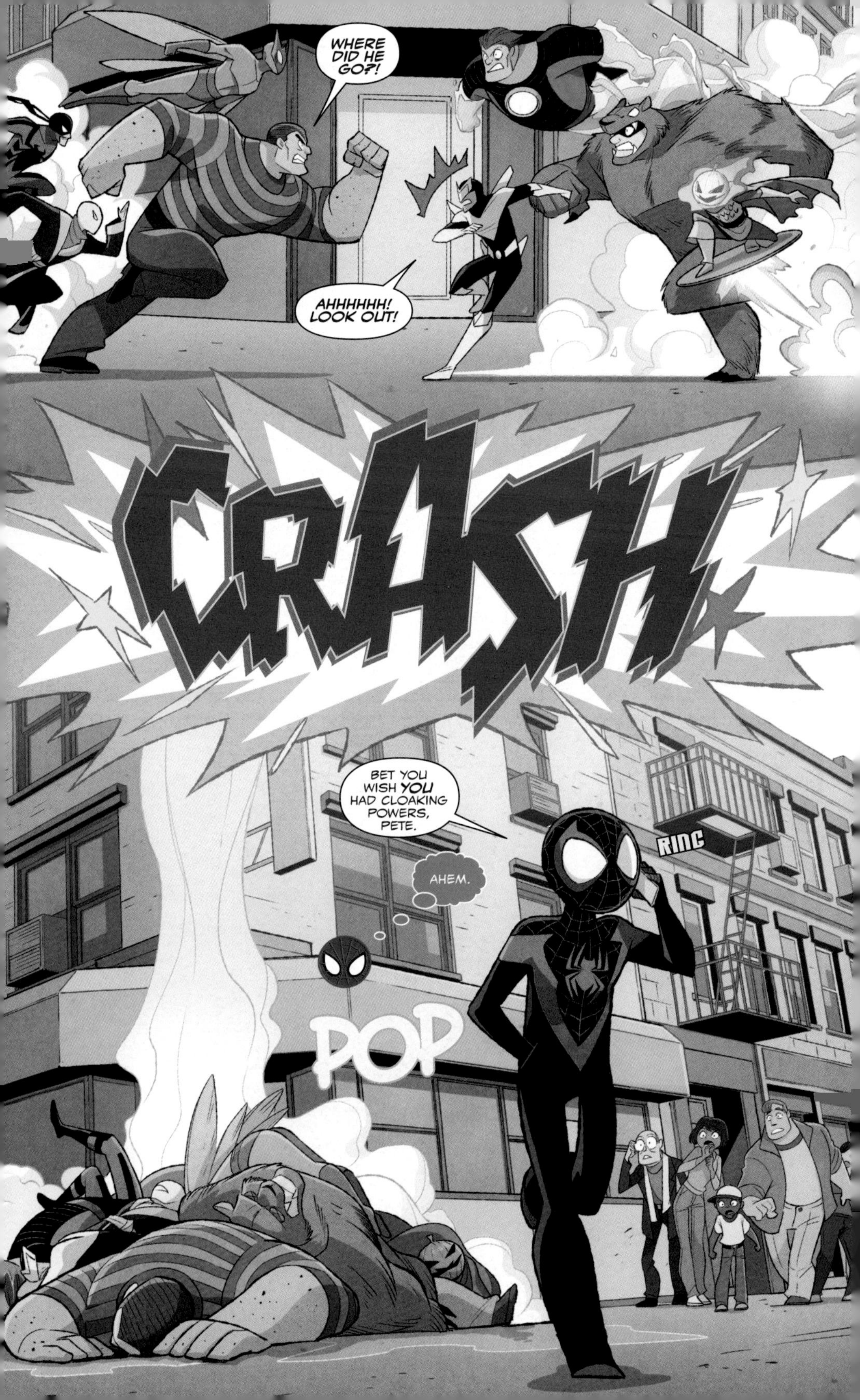
WHERE DID HE GO?!
AHHHHHH! LOOK OUT!
CRASH
BET YOU WISH YOU HAD CLOAKING POWERS, PETE.
RING
AHEM.
POP

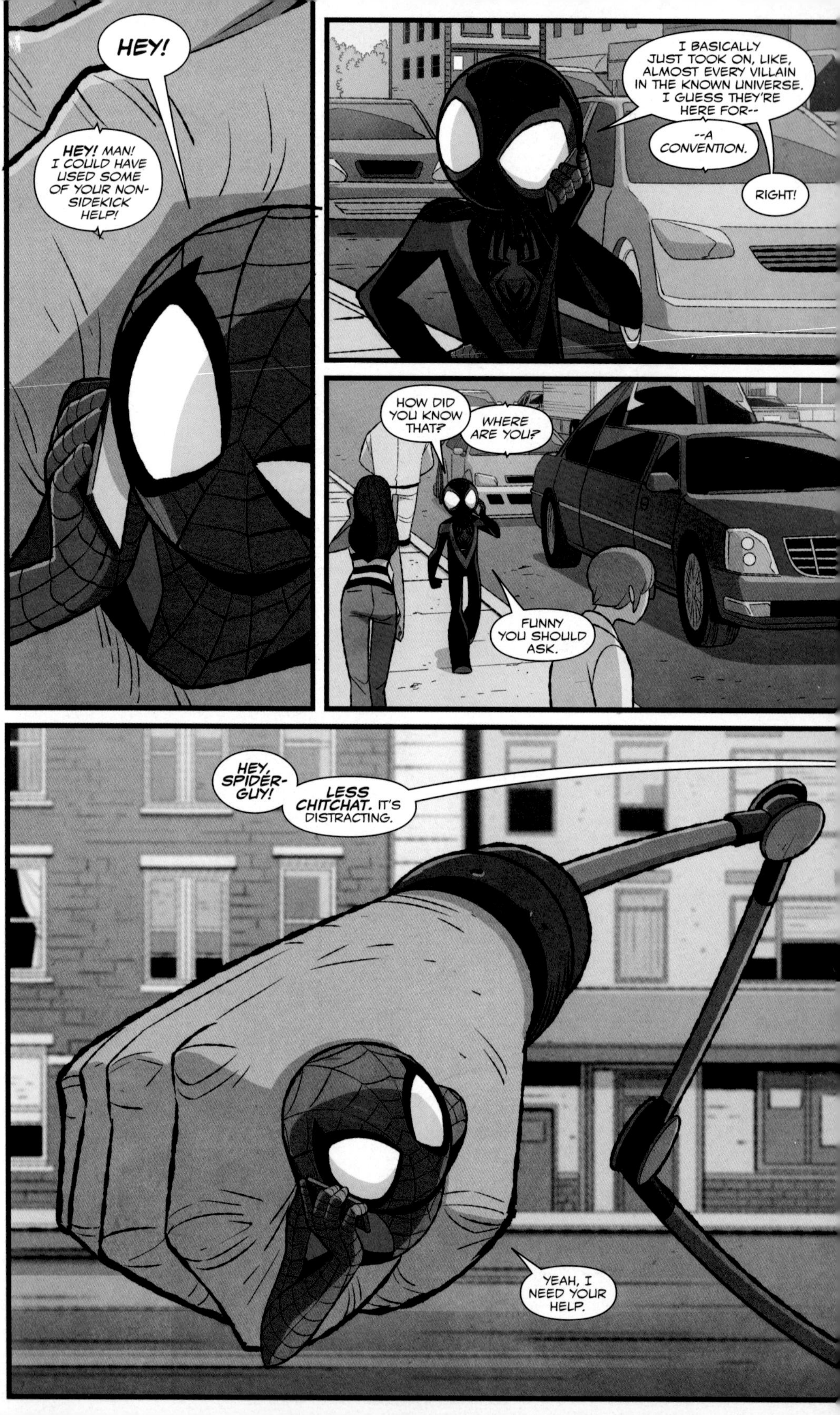
HEY!
HEY! MAN! I COULD HAVE USED SOME OF YOUR NON-SIDEKICK HELP!
I BASICALLY JUST TOOK ON, LIKE, ALMOST EVERY VILLAIN IN THE KNOWN UNIVERSE. I GUESS THEY'RE HERE FOR--
--A CONVENTION.
RIGHT!
HOW DID YOU KNOW THAT?
WHERE ARE YOU?
FUNNY YOU SHOULD ASK.
HEY, SPIDER-GUY!
LESS CHITCHAT. IT'S DISTRACTING.
YEAH, I NEED YOUR HELP.

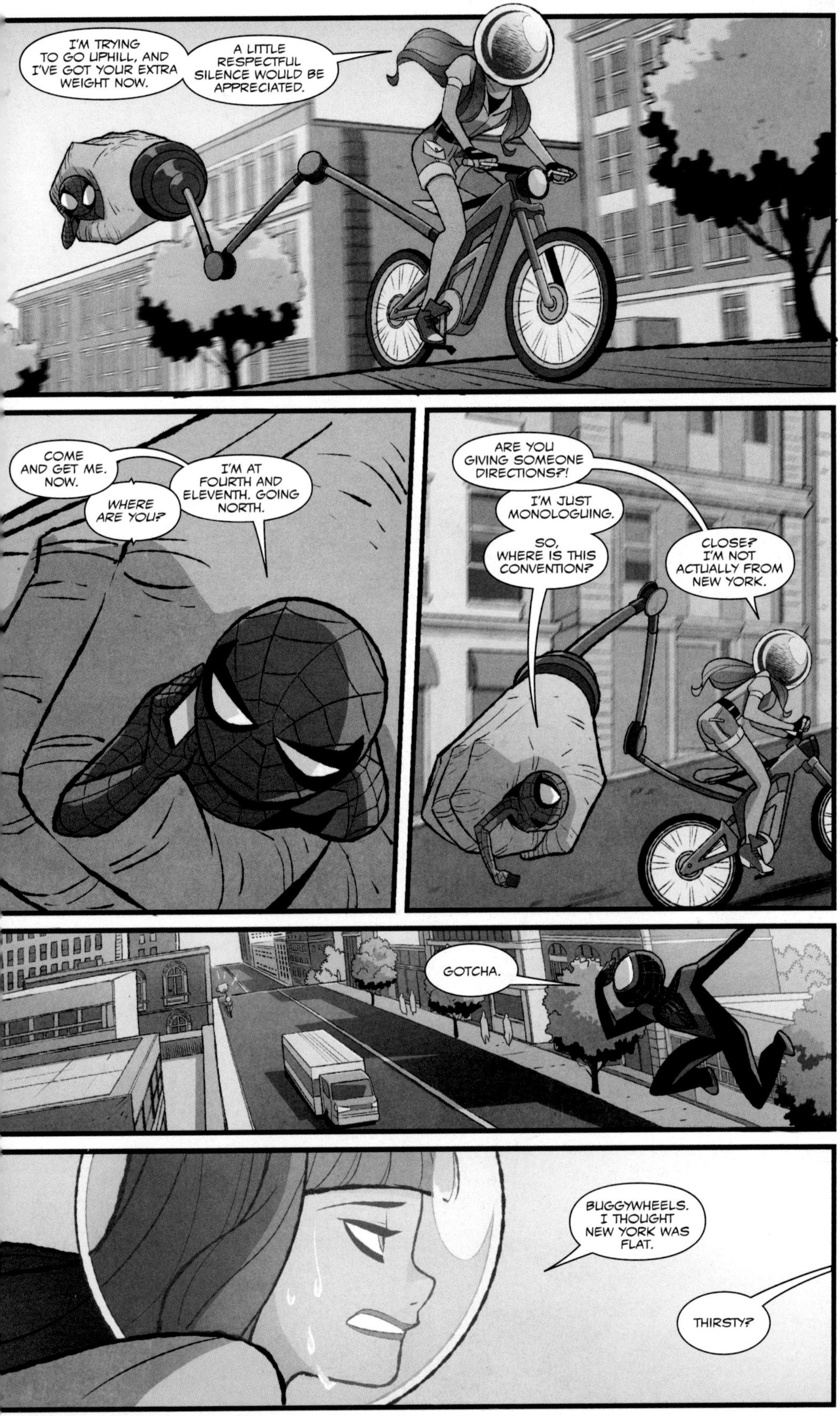
I'M TRYING TO GO UPHILL, AND I'VE GOT YOUR EXTRA WEIGHT NOW.
A LITTLE RESPECTFUL SILENCE WOULD BE APPRECIATED.
COME AND GET ME. NOW.
WHERE ARE YOU?
I'M AT FOURTH AND ELEVENTH. GOING NORTH.
ARE YOU GIVING SOMEONE DIRECTIONS?!
I'M JUST MONOLOGUING.
SO, WHERE IS THIS CONVENTION?
CLOSE? I'M NOT ACTUALLY FROM NEW YORK.
GOTCHA.
BUGGYWHEELS. I THOUGHT NEW YORK WAS FLAT.
THIRSTY?

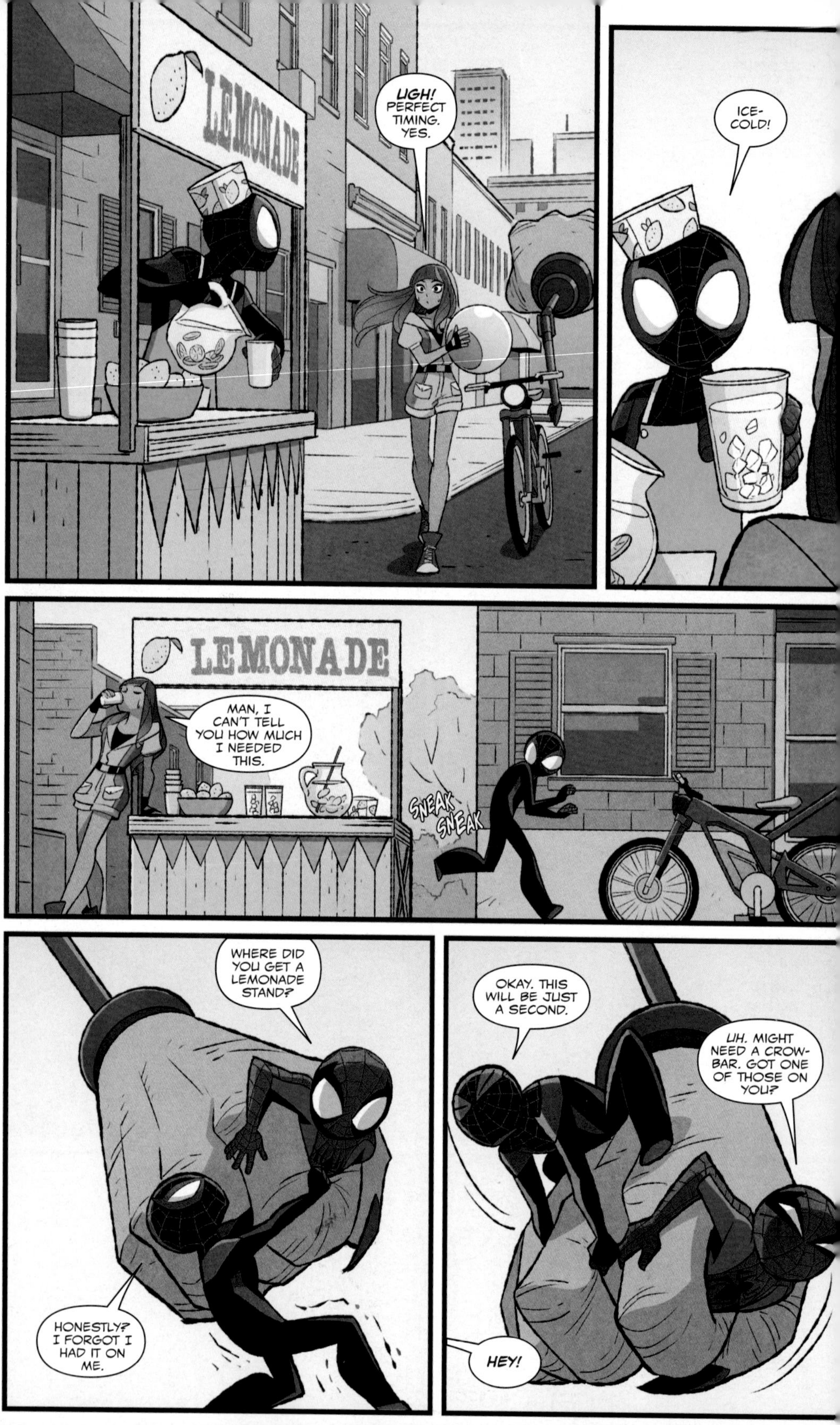

UGH! PERFECT TIMING. YES.
LEMONADE
ICE-COLD!
LEMONADE
MAN, I CAN'T TELL YOU HOW MUCH I NEEDED THIS.
SNEAK SNEAK
WHERE DID YOU GET A LEMONADE STAND?
HONESTLY? I FORGOT I HAD IT ON ME.
OKAY. THIS WILL BE JUST A SECOND.
UH. MIGHT NEED A CROW-BAR. GOT ONE OF THOSE ON YOU?
HEY!

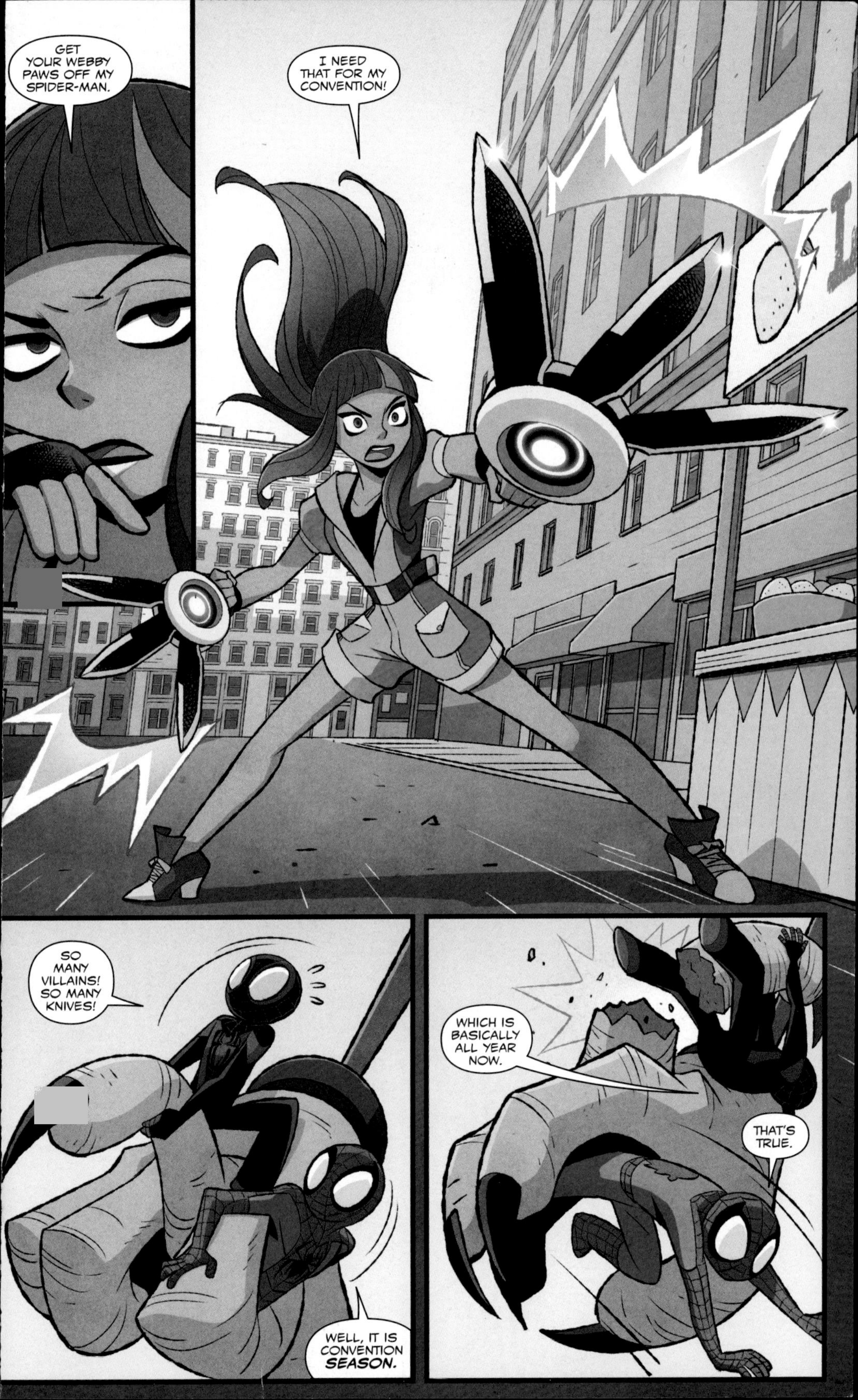
GET YOUR WEBBY PAWS OFF MY SPIDER-MAN.
I NEED THAT FOR MY CONVENTION!
SO MANY VILLAINS! SO MANY KNIVES!
WELL, IT IS CONVENTION **SEASON.**
WHICH IS BASICALLY ALL YEAR NOW.
THAT'S TRUE.

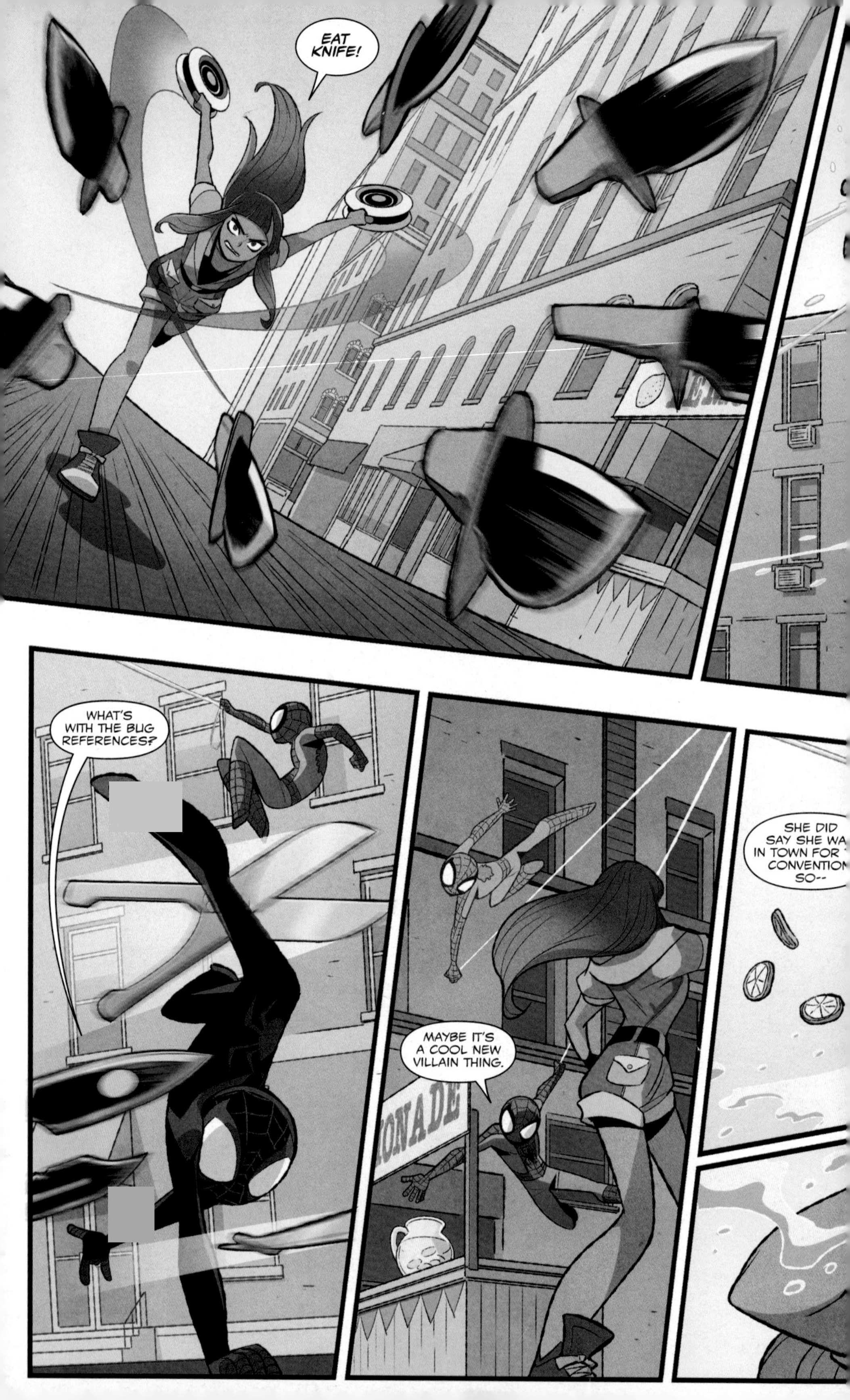
EAT KNIFE!
WHAT'S WITH THE BUG REFERENCES?
MAYBE IT'S A COOL NEW VILLAIN THING.
ONADE
SHE DID SAY SHE WA IN TOWN FOR CONVENTIO SO--

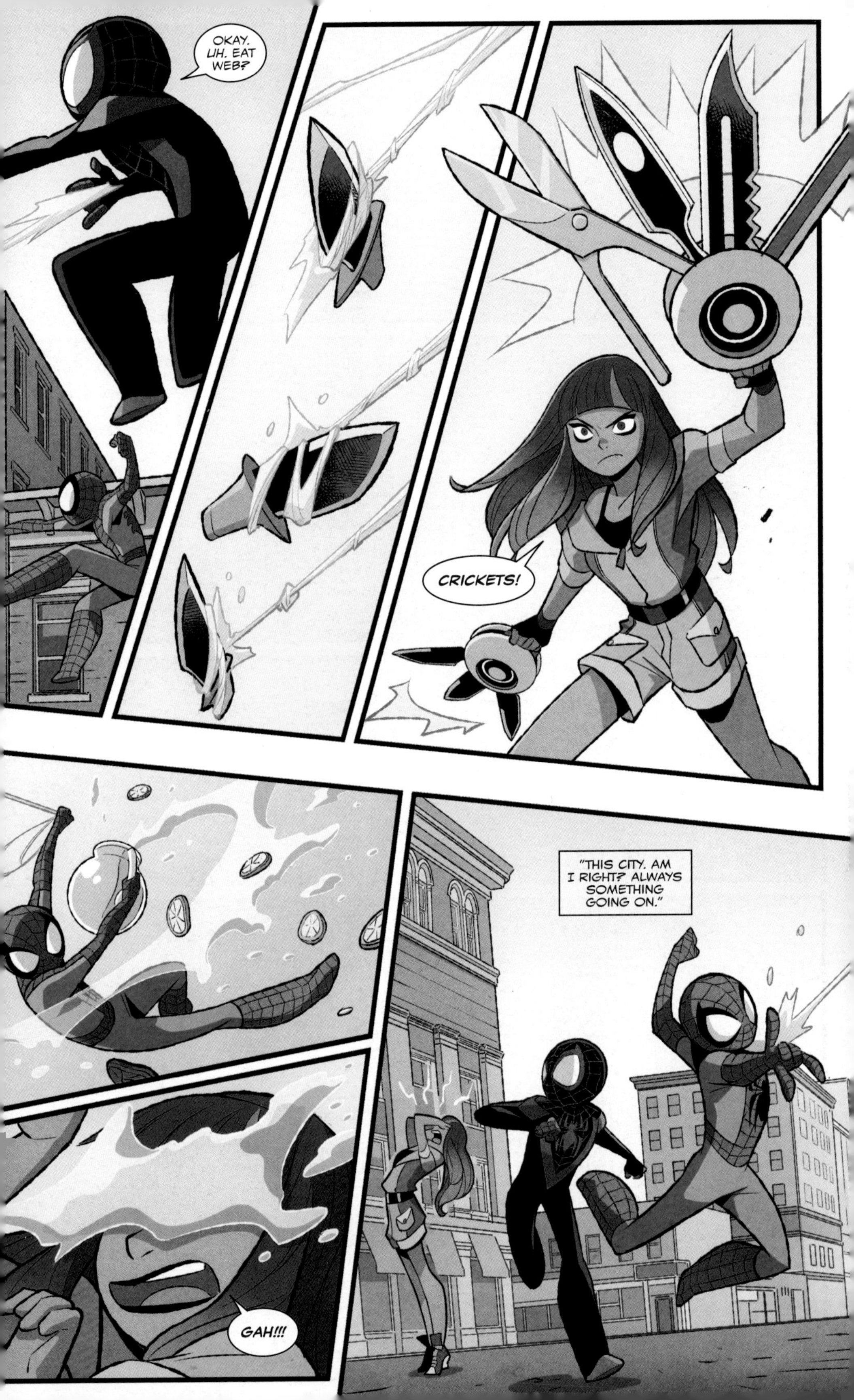
OKAY. UH. EAT WEB?
CRICKETS!
"THIS CITY. AM I RIGHT? ALWAYS SOMETHING GOING ON."
GAH!!!

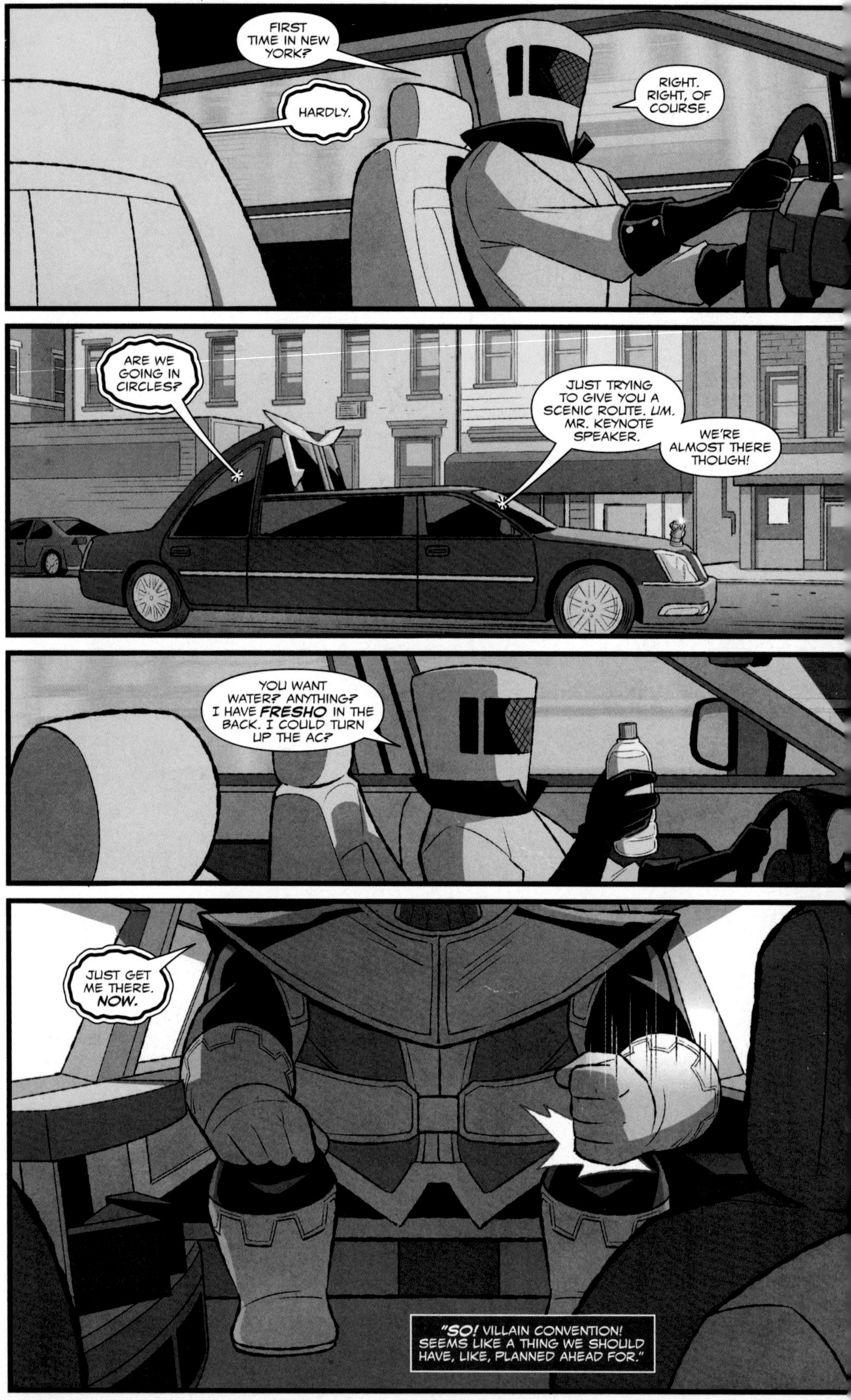
FIRST TIME IN NEW YORK?
HARDLY.
RIGHT. RIGHT, OF COURSE.
ARE WE GOING IN CIRCLES?
JUST TRYING TO GIVE YOU A SCENIC ROUTE. UM. MR. KEYNOTE SPEAKER.
WE'RE ALMOST THERE THOUGH!
YOU WANT WATER? ANYTHING? I HAVE FRESHO IN THE BACK. I COULD TURN UP THE AC?
JUST GET ME THERE. NOW.
"SO! VILLAIN CONVENTION! SEEMS LIKE A THING WE SHOULD HAVE, LIKE, PLANNED AHEAD FOR."

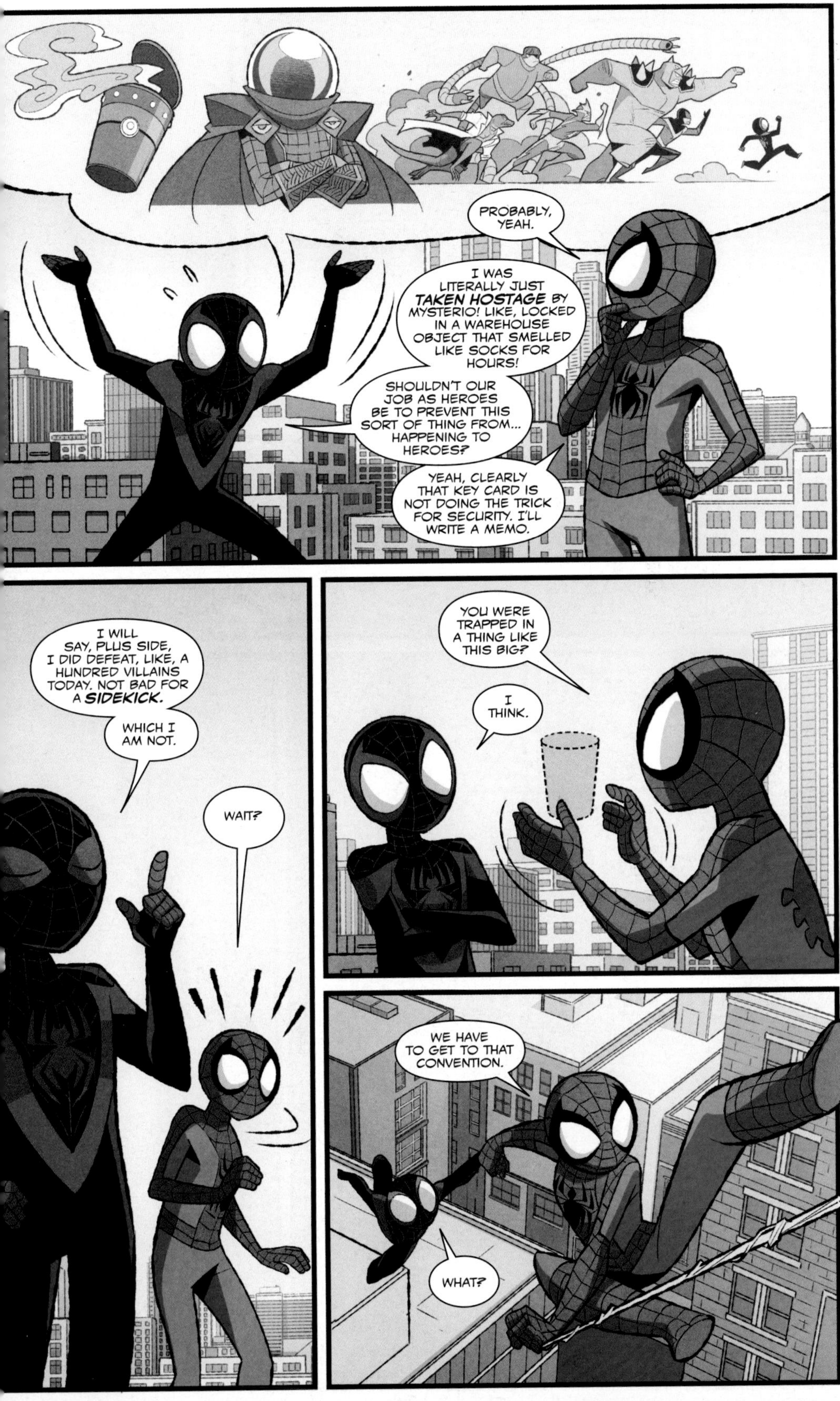
PROBABLY, YEAH.
I WAS LITERALLY JUST TAKEN HOSTAGE BY MYSTERIO! LIKE, LOCKED IN A WAREHOUSE OBJECT THAT SMELLED LIKE SOCKS FOR HOURS!
SHOULDN'T OUR JOB AS HEROES BE TO PREVENT THIS SORT OF THING FROM... HAPPENING TO HEROES?
YEAH, CLEARLY THAT KEY CARD IS NOT DOING THE TRICK FOR SECURITY. I'LL WRITE A MEMO.
I WILL SAY, PLUS SIDE, I DID DEFEAT, LIKE, A HUNDRED VILLAINS TODAY. NOT BAD FOR A SIDEKICK.
WHICH I AM NOT.
WAIT?
YOU WERE TRAPPED IN A THING LIKE THIS BIG?
I THINK.
WE HAVE TO GET TO THAT CONVENTION.
WHAT?

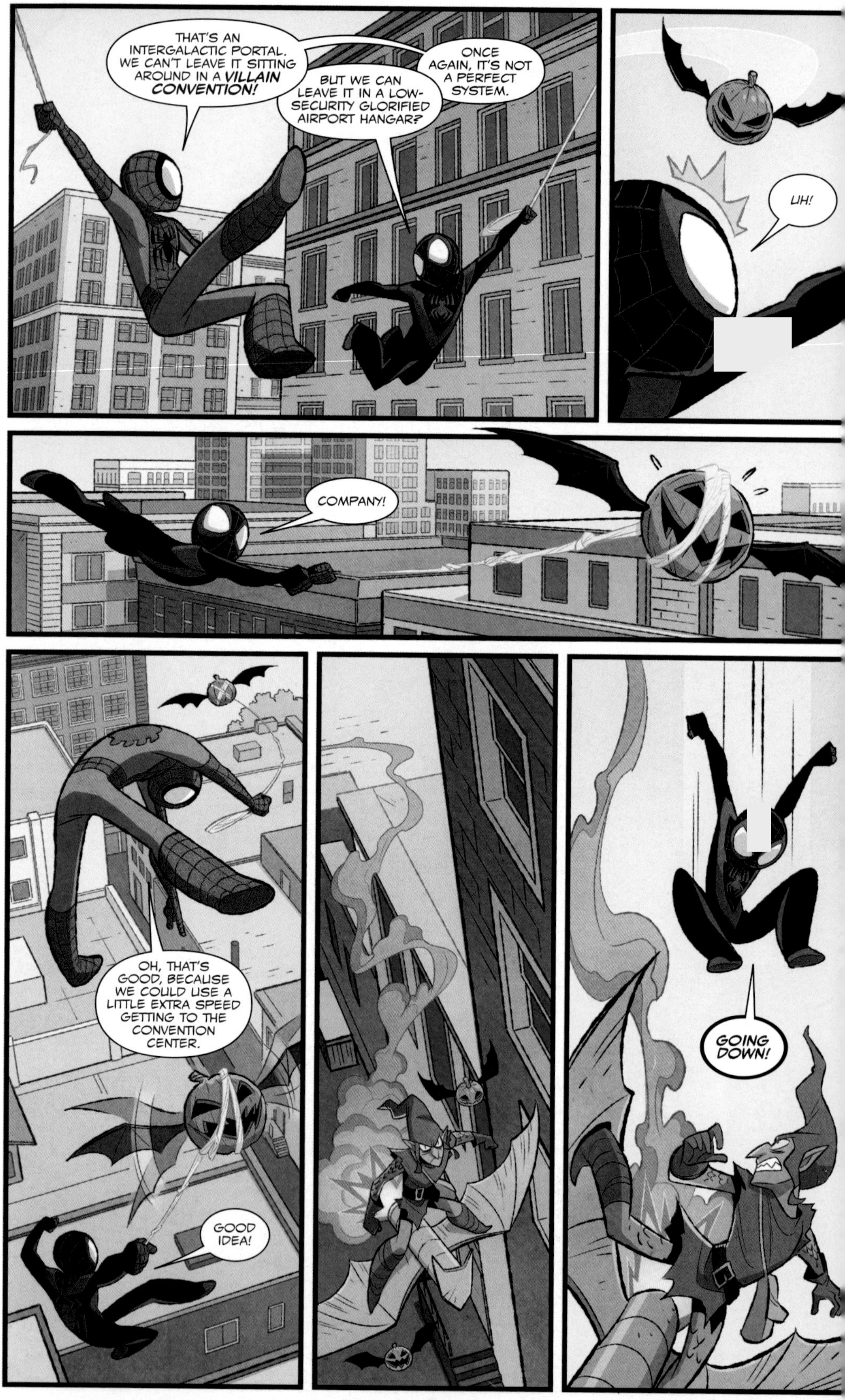
THAT'S AN INTERGALACTIC PORTAL. WE CAN'T LEAVE IT SITTING AROUND IN A *VILLAIN CONVENTION!*
BUT WE CAN LEAVE IT IN A LOW-SECURITY GLORIFIED AIRPORT HANGAR?
ONCE AGAIN, IT'S NOT A PERFECT SYSTEM.
UH!
COMPANY!
OH, THAT'S GOOD, BECAUSE WE COULD USE A LITTLE EXTRA SPEED GETTING TO THE CONVENTION CENTER.
GOOD IDEA!
GOING DOWN!

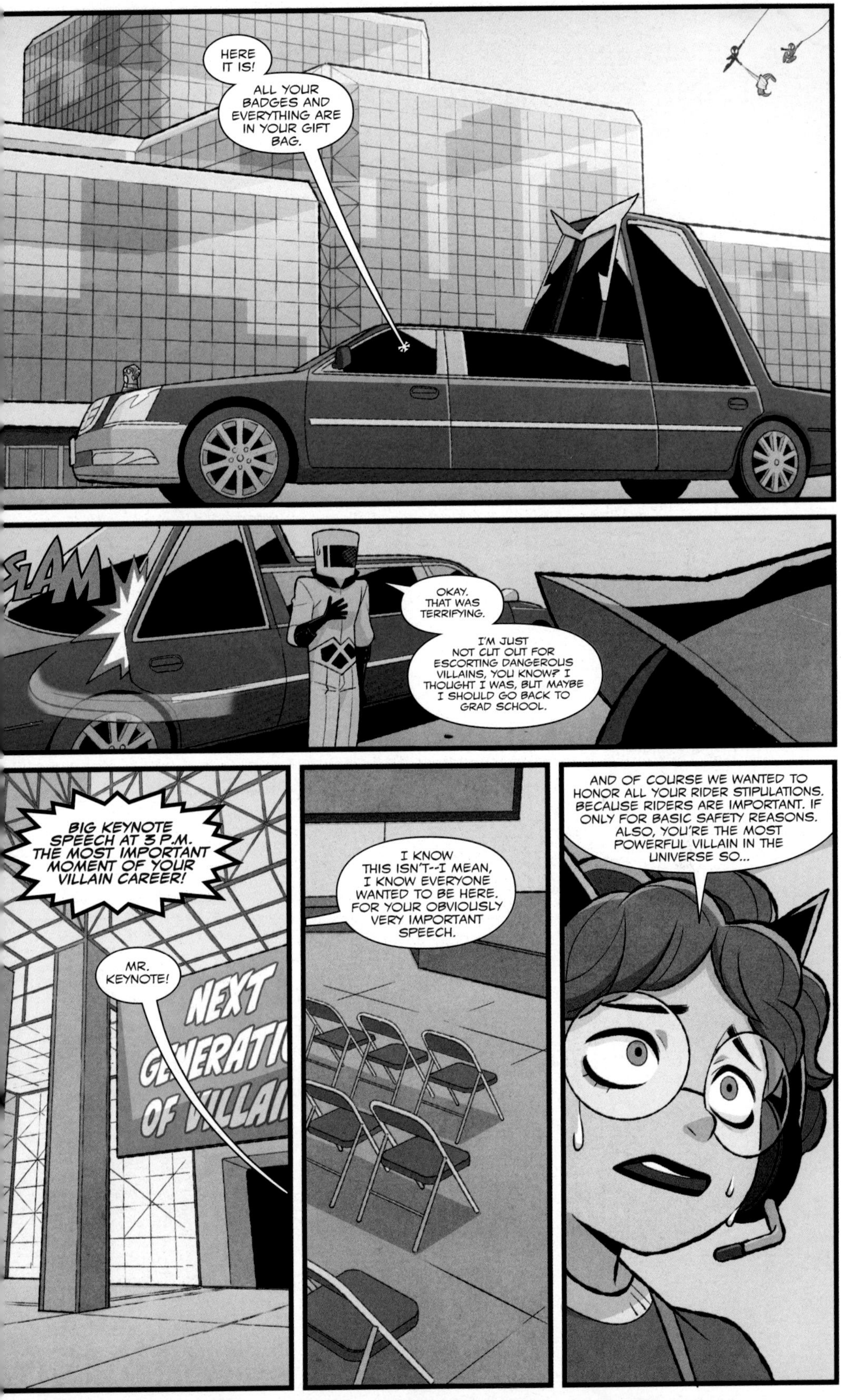
HERE IT IS!
ALL YOUR BADGES AND EVERYTHING ARE IN YOUR GIFT BAG.
SLAM
OKAY. THAT WAS TERRIFYING.
I'M JUST NOT CUT OUT FOR ESCORTING DANGEROUS VILLAINS, YOU KNOW? I THOUGHT I WAS, BUT MAYBE I SHOULD GO BACK TO GRAD SCHOOL.
BIG KEYNOTE SPEECH AT 3 P.M. THE MOST IMPORTANT MOMENT OF YOUR VILLAIN CAREER!
MR. KEYNOTE!
I KNOW THIS ISN'T--I MEAN, I KNOW EVERYONE WANTED TO BE HERE. FOR YOUR OBVIOUSLY VERY IMPORTANT SPEECH.
AND OF COURSE WE WANTED TO HONOR ALL YOUR RIDER STIPULATIONS. BECAUSE RIDERS ARE IMPORTANT. IF ONLY FOR BASIC SAFETY REASONS. ALSO, YOU'RE THE MOST POWERFUL VILLAIN IN THE UNIVERSE SO...

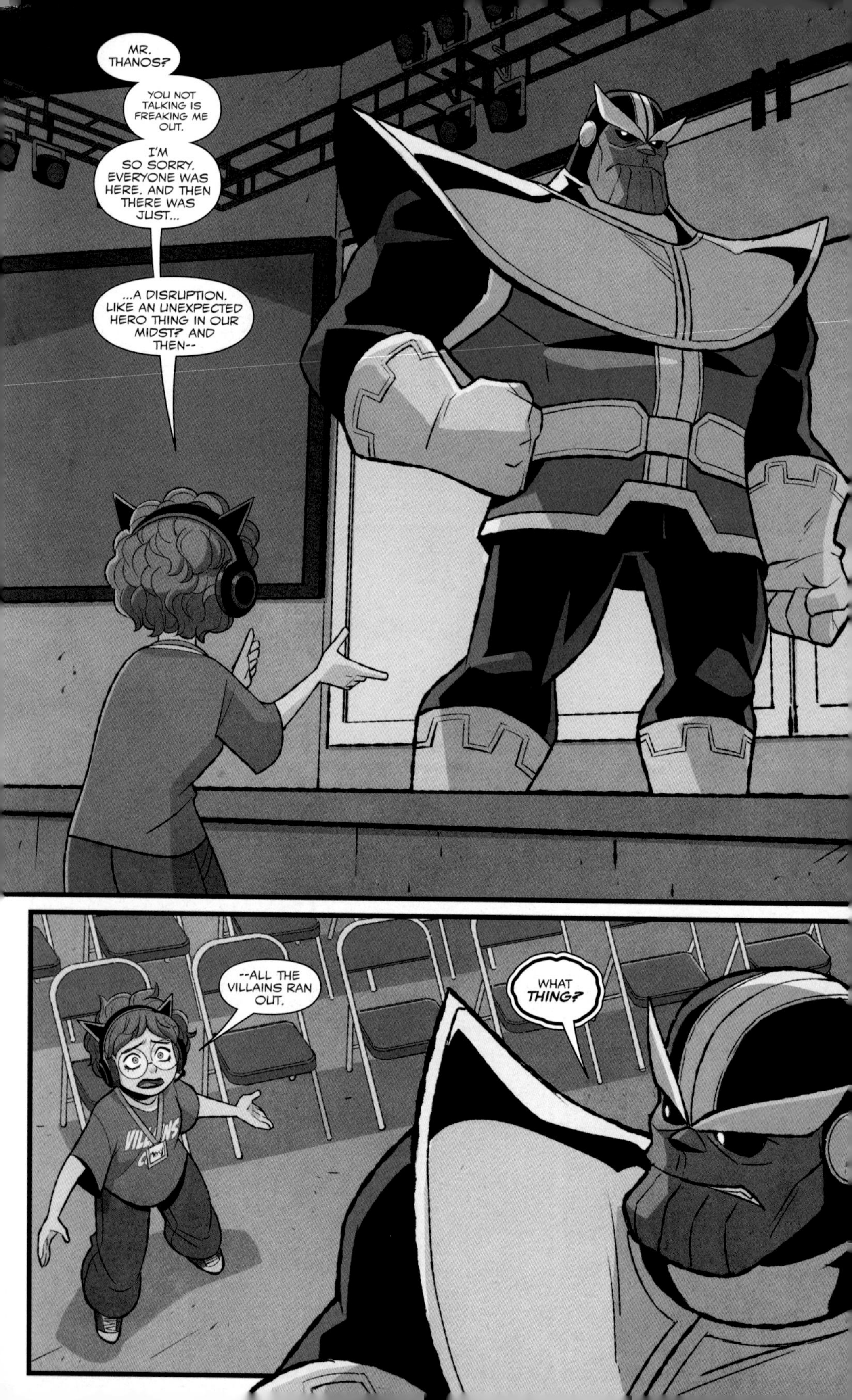
MR. THANOS?
YOU NOT TALKING IS FREAKING ME OUT.
I'M SO SORRY. EVERYONE WAS HERE. AND THEN THERE WAS JUST...
...A DISRUPTION. LIKE AN UNEXPECTED HERO THING IN OUR MIDST? AND THEN--
--ALL THE VILLAINS RAN OUT.
WHAT *THING?*

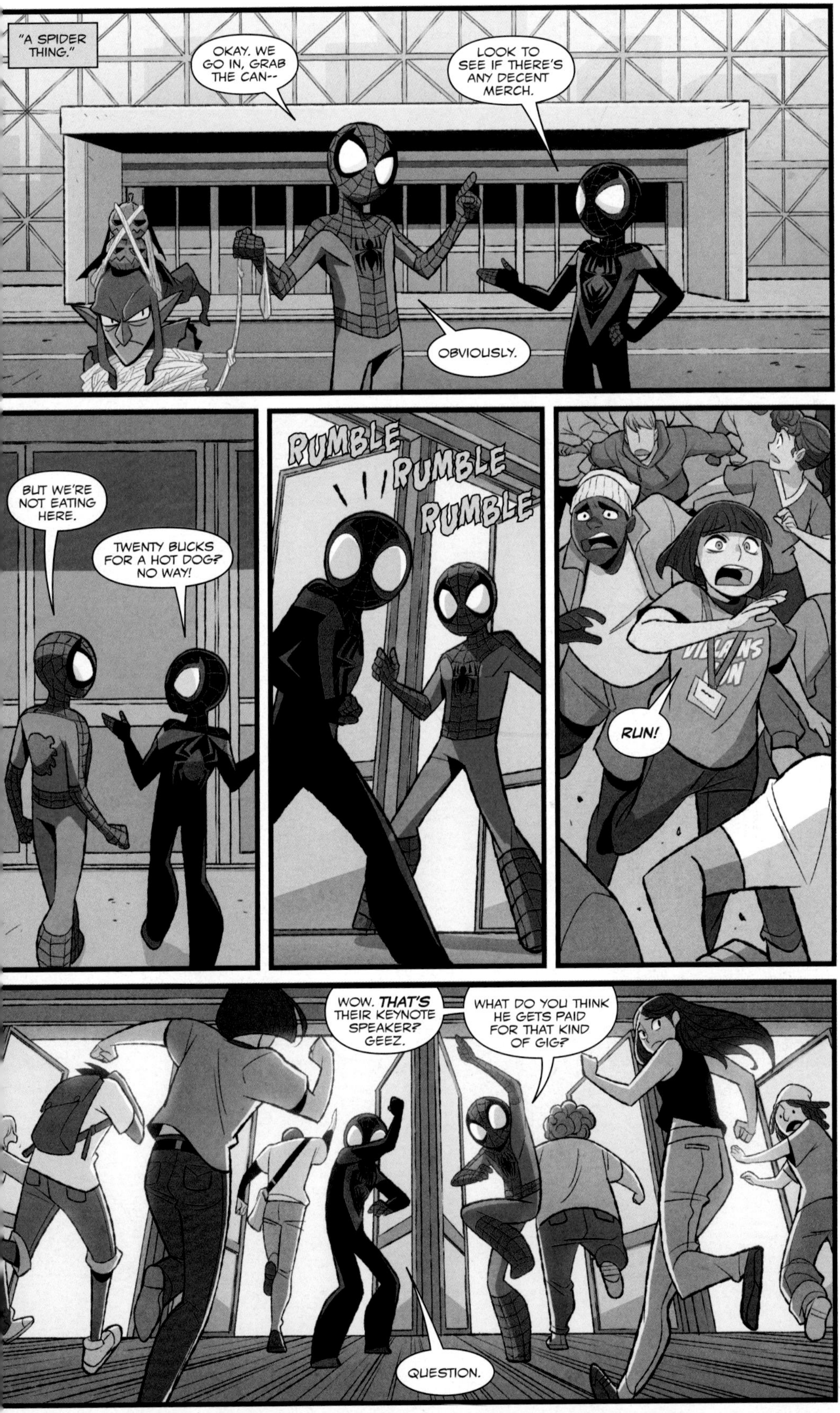
"A SPIDER THING."
OKAY. WE GO IN, GRAB THE CAN--
LOOK TO SEE IF THERE'S ANY DECENT MERCH.
OBVIOUSLY.
BUT WE'RE NOT EATING HERE.
TWENTY BUCKS FOR A HOT DOG? NO WAY!
RUMBLE
RUMBLE
RUMBLE
RUN!
WOW. THAT'S THEIR KEYNOTE SPEAKER? GEEZ.
WHAT DO YOU THINK HE GETS PAID FOR THAT KIND OF GIG?
QUESTION.

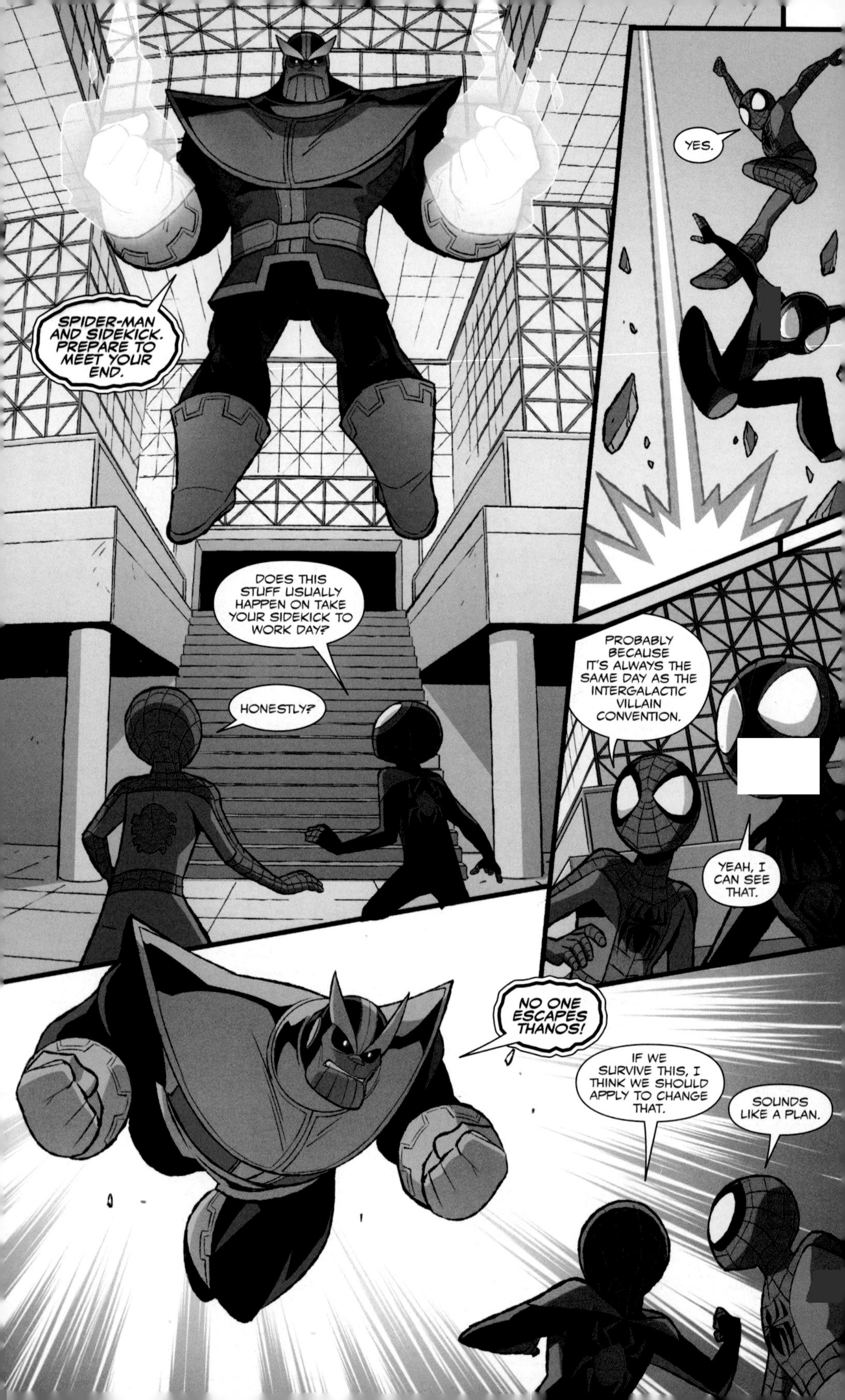

SPIDER-MAN AND SIDEKICK. PREPARE TO MEET YOUR END.
DOES THIS STUFF USUALLY HAPPEN ON TAKE YOUR SIDEKICK TO WORK DAY?
HONESTLY?
YES.
PROBABLY BECAUSE IT'S ALWAYS THE SAME DAY AS THE INTERGALACTIC VILLAIN CONVENTION.
YEAH, I CAN SEE THAT.
NO ONE ESCAPES THANOS!
IF WE SURVIVE THIS, I THINK WE SHOULD APPLY TO CHANGE THAT.
SOUNDS LIKE A PLAN.

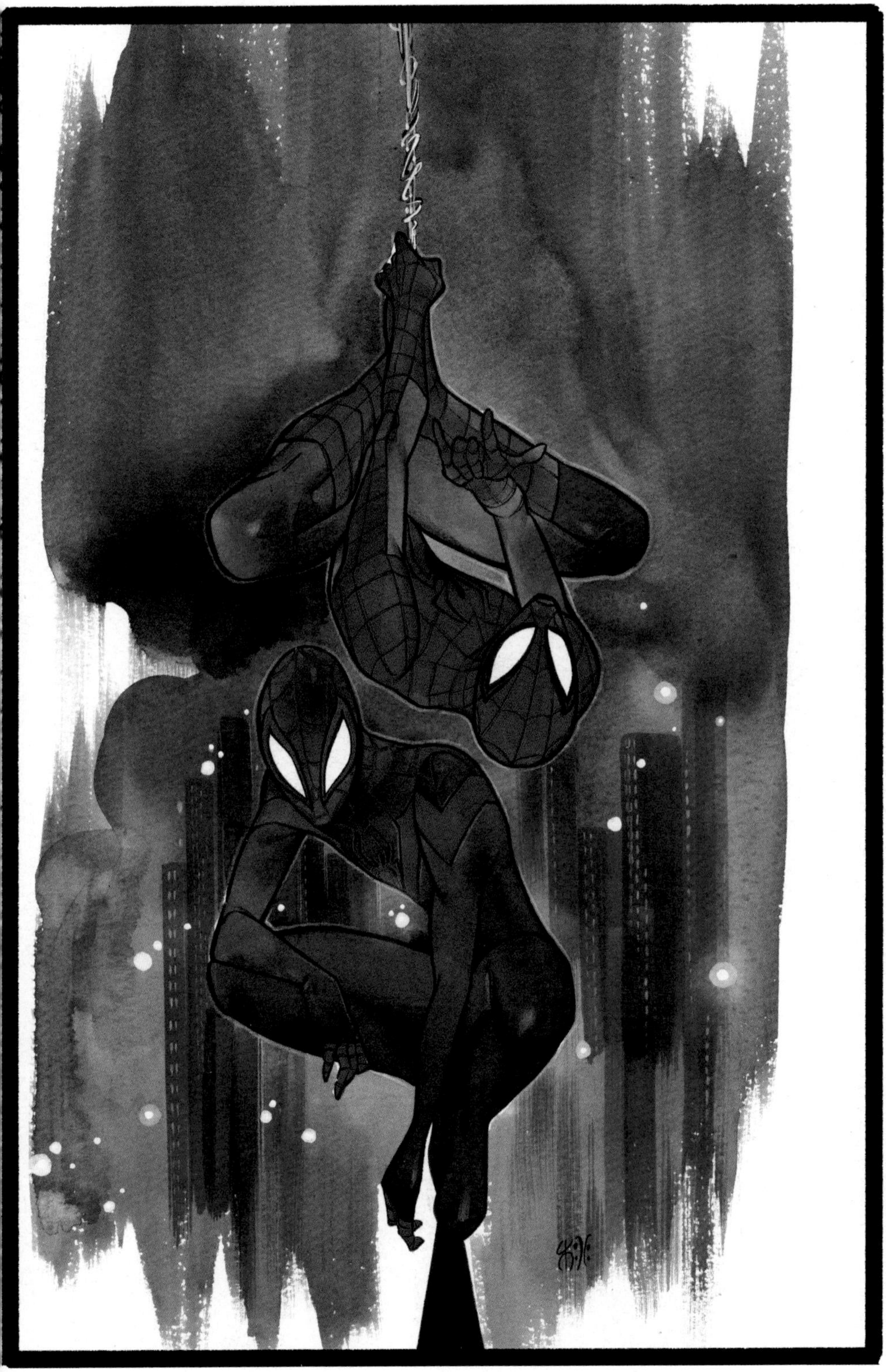

#1 VARIANT BY **PEACH MOMOKO**

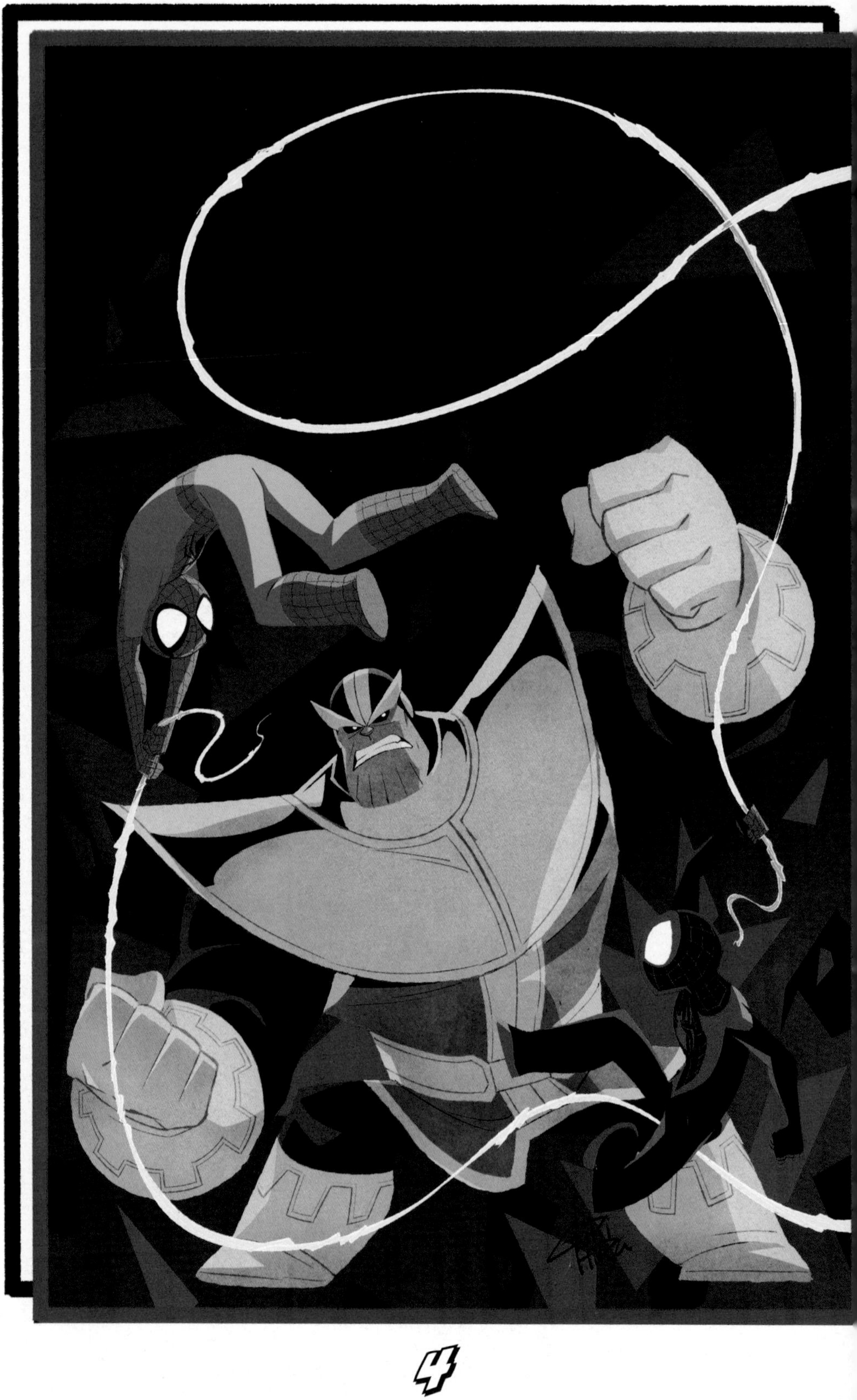

4

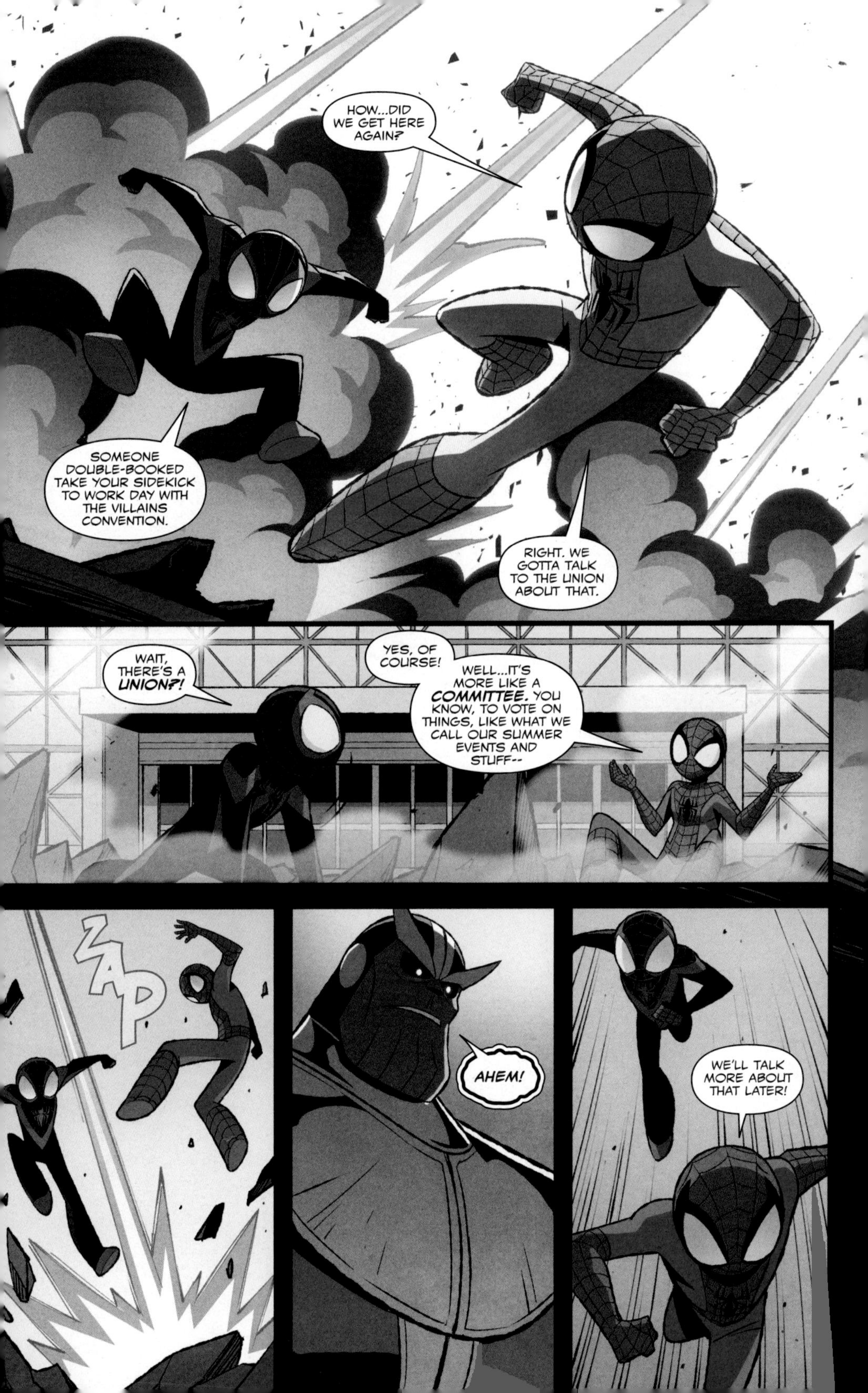
HOW...DID WE GET HERE AGAIN?
SOMEONE DOUBLE-BOOKED TAKE YOUR SIDEKICK TO WORK DAY WITH THE VILLAINS CONVENTION.
RIGHT. WE GOTTA TALK TO THE UNION ABOUT THAT.
WAIT, THERE'S A UNION?!
YES, OF COURSE!
WELL...IT'S MORE LIKE A COMMITTEE. YOU KNOW, TO VOTE ON THINGS, LIKE WHAT WE CALL OUR SUMMER EVENTS AND STUFF--
ZAP
AHEM!
WE'LL TALK MORE ABOUT THAT LATER!

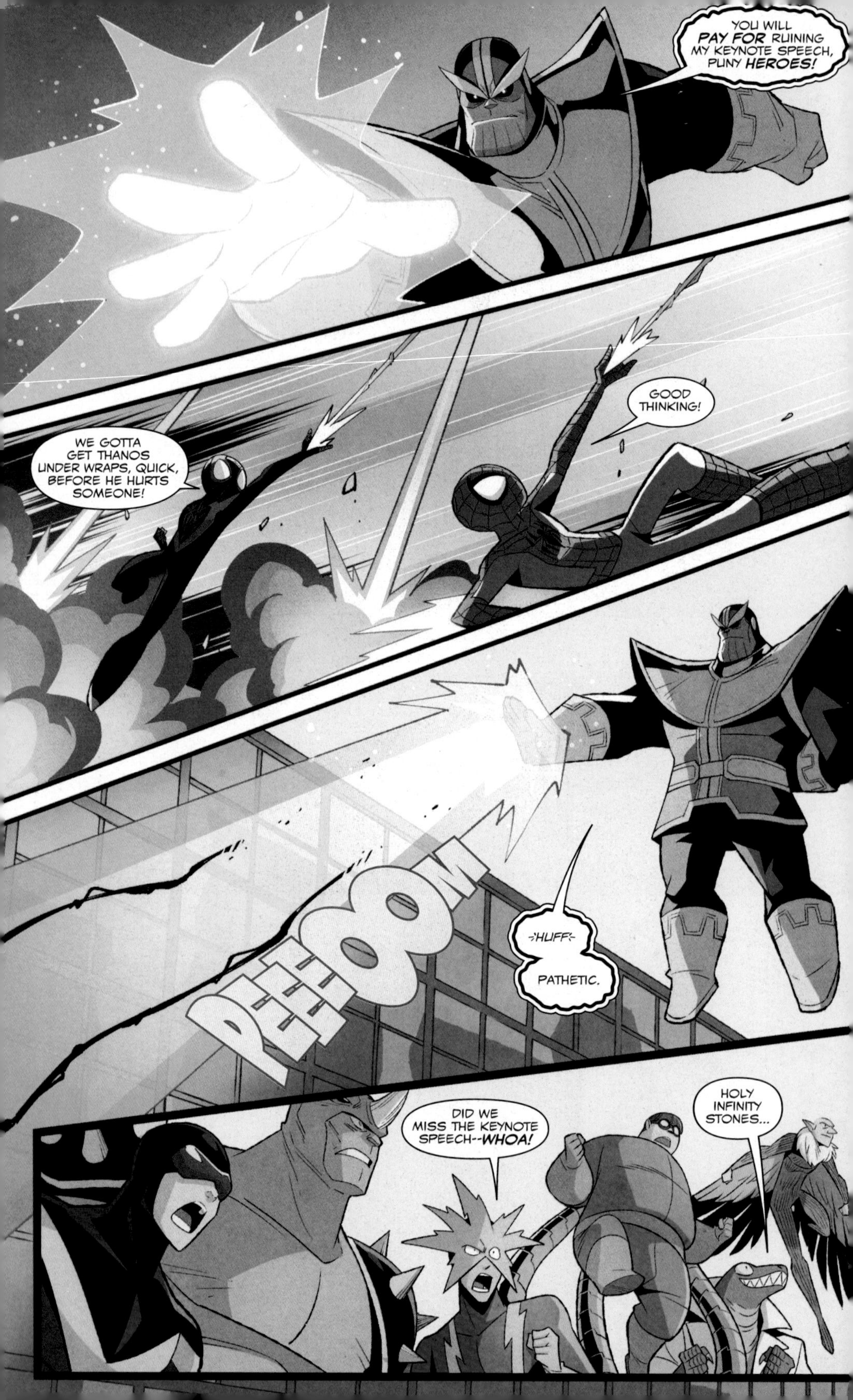
YOU WILL PAY FOR RUINING MY KEYNOTE SPEECH, PUNY HEROES!
WE GOTTA GET THANOS UNDER WRAPS, QUICK, BEFORE HE HURTS SOMEONE!
GOOD THINKING!
PEEBOOM
-HUFF-
PATHETIC.
DID WE MISS THE KEYNOTE SPEECH--WHOA!
HOLY INFINITY STONES...

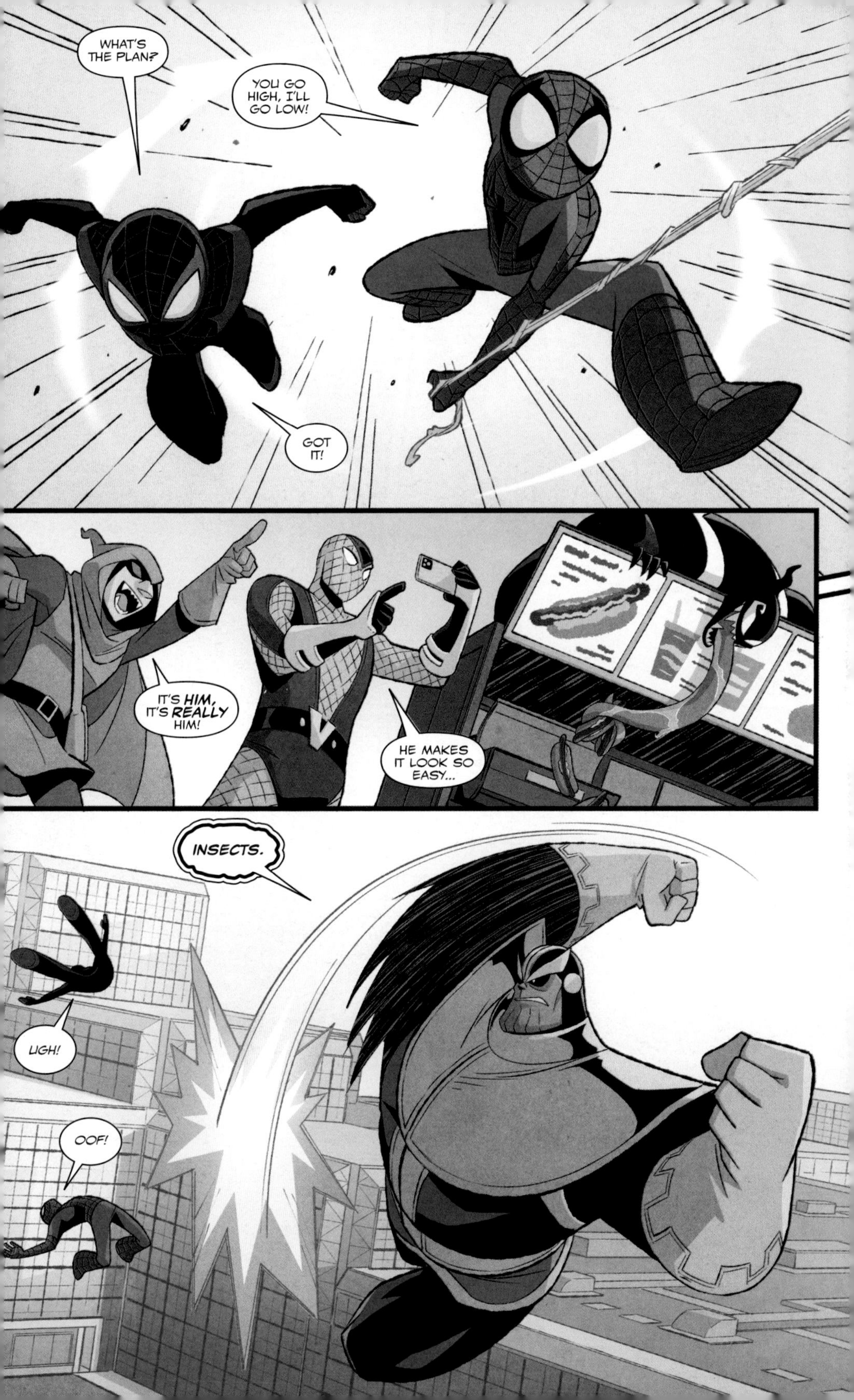
WHAT'S THE PLAN?
YOU GO HIGH, I'LL GO LOW!
GOT IT!
IT'S HIM, IT'S REALLY HIM!
HE MAKES IT LOOK SO EASY...
INSECTS.
UGH!
OOF!

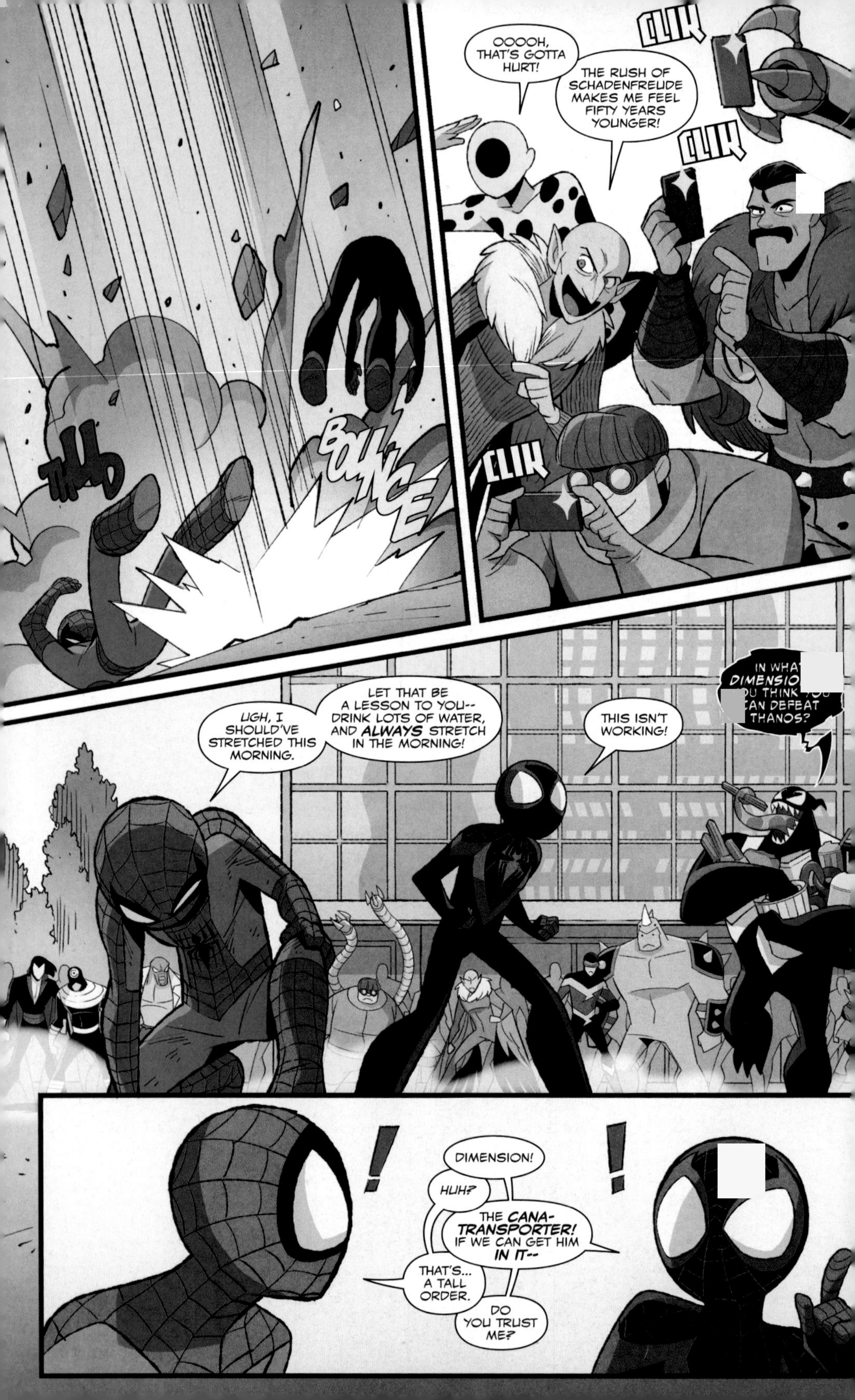
THUD
BOUNCE
OOOOH, THAT'S GOTTA HURT!
THE RUSH OF SCHADENFREUDE MAKES ME FEEL FIFTY YEARS YOUNGER!
CLIK
CLIK
CLIK
UGH, I SHOULD'VE STRETCHED THIS MORNING.
LET THAT BE A LESSON TO YOU-- DRINK LOTS OF WATER, AND ALWAYS STRETCH IN THE MORNING!
THIS ISN'T WORKING!
IN WHA
DIMENSIO
OU THINK YOU
AN DEFEAT
THANOS?
!
!
DIMENSION!
HUH?
THE CANA-TRANSPORTER! IF WE CAN GET HIM IN IT--
THAT'S... A TALL ORDER.
DO YOU TRUST ME?

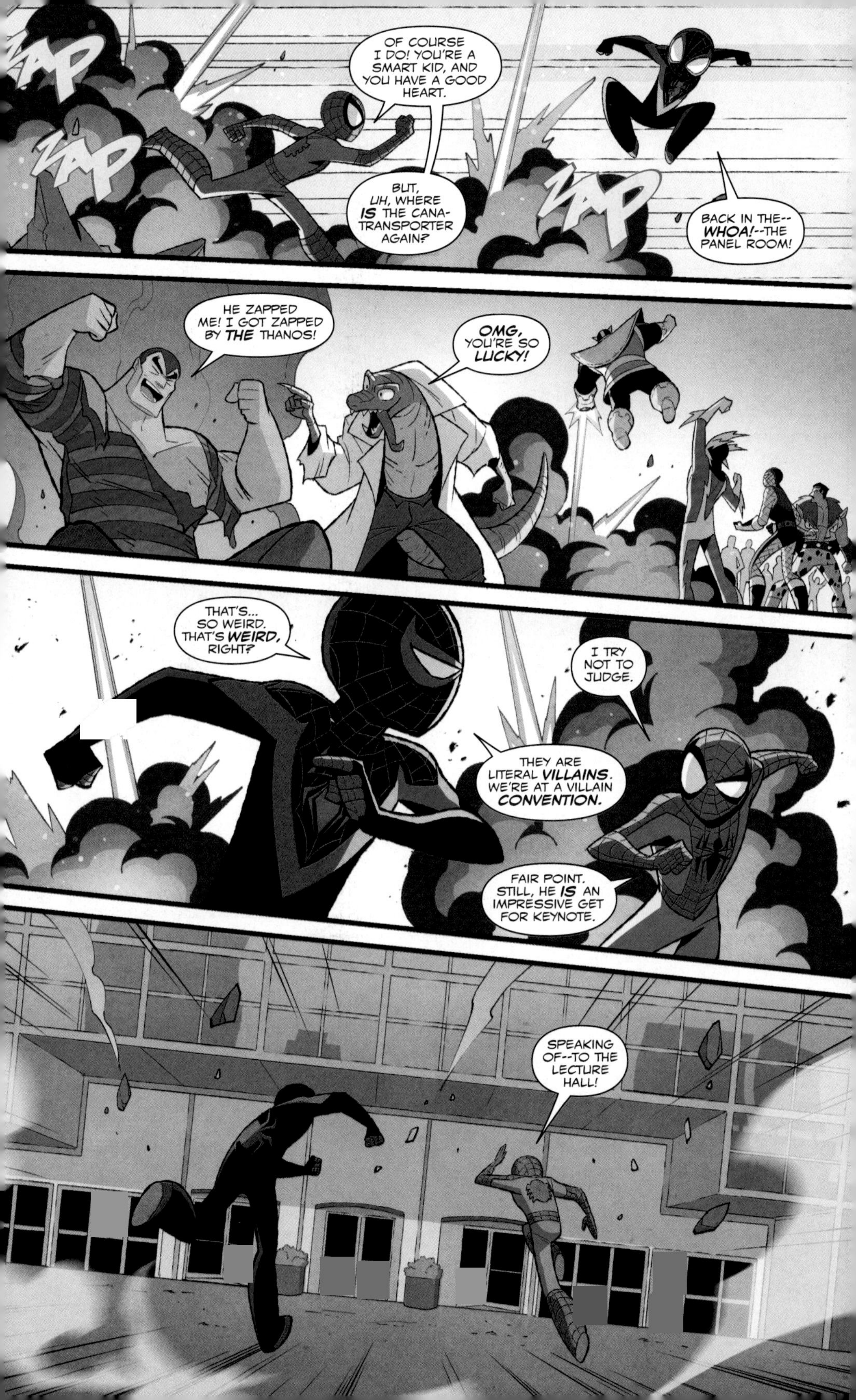
ZAP
ZAP
OF COURSE I DO! YOU'RE A SMART KID, AND YOU HAVE A GOOD HEART.
BUT, UH, WHERE **IS** THE CANA-TRANSPORTER AGAIN?
ZAP
BACK IN THE-- **WHOA!**--THE PANEL ROOM!
HE ZAPPED ME! I GOT ZAPPED BY **THE** THANOS!
OMG, YOU'RE SO **LUCKY!**
THAT'S... SO WEIRD. THAT'S **WEIRD,** RIGHT?
I TRY NOT TO JUDGE.
THEY ARE LITERAL **VILLAINS**. WE'RE AT A VILLAIN **CONVENTION.**
FAIR POINT. STILL, HE **IS** AN IMPRESSIVE GET FOR KEYNOTE.
SPEAKING OF--TO THE LECTURE HALL!

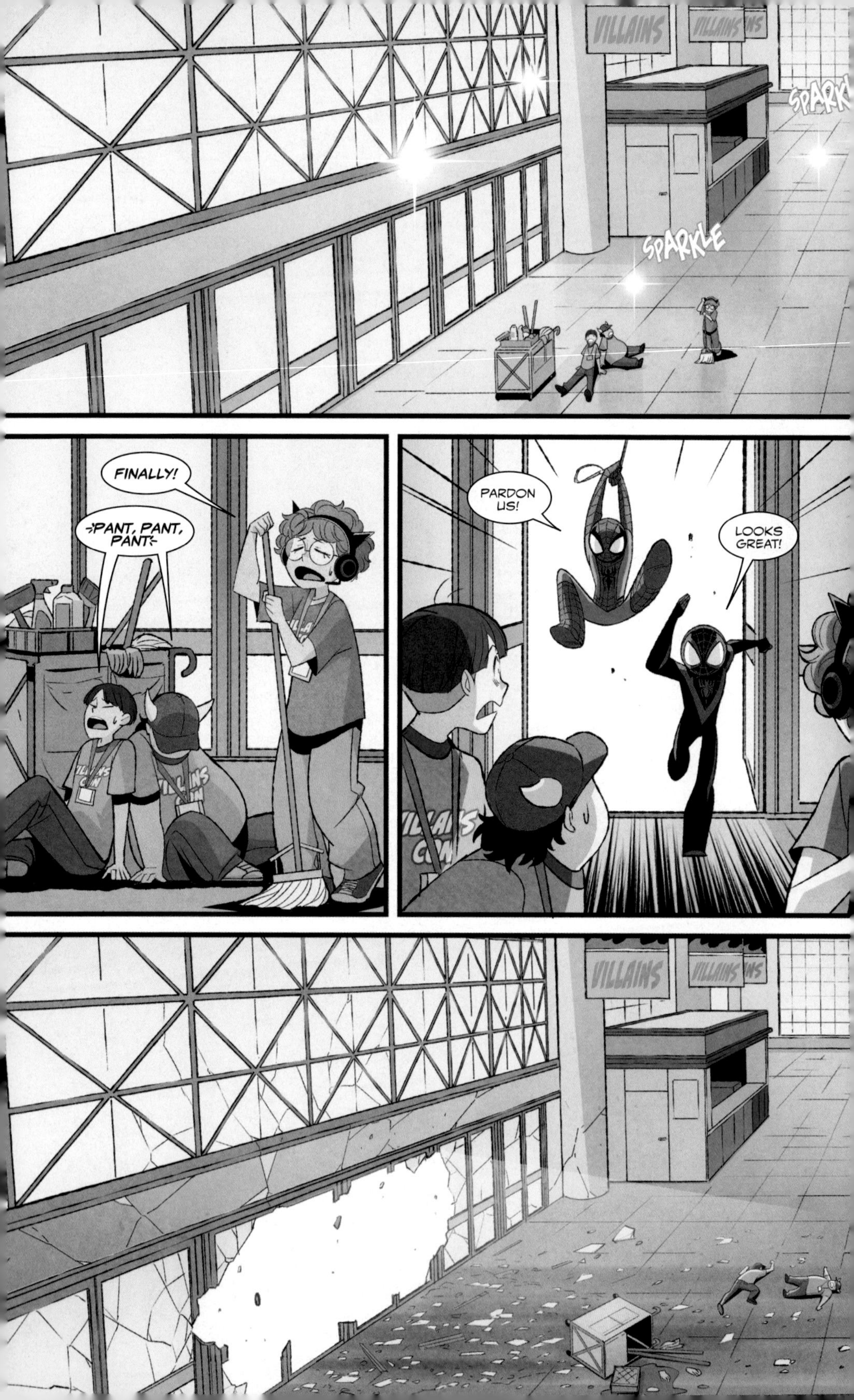
VILLAINS
VILLAINS
SPARK!
SPARKLE
FINALLY!
PANT, PANT, PANT
PARDON US!
LOOKS GREAT!
VILLAINS

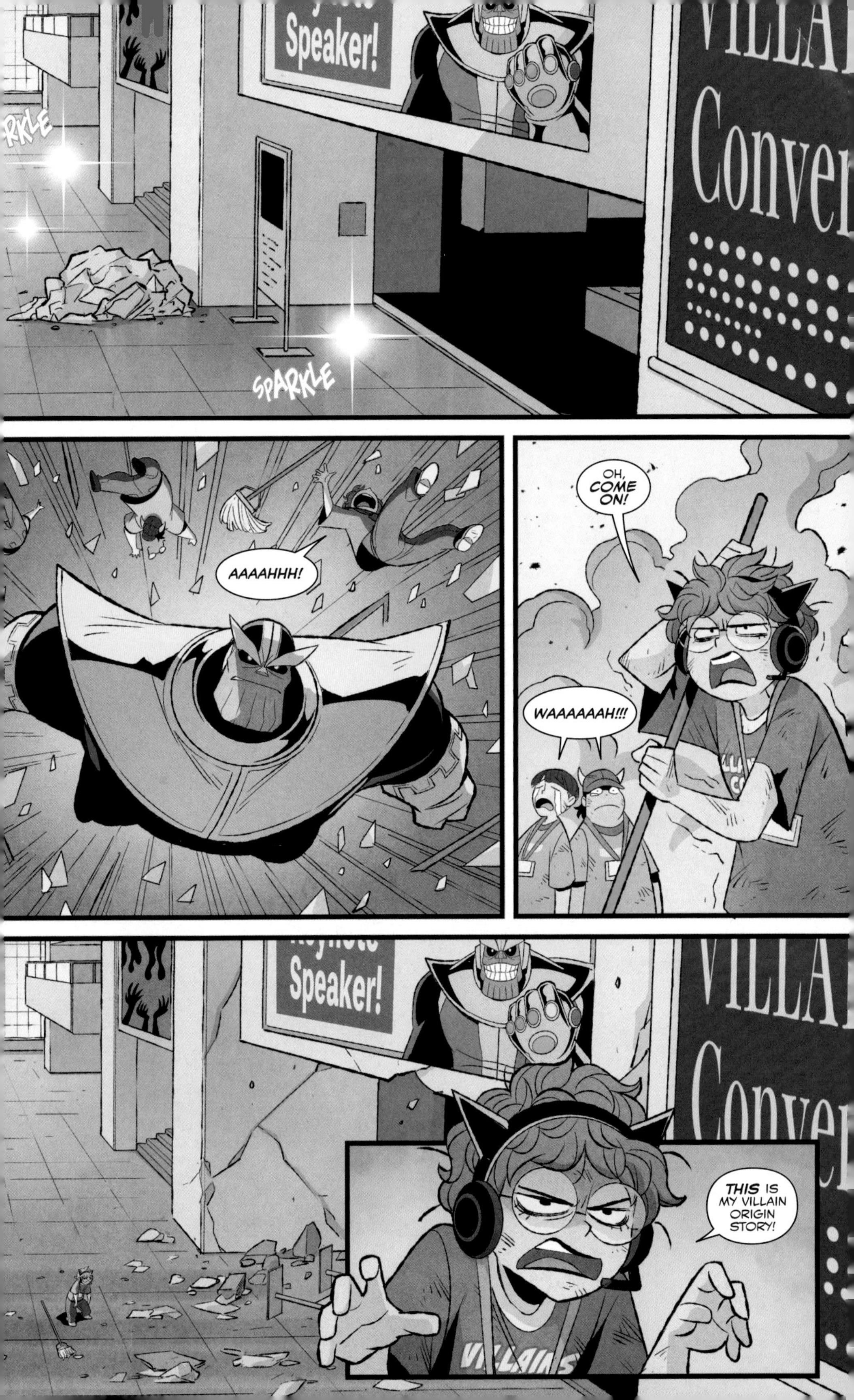
Speaker!
Conven
RKLE
SPARKLE
AAAAHHH!
OH, COME ON!
WAAAAAAH!!!
Speaker!
THIS IS MY VILLAIN ORIGIN STORY!
VILLAINS

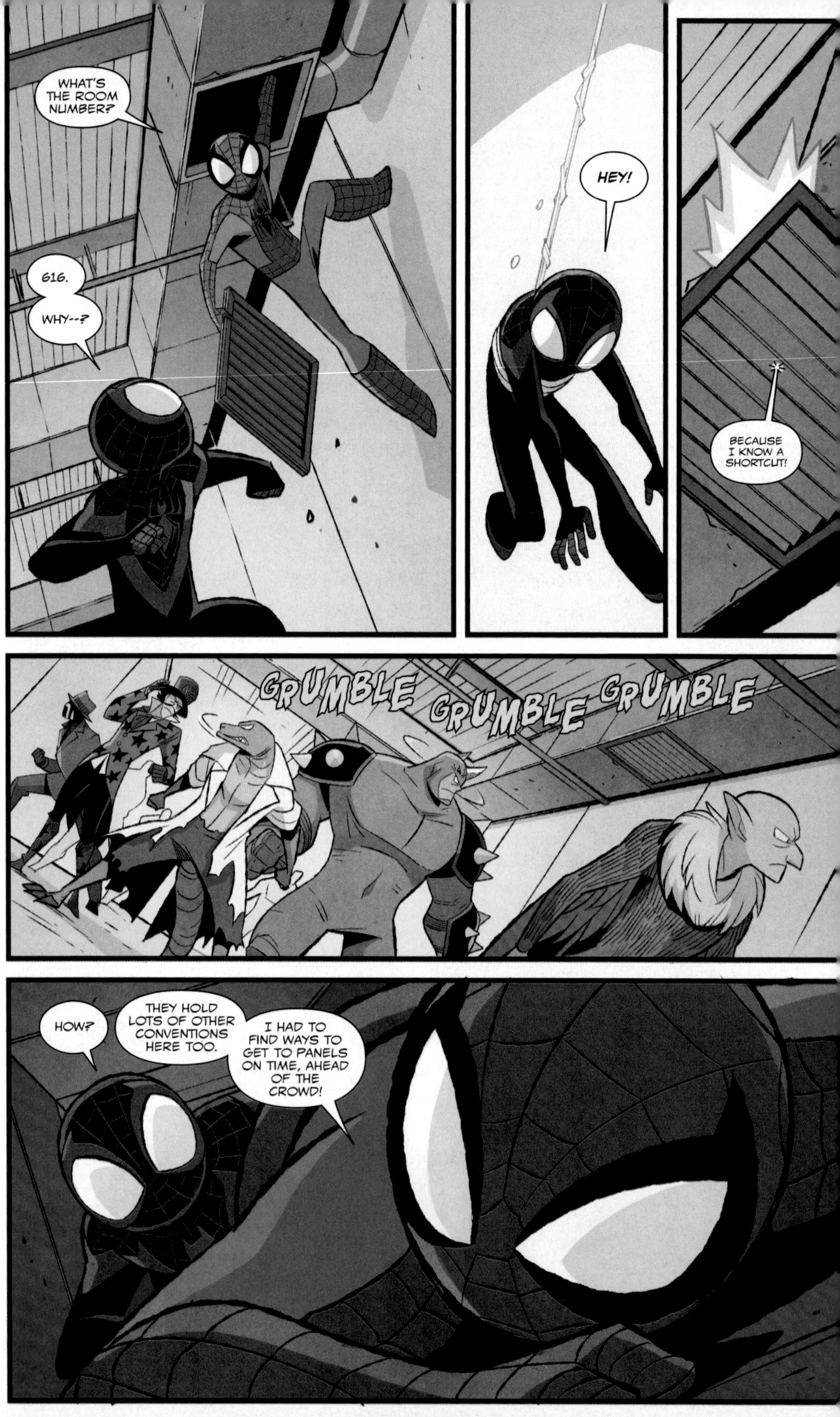
WHAT'S THE ROOM NUMBER?
616.
WHY--?
HEY!
BECAUSE I KNOW A SHORTCUT!
GRUMBLE GRUMBLE GRUMBLE
HOW?
THEY HOLD LOTS OF OTHER CONVENTIONS HERE TOO.
I HAD TO FIND WAYS TO GET TO PANELS ON TIME, AHEAD OF THE CROWD!

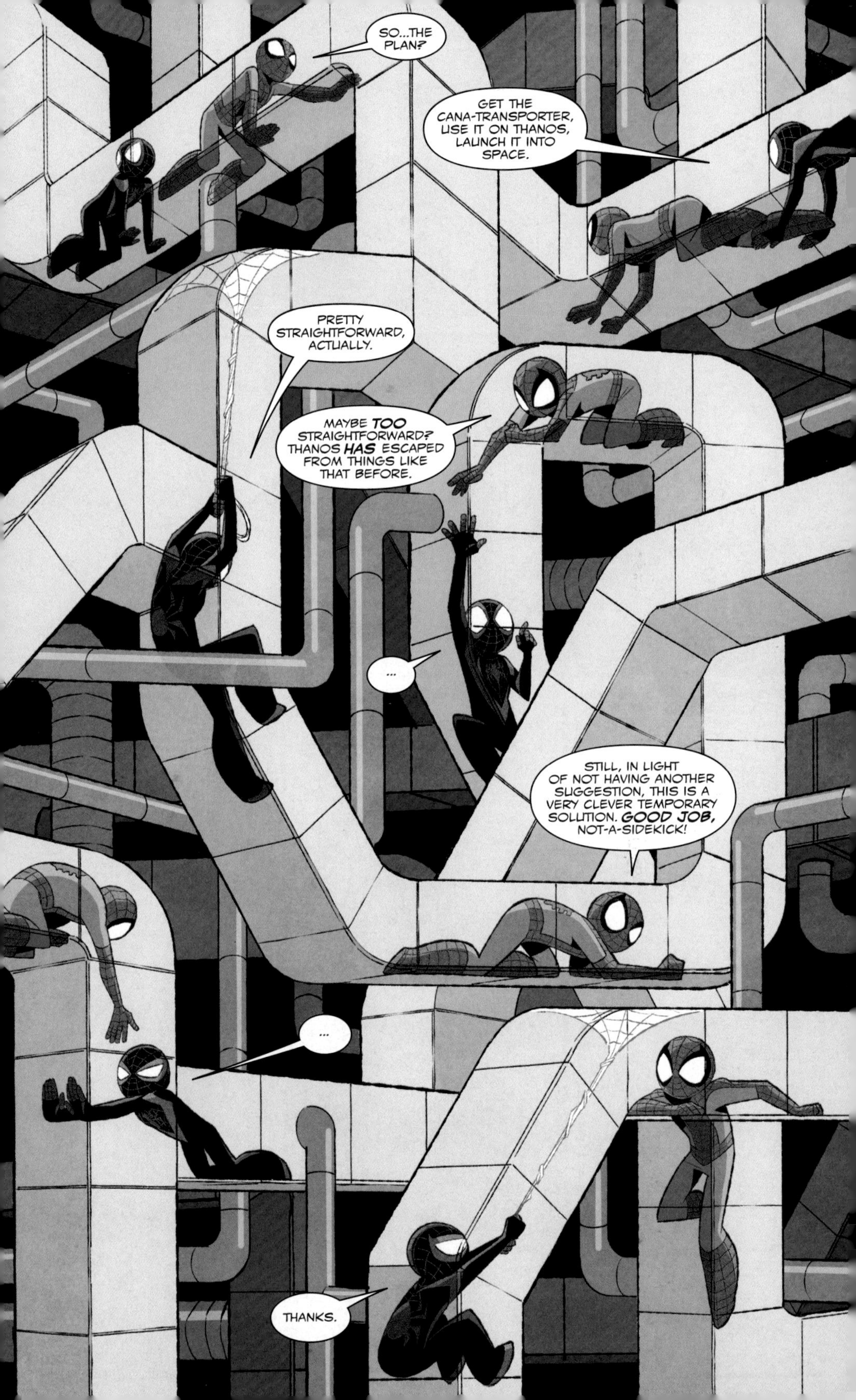
SO...THE PLAN?
GET THE CANA-TRANSPORTER, USE IT ON THANOS, LAUNCH IT INTO SPACE.
PRETTY STRAIGHTFORWARD, ACTUALLY.
MAYBE **TOO** STRAIGHTFORWARD? THANOS **HAS** ESCAPED FROM THINGS LIKE THAT BEFORE.
...
STILL, IN LIGHT OF NOT HAVING ANOTHER SUGGESTION, THIS IS A VERY CLEVER TEMPORARY SOLUTION. **GOOD JOB,** NOT-A-SIDEKICK!
...
THANKS.

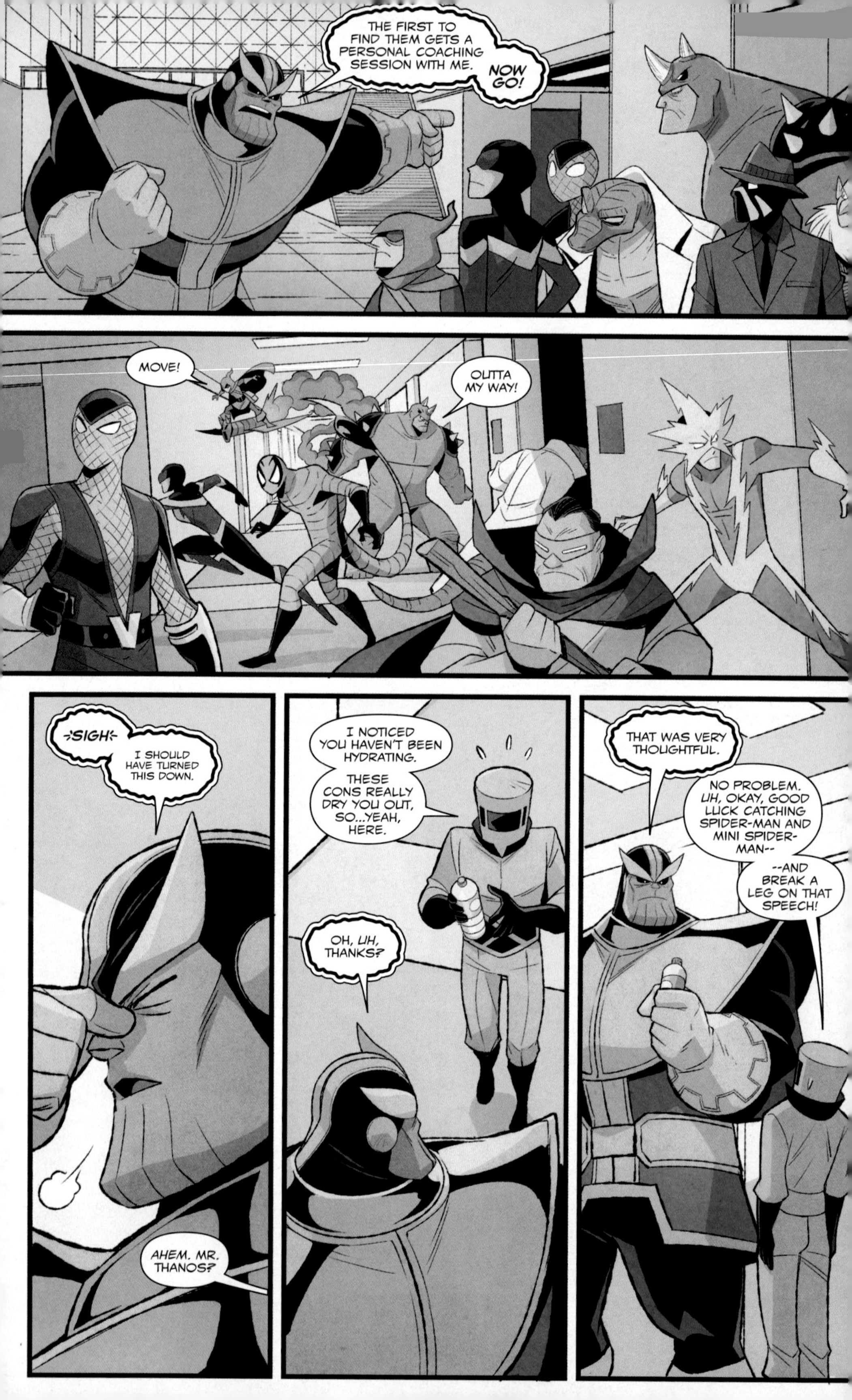
THE FIRST TO FIND THEM GETS A PERSONAL COACHING SESSION WITH ME.
NOW GO!
MOVE!
OUTTA MY WAY!
-SIGH-
I SHOULD HAVE TURNED THIS DOWN.
AHEM. MR. THANOS?
I NOTICED YOU HAVEN'T BEEN HYDRATING.
THESE CONS REALLY DRY YOU OUT, SO...YEAH, HERE.
OH, UH, THANKS?
THAT WAS VERY THOUGHTFUL.
NO PROBLEM. UH, OKAY, GOOD LUCK CATCHING SPIDER-MAN AND MINI SPIDER-MAN--
--AND BREAK A LEG ON THAT SPEECH!

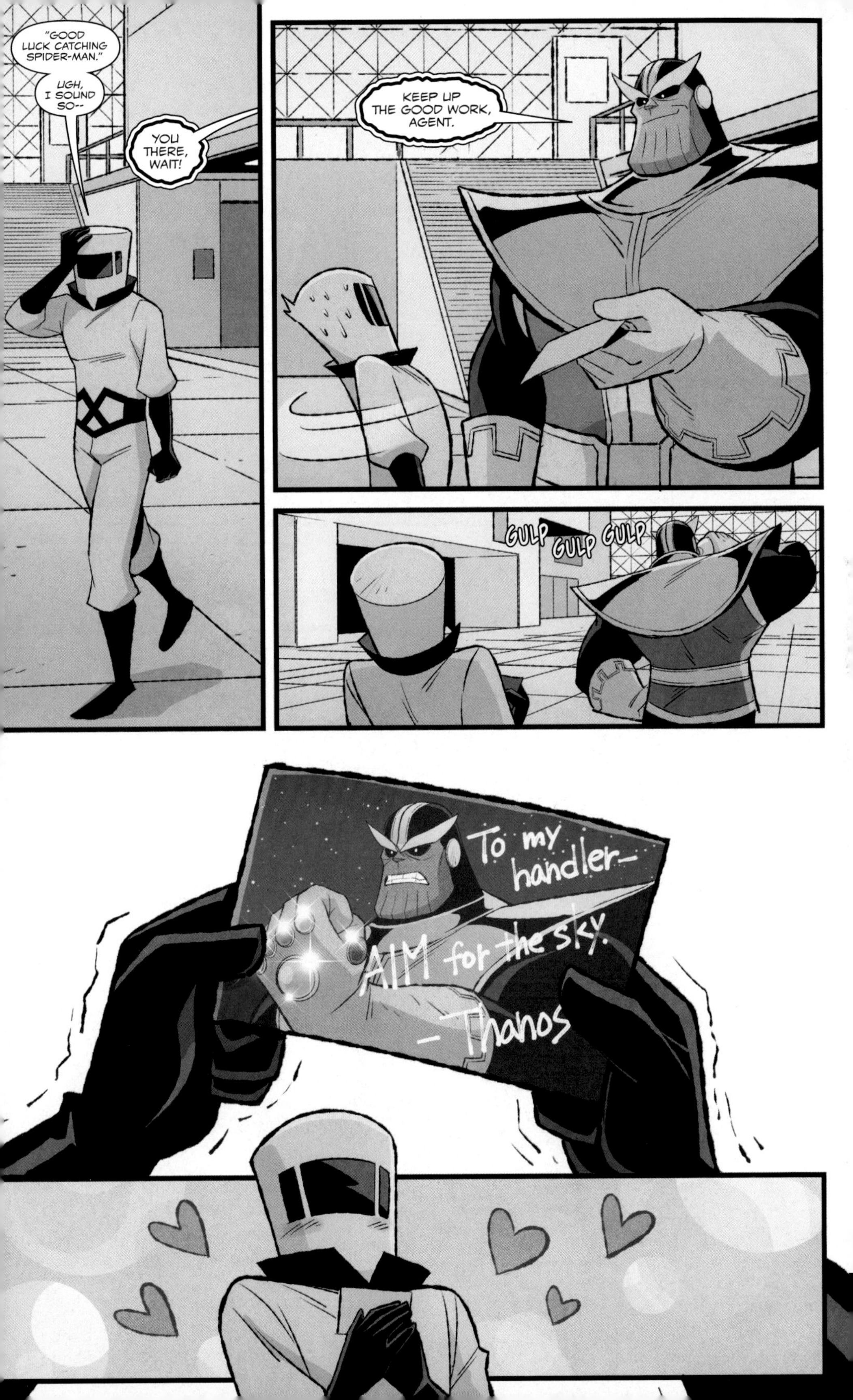
"GOOD LUCK CATCHING SPIDER-MAN."
UGH, I SOUND SO--
YOU THERE, WAIT!
KEEP UP THE GOOD WORK, AGENT.
GULP GULP GULP
To my handler-
AIM for the sky.
-Thanos

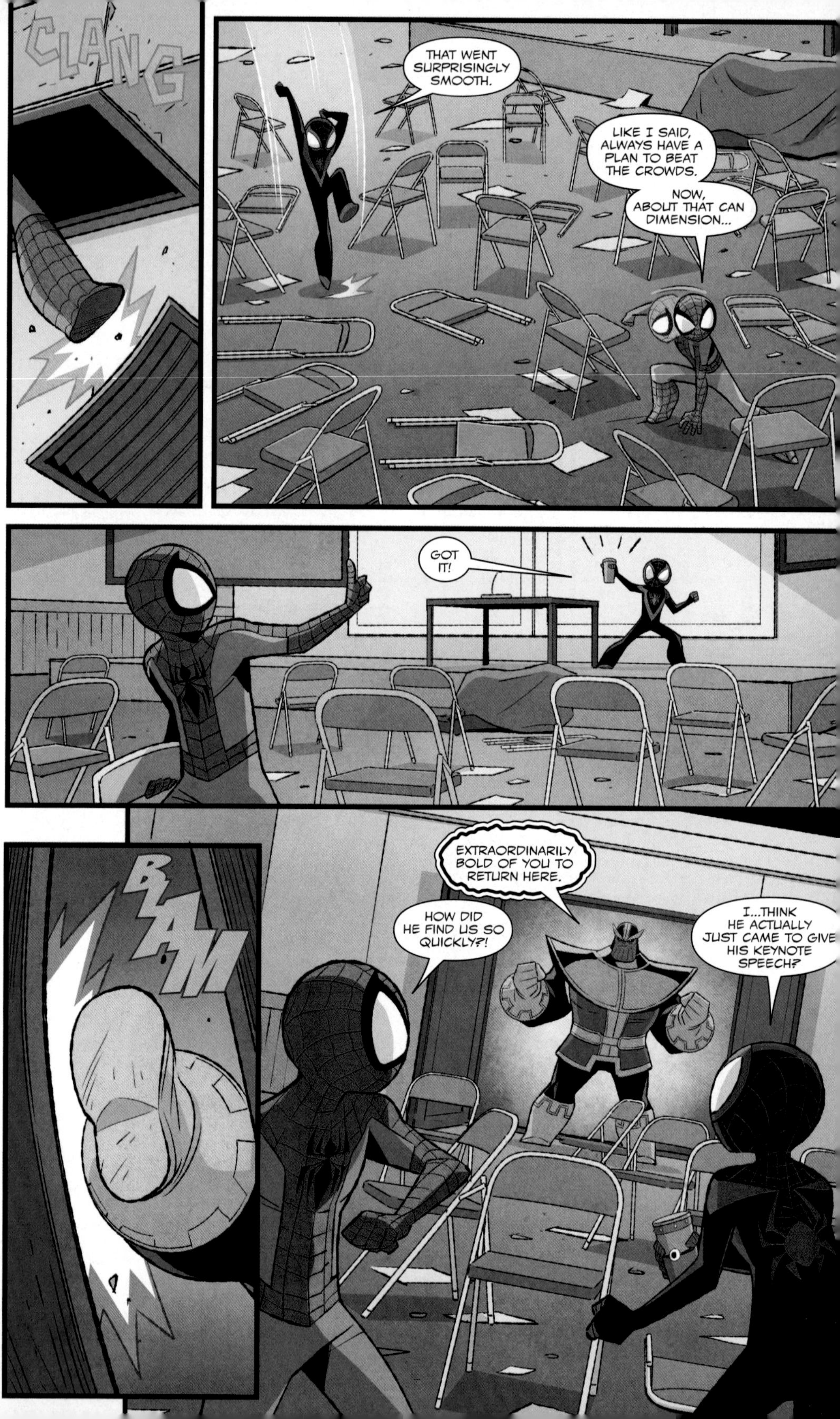
CLANG
THAT WENT SURPRISINGLY SMOOTH.
LIKE I SAID, ALWAYS HAVE A PLAN TO BEAT THE CROWDS.
NOW, ABOUT THAT CAN DIMENSION...
GOT IT!
BLAM
EXTRAORDINARILY BOLD OF YOU TO RETURN HERE.
HOW DID HE FIND US SO QUICKLY?!
I...THINK HE ACTUALLY JUST CAME TO GIVE HIS KEYNOTE SPEECH?

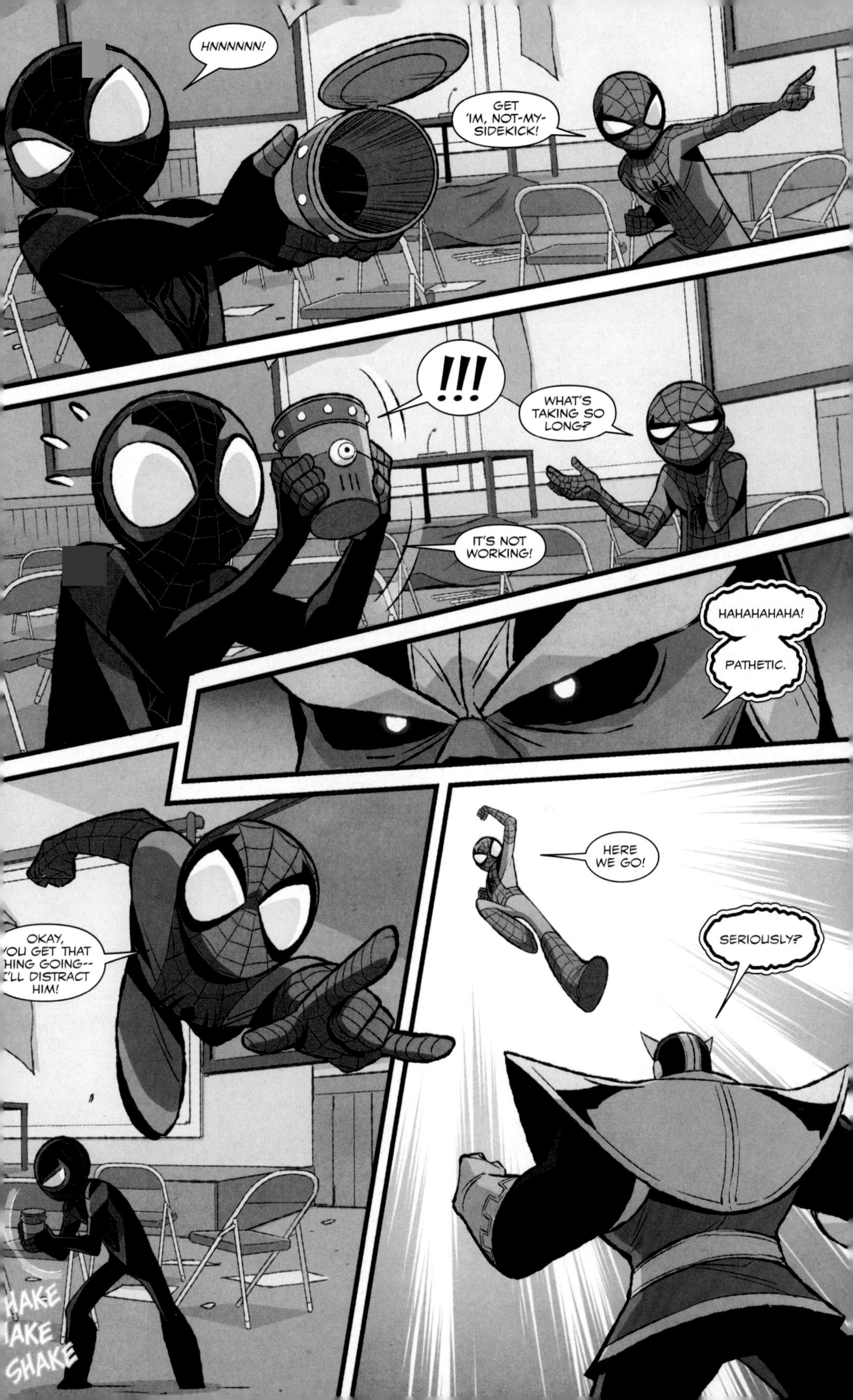
HNNNNNN!
GET 'IM, NOT-MY-SIDEKICK!
!!!
WHAT'S TAKING SO LONG?
IT'S NOT WORKING!
HAHAHAHAHA!
PATHETIC.
OKAY, OU GET THAT HING GOING-- 'LL DISTRACT HIM!
HAKE
AKE
SHAKE
HERE WE GO!
SERIOUSLY?

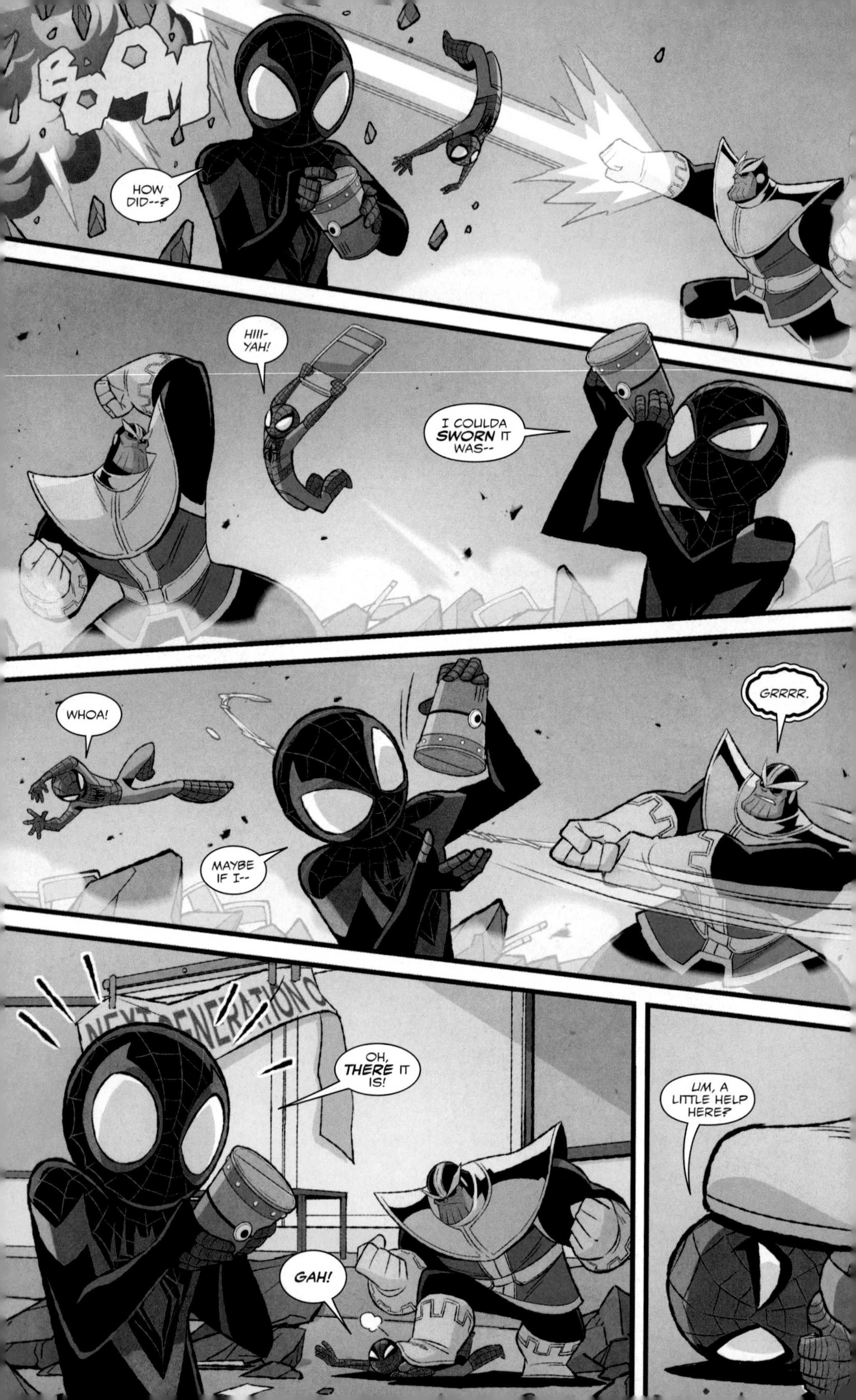
BOOM
HOW DID--?
HIII-YAH!
I COULDA SWORN IT WAS--
WHOA!
GRRRR.
MAYBE IF I--
NEXT GENERATION C
OH, THERE IT IS!
GAH!
UM, A LITTLE HELP HERE?

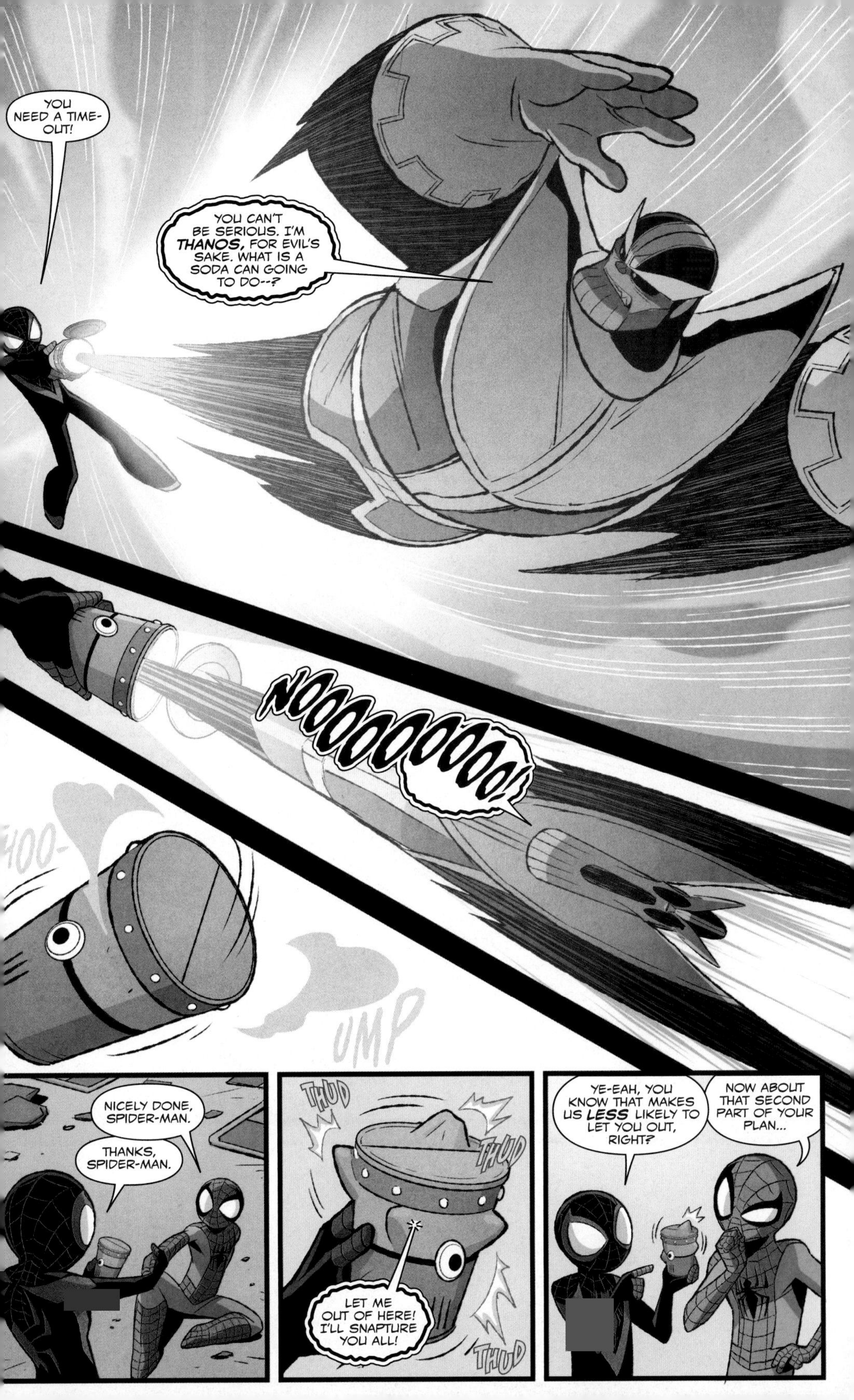
YOU NEED A TIME-OUT!
YOU CAN'T BE SERIOUS. I'M **THANOS,** FOR EVIL'S SAKE. WHAT IS A SODA CAN GOING TO DO--?
NOOOOOOOOO!
HOO-
UMP
NICELY DONE, SPIDER-MAN.
THANKS, SPIDER-MAN.
THUD
THUD
LET ME OUT OF HERE! I'LL SNAPTURE YOU ALL!
THUD
YE-EAH, YOU KNOW THAT MAKES US **LESS** LIKELY TO LET YOU OUT, RIGHT?
NOW ABOUT THAT SECOND PART OF YOUR PLAN...

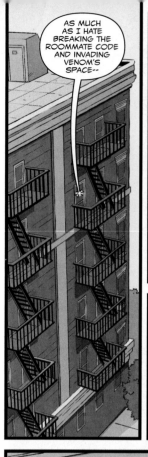

AS MUCH AS I HATE BREAKING THE ROOMMATE CODE AND INVADING VENOM'S SPACE--

--HE HAS *JUST* THE THING TO GET THE JOB DONE.

ALSO, I'M PRETTY SURE HE STOLE IT FROM THE WAREHOUSE ANYWAY!

WE HAVE TO HURRY-- I CAN FEEL HIM BLASTING AWAY IN THERE.

WOULD YOU LIKE TO DO THE HONORS?

THANKS!

OF COURSE! YOU EARNED IT TODAY!

SHUNK

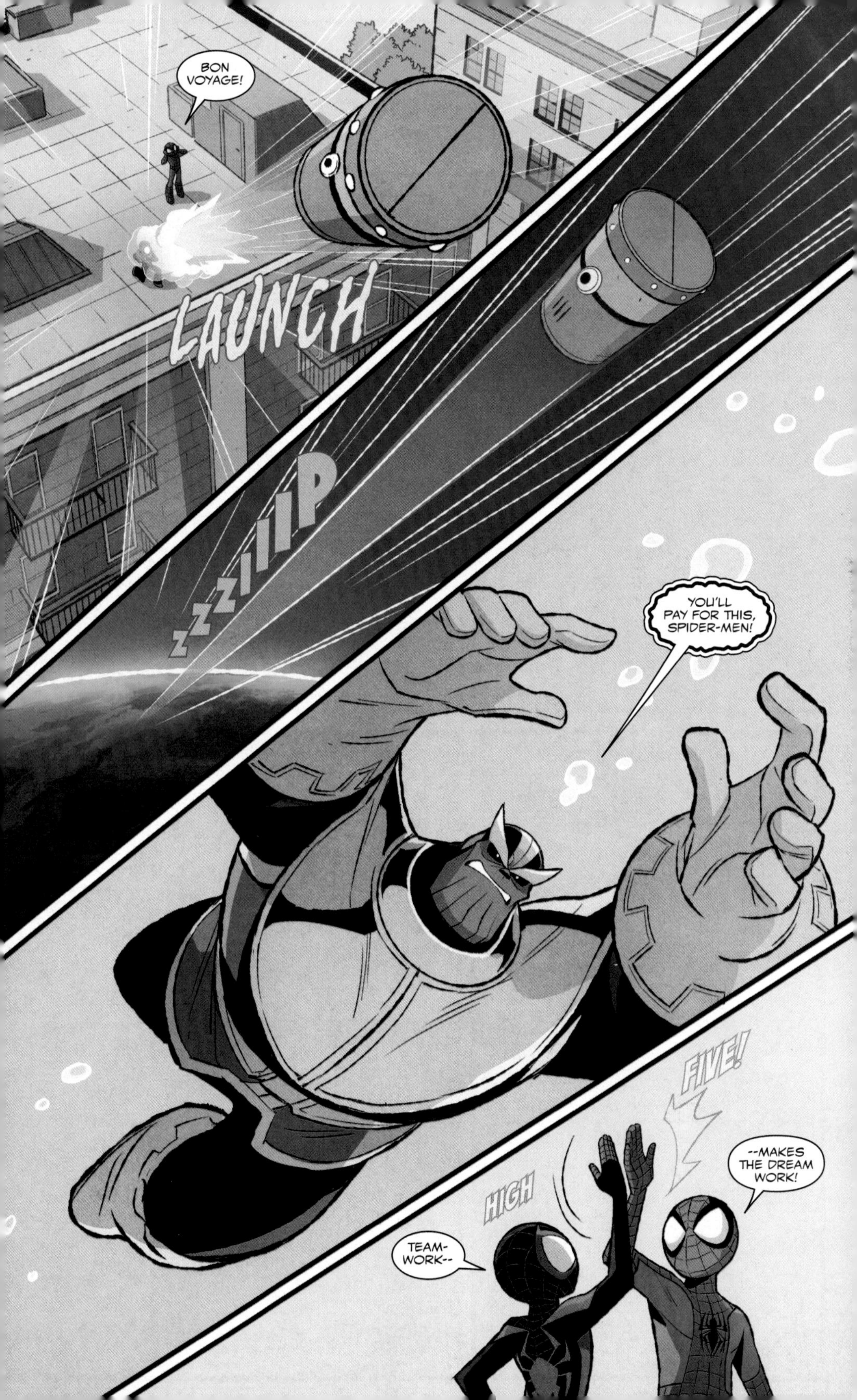
BON VOYAGE!
LAUNCH
ZZZIIIIP
YOU'LL PAY FOR THIS, SPIDER-MEN!
TEAM-WORK--
HIGH
FIVE!
--MAKES THE DREAM WORK!

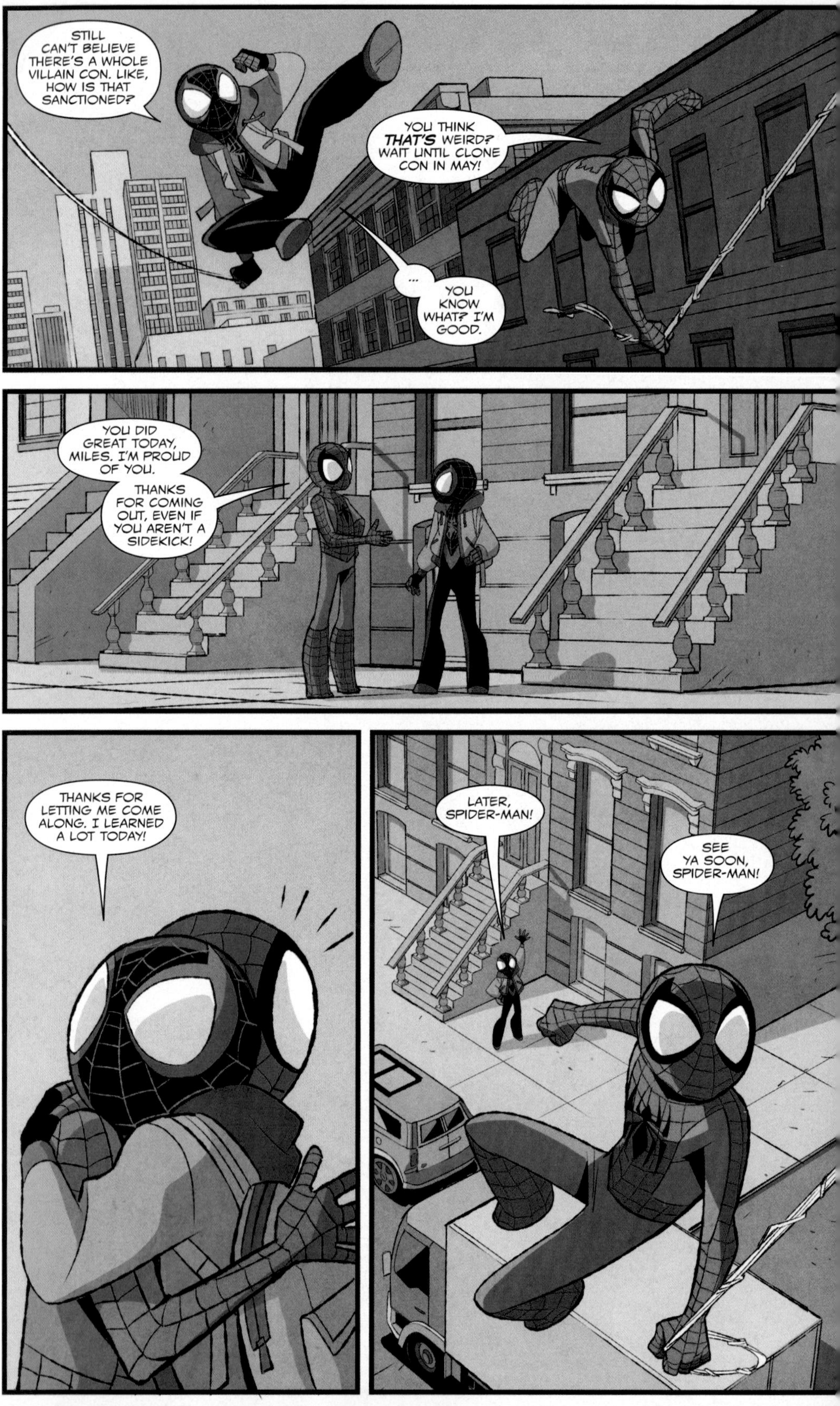
STILL CAN'T BELIEVE THERE'S A WHOLE VILLAIN CON. LIKE, HOW IS THAT SANCTIONED?
YOU THINK *THAT'S* WEIRD? WAIT UNTIL CLONE CON IN MAY!
...
YOU KNOW WHAT? I'M GOOD.
YOU DID GREAT TODAY, MILES. I'M PROUD OF YOU.
THANKS FOR COMING OUT, EVEN IF YOU AREN'T A SIDEKICK!
THANKS FOR LETTING ME COME ALONG. I LEARNED A LOT TODAY!
LATER, SPIDER-MAN!
SEE YA SOON, SPIDER-MAN!

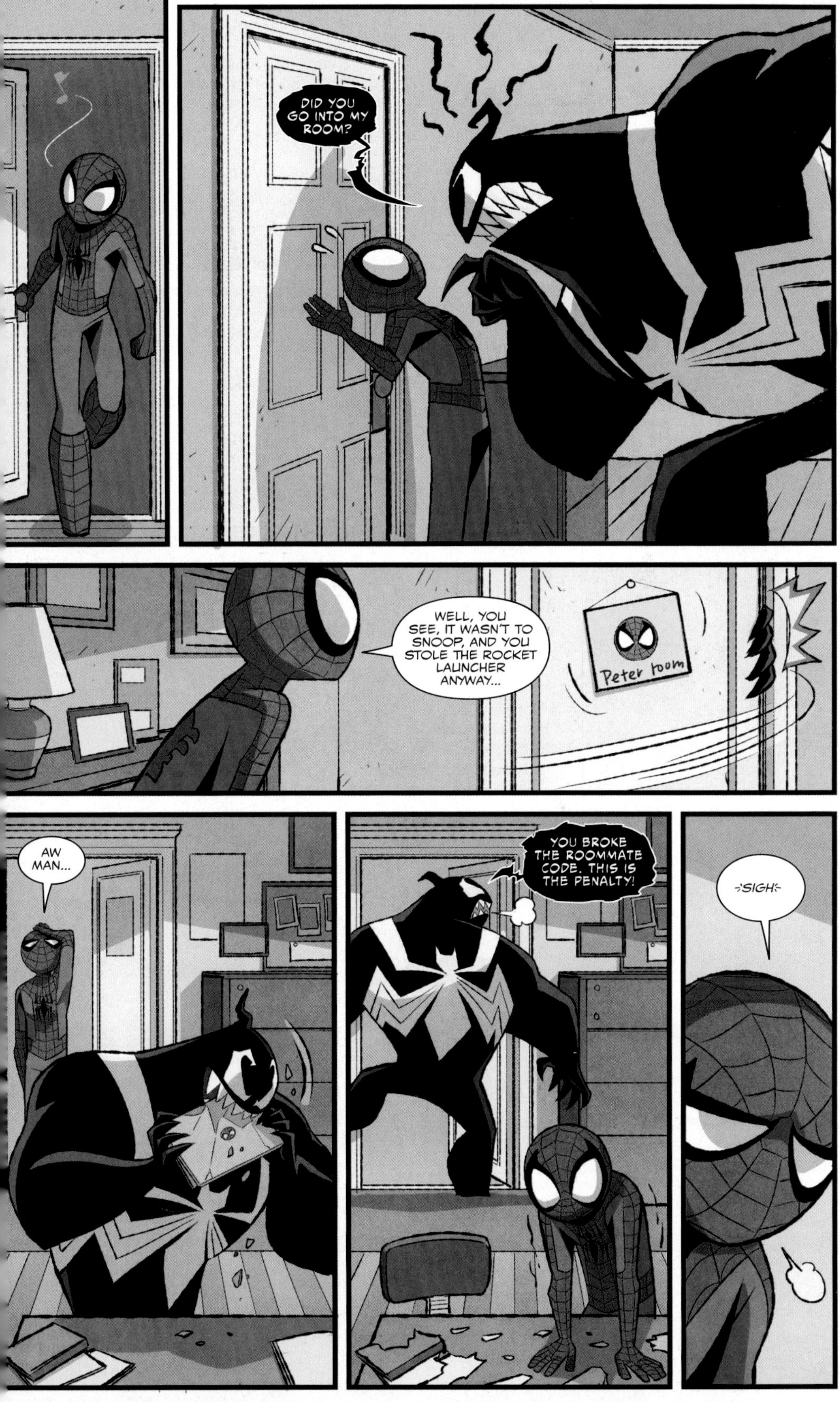
DID YOU GO INTO MY ROOM?
WELL, YOU SEE, IT WASN'T TO SNOOP, AND YOU STOLE THE ROCKET LAUNCHER ANYWAY...
Peter room
AW MAN...
YOU BROKE THE ROOMMATE CODE. THIS IS THE PENALTY!
SIGH

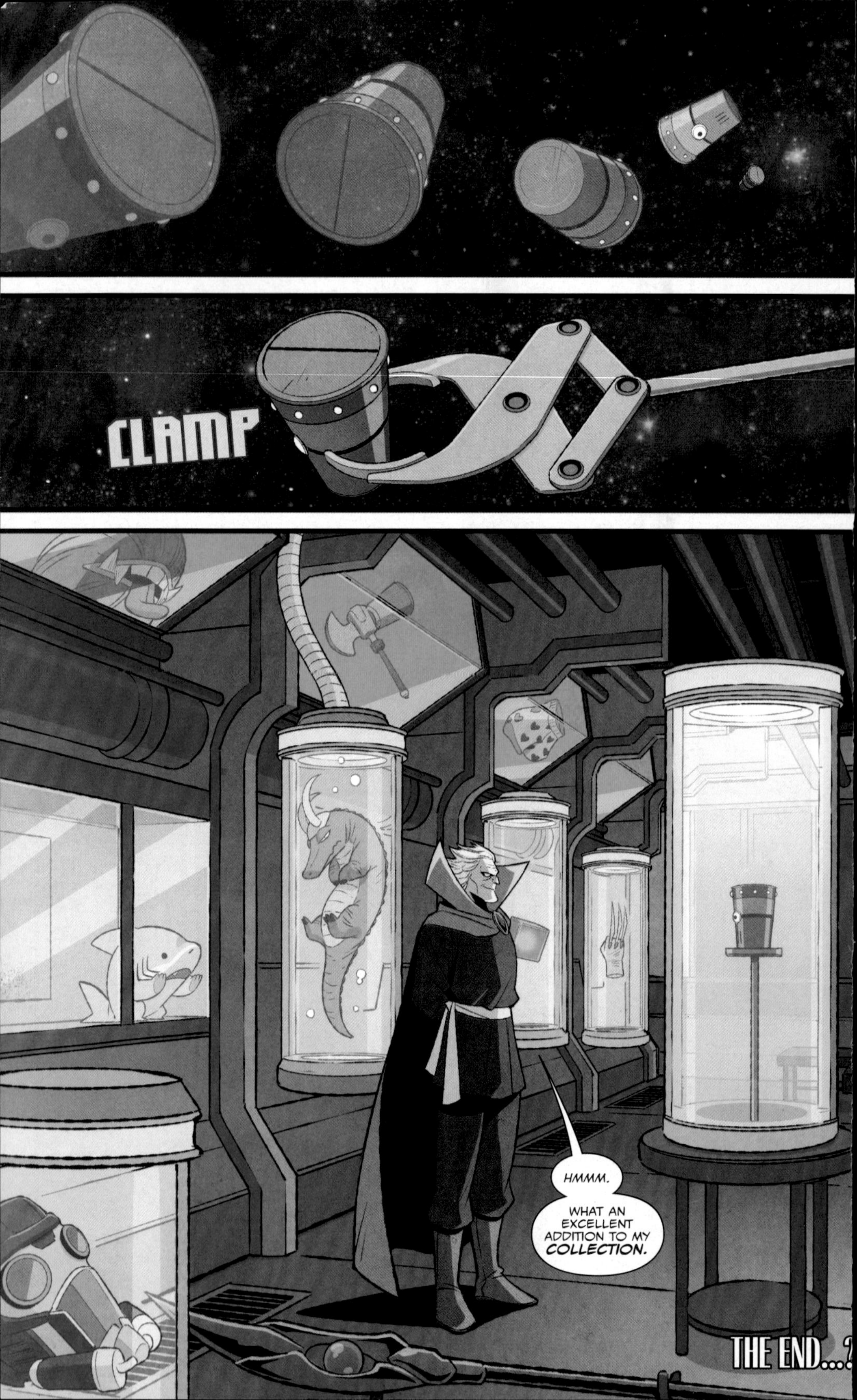
CLAMP
HMMM.
WHAT AN EXCELLENT ADDITION TO MY *COLLECTION.*
THE END...?

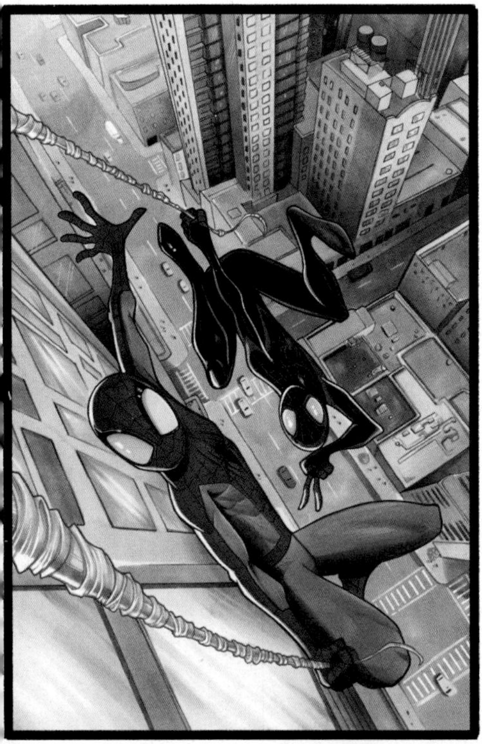

#1 VARIANT BY **CHRISSIE ZULLO**

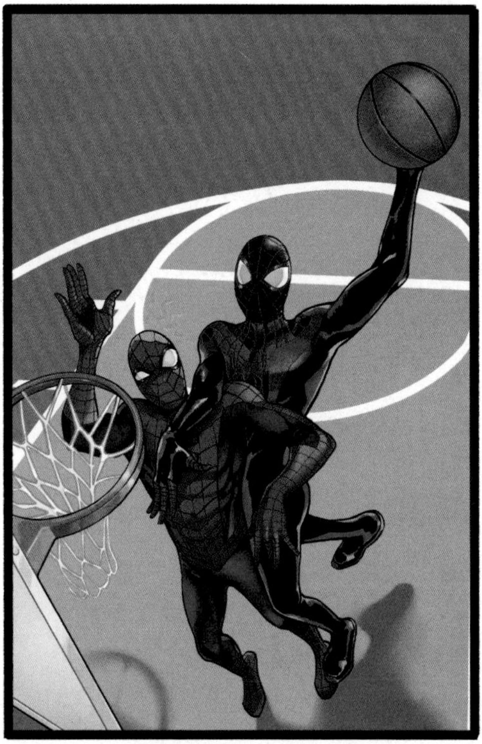

#1 VARIANT BY **ROMY JONES**

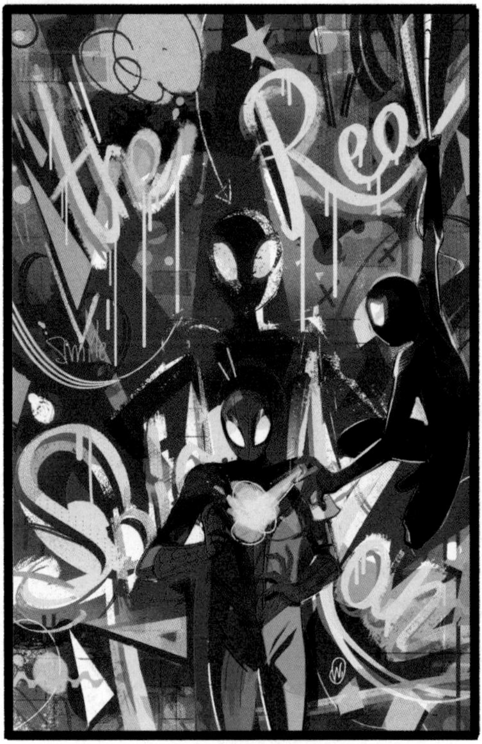

#2 VARIANT BY **NICOLETTA B ALDARI**

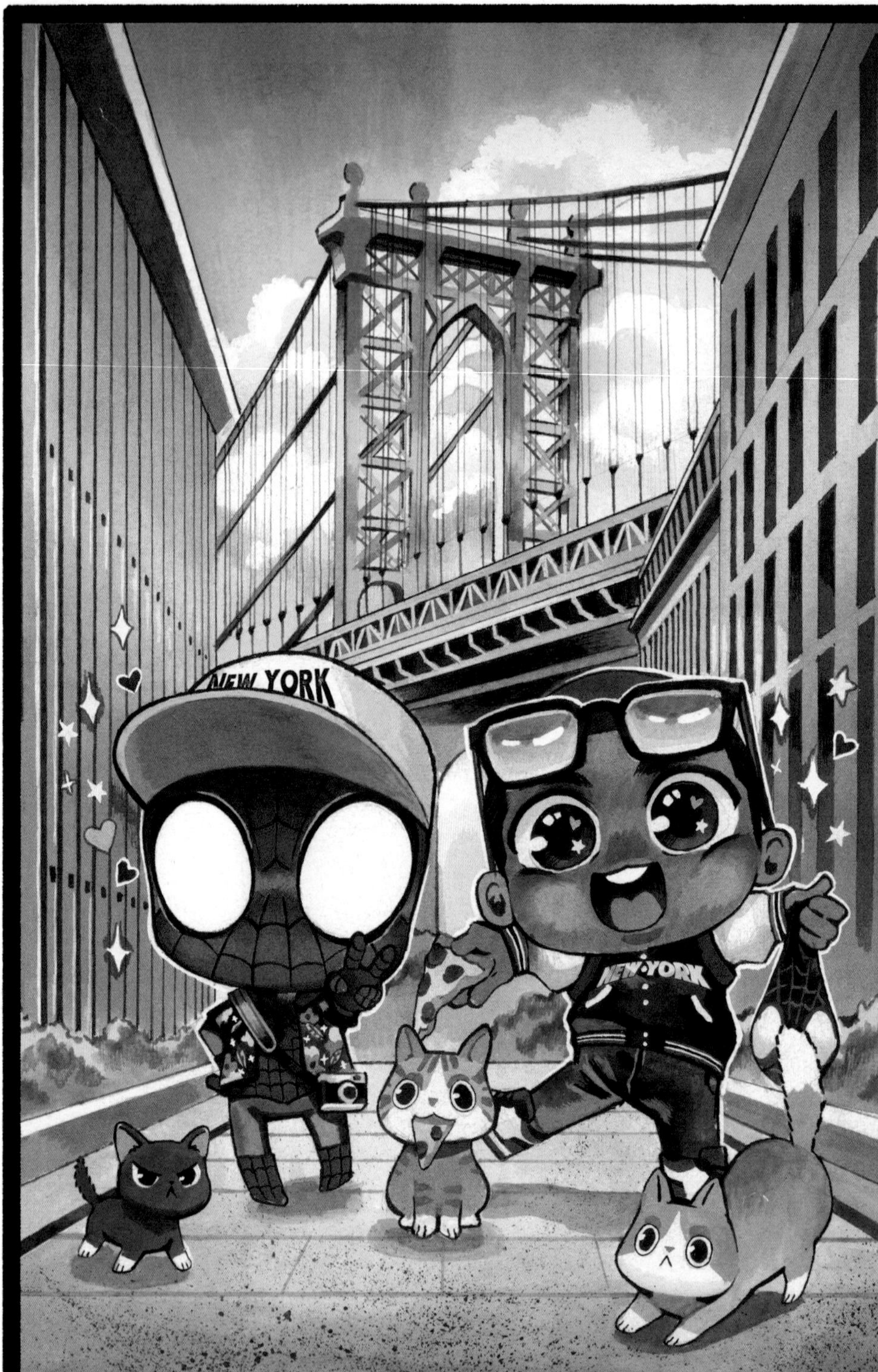
NEW YORK
NEW YORK

#3 VARIANT BY **RIAN GONZALES**

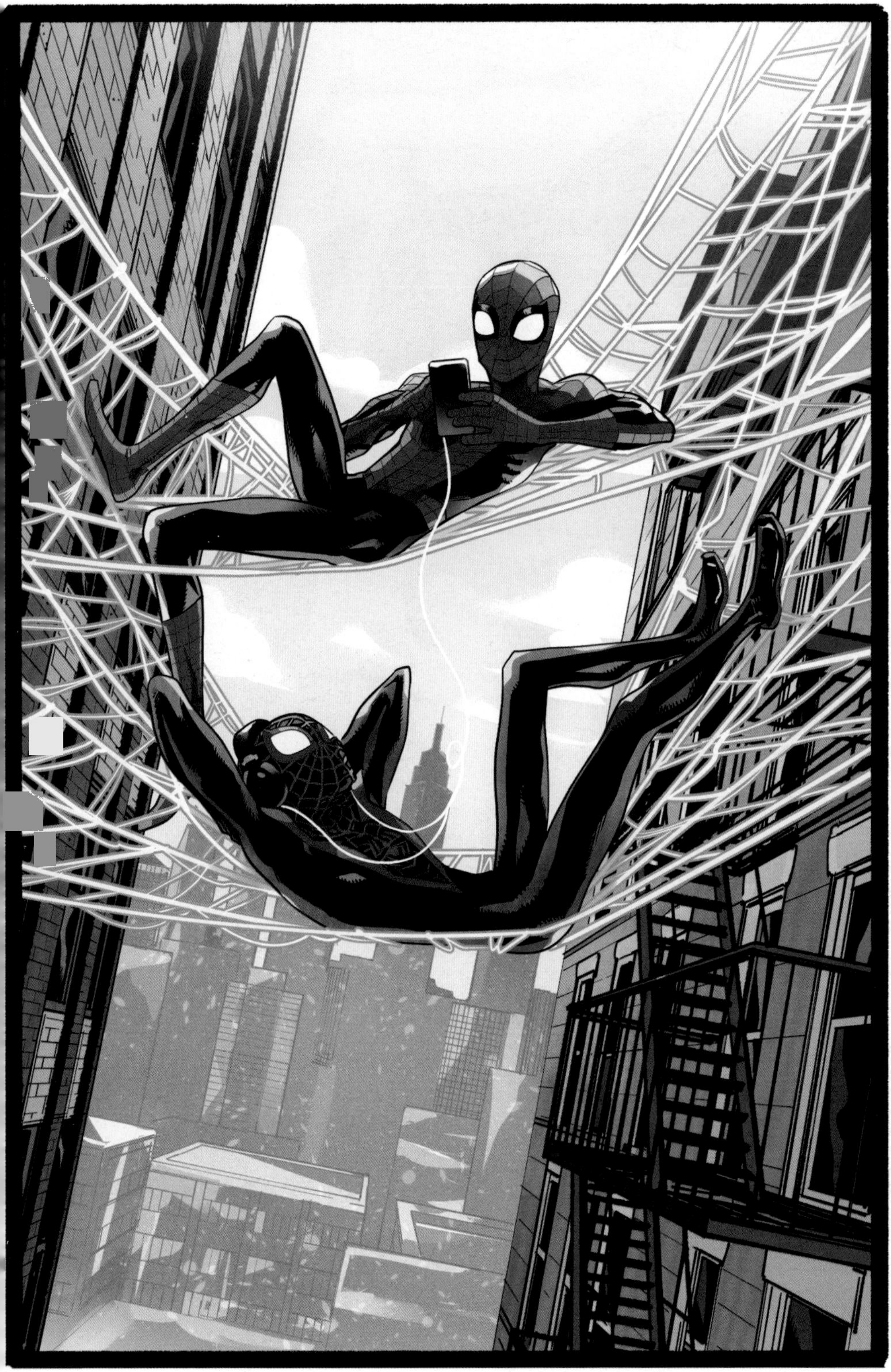

#4 VARIANT BY **NAO FUJI**

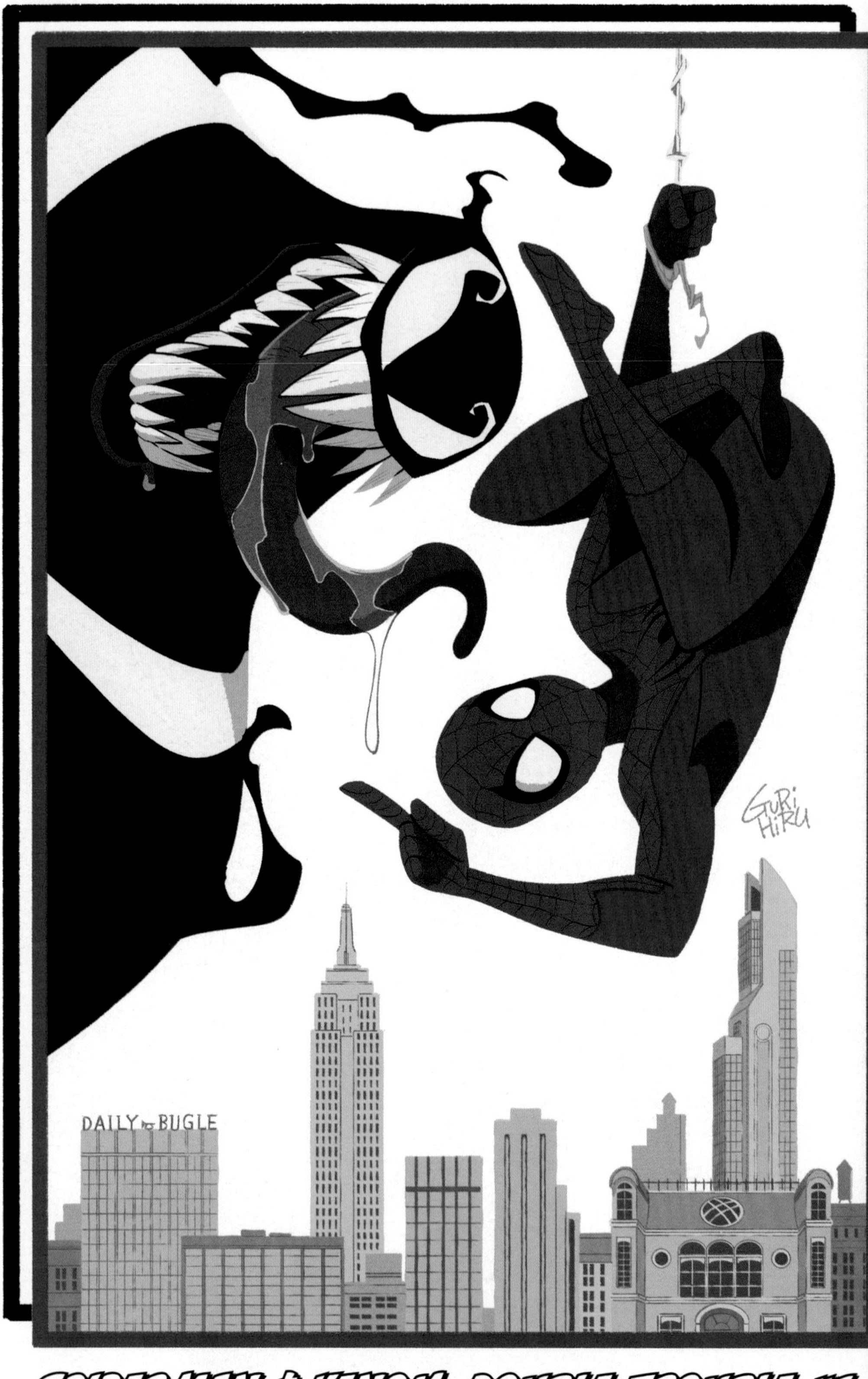
GURI
HIRU
DAILY BUGLE

SPIDER-MAN & VENOM: DOUBLE TROUBLE #1

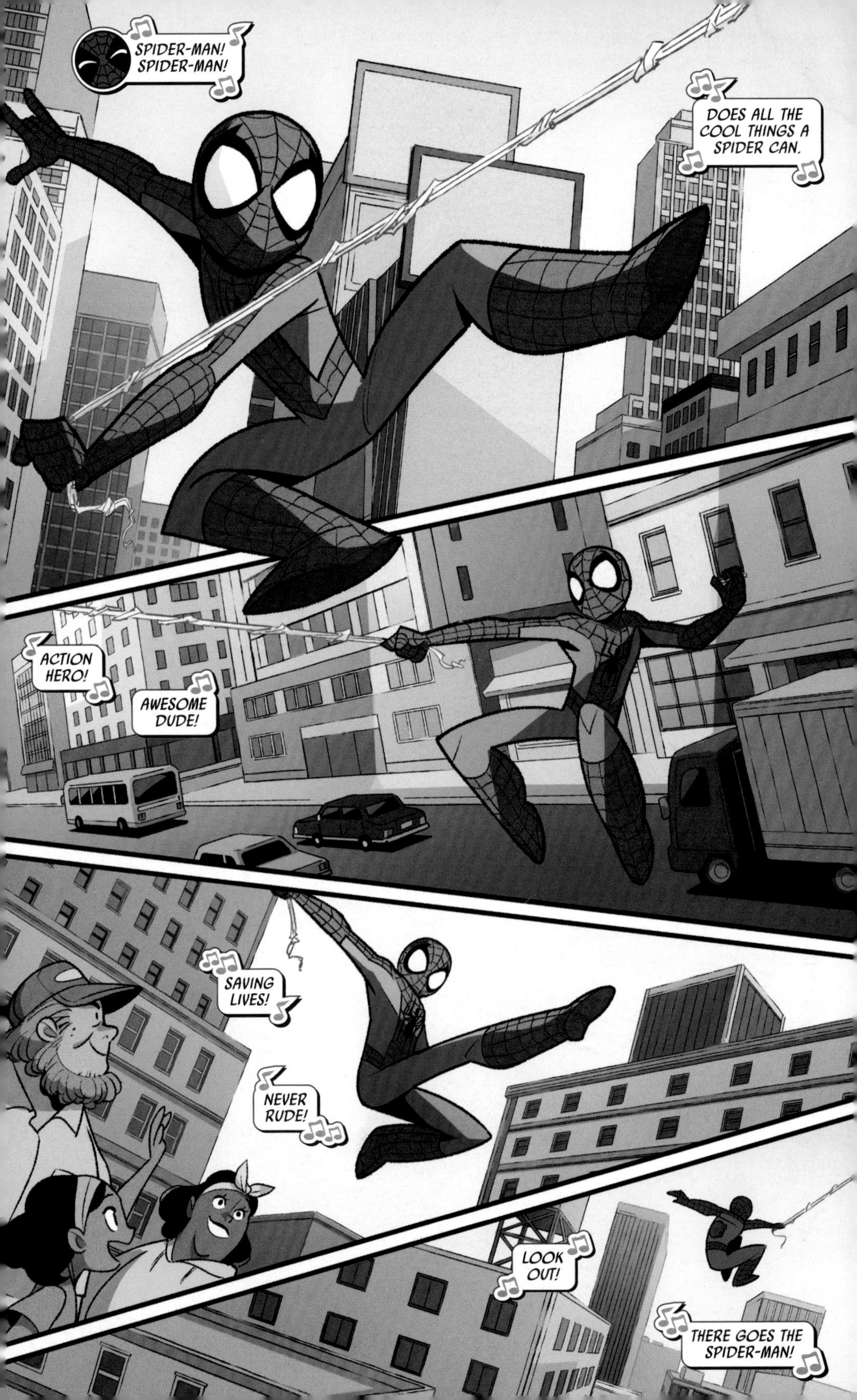
SPIDER-MAN! SPIDER-MAN!
DOES ALL THE COOL THINGS A SPIDER CAN.
ACTION HERO!
AWESOME DUDE!
SAVING LIVES!
NEVER RUDE!
LOOK OUT!
THERE GOES THE SPIDER-MAN!

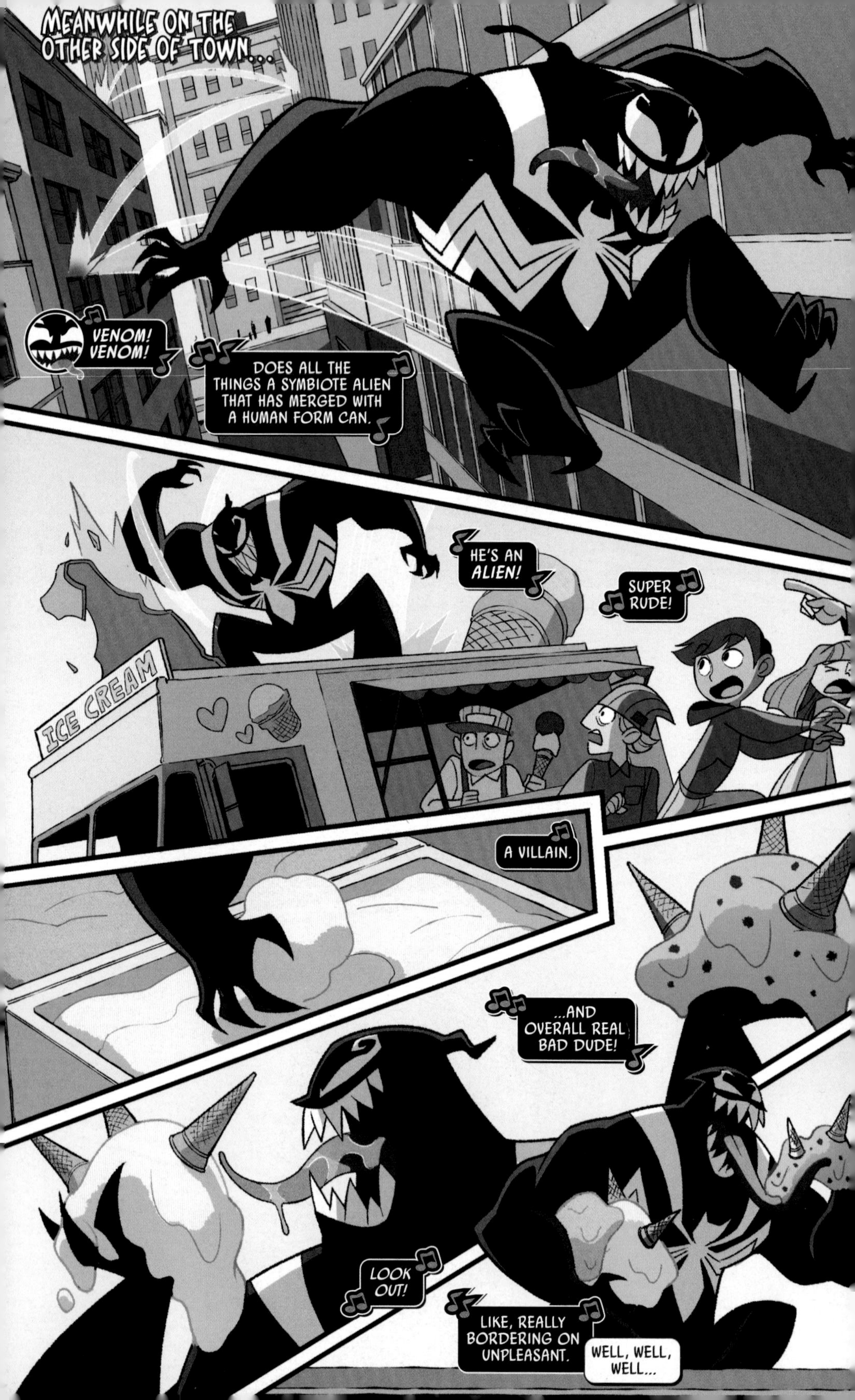
MEANWHILE ON THE OTHER SIDE OF TOWN...
VENOM! VENOM!
DOES ALL THE THINGS A SYMBIOTE ALIEN THAT HAS MERGED WITH A HUMAN FORM CAN.
HE'S AN ALIEN!
SUPER RUDE!
ICE CREAM
A VILLAIN.
...AND OVERALL REAL BAD DUDE!
LOOK OUT!
LIKE, REALLY BORDERING ON UNPLEASANT.
WELL, WELL, WELL...

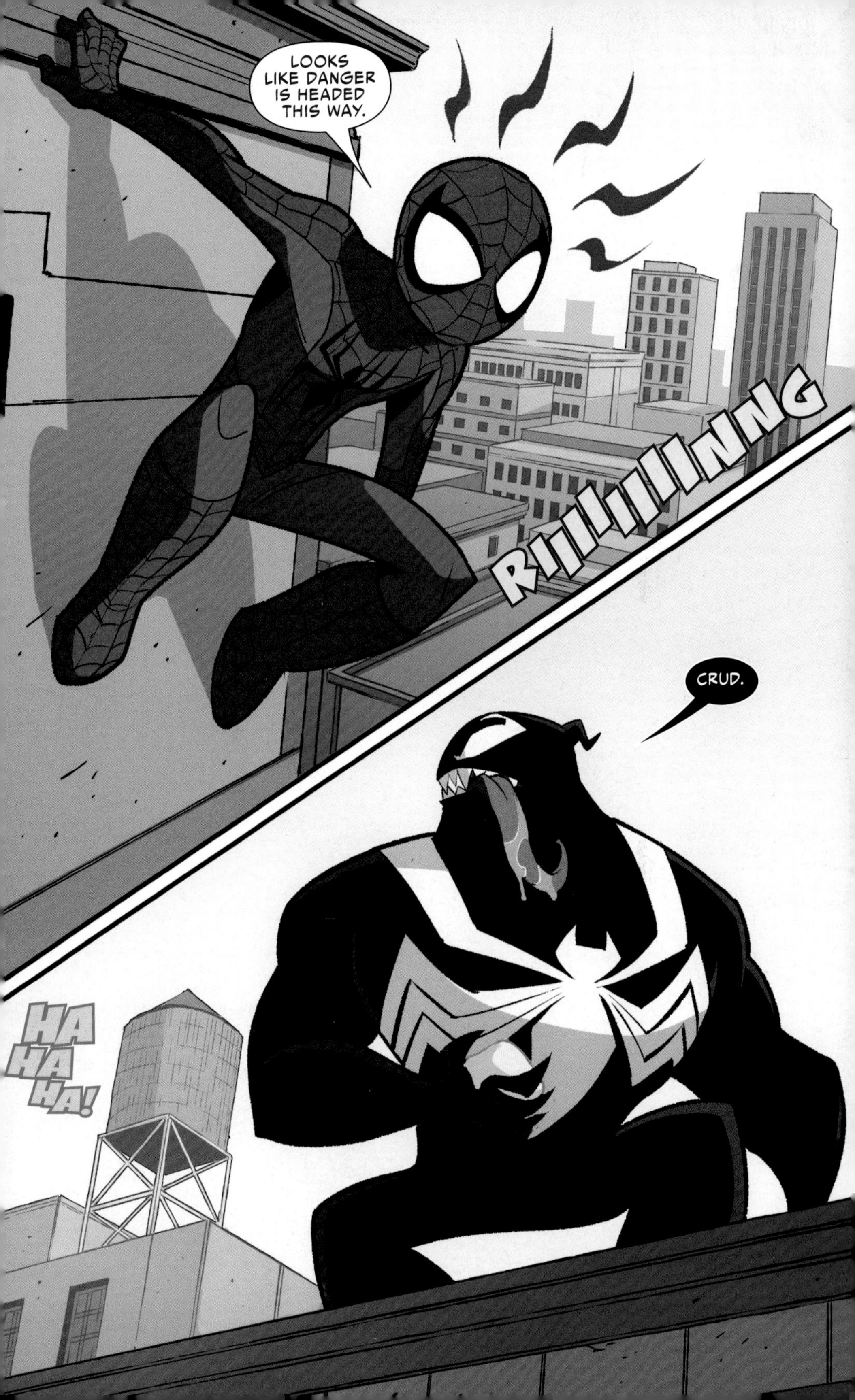
LOOKS LIKE DANGER IS HEADED THIS WAY.
RIIIIIIINNG
CRUD.
HA HA HA!

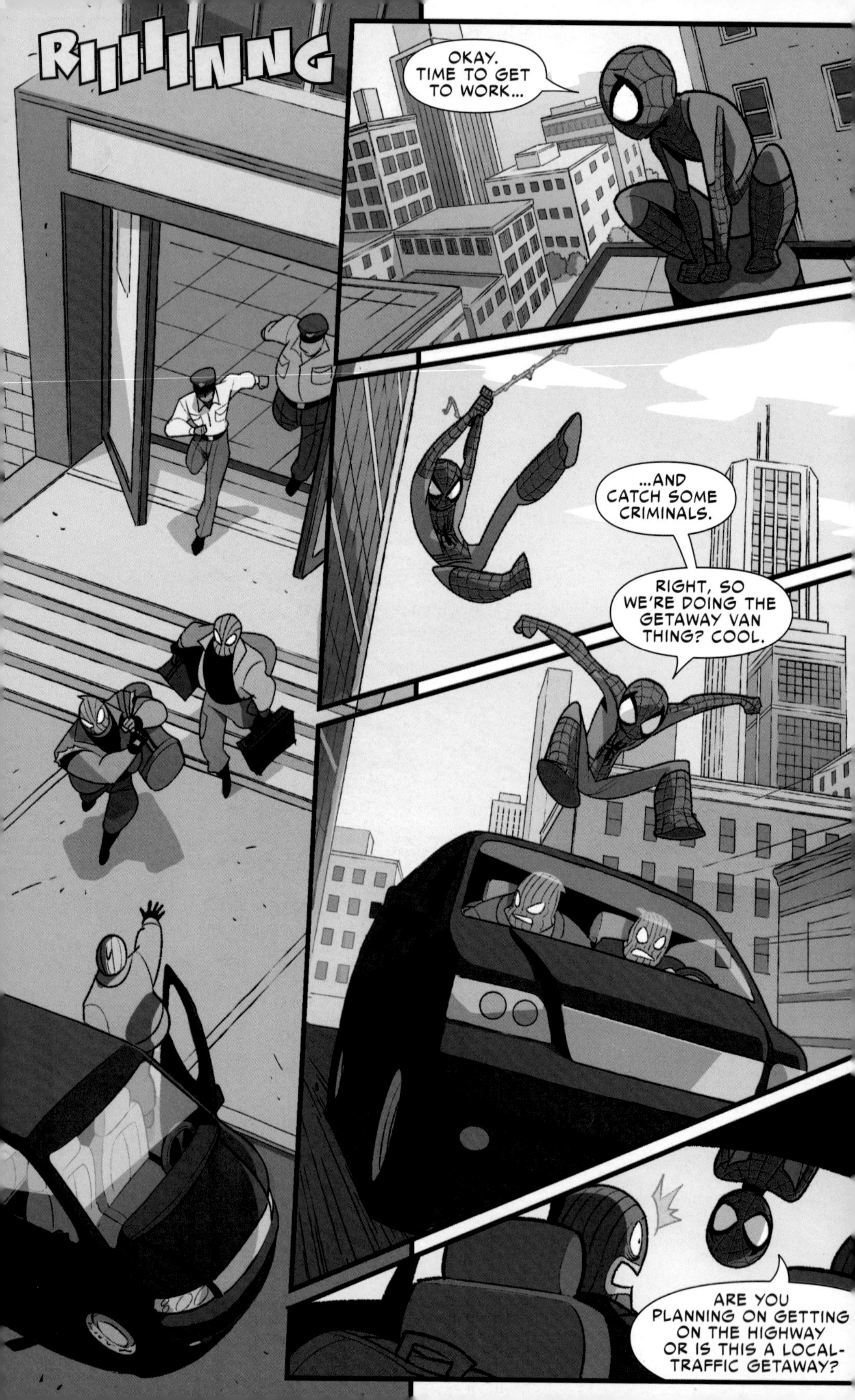
RIIIIINNG
OKAY. TIME TO GET TO WORK...
...AND CATCH SOME CRIMINALS.
RIGHT, SO WE'RE DOING THE GETAWAY VAN THING? COOL.
ARE YOU PLANNING ON GETTING ON THE HIGHWAY OR IS THIS A LOCAL-TRAFFIC GETAWAY?

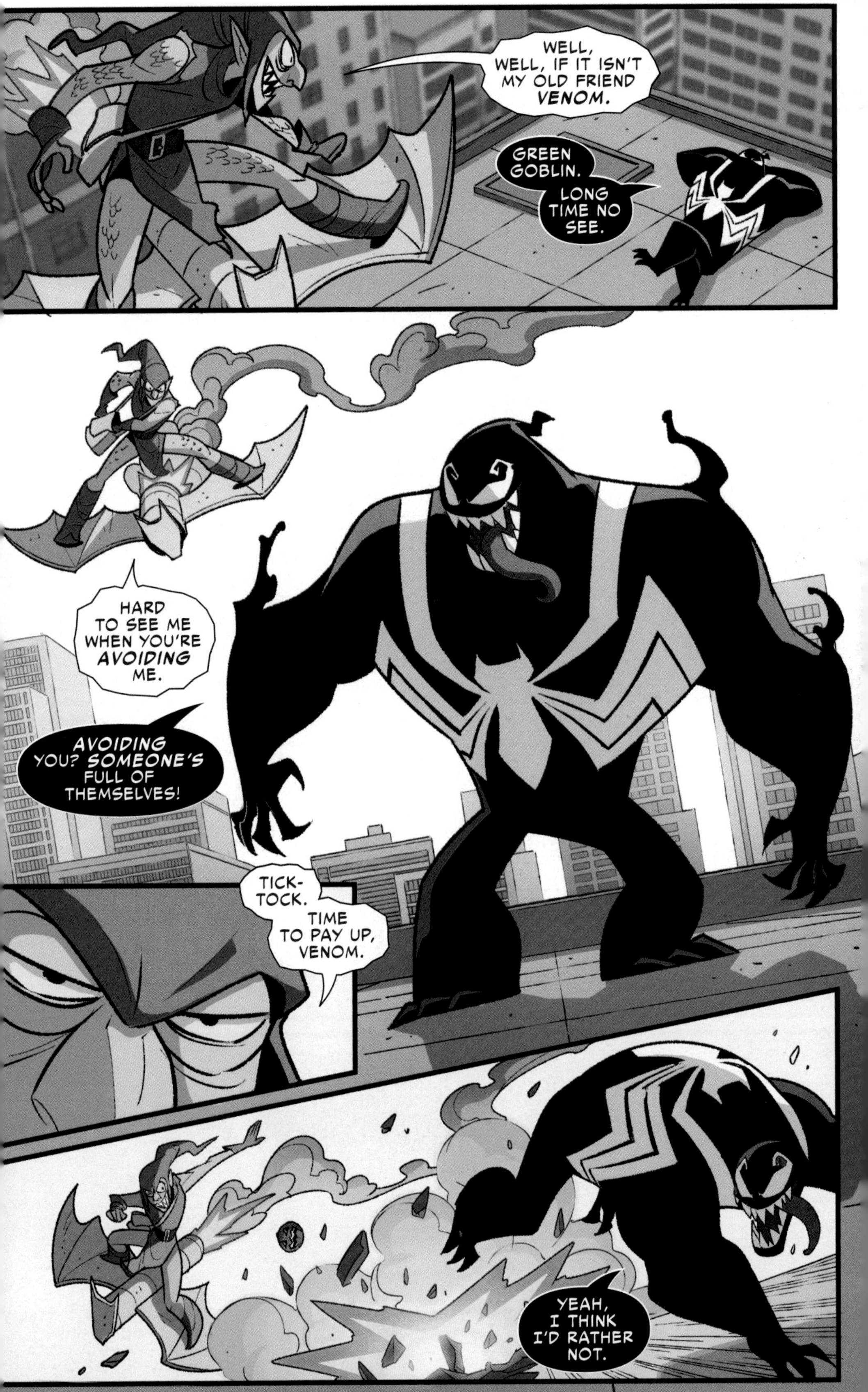
WELL, WELL, IF IT ISN'T MY OLD FRIEND VENOM.
GREEN GOBLIN.
LONG TIME NO SEE.
HARD TO SEE ME WHEN YOU'RE AVOIDING ME.
AVOIDING YOU? SOMEONE'S FULL OF THEMSELVES!
TICK-TOCK.
TIME TO PAY UP, VENOM.
YEAH, I THINK I'D RATHER NOT.

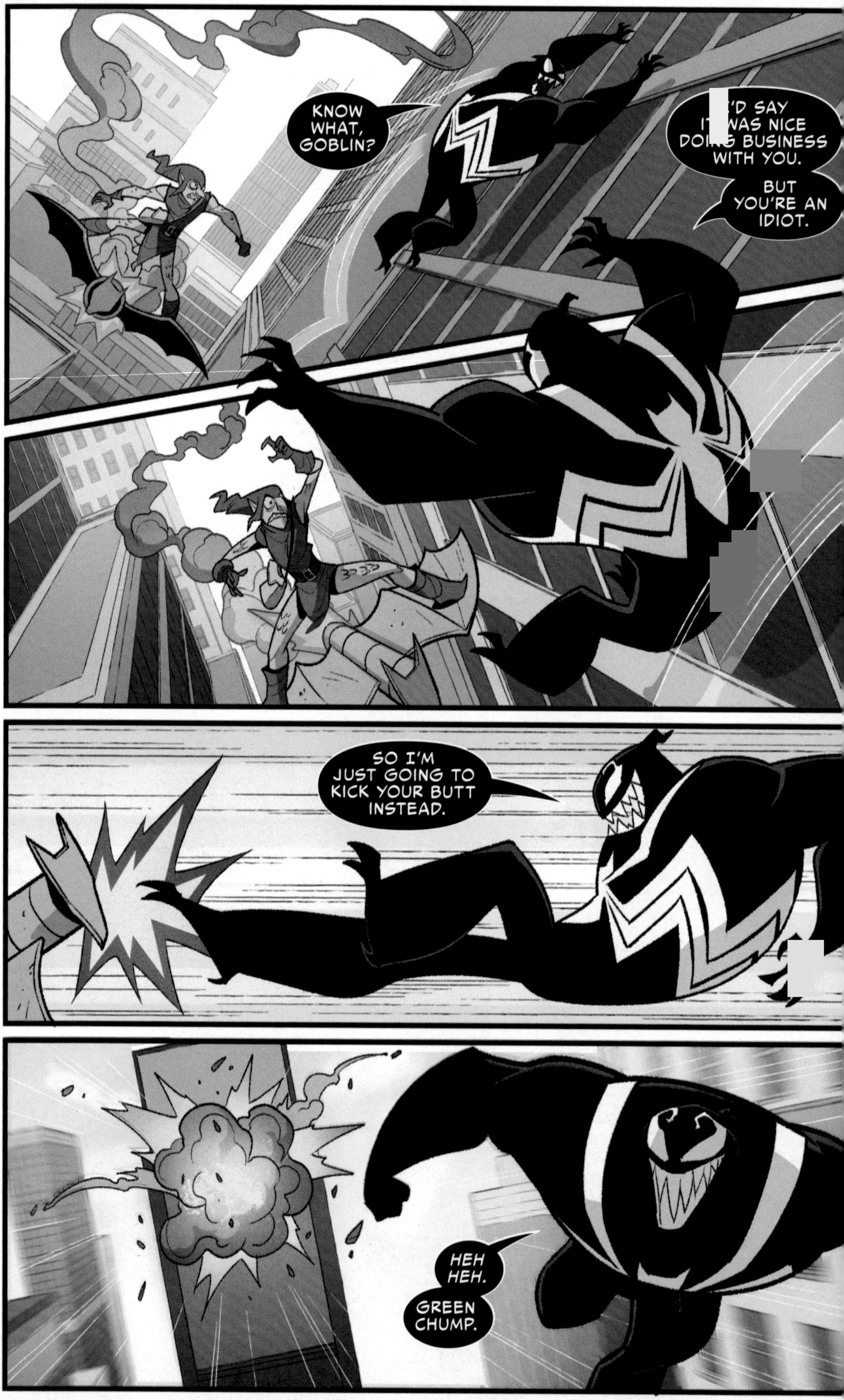
KNOW WHAT, GOBLIN?
I'D SAY IT WAS NICE DOING BUSINESS WITH YOU.
BUT YOU'RE AN IDIOT.
SO I'M JUST GOING TO KICK YOUR BUTT INSTEAD.
HEH HEH.
GREEN CHUMP.

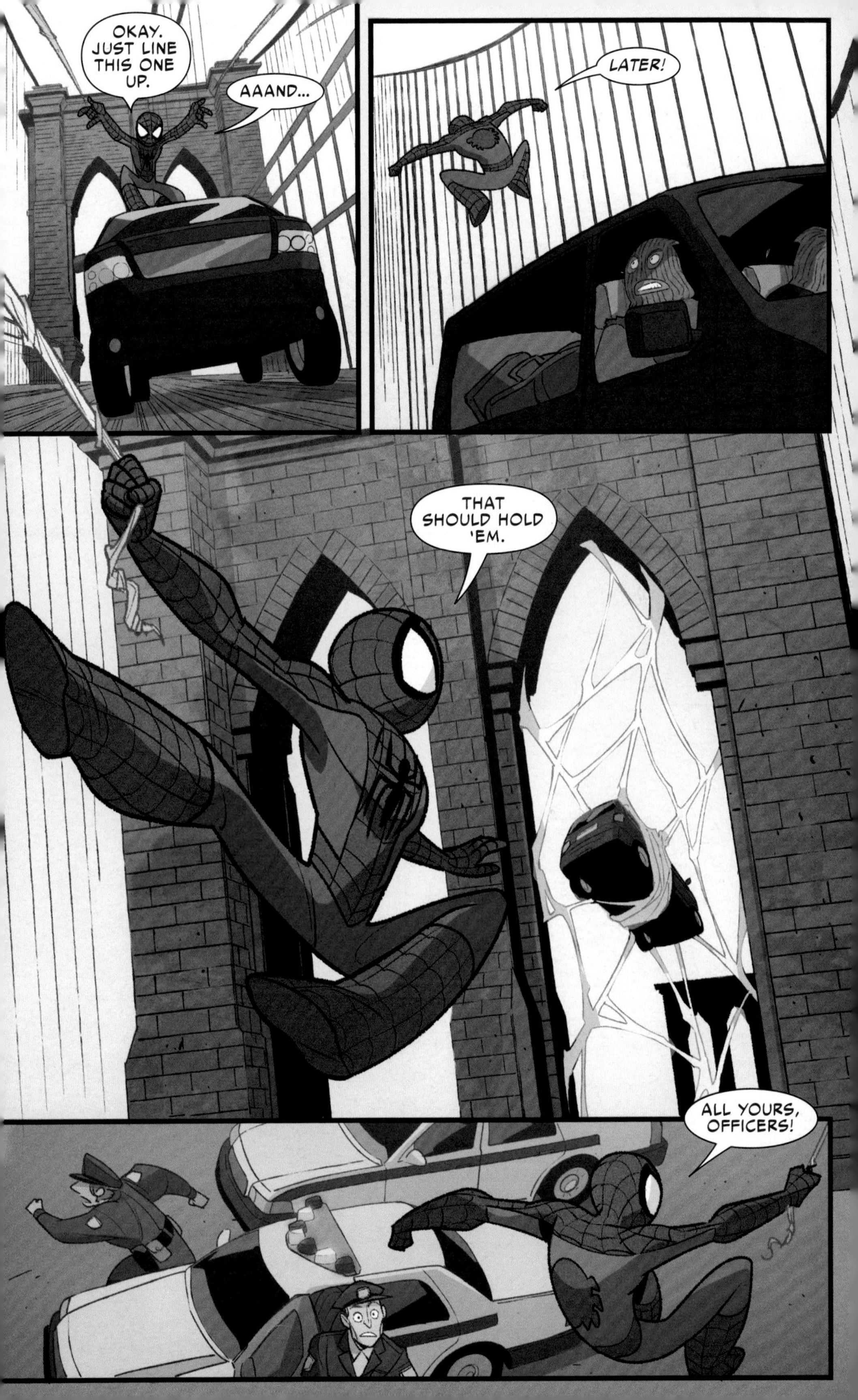
OKAY. JUST LINE THIS ONE UP.
AAAND...
LATER!
THAT SHOULD HOLD 'EM.
ALL YOURS, OFFICERS!

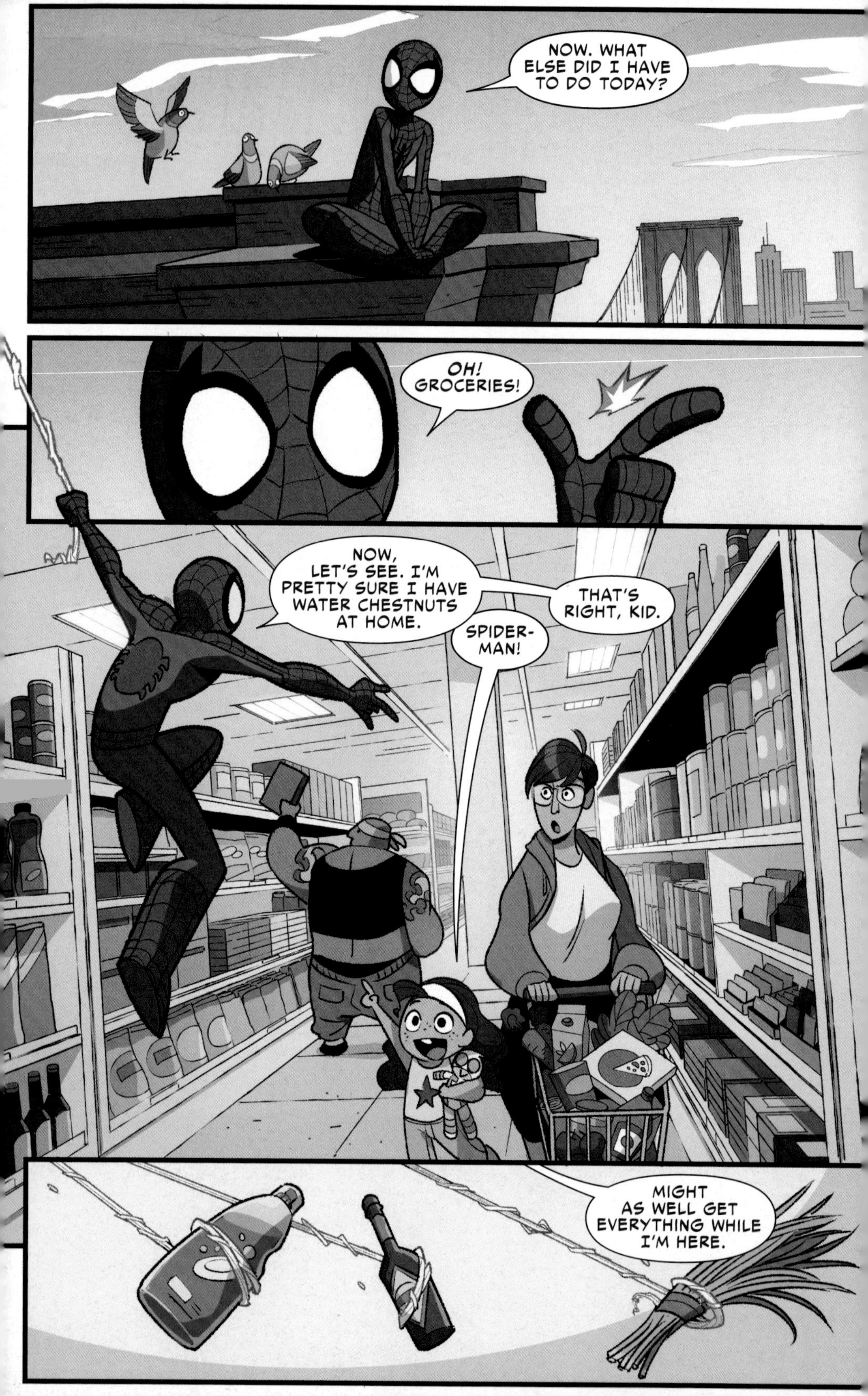
NOW. WHAT ELSE DID I HAVE TO DO TODAY?
OH! GROCERIES!
NOW, LET'S SEE. I'M PRETTY SURE I HAVE WATER CHESTNUTS AT HOME.
THAT'S RIGHT, KID.
SPIDER-MAN!
MIGHT AS WELL GET EVERYTHING WHILE I'M HERE.

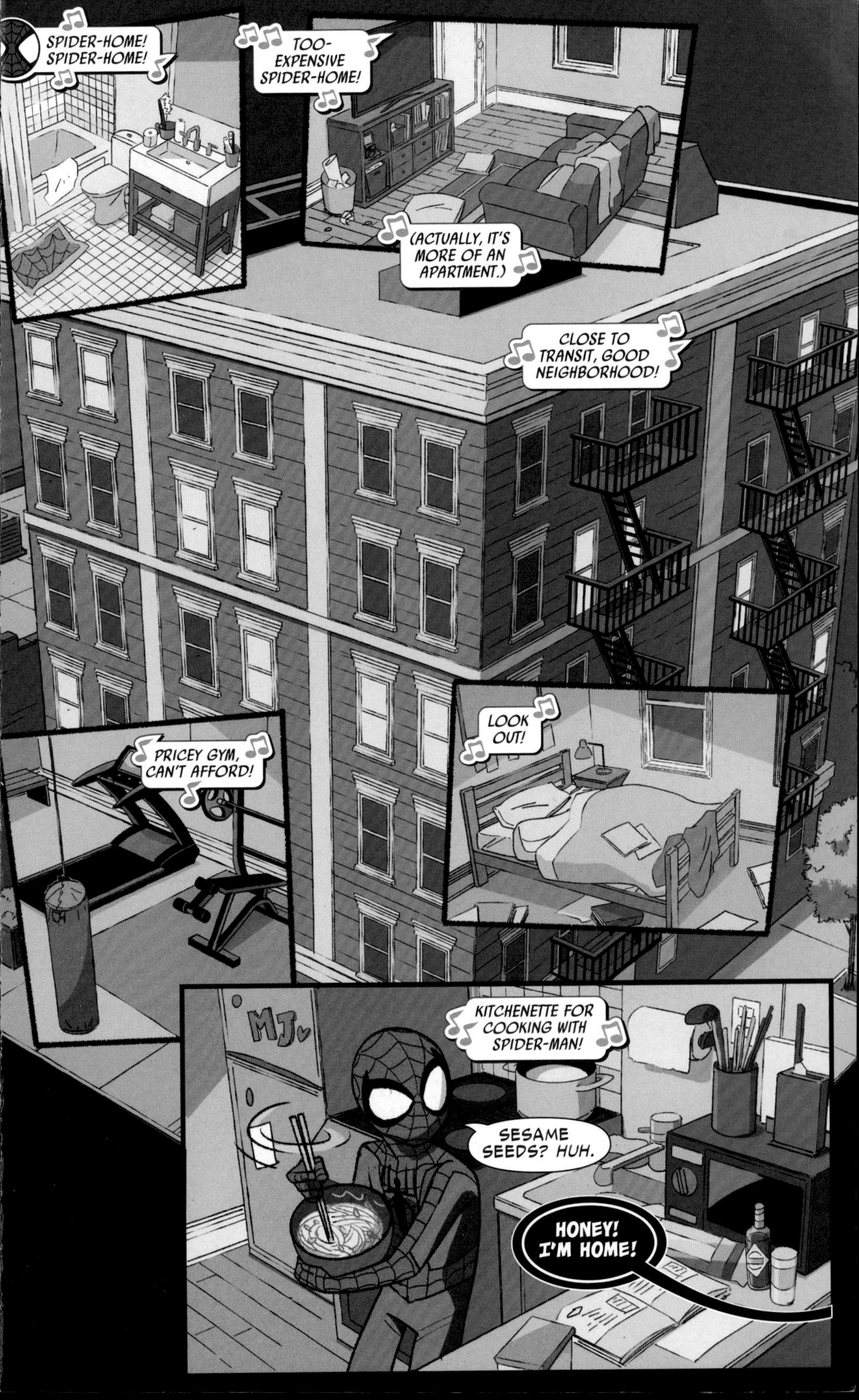
SPIDER-HOME! SPIDER-HOME!
TOO-EXPENSIVE SPIDER-HOME!
(ACTUALLY, IT'S MORE OF AN APARTMENT.)
CLOSE TO TRANSIT, GOOD NEIGHBORHOOD!
PRICEY GYM, CAN'T AFFORD!
LOOK OUT!
KITCHENETTE FOR COOKING WITH SPIDER-MAN!
MJ
SESAME SEEDS? HUH.
HONEY! I'M HOME!

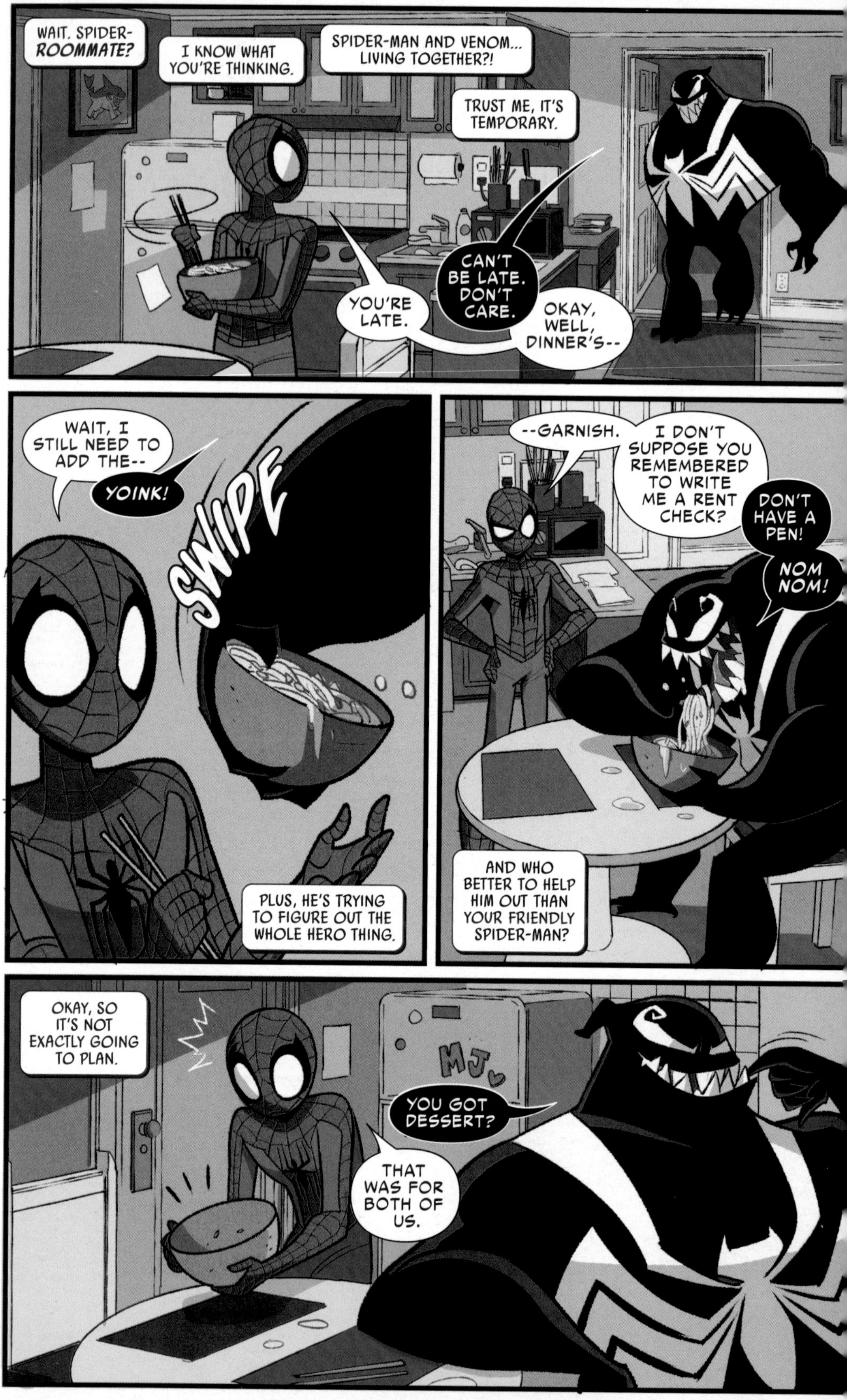

WAIT. SPIDER-ROOMMATE?
I KNOW WHAT YOU'RE THINKING.
SPIDER-MAN AND VENOM... LIVING TOGETHER?!
TRUST ME, IT'S TEMPORARY.
YOU'RE LATE.
CAN'T BE LATE. DON'T CARE.
OKAY, WELL, DINNER'S--
WAIT, I STILL NEED TO ADD THE--
YOINK!
SWIPE
PLUS, HE'S TRYING TO FIGURE OUT THE WHOLE HERO THING.
--GARNISH.
I DON'T SUPPOSE YOU REMEMBERED TO WRITE ME A RENT CHECK?
DON'T HAVE A PEN!
NOM NOM!
AND WHO BETTER TO HELP HIM OUT THAN YOUR FRIENDLY SPIDER-MAN?
OKAY, SO IT'S NOT EXACTLY GOING TO PLAN.
MJ
YOU GOT DESSERT?
THAT WAS FOR BOTH OF US.

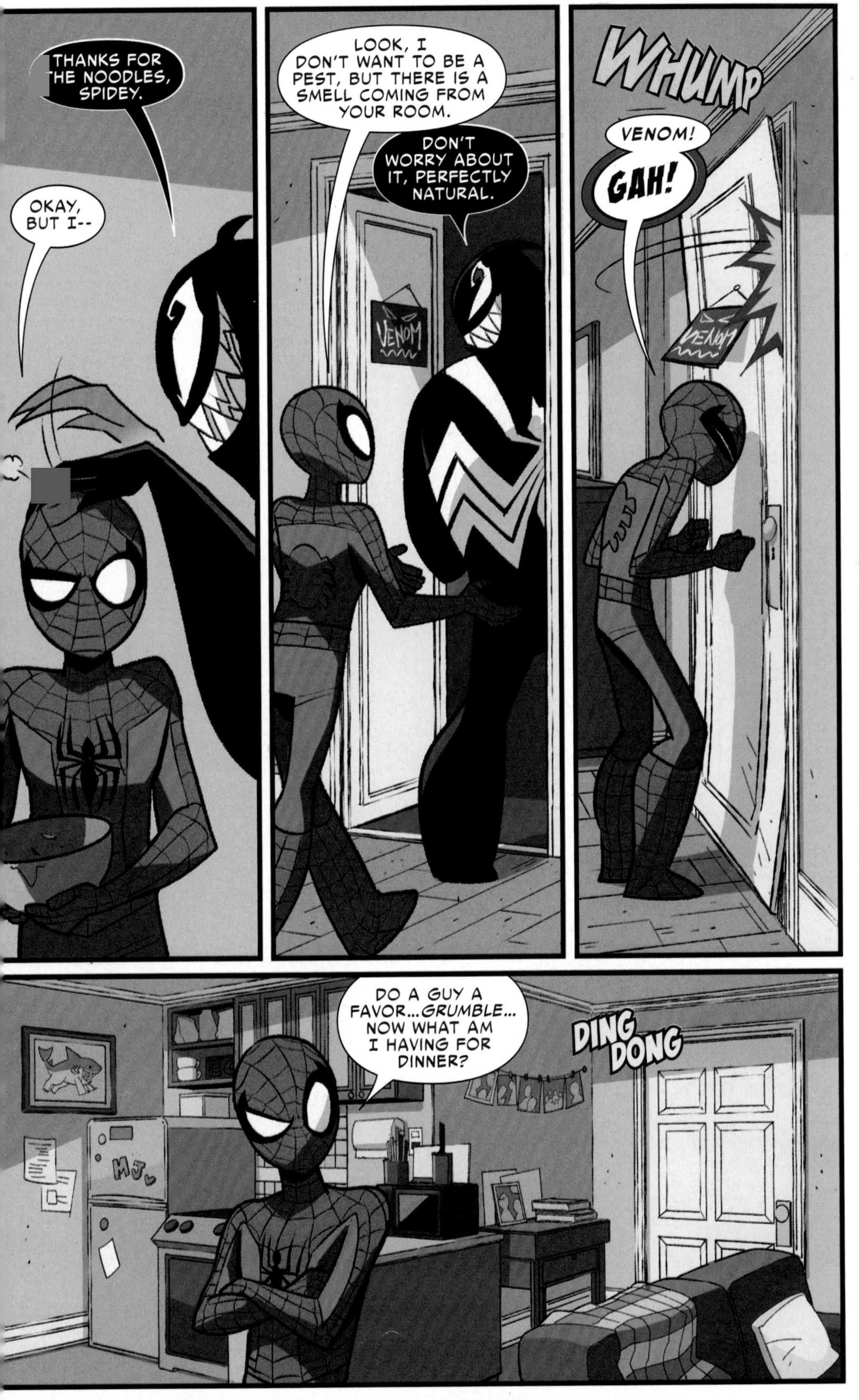
THANKS FOR THE NOODLES, SPIDEY.
OKAY, BUT I--
LOOK, I DON'T WANT TO BE A PEST, BUT THERE IS A SMELL COMING FROM YOUR ROOM.
DON'T WORRY ABOUT IT, PERFECTLY NATURAL.
VENOM
WHUMP
VENOM!
GAH!
DO A GUY A FAVOR...GRUMBLE... NOW WHAT AM I HAVING FOR DINNER?
DING DONG
MJ

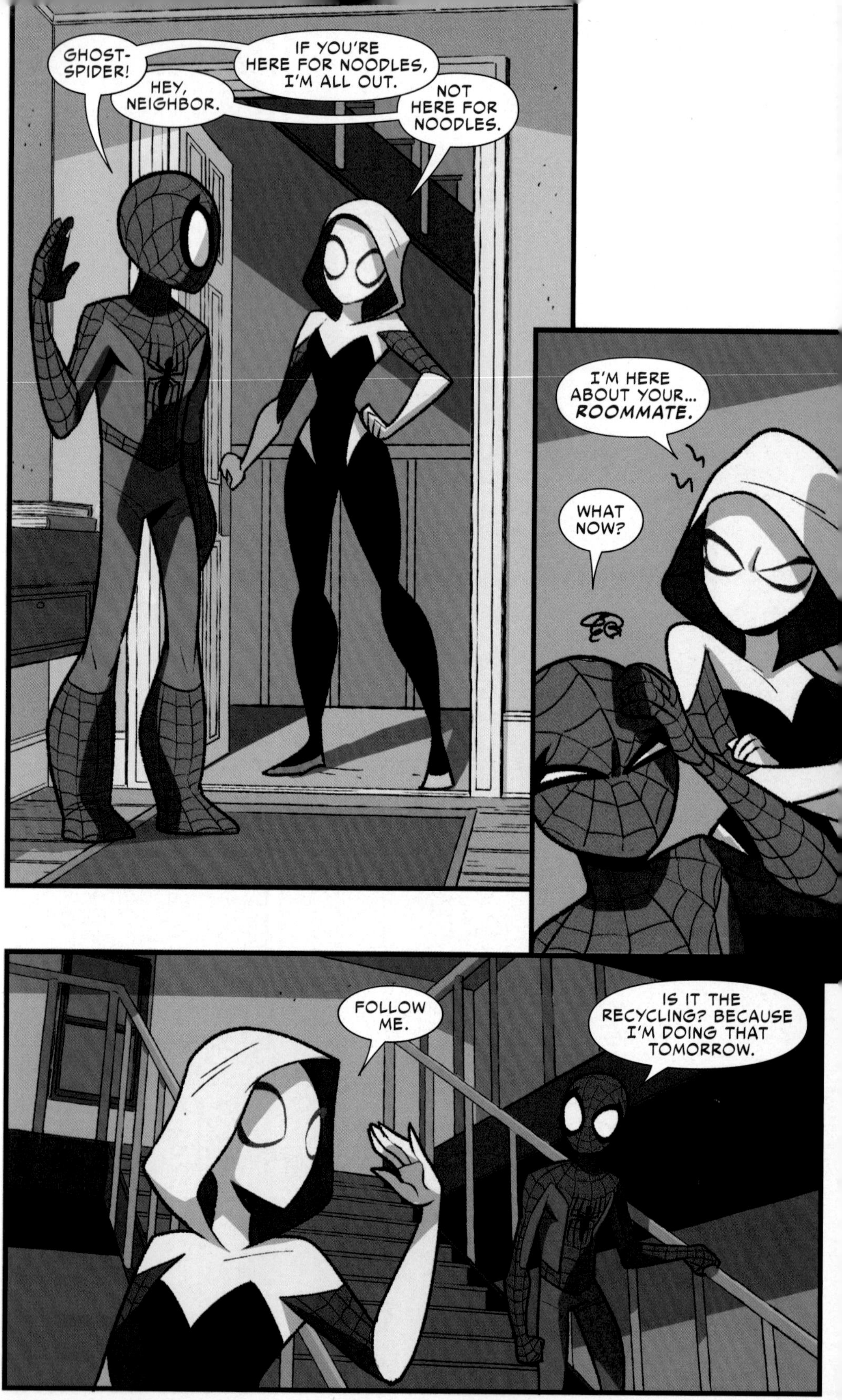
GHOST-SPIDER!
IF YOU'RE HERE FOR NOODLES, I'M ALL OUT.
HEY, NEIGHBOR.
NOT HERE FOR NOODLES.
I'M HERE ABOUT YOUR... *ROOMMATE.*
WHAT NOW?
FOLLOW ME.
IS IT THE RECYCLING? BECAUSE I'M DOING THAT TOMORROW.

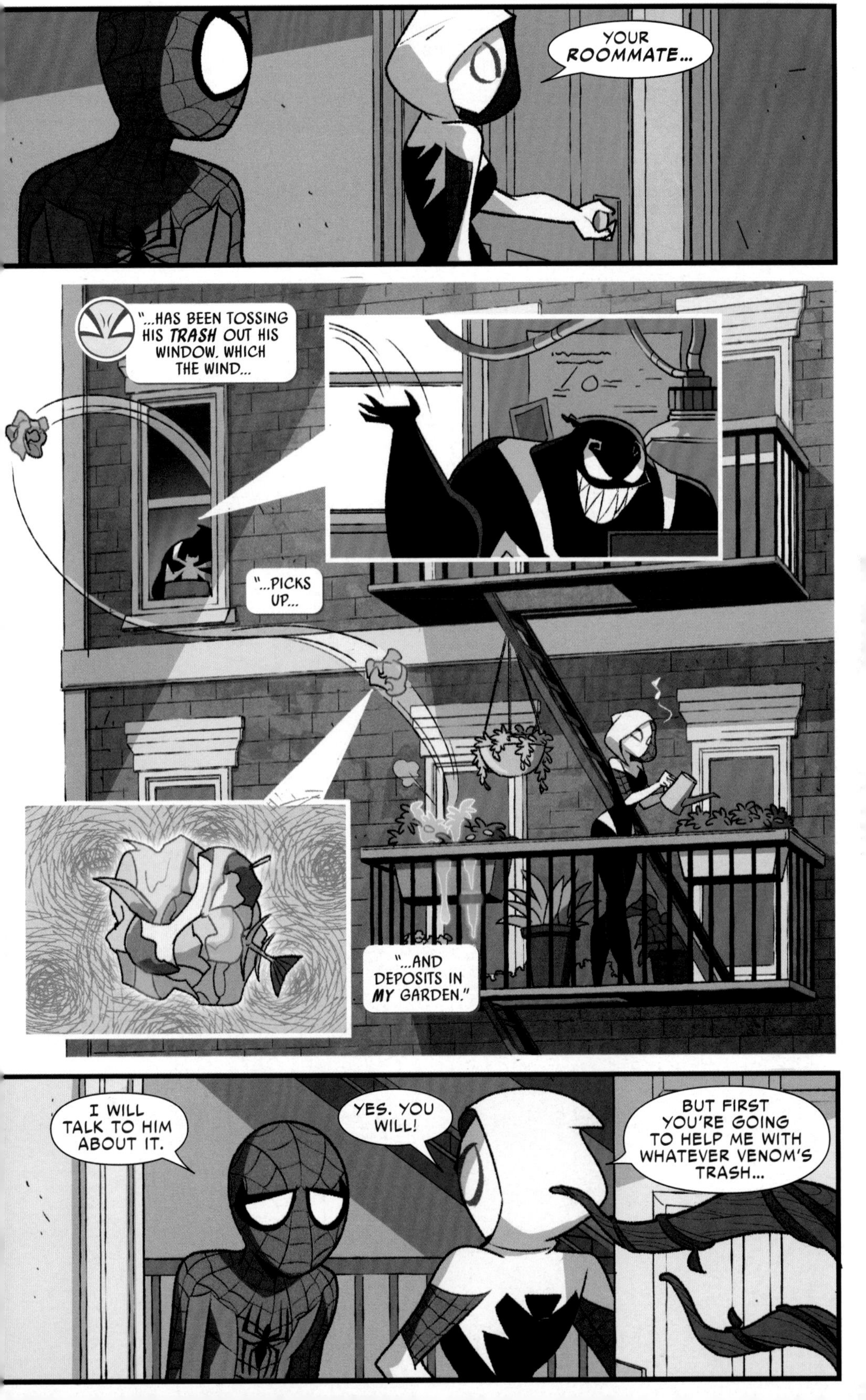
YOUR ROOMMATE...
"...HAS BEEN TOSSING HIS TRASH OUT HIS WINDOW. WHICH THE WIND...
"...PICKS UP...
"...AND DEPOSITS IN MY GARDEN."
I WILL TALK TO HIM ABOUT IT.
YES. YOU WILL!
BUT FIRST YOU'RE GOING TO HELP ME WITH WHATEVER VENOM'S TRASH...

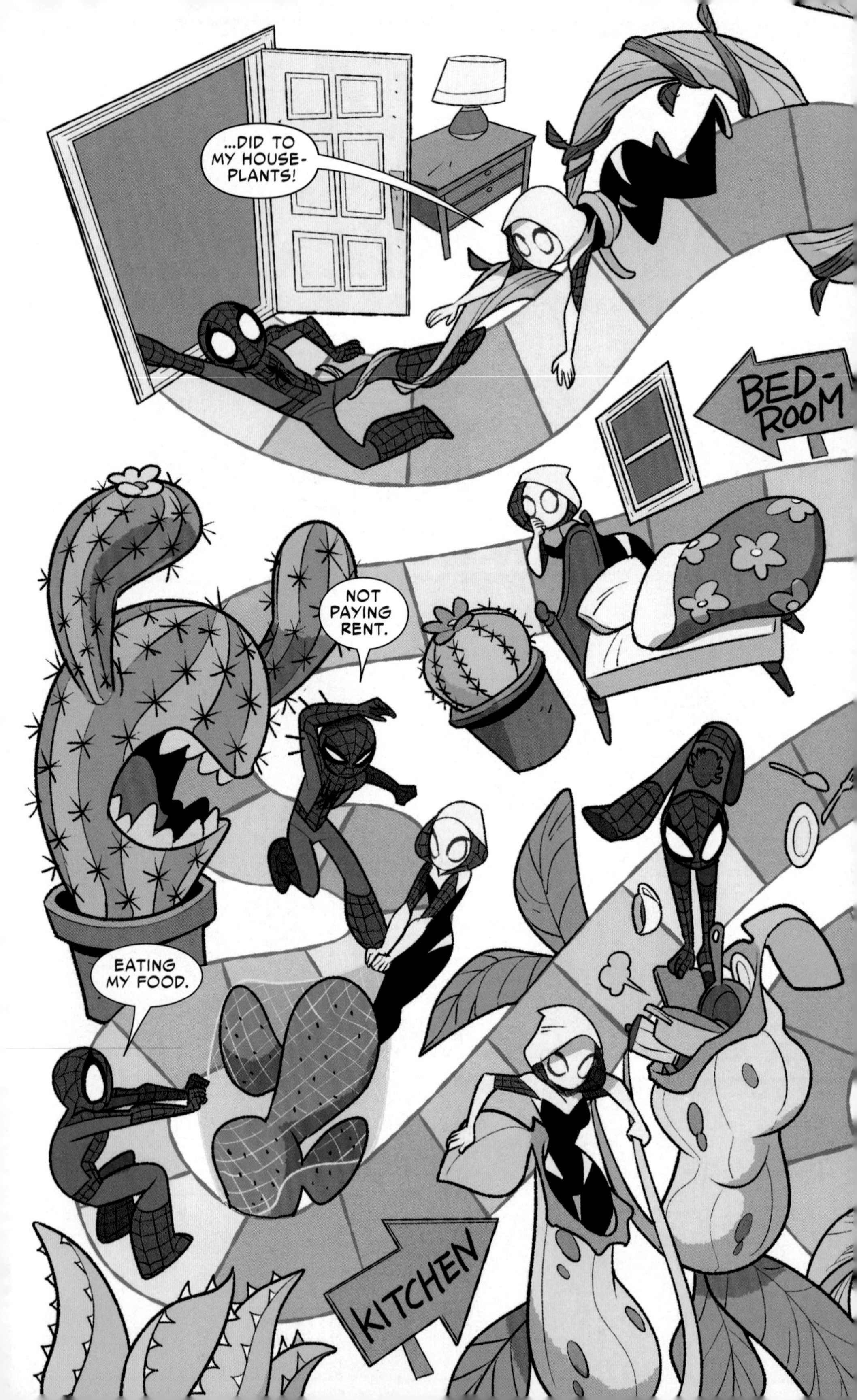

...DID TO MY HOUSE-PLANTS!
BED-ROOM
NOT PAYING RENT.
EATING MY FOOD.
KITCHEN

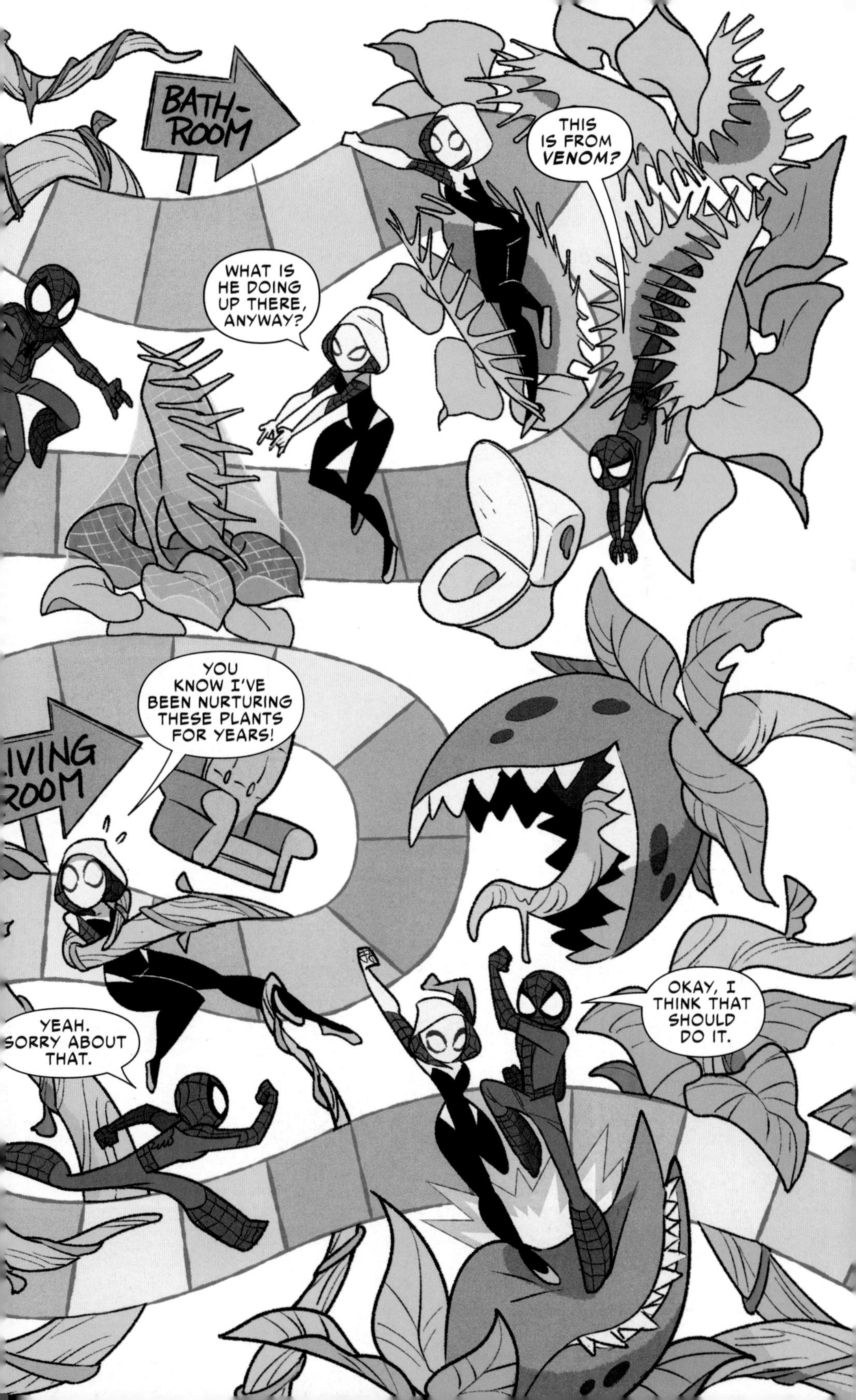
BATH-ROOM
THIS IS FROM VENOM?
WHAT IS HE DOING UP THERE, ANYWAY?
YOU KNOW I'VE BEEN NURTURING THESE PLANTS FOR YEARS!
IVING ROOM
YEAH. SORRY ABOUT THAT.
OKAY, I THINK THAT SHOULD DO IT.

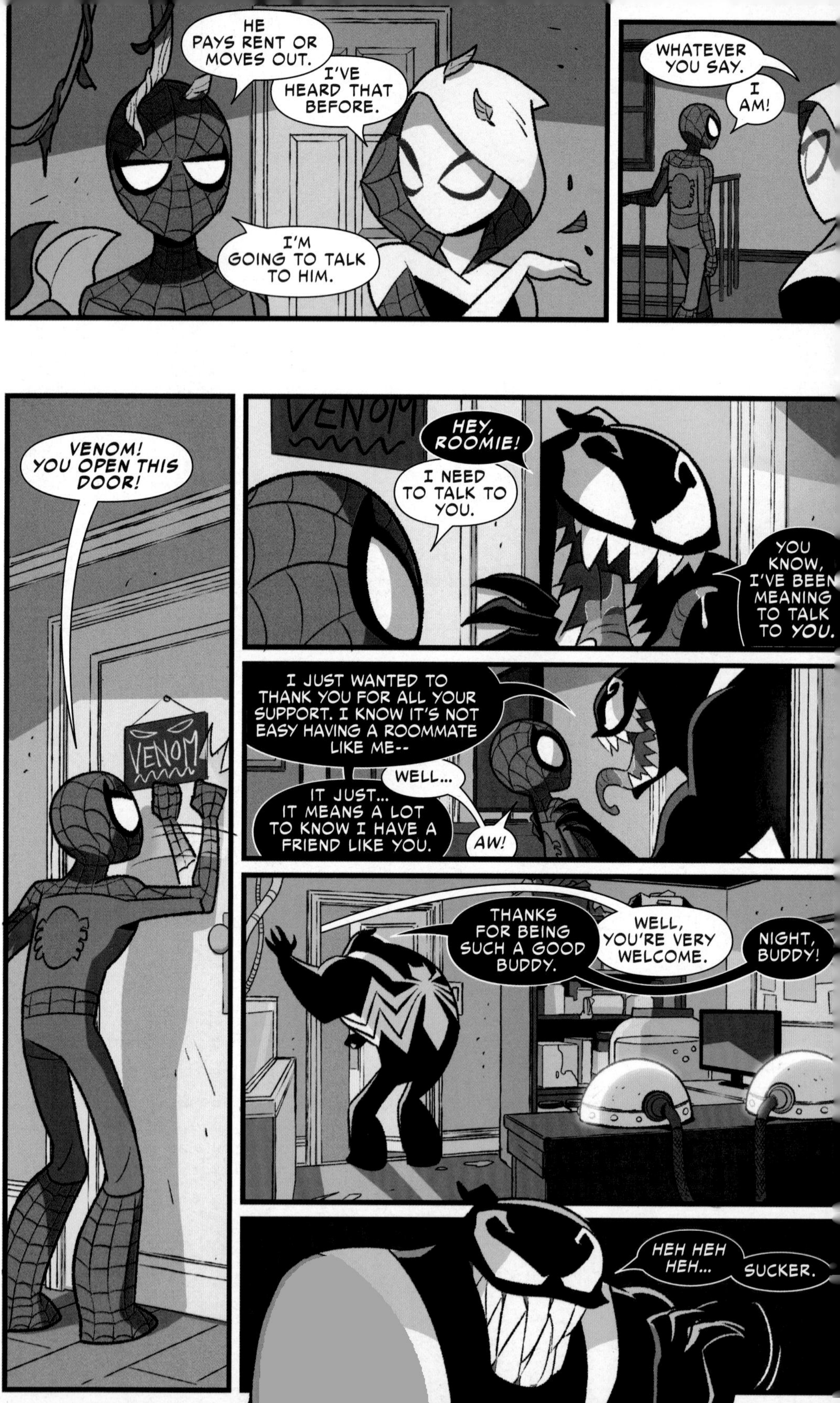
HE PAYS RENT OR MOVES OUT.
I'VE HEARD THAT BEFORE.
I'M GOING TO TALK TO HIM.
WHATEVER YOU SAY.
I AM!
VENOM! YOU OPEN THIS DOOR!
VENOM
HEY, ROOMIE!
I NEED TO TALK TO YOU.
VENOM
YOU KNOW, I'VE BEEN MEANING TO TALK TO YOU.
I JUST WANTED TO THANK YOU FOR ALL YOUR SUPPORT. I KNOW IT'S NOT EASY HAVING A ROOMMATE LIKE ME--
WELL...
IT JUST... IT MEANS A LOT TO KNOW I HAVE A FRIEND LIKE YOU.
AW!
THANKS FOR BEING SUCH A GOOD BUDDY.
WELL, YOU'RE VERY WELCOME.
NIGHT, BUDDY!
HEH HEH HEH...
SUCKER.

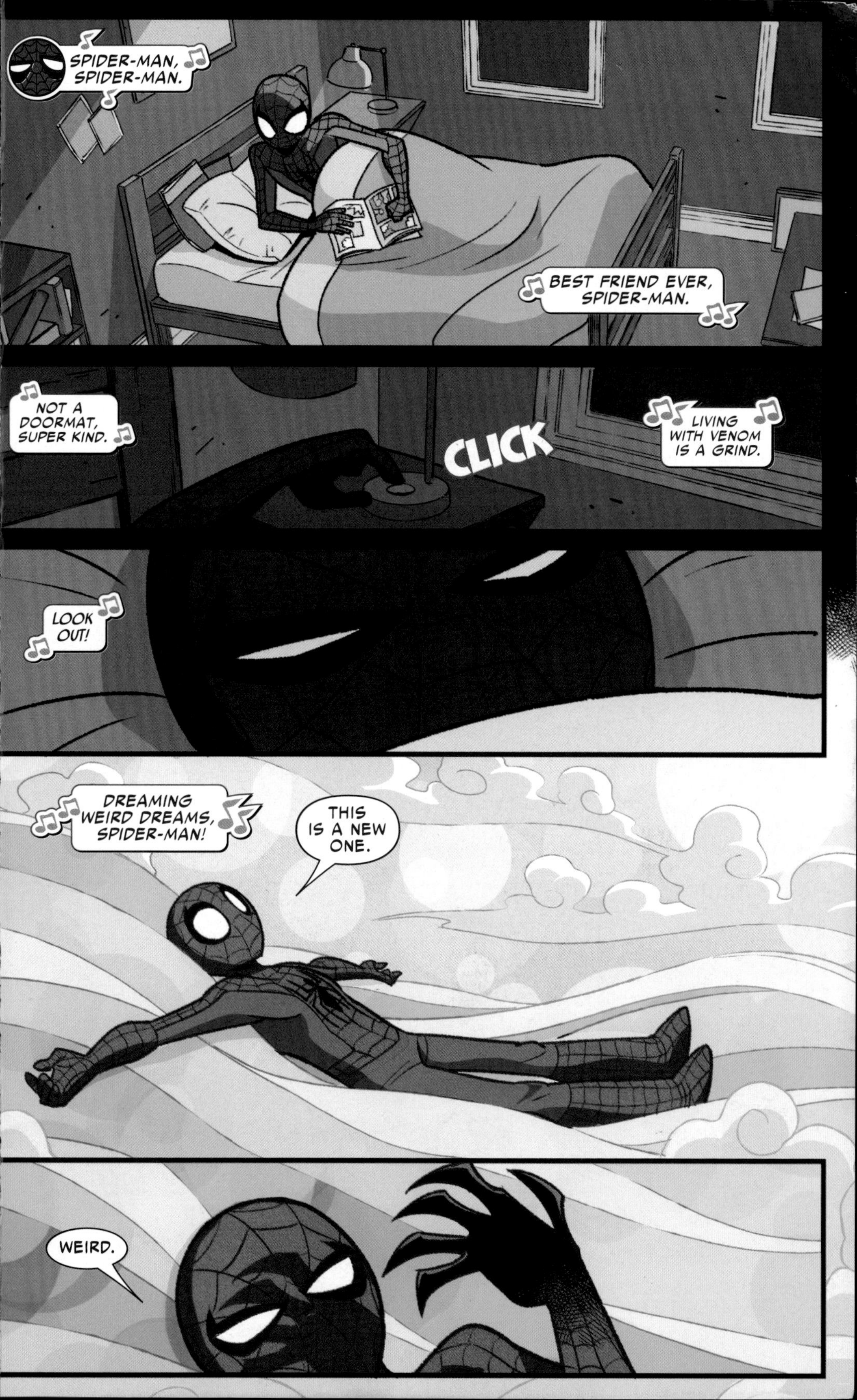
SPIDER-MAN, SPIDER-MAN.
BEST FRIEND EVER, SPIDER-MAN.
NOT A DOORMAT, SUPER KIND.
CLICK
LIVING WITH VENOM IS A GRIND.
LOOK OUT!
DREAMING WEIRD DREAMS, SPIDER-MAN!
THIS IS A NEW ONE.
WEIRD.

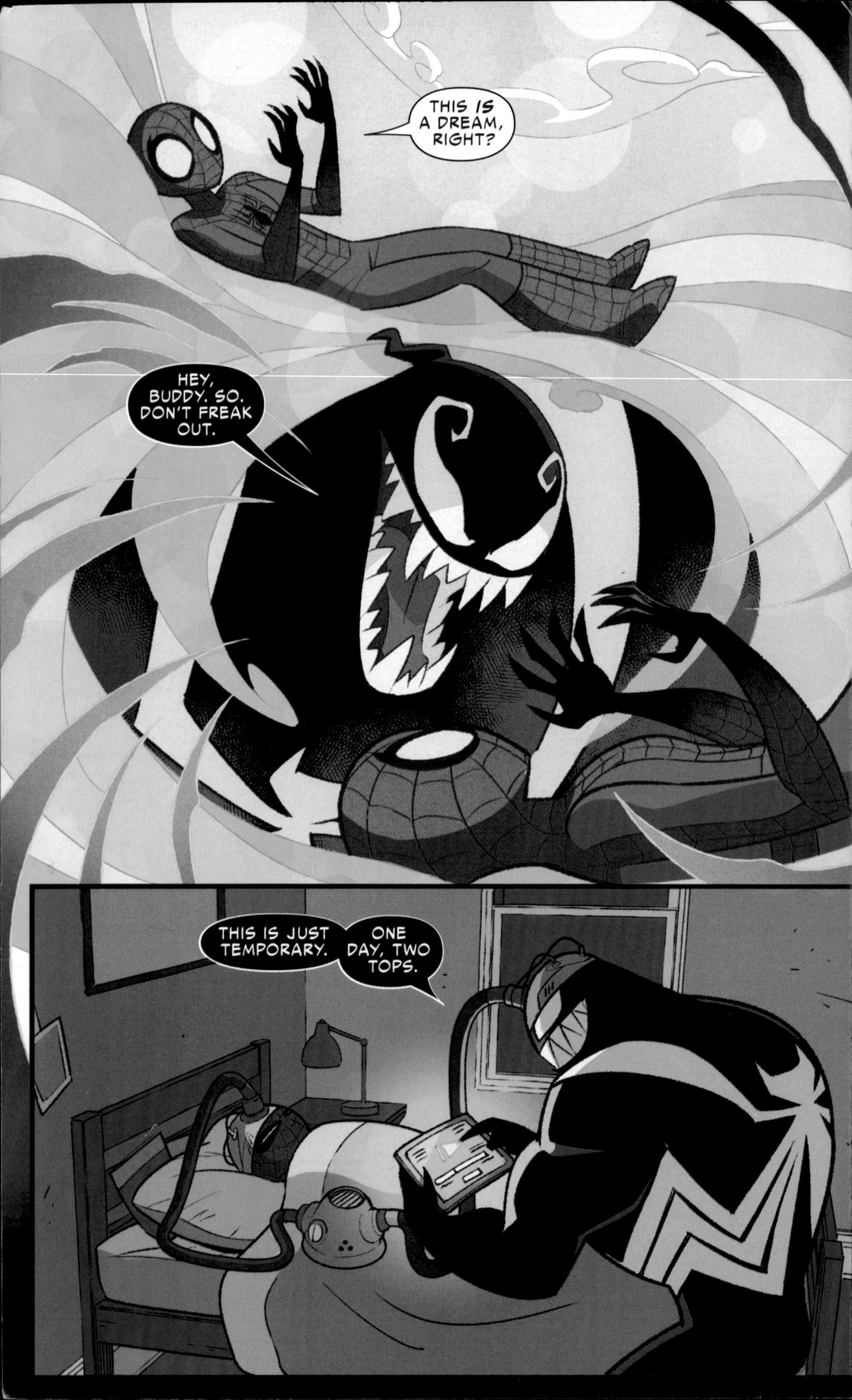
THIS IS A DREAM, RIGHT?
HEY, BUDDY. SO. DON'T FREAK OUT.
THIS IS JUST TEMPORARY.
ONE DAY, TWO TOPS.

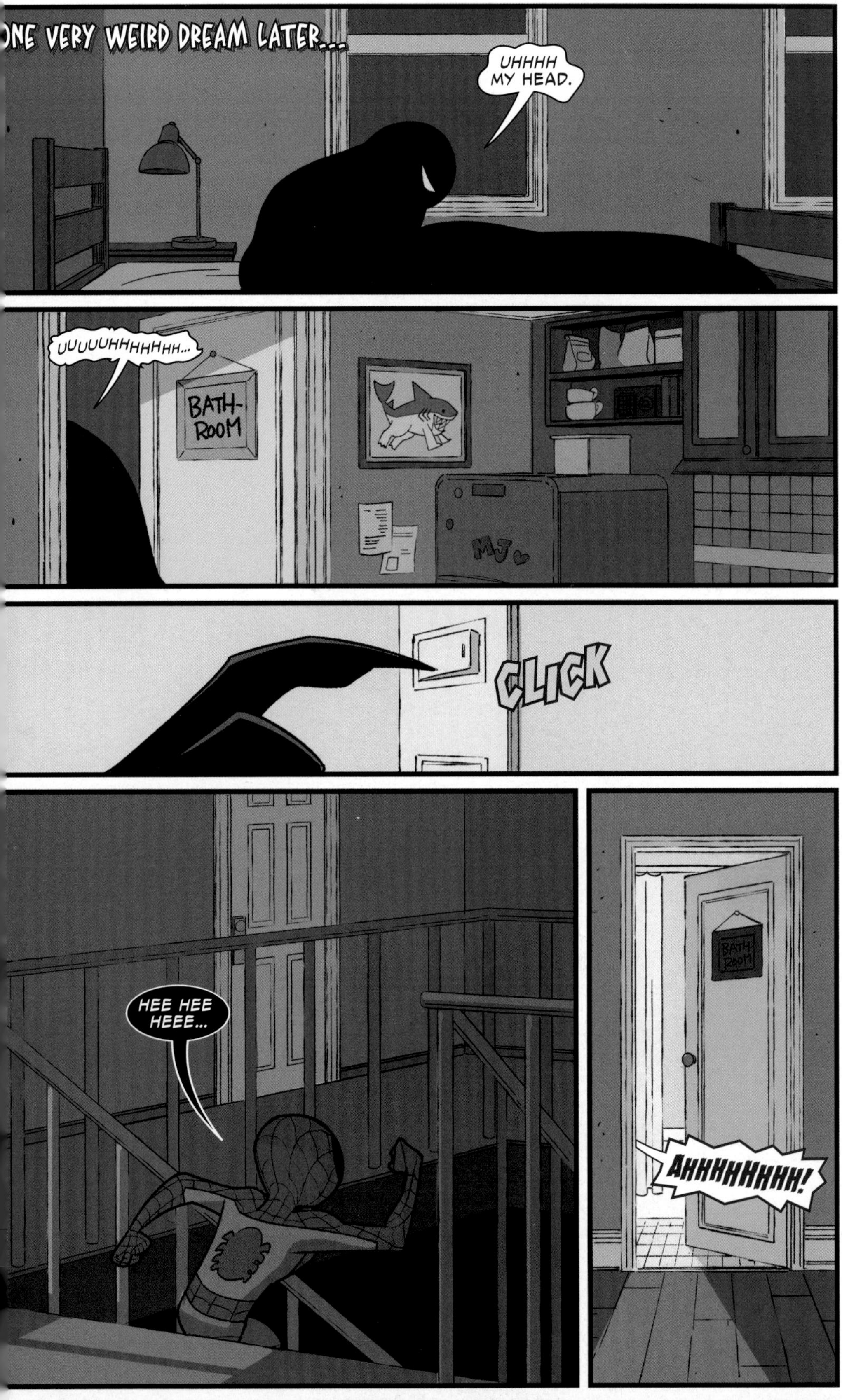
ONE VERY WEIRD DREAM LATER...
UHHHH MY HEAD.
UUUUUHHHHHH...
BATH-ROOM
MJ
CLICK
HEE HEE HEEE...
BATH ROOM
AHHHHHHHH!

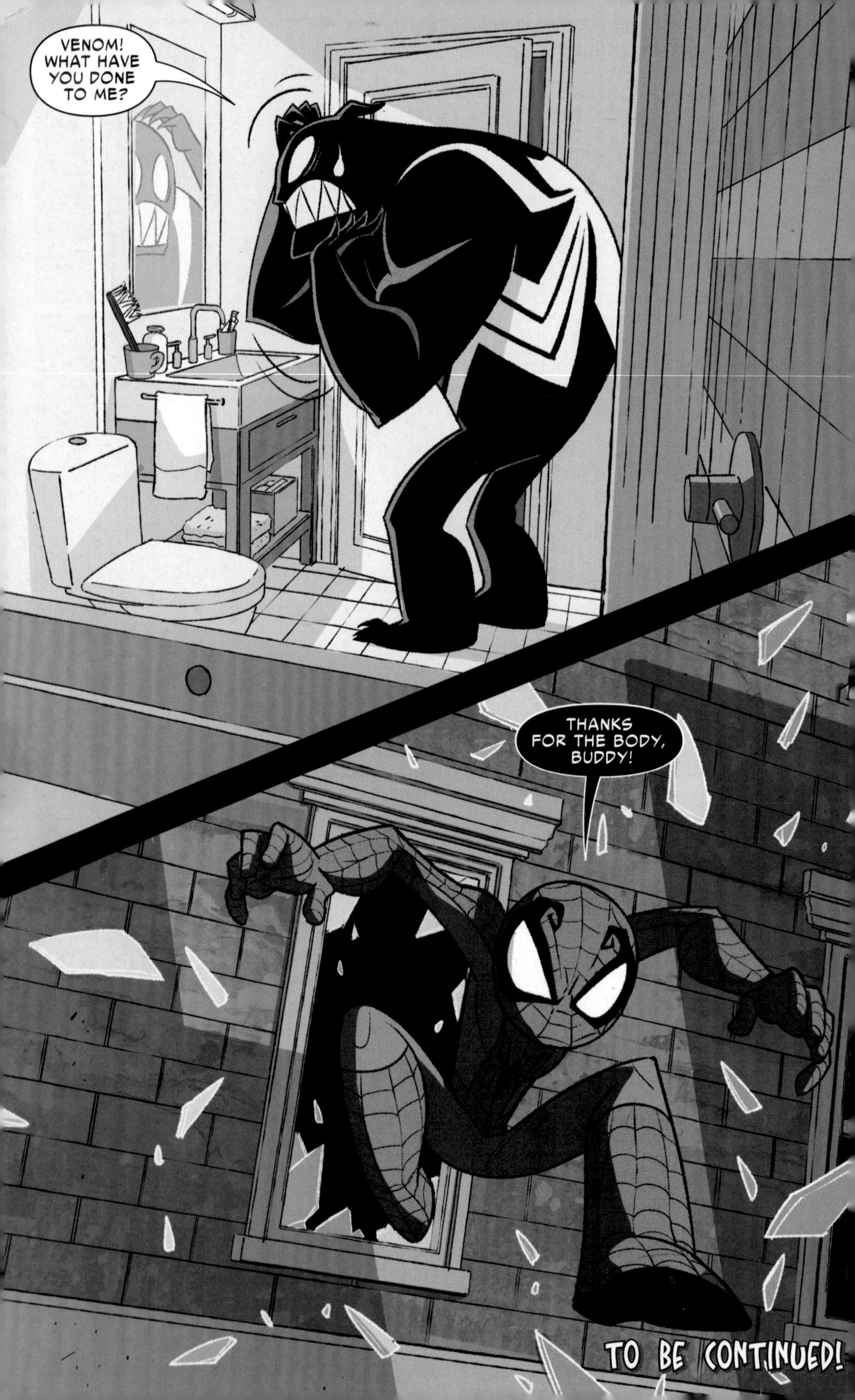
VENOM! WHAT HAVE YOU DONE TO ME?
THANKS FOR THE BODY, BUDDY!
TO BE CONTINUED!